# FROM
# NOWHERE

Julia Navarro is a journalist, a political analyst, and the internationally bestselling author of eight novels, including *The Brotherhood of the Holy Shroud*, *Tell Me Who I Am* and *Story of a Sociopath*. Her fiction has reached millions of readers all around the world through translations sold in over thirty countries. She lives in Madrid.

**f** www.julianavarro.es
Julia.Navarro/Oficial

# JULIA NAVARRO

---

# FROM NOWHERE

Translated by Rosemary Peele

GRUPO BOOKS

Grupo Books is an imprint of Penguin Random House Grupo Editorial, S. A. U.

©2021, by Julia Navarro
©2023, by Penguin Random House Grupo Editorial, S. A. U.
Travessera de Gràcia, 47-49. 08021 Barcelona, Spain
English translation ©2023, by Rosemary Peele
Originally published in Spanish in 2021 by Penguin Random House Grupo Editorial
as *De ninguna parte*

ISBN: 978-1-64473-731-6

Printed in USA

*To my dear Fernando Escribano.*
*It is a privilege to be your friend.*

*For Jesús Barderas and José María San Juan,*
*with whom I have had decades of shared*
*friendship. This novel may have been forged many*
*years ago during a trip we took together in the*
*Middle East.*

*And just when I thought I had no room for more friends,*
*José Manuel Lorenzo appeared like a whirlwind*
*with his infectious vitality.*

*Also, to Enrique Arnaldo, always lavish in offering*
*his friendship.*

*For Alba Fernández, whose life is still unwritten,*
*and for Juan Manuel, her grandfather.*

# Book I

*I've never slept beside a woman. I can't allow myself to do it. I might dream, talk in my sleep and let something incriminating slip. My life has been reduced to killing and fleeing. Killing and fleeing. Killing and fleeing.*

*The woman I met last night said goodbye to me in the doorway through a yawn. She seemed relieved to see me go. In a few minutes, she wouldn't remember my face, and I wouldn't remember her name.*

*I always seek out professionals because all I'm looking for is a quick release. A few times they've tried to stay the night, but I haven't let them because I was afraid of falling asleep.*

*I enjoy walking alone. I pass by women who display their flesh on street corners while the men they work for stand watch, smoking in anonymous doorways.*

*I wonder what it would be like to spend a whole night with a woman. I'll probably never know. When I was a teenager, I dreamed of a future where I could share my days and nights with Marion.*

*I walk towards the 10th arrondissement. Soon I'll pass right by the apartment where she lived with her sister Lissette. It's not like I'm hoping I'll see her. She left years ago, but being on this street makes her feel closer to me.*

*Marion, soon we'll see each other again. I promised you I would do something big.*

*Tonight, like so many other nights, the past visits me and I can barely recognize myself in the teenager I used to be. I still feel a shiver when I remember the day I arrived in Paris with my brother Ismail and my uncle Jamal.*

*Abir and Ismail, two scared boys with no options left. It was the fallout of a tragedy. My tragedy. The murder of our parents in Ain al-Hilweh, and the Israeli command that made us into orphans.*

*I close my eyes to remember it more clearly, even though I dread reliving what happened then, and it still haunts the present as part of the torture that keeps me from sleeping.*

\*

Abir took a deep breath and let the memories drag him down into the past.

It still burned in his memory, that early morning in Ain al-Hilweh when the Jews burst in while his family slept. They weren't looking for them; they were looking for Sheikh Mohsin. The sheikh had come to visit his mother's brother-in-law.

His father, Jafar, ordered them to flee and Abir grabbed Ismail's hand as his mother, Ghada, followed them with his little sister, the sweet Dunya, in her arms. They jumped from a window. The sound of gunshots shrouded the dawn. His mother tripped and fell down hard. Dunya's head smashed onto the ground and blood began to pour out as her mother screamed. Abir turned around and was desperate to help them, but right then he heard gunshots followed by an explosion and Sheikh Mohsin screamed at them to run. Instead, he crouched down and tried to pull his mother up by the hand. He was horrified to see she had been wounded. When the sheikh had fired at the Jews, she had put herself between them to shield the sheikh. And there, in the street, she died. Abir then snatched up a rock and shook it in his fist, screaming at those dogs that he would kill them. He would keep his promise. He was keeping it.

After their parents' murder, the boys stayed in Ain al-Hilweh for a time. It was a refugee camp, but they felt safe there, being so familiar. Later, the family decided they would be better off in Beirut. His cousins, Gibram, Sami and Rosham, did everything possible to comfort him.

They stayed there until Jamal Adoum, his father's uncle, came to get them. When he found out what had happened, he wasted no time returning to Lebanon to take charge of the two orphans from his nephew Jafar, Ghada's husband. It was his family obligation.

Uncle Jamal was a humble working man, an electrician. He had first emigrated to France in search of work and then … then, because of Noura, he'd had to try his luck in Belgium, settling down in Brussels. Aunt Fatima was a good woman and Cousin Farid had gained the respect of the entire family with his piety and wisdom. As for Noura, Abir couldn't help caring for his cousin, as ashamed as he was of her indecent behavior.

He felt grateful to his uncle because he had adopted them. He gave them his last name and showed them how to be good, fearful believers of Allah. He made sure that Abir and little Ismail never missed going to the mosque, even once. If one of them was sick and his wife asked if they could stay home, Jamal refused. There was no excuse to miss a single Friday of prayer alongside their brothers as it was the only thing that could possibly uphold the faith in that sinful city.

His uncle didn't believe they had to be grateful to the infidels. They had been allowed to live amongst them, yes, but they'd earned that. Nobody had given it to them, and so they owed them nothing. They worked hard and got paid. They didn't consider him one of them nor did he have any desire to belong in this place. One day, Europe would fall like ripe fruit into the hands of the believers.

Jamal never forgave the Jews and taught his children and his two nephews to hate the murderers. He never let them forget, or even heal their wounds.

Abir had to learn to survive in Paris. He got good grades to win the teachers' approval, forced himself to do the same things the other boys did; even, unbeknownst to his uncle, smoking and drinking. He didn't want to admit it, even to himself, but he still remembered how much he liked the taste of wine. His friends at school laughed at him for never trying to sneak a hand up the girls' skirts. Until one day he did.

The truth was that he imitated the behavior of the other boys to feel like he was part of their world and avoided other Muslims. He didn't want to be different. He strove to be seen as French, but those boys would never stop seeing him as an *Arabe*, taunting and laughing at him as they used the word. His skin color, his clothes, his guttural accent — as hard as he tried, he would never be like the rest of them. He even went through a rebellious phase where he refused to speak Arabic at home. He only wanted to speak French and began to loathe his Aunt Fatima's cooking. Several times, his uncle punished him with a belt. He still had a few of the scars on his back. Jamal ordered him to behave like a good Muslim and not try to turn himself into something he would never be.

"Why should we have to renounce our beliefs and customs to please them? One day all of Europe will be ours and the infidels will convert."

How right his uncle was. Now he was sure they would accomplish it. Europeans were weak, faint-hearted. They were too busy wrapped up in trying to keep up appearances. They had reluctantly opened the doors to the continent and before they knew it, they would all be part of Islam.

He lit a cigarette and drew in the smoke until it filled his lungs. He continued to talk to himself, letting his thoughts drift.

He would have liked to go by the apartment he'd once lived in with his aunt and uncle. But someone might recognize him and that would put him in danger.

He put his hand in his pocket and felt the key to the apartment where he could rest. It belonged to a man he didn't know in charge of finding safe houses for the brothers who belonged to the Circle's groups in Europe, fighters and members of the sleeper cells.

Abir had become one of Sheikh Mohsin's lieutenants who guided the Circle's fighters. The sheikh had never forgotten how Abir's parents had sacrificed their lives to protect him. And because they had a distant family connection, he trusted him enough to let him organize some of the attacks they took part in, though sometimes Abir left before they were carried out. Sheikh Mohsin said he still wanted him alive, that his moment for martyrdom would come soon enough.

He felt proud to have the sheikh's trust; this made the other men respect him, but this also forced him to display his bravery unfalteringly.

He'd been walking for almost two hours, and he was tired. He got to the street where his hideout was located. He stopped to light another cigarette and check if anything caught his eye. The street was deserted, and he walked calmly toward the doorway. He opened the door and went stealthily up the stairs. He was relieved to be somewhere safe.

In a few days, he would travel to Brussels, but first he had to meticulously plan the details of his operation. The whole world would be crushed at his feet. He was going to humiliate the infidels as no one had ever dared before. And Marion would admire him for it in spite of herself.

*Tel Aviv. 5 a.m.*
*Jacob*

"I'll find you! I'll kill you all and you'll pay for what you've done!" The screams ricocheting in his head had woken him. In the shadowy room, he believed he could still make out the silhouette of that desperate teenager with a weapon in his hand.

It was the recurring dream he had never managed to conquer. He still feared the child's eyes filled with tears and pain, his fist clenched threateningly.

He had never been the same again. He couldn't be. He questioned who he was, what he was doing, what he wanted. But he hadn't found the answers, and he felt he had lost control of his life, though he was unsure that he had ever really had it in the first place.

He berated himself for his tendency to probe every single thing he lived through, no matter how insignificant. He tried to shake off thoughts of the past. This happened to him all the time. He would sink into thinking about what was, and what could have been, scrutinizing every instant and sure that his life had taken a wrong turn. He didn't doubt that Tel Aviv was the new Silicon Valley, and as such the best place for his work. But he felt it wasn't a normal city, because Israel wasn't a normal country, though the Israelis didn't seem to realize it, and they acted like the anomalous existence of their nation was normal. Still, he admired them.

What worried him most was losing perspective and ending

up one of them, because that would mean renouncing what he had always wanted to be. He would never stop resenting his mother for deciding to leave Paris behind and settle in Israel. It's wasn't that he remembered Paris nostalgically. He hadn't felt he belonged in that city either, though his mother hadn't actually given him the time or the opportunity to try and build a life of his own there.

He would have liked to have a carefree attitude like his colleagues at work. But he couldn't help it: he needed to scrutinize every moment of his life in order to understand himself, even though this wasn't the time to think about the past. At 7:30 a.m. he had an appointment at the psychiatric clinic of Tel Aviv's Sheba Hospital. He'd had a hard time deciding whether to speak with a psychiatrist, until his boss, Natan Lewin, convinced him he should. "It'll help you confront your ghosts. Plus, she's required to keep all information confidential. You can tell her anything. She treated me for a while. You won't be the first or the last of us who needs their head screwed on straight, and I can assure you, Dr. Tudela is special."

Fine, he would go, but if she turned out to be a charlatan, he wouldn't waste even a minute with her.

He took a quick shower and sat down in front of the computer. He had to finish coding a computer program before he went to the hospital. He didn't mind; he liked his work, and if it weren't for the ghosts cluttering his brain, he would have almost been happy.

A long time passed before he looked at his watch. He was going to be late. He hoped Dr. Tudela wouldn't take it badly if he showed up wearing his old army pants. They were comfortable and good at fighting off the cold and damp in the first hours of the day.

When he arrived at the hospital, he was already five minutes late. The staff pointed out where Dr. Tudela's office was, and he ran down the hallway until he found it.

He had barely grazed the door with his knuckles when he heard a pleasant and emphatic voice say, "Come in." He entered and found a woman his mother's age, or at least that's how she appeared. She wore her hair short and undyed; it must have been brown once, but now it was peppered with gray. Dark eyes and olive skin. Not pretty or ugly, but her eyes drew him in like a magnet.

"Jacob Baudin?"

"Yes, sorry I'm late."

"Don't worry. Were you thinking twice about coming?"

"No ... well, the truth is I'm not completely sure that talking to you is going to help with anything."

"That's something you'll have to determine for yourself."

The answer disconcerted him. There was no animosity in her tone, but there was the conviction of a woman who was not prepared to be questioned.

"You know what I do for a living, but what do you do, really? Cure sick souls?" Jacob asked with a trace of impertinence.

"Souls? I can recommend the novel, *The Master of Souls*, written by Iréne Némirovsky. You'll like it."

"I don't know who Iréne Némirovsky is."

"Read the book and you'll get to know her. She was an extraordinary novelist who wrote with great sensitivity. She died in Auschwitz."

They fell silent and then the doctor pulled him back from his thoughts.

"We need to be listened to. Sometimes, when we translate our problems and our most intimate thoughts into words, we can start on a path to self-knowledge and, in some cases, resolution."

"So you're a master of souls."

"Well, I hope not, or at least I wouldn't want to be compared to the character in Némirovsky's novel. Although not everything about him was bad. He deceived his patients, but he also helped some of them save themselves. I can assure you, I don't deceive my patients."

"I didn't mean to upset you."

"You haven't. So, you work in IAI. You're lucky, that's one of the top technology firms in the world. What do you do exactly?"

"Design, computers, drones, programs … a little of everything."

"You must be very good. Your boss, Natan Lewin, only hires the best."

Jacob shrugged. He wasn't going to contradict her. Yes, he was good at his work, very good. He understood algorithms better than people.

"Well, you didn't come to talk about drones, or at least I don't think you did."

"No. The thing is … well, my problem is with dreams."

"You don't like what you dream."

"They're a real source of torment."

"Because they are about something you have lived through, or something you are afraid of living through?"

"I guess both."

"The past accompanies us in the present and it will continue to do so in the future. We can't change it, but we can try to stop that past from becoming an unsolvable problem, or at least learn to endure it."

"That sounds easy, but it's not."

"No, it's not. That's why you're here."

They looked at each other. He hesitated, but then he let his words bubble up before he could think about it.

"The problem is, I don't understand this country. I'm Jewish, but I don't know how to be Jewish. I have enemies I didn't choose. I don't know if I want to be here, but I also don't know where else to go."

"Where do you feel you're from?"

"Nowhere."

Dr. Tudela let the silence linger between them for a few seconds. She seemed to be meditating on what she had just heard.

"Have you always felt that you're from nowhere?"

"My parents, André and Joanna, were born and raised in France. I was born in Beirut and grew up there because my parents worked in the city. My mother tongue was French, but my world was Lebanese. The language I spoke most of the day was Arabic. My friends, my teachers, the people my parents worked with, the city, the flavors, the sounds, the smell of the sea … all that was part of Beirut. I felt safe there, happy. It was devastating for me when they brought me to France."

"What happened?"

And so Jacob recalled everything for her and told her about the anguish of leaving Beirut.

*

One night his father came to him and explained that he was sick. He had pancreatic cancer that was probably incurable, but he was going to do everything he could to survive. That's why they were leaving Lebanon to settle in Paris, where, he said, he could receive adequate treatment.

It was difficult for him to adapt to the city. In the beginning, the other boys at school laughed at him because, they said, he spoke French with an accent, but he made friends and little by little got used to living in the family's stately house in the 16th arrondissement, though he missed the sea. But his father's illness cast a shadow over any glimmer of happiness he might have felt. It was hard for him to admit that that strong and determined man he knew could barely get out of bed. His tanned face had taken on a yellow tinge, that the muscles of his arms had withered, leaving him weak.

The worst came when they moved him to the hospital for good. His father died the day he turned 12 and since then he didn't celebrate a single birthday. He felt as though that day were cursed.

He remembered his mother shaking him awake earlier than normal, urging him to hurry. "We have to go to the hospital," she told him. They barely spoke on the way there. When they arrived, the doctor was waiting for them at the door of his father's room.

"I'm sorry to have alarmed you, but I'm afraid there's not much time left, and your husband asked us to tell you and bring your son. He wants to say goodbye to him. He has just had confession and was given last rites. Father Antoine told me he is at our service. He's going to the chapel now to pray for him. Please know, madame, that when he received the last rites his spirits improved," the doctor informed them.

His mother pressed her lips together and clenched her son's hand. When they entered the room, she immediately changed her bitter expression for a smile.

"André, we're here, and Jacques has come to give you a hug. You know today is his birthday."

His father stroked his face and used every ounce of strength to speak. "Jacques, when I'm not here, you'll have to take care of your mother. Be good and patient with her ... we both know she has a temper, but she loves us so much. She ... she ... has suffered a lot. Obey her and never abandon her. Do you promise me?

"Yes, father, ... but you're not going to leave, right?"

His father grabbed his hand and tried to sit up.

"My God, André, don't move!" his mother gasped, as she tried to prop up the pillows to allow him to sit up.

"Son, I don't have much time left. I've fought hard, but the illness is stronger than me ... but I've fought, Jacques, and I will until the very last moment. We should always fight and never give up, even if we know we can't win."

"Father ... please, don't go ..."

But his father's eyes closed, and the doctor approached the bed, giving Jacques a look so he would move out of the way. Then he gave a signal that only the nurse understood, and she came over with a syringe in her hand.

They gave him an injection and his father plunged into sleep. And Jacques and his mother stayed there the rest of the day. Occasionally, his father opened his eyes, and seemed to be trying to smile. The doctor visited a few times throughout that interminable day, which became an even more interminable night, until his father finally passed away.

He and his mother hadn't moved from the room, stroking his face, squeezing his hands, murmuring soothing words to him. Every time he let tears well up, his mother would glare at him so angrily that he managed to hold them in. No, he couldn't cry, she whispered in his ear, his father had to go in peace feeling both of them by his side. And so it was.

The loss of his father shattered him so much that he didn't speak for days. His mother didn't make him. She was facing her own pain. Each of them found relief in the silence of their rooms and didn't even share their meals. Jacques went to the fridge and made do with what he found. He wasn't hungry.

It went on this way for a week. Then his mother burst into his room. She seemed to have gotten older.

"We're never going to stop crying for him, but now we have to keep living and get used to him not being here anymore. Tomorrow, you're going back to school."

"I don't want to," he dared to say.

"But you will. And I will look for a job. We have no choice but to live, and since that's all we can do, we'll do it as best we can."

"What if I don't want to live anymore?"

"You don't have that option, Jacques, so you better get used to the idea that you have to endure your father's absence."

"How did you survive when your parents died? You've never told me anything about my grandparents."

In that moment she fell silent and left the room. But the next day, she dragged him out of bed and took him to school.

Six months passed before his mother would reveal the big secret to him.

"We're Jewish, Jacob."

"Jacob? Why are you calling me Jacob, Mother? You know my name is Jacques…"

"Jacques is the same as Jacob."

"Well, if it's the same, then call me Jacques."

She told him the time had come to return 'home.' No place had felt like home for him besides Beirut. But that's when he discovered that, for his mother, her 'home' was Israel, where, she said, they had a cousin. He couldn't refuse. He wasn't even 13 years old yet, so he had to go with her and undertake a new life in a country where the language was completely foreign to him. Even more foreign was the common link among Israelis, which was first and foremost their religion.

When his parents got married, they had reached an agreement on their religious differences. Up until that moment, Jacob hadn't known his mother was Jewish, so he never knew of his father's approval for him to be circumcised, though they baptized him too. It wasn't easy to accept that he was Jewish. Many of his friends from school detested Jews and suddenly, his mother told him he was one of them. He rebelled. He insisted he was Catholic, he'd had a First Communion, and in Beirut he'd gone to a Catholic school, and anyway, he had no interest in converting to Judaism.

"You don't have to convert, Jacob, it's who you are, and it's who you are because I'm Jewish, and Judaism is passed down through the mother."

"But I could choose…"

"No, you can't, you are who you are."

"I'm Catholic like my father."

"Well, you're Catholic too, but now you will be Jewish."

In Israel, Jacob was unhappy from day one. Everything seemed foreign to him. The people, direct and rude, didn't waste time with roundabout conversation like they did in Beirut, or on using good Parisian manners. Hebrew felt impossible to learn, though he did finally end up mastering it. But above all, in Israel he learned for the first time what it was to feel alone. At first, the language separated him from the rest of the residents, even though his mother, in an effort to keep him from feeling lost, had decided to choose what was considered to be a more cosmopolitan place, a kibbutz in Galilee called the Ein Gev, or Pearl of the Sea of Galilee. It operated as a hotel. She chose well, given that travelers from all walks of life stayed there.

His mother found work at the reception desk. Her choice was intended to smooth Jacob's arrival in a country that felt as foreign as Mars. She dedicated her time to working and to making her son into a good Jew. She forced him to have a Bar Mitzvah. As soon as he turned 13, the Rabbi explained that the time had come for his soul to pass to another level called *neshama*; it involved beginning to take on responsibilities.

A few of his mother's new friends, all of whom lived in the kibbutz, attended his Bar Mitzvah ceremony.

Sometimes Jacob would ask about their cousin.

"Why doesn't he ever come see us or why don't we go see him?" Wasn't that cousin the real reason they were here? She would reply that he traveled a lot and was very busy, but that one day they would meet him.

He wasn't miserable, but he wasn't happy either. He admired the founders of the nascent Israel, but he never managed to stop feeling like a foreigner. "You're Jewish," his mother repeated to him, and that assertion burdened him so much that if he could have, he would have run away.

25

One day as they walked along the beach, he dared to ask why she had never told him earlier that he was Jewish, but most of all, why, when they lived in Beirut and then later in Paris, had she gone to church and participated in the sacraments, and why had she even wanted him to have his First Communion when he turned eight.

"Because I was Catholic."

"So, you're like me? You're Jewish and you're Catholic. I don't understand. How can you be both things? You raised me as Catholic and now you insist that I practice Judaism."

That was when she hardened her face to restrain any emotion and revealed her secret. "I was born in Paris. When the Nazis came, my parents hid in the house of my mother's friend, Claudine. Claudine was older than her, but they got along well and had a lot of affection for each other. She had been widowed and had gone to live in the country on her parents' farm. At first, they didn't want my parents to stay there too long. They were afraid. But they were good people and they ended up allowing them to seek refuge on the farm. They put a mattress in the attic of a granary so my parents could sleep, a table and a couple of chairs, an old wardrobe. In the end, they did what they could to make sure my parents would be all right. But just before the Nazis lost the war, my mother, who had gotten pregnant and given birth, fell ill and had to seek help from a doctor, who then reported them. When the police arrived to take them away, my mother asked her friend to save me.

"Claudine bundled me in a torn sheet and sent her daughter, who at that time would have been about ten years old, to take me to a convent in a nearby village. In that area, many orphans were taken in by the nuns. It wasn't exactly an orphanage, more like a refuge in which about a dozen children ended up living. That girl, Élise, Claudine's daughter, risked her life for me. She carried me huddled against her body, placed me on the doorstep of the convent, rang the bell and then took off running. It was May 30, 1944, and only a few weeks later the Allies would liberate Paris. My parents and Élise's family had had terrible luck.

"The nuns took care of me and decided to baptize me according to that feast day, which was for Saint Joan of Arc. Most importantly, they kept the gold chain with the Star of David that my mother had put around my neck. Naturally, the nuns raised me as Catholic, they couldn't have done otherwise. I have to confess that I even considered becoming a nun. Life in the convent was always peaceful and those good women gave me and the other orphans all the affection they could.

"When I turned 18, the Mother Superior called me in to talk. A few months before, I had expressed my wish to be a novice, and then become a nun and stay there forever. But Sister Marie de l'Enfant Jésus was a wise woman, and she knew how to read what was inside me and sensed that I was afraid to face life. The idea of leaving the convent made me lightheaded. She convinced me that I should try my luck 'outside' and if in the end, I really felt it was a true vocation, I could come back. But I would only know this if I had experienced secular life. Before I left, she gave me the chain with the Star of David. I took it without knowing what to do with it and tried to get her to reveal something about my parents. But she was telling the truth when she swore that all she knew was that on the night of May 30, someone had knocked on the door of the convent and when they opened it, there was a bundle on the floor. There I was, a newborn baby. She couldn't give me any more information. I had to make do with that chain with the Star of David. I asked her fearfully whether she thought my parents had been Jewish. She told me it was very likely. So they sent me to Paris, to a young women's residence where they gave me room and board in exchange for looking after the library. It was a modest place, for provincial girls without economic means who wanted to study in Paris. I matriculated at the Sorbonne to study history. The truth was I had no defined vocation besides the idea of being a nun. As well as working at the library of the residence, I found a job taking care of children in the afternoon. Their parents worked and needed someone to pick them up from school and help with homework. It was just a few hours a week, but it was enough to earn a few francs. I was 20 years old. It was there in their home that I met your father."

"This sounds like a sappy novel," Jacob said to her suspiciously.

"Yes, that's what it was like. Your father was related to the children's mother. They were cousins, and they had even gone to the same university, studying at the ENA."

"And you fell in love and got married?"

"We met, we started to see each other … and yes, we fell in love, but not immediately. We actually stopped seeing each other for a long time. Your father traveled a lot in the Middle East, because he worked for an import-export business with interests in various countries. And I finished my degree and stopped taking care of the children, but I kept in touch with the family. Every now and again they would invite me over for coffee, and six or seven years passed until during one of those visits, we met again. It was the early seventies. So it wasn't as fast as you think. What had happened at the start was that when I met him, it shook my decision to be a nun. I told Sister Marie, who laughed and told me, 'I knew it. I'm happy for you. The only thing I want, and what we pray for, is that when you get married you form a Christian home.' But as I told you, several years had passed before we saw each other again. Even so, your father wasted no time asking me to marry him. I had to be honest with him and tell him that I didn't really know who I was. He asked me what I wanted to do, and I told him I'd like to know why I'd been abandoned with a Star of David around my neck.

"It was his idea to put an announcement in the newspapers of the region where the convent was located. A very simple announcement that read 'On May 30, 1944, someone left a child wearing a thin gold chain with the Star of David on the doorstep of the Couvent de Sainte Thérèse. Please, if you know anything about this matter, we request that you contact the Mother Superior of the convent.' I didn't think my parents would suddenly appear—maybe they were dead, or circumstances had forced them to get rid of me, and if they hadn't come to look for me after all these years, it was going to be difficult to find any clues. Time passed, and just when we had lost all hope of anyone turning up, Élise appeared...yes, Claudine's daughter, my mother's friend. She asked to speak with the nun and told her she had been the one who left me there that day."

"And you were able to meet her?"

"Yes, the nuns set up a meeting. We cried in each other's arms for a long time. Her mother and grandparents had been arrested for hiding my parents, who were Jewish. They tortured them, imprisoned them, and subjected them to all kinds of degradation. Élise was left an orphan. Her mother died at the hands of the Gestapo. A distant aunt took her and her brother to live in Bordeaux. She hadn't returned to the region until two years earlier. She had been set on reclaiming her grandparents' farm, and though she hadn't managed it, she decided to stay in the area. When she read the announcement in the newspaper, she hesitated; she had really loved my parents when she was little, but at the same time, she blamed them for her misfortune. If her mother and her grandparents hadn't taken in my parents, they wouldn't have lost their lives. But Élise is a good person and decided that the little girl she had saved deserved to know who she was. The most difficult part for her was telling me that my parents were sent to Auschwitz. Your father helped me confront the despair I felt knowing my parents had died in a concentration camp.

"We traveled to Poland and to Auschwitz, and there I had to accept that I was Jewish. But what did being Jewish mean? I asked Sister Marie, and that good woman, who wasn't an intellectual at all, tried to console me by saying that being Jewish was the same as being Christian, because after all Our Lord Jesus had been Jewish, and so there was nothing wrong with being Jewish. She asked me to pray and told me I would find my path within. She gave me only one piece of advice: 'It doesn't matter what you call God. The important thing is that you believe in Him and you follow His commandments.'

"But back to your question, I have lived as a Catholic, and, as an adult, when your father got sick and we went to Paris, I started to study Judaism in depth. I've never stopped feeling Catholic, but now I feel Jewish too, even if that might be a contradiction. When your father died, I decided the time had come to accept who we really are. That's why I wanted to come to Israel. I can't change the past, but I can't run away from it either."

"Then why did you go live in Beirut?"

"Because your father was offered a position by his company to be their Middle East representative. He couldn't turn it down. It was a good position with an excellent salary, and on top of everything else they gave him shares in the company. He had an office with 20 employees. You were born in Beirut, and we were very happy there. But long before we had moved, when your father and I were still engaged, I had gotten a call from Sister Marie. The Jewish community in France had seen the announcement published in the newspaper and wanted to know the story behind it. She gave them my number, asking them to be considerate with me, and they were. They offered me support, work, anything I needed, and of course they invited me to practice Judaism."

"And you told them no?"

"I told them the truth, that I wasn't prepared to stop being who I was, to change my identity, take on a different religion and call God by a different name. They understood and didn't persist. Still, we didn't lose contact. When I went with your father on his trips to Paris, I was even able to participate in some activities with the Jewish community. That's how I met some of the people who, over time, became our friends.

"Also, it wouldn't have been good to renounce Catholicism just as we were going to live in Lebanon. You were lucky to be born one year before the war of '82. We baptized you in the church of Saint Simon. When you were little, we would always go there to celebrate the religious holidays. It's in the Sabtiyeh neighborhood, do you remember? We would also pray at Saint Charbel. It's a special place because both Christians and Muslims go there to ask for protection from the saint."

"The only thing I remember is that I liked living in Beirut," Jacob responded sullenly. "I was happy there, and I had a lot of friends."

"We couldn't stay there. Your father's business started to go badly because of the political situation, but above all his illness was the main reason we went back to France."

"I remember that house in Raouché, we could see the two rocks from our terrace…"

"Yes, it was the best neighborhood in Beirut. During the war of '82, our neighborhood felt immune to what was going on."

"I've never tasted hummus as good as Karima made."

"You loved her *kibbeh* too. She was a wonderful girl. But we can't look back. Now we're here, reclaiming our identities."

Jacob wasn't sure they'd managed it. He still missed the Beirut of his childhood because it had been so difficult for him to find his place in Paris. He hadn't had time to feel French. He still felt the rage brought on by the boys who imitated his accent and his habit of sprinkling the language with Arabic expressions.

He had two mother tongues: one from his mother and the other from Karima, who had looked after him when he was little. Going out in the street with Karima was an adventure, because she took him to places his parents would never have gone. The visits he enjoyed most were those with her family, who lived in a neighborhood in the south of the city, Bourj el-Barajneh.

Now that area belonged to Hezbollah, but back then it was Karima's neighborhood. She let him play with other children in the doorway of the house where her parents lived.

Arabic was his language, the language of playing, the language of friends chosen by him and not his parents. The language they spoke in those neighborhoods. But in Paris, his Beirut accent became an inconvenience. His classmates muttered that he wasn't really French but Arab, and their words carried a level of disdain that bordered on insulting.

In Paris, it was difficult for him to adapt to the formalness that ruled social relationships. His parents' friends lacked the joviality of their friends from Beirut. Even his teachers treated him condescendingly, as if being born in Lebanon marked him as different from the rest of the children.

He never made a real friend in Paris. His mother spent every hour of her day tending to his father, though every now and again she would force him to invite some classmates from school to their house to 'keep him company.' But those boys hardly ever accepted the invitation. At first, they did, more out of curiosity than sympathy. But he still remembered how much it had hurt to overhear the school director explaining to one of the boy's mothers that she shouldn't worry about letting her son go to the Baudin house because they were a French family and, moreover, they were quite well-off. No, they weren't Arab immigrants, they were French, but they had lived in Beirut.

He managed to keep his parents from sensing how difficult it was for him to feel like a foreigner. He didn't complain, but he prayed his father would be cured of the disease that consumed him, and that they would be able to return to Beirut. He felt rejected by the city, and he returned the sentiment, even when it became familiar and he began to recognize its beauty. He spent a lot of time in his room on the computer, clicking the mouse and traveling to places his parents couldn't have known existed.

He was gifted, according to his teachers, and his father would often joke about it, calling him a genius. But he didn't laugh when he learned Jacob had become a hacker. He hacked into the computers of the principal, the manager of the store where they bought food, and even his father's friend, a member of parliament. He was fascinated by the secrets to be discovered in a computer. Though he promised his father he would stop, he kept doing it.

It was difficult to adapt to France and accept that he was French, but it was much more difficult to feel Israeli. Arriving in Israel at almost 13 was like jumping into an abyss. But his mother insisted that they had to get over who they'd been, which brought him to the conclusion that he was from nowhere. He had stopped being Lebanese, they hadn't given him time to be French, and being Israeli wasn't easy. The history of the Jewish people had been forged through exiles and persecutions. He always wondered why they were persecuted throughout history, and what made them so hated in everyone else's eyes.

Being Jewish was difficult. But these were people who had the virtue of endurance. They had endured every type of degradation, genocide and banishment. They had never been wanted anywhere and it had taken centuries to return to the piece of land they were given by Yahweh himself, God of Israel. It was all they had, the teachers told him, and if they didn't want to be exiles again, they needed to fight to preserve it. It was their only home. But to do this, their defense meant sharing a strip of land with the Palestinians.

During the time they lived in Ein Gev, Jacob alternated between school and work in the kibbutz. He did IT work for the community and fixed the computers. Just as when he was younger, hours would easily evaporate in front of the computer. He dreamed of traveling to California, to Silicon Valley, but his mother insisted Tel Aviv was the new Silicon Valley. And she was right.

Shortly before he was to enlist in military service, Jacob's mother decided to move to the capital. He wavered between a career in quantum engineering and becoming a computer engineer. What interested him was the virtual world; it seemed more fascinating to him than the real one.

What his mother couldn't have foreseen was that he would refuse to serve in the Occupied Territories, and that this would produce an endless number of problems. Being a conscientious objector in a country like Israel, which was in a permanent state of war, was daring and maybe even stupid, she would say when they argued about it. She was probably right. In any case, she had no doubt that he should learn to defend this scrap of land, the only thing the Jewish people could call their own.

*

The sound of his cell phone pierced through the story. Dr. Tudela gestured for him to answer, and for a few seconds he listened to the flustered voice of one of the programmers at IAI. There was a glitch in one of the programs he'd developed for a Swiss hospital, and it was about to be shown that same day to a group of executives from the center. They needed him right away; he was, after all, the creator of the program.

Unable to say no, Jacob apologized to the doctor.

"The time has flown by."

"It's good for you to talk about yourself out loud. It helps with evaluating problems," she said.

"When do I have to come back?"

"Whenever you want."

"I'll be back then."

When he left the psychiatrist's office, he thought about why he had been so honest with a complete stranger. He wondered if the fact that she wore a white coat made him trust her more.

He had unburdened himself as if he had been with a priest. Suddenly, he realized that he missed confession. As a teenager, it had calmed him to kneel in the confessional and tell the priest about what he believed might be his sins. When he finished his confession, he'd always felt clean and ready to carry on.

It was one of the advantages of being Catholic, he thought. They could pour all their anxieties, fears, dilemmas, and shame into the ears of the priest, safe in the knowledge that it would stay there and go no further.

He drove quickly, and when he arrived at the IAI, Natan Lewin himself had been trying to fix the program.

"Did you manage it?" Jacob asked facetiously.

"Of course not! One of your damn inventions! There's no way to get it working."

"That's the idea, not just anybody should be able to fix it. You just don't know where the entry point is."

He sat down in front of the computer and a few minutes later the program came back to life. His colleagues seemed relieved and a few of them slapped him on the back, but he noticed his boss was annoyed he hadn't been the one to find the way into the program, assuming himself to be the top expert in all technological matters.

"Now that you've annoyed us for long enough, get to work—the plane from Switzerland has just landed."

*Paris.*
*Noura and Marion*

Abir tossed and turned in bed, unable to get to sleep. He never managed to sleep more than three or four hours.

He'd been in Paris for two days and had almost completed his task. One more day, and he would travel to Brussels. He trusted the men who were going to help him. Their mission was going to bring about the biggest humiliation the West had ever suffered.

He hadn't sought out the company of any more women. Sheikh Mohsin had trained him well, insisting on moderation. It was bad to seek easy pleasure, but it was even worse to turn it into a necessity.

Searching for sleep, he closed his eyes only to have the image of his cousin Noura float into his memory. She had shamed the family, but he had never been able to shun her. He remembered her friendliness and kindness when he and Ismail arrived at their uncle's house. She made sure to help them and guide them during their first months in the city. Noura was like her mother, Fatima: happy and trusting, and always there for anyone in need. But she renounced who she was. At school, she asked to be called Nora and adopted the shameless behavior of her French classmates.

His uncle had felt a special dislike for her friend Marion. Together with Noura, she was the prettiest girl in the class. Both girls were the center of attention for all their classmates

37

and enjoyed seducing them. The boys worshiped them, and the other girls were jealous. Their teachers grew frustrated as they ignored their studies, although Marion was smart enough to pass most of her exams with flying colors.

And Abir, like all the other boys, fell in love with Marion and her dark blond hair, her honey-colored eyes, her endless legs, her generous cleavage, and, most of all, the bold way she looked at him.

Marion had been a bad influence on Noura. It was Marion who lent her miniskirts, spaghetti-strap tank tops and high heels. She and Noura shared a box of makeup, spreading it onto their faces, painting their lips red. Their toenails glittered with different colors: one green, the others red, yellow, or blue.

Noura wore a hijab when she left the house, but as soon as she got to school, she would rush to the bathroom where Marion was waiting and transform herself. Abir knew about his cousin's daily transformation, but he was too in love with Marion to tell on Noura and feared losing the little attention her friend paid to him.

It was also true that back then he wanted to be like the other boys, and it pained him to be reminded he wasn't really French. Some of his classmates couldn't be bothered to speak to him, as if he were inferior, and even excluded him from games at recess.

Marion didn't pay him any attention either. If she spoke to him, it was because he was Noura's cousin, but she never really noticed him. Until 'it' happened. They must have been 16. That weekend, Marion had thrown a party at the apartment she lived in with her older sister. Her father, who made a living teaching English, had abandoned them when they were teenagers, and her mother, the daughter of a Spanish immigrant, had died of cancer only a few years before, leaving the sisters on their own. Lissette made little effort in Marion's upbringing, and had a boyfriend who lived in the outskirts of Paris. Whenever she went to spend the weekend with him, Marion made the most of her freedom.

Noura convinced her father to let her go to her friend's home for an afternoon snack. He allowed her to go, but on the condition that Abir come with her, and of course, they must come home no later than 7 p.m. She accepted. She had no other choice. It still shamed him to think about what happened. Marion had asked the boys in the class to bring something strong to drink. On the way to the apartment, Noura forced him to go into a small shop and spend his own money on a bottle of wine. The other boys brought whiskey or gin. They drank and danced, and when it was nearly 7 p.m. and Abir reminded his cousin that they had to leave, Marion objected, saying that the best part of the party was starting. They would turn off the lights and, in the darkness, without seeing each other, they would pair up. The lights would be off for one hour, and everyone could do whatever they wanted with whomever they were with.

The girls objected. Turning the lights off was fine, but they wanted to know who they would spend their hour with. Marion stood firm. It was to be a surprise, and when they turned on the light they would discover who their partner was. The boys protested too, but finally they gave in.

That hour. He would never forget it. Abir had positioned himself near Marion, calculating where he would have to be to be paired with her. One hour. A whole hour listening to laughter, moans, floating words and tearful murmurings. For an hour, Marion—he knew it was Marion—made him feel like a man. One hour. Just one hour. The ringing of an alarm clock was the signal for her to escape from his arms and flick on the light. Some girls tried to fasten the clasp of their bra, others hurried to find their pants, and the room was filled with laughter, yes, nervous laughter, guilty laughter. Noura was dressed and seemed calm. As soon as they left the party, Abir asked his cousin if she had done anything inappropriate. She blushed and laughed at him, telling him it was none of his business.

They went home knowing their lateness would have consequences. And it did.

Uncle Jamal was waiting for them with a belt in his hand. Neither their excuses, meant nor Fatima begging her husband not to hurt them, had any effect.

The belt lashed against their bodies. Abir tried to protect his cousin, but he couldn't stop all the blows. Blood poured down his face.

When they returned to school on Monday, Abir trembled as he approached Marion. After what had happened during that hour, he assumed they were at least engaged. He was ready to marry her as soon as possible. Marion laughed. How could you think we're dating? What a ridiculous idea! Yes, she had noticed it was Abir's first time.

"You were really clumsy and boring," she told him, the words wounding him more than his uncle's belt.

Still, he didn't give up. He became Marion's shadow. He followed her everywhere and waited expectantly for her to look at him. Being Noura's cousin worked in his favor, because sometimes the two friends would allow him to go out with them. They spoke in front of him as if he didn't exist, and he listened to their secrets, to how badly some boys kissed and how skilled others were. The two girls brazenly shared their experiences. Abir tried to stay calm, telling himself that at least his cousin didn't seem to have lost her virginity. Kisses, letting a hand slip under her bra too, even up her skirt, yes, but she hadn't lost her virtue, or at least that's what he preferred to believe. Sometimes apprehension jumped into his head. What exactly had Noura done that afternoon in Marion's apartment when the lights were off? He shook off those thoughts; his priority was getting Marion's attention.

One day, Abir asked his cousin to help him with Marion. He was afraid she would make fun of him, but instead Noura grabbed his hand affectionately.

"What do you mean you're in love? Abir, you must understand, we're never getting married, ever. We want to be free and do what we want with our lives without having to obey a husband. Don't make that face. Abir, you don't know Marion. She just wants to have fun for now."

"And you? Are you like her?" he asked, both angry and devastated.

"You know what Cousin? I want to be a singer, and that's what I'm going to be. I refuse to spend the rest of my life hiding in a trench coat and covering up my hair. And Marion is never going to belong to anyone. She wants to be important. And she will be. She still doesn't know what she's going to do when she finishes school, but if she's clear about anything it's that she doesn't want to live in a suburb, or become a salesgirl, or teach a bunch of brats or get married and devote herself to washing her husband's clothes. Forget about Marion."

But Abir refused to give up and begged her to put a good word in for him. Noura touched his face, and with a sigh of resignation promised she would talk to her.

Only a few days passed before he started pestering his cousin for information. Noura looked down; she couldn't seem to find the right words to avoid hurting him. Finally, she spoke.

"Look, she doesn't feel anything for you. She got annoyed when I asked if she was sure she could never love you. She told me that there's nothing about you she likes, that you're just some boy who has nothing to offer her. She thinks you'll never get out of this neighborhood, that you have no future. You have to accept it, Abir. She doesn't like you and she'll never love you. She's not the one for you, and you're not the one for her. I'm begging you, Cousin, forget her."

But he couldn't forget that hour with Marion. And he never forgot her indifference or how much he'd dreamed of her.

A year later, in their final year, Uncle Jamal appeared at school one afternoon with no warning. As they filed out of class, Noura wasn't wearing her hijab. She flaunted her coppery hair in the fresh air wearing a miniskirt that Marion had lent her. The top buttons of her blouse were undone, allowing a glimpse of cleavage. Her lips were painted crimson red, and if that weren't enough, she was holding hands with a boy.

His uncle went pale and rushed furiously towards his daughter, grabbing her by the arm and dragging her along as he insulted her. Abir didn't know what to say and endured the slap across the face his uncle gave him, reproaching him for his ingratitude.

The worst came once they got home. Noura showed no regret, despite the blows. Jamal had to hear from his daughter's lips that he could kill her if he wanted to, but she was never going to wear a hijab again. She also announced that as soon as she was 18, she was leaving. This was France and he couldn't keep her there against her will. When she couldn't stand being beaten anymore, she stood up and told him that if he kept hitting her, she would go to the police to report him and ask for protection from social services.

Abir felt ashamed. He had been deceiving his aunt and uncle. He had allowed Noura's dishonor to take place. He had been complicit in her lies to her parents. He got on his knees and begged his uncle to punish him instead. He confessed that he had drifted away from religion, that he had wanted to be like the other boys, to not be seen as a poor Muslim with no homeland, that's why he smoked, that's why he drank, yes, that's why he'd been willing to break away from all the teachings of the Prophet and disrespect the Almighty. Noura wasn't guilty, he was. Wanting to be accepted by the others, he had sacrificed his cousin's honor, allowing her to put her hijab in her bag when she left the apartment and borrow Marion's clothes. Jamal stayed quiet listening to him. Fatima was crying, despairing of the shame that was pulling apart her home.

Farid offered to punish his sister for her sins. It has to be done, he said to his father.

"She has dishonored us. What kind of men are we if we allow it?" he argued, his words dripping with disdain and hatred.

Abir feared the punishment. He knew they could take her life and found himself begging his relatives to punish him and forgive Noura.

His uncle said he would consult with the imam. He would know what to do.

They locked Noura in her room. Jamal threatened to disown his wife if she let their daughter out.

Noura seemed to accept her father's punishment, but her submissive attitude was a trap. She was just lying in wait for him to open the door to her room.

The imam advised Jamal to marry Noura off immediately. A husband was what she needed, but first they had to determine if she'd lost her virginity. Fatima asked Abir if it were possible, but he didn't want to talk about the afternoon they turned off the lights in Marion's house. He lied. He said that he had never seen Noura let any boy touch her, but his uncle didn't believe him and allowed the imam to send a woman to examine her. To the great relief of the family, the woman assured them that Noura was intact. During those long days, Noura and Abir stayed home as Jamal had forbidden them from leaving. Finally, Jamal allowed Abir to return to school, but not Noura. She would stay at home until he could find her a husband. A friend's son might be interested.

When Abir got to school, Marion met him out front.

"Where's Nora?" she asked angrily. "Why isn't she back in class? I called your house and your aunt hung up when I asked about her."

"Stop calling her Nora, you know her name is Noura, and she's never coming back. She's getting married. That's what her father has decided, and until he finds a husband she'll be staying at home. They're not going to let her out."

"But they can't do that! They can't force her!"

"Yes, they can. It's for the best. She has to get married as soon as possible. She has dishonored the family."

"Dishonored? What the hell are you talking about?" Marion shouted.

"You don't understand. You're not like us. Women don't do … they don't do what you've both been doing."

"And what is it we do exactly, Abir? Tell me, what is it?"

"Smoking, drinking, wearing short skirts, showing off, your hair uncovered. You aren't modest. You parade around in front of everybody instead of saving yourselves for your husband."

"What are you talking about? I never thought you were very smart, you always seemed like a stupid, lovestruck Arab. But now I see you're much worse than that."

Marion looked at him with so much hatred that Abir felt decimated. Somehow, he found the courage to answer her.

"You're a bad influence on Noura. She copied you and—"

"Nora doesn't copy me! You're such an idiot!"

"You're unchaste, Marion. I know that firsthand. You'll be with anyone and…and…well, that day in your house…I was the first, right?"

"The first? You?" Marion started laughing as she flipped her hair out of her face.

"Stop laughing!" Abir shouted.

"I feel sorry for you, really sorry for you. No, you weren't the first, and I was just unlucky you were beside me that day. You did it on purpose. I didn't want to be with you. I had to force myself because I was so grossed out by your BO and your breath reeking of spices. I only did it for Nora, so she wouldn't be embarrassed because I rejected you."

He hated her. Yes, in that moment he felt so much hatred, he could have killed her. But her obvious disdain for him left him feeling powerless.

"You know what, Abir? Your family can't do this to Nora. They can't. They'll have to kill her, because they won't be able to force her to get married."

"Yes, we can. And she'll do it. She's already accepted it."

Marion looked at him and began to laugh so hard it felt like a slap.

"You don't know her, Abir, you don't know her. She won't get married. Nora's not like you."

"And what am I?" Abir asked insolently.

"A poor boy who won't amount to anything. You'll never get out of this neighborhood. You'll always do what they tell you. You're a nobody, Abir, you'll never be anybody. You know what? The most important thing that was ever going to happen in your life was that hour with me. You're never going to forget it for the rest of your days."

Marion was right. He would never forget it for the rest of his life. He had lost track of how many nights he had woken up imagining he was with her. He couldn't get her out of his head. At the same time, she had planted a seed of hatred in him with her disdain. And she had touched a nerve telling him he was a nobody. He *was* a nobody because he was from nowhere. He didn't belong in Ain al-Hilweh, the village where he was born, where he had grown up, where he had faced death. He wasn't French either. They had never allowed him to dream of being one of them, not even for a single day. No, he was from nowhere, and that made him a nobody. But someday, he would be someone. He would show Marion what he was made of. No, he wouldn't just be a boy from an immigrant neighborhood.

He shook his head to clear the fog of the past and return to the present. He turned on the TV, hoping it would help him sleep. He looked at his watch. Two hours had passed. Yes, he'd spent two whole hours thinking about Marion.

He lit another cigarette and stared at the screen while his mind carried him back to his teenage years.

One night, Uncle Jamal announced that after Friday prayer at the mosque, they would be visited by his good friend Ali Amri and his youngest son, Brahim. They would reach an agreement to marry Noura to Brahim. His uncle would have preferred a Lebanese husband for her, but given the rush, the imam had found Brahim, a young man who was devout and pious, and above all, always prepared to obey his father. Moreover, Ali Amri was a distant cousin of the imam, and for Jamal it was an honor to marry Noura into the imam's family.

Ali Amri was an honorable and upstanding carpenter who worked hard to keep a small workshop and support his wife and his five children. He had left Algiers in the late '90s, fleeing the radical Islamism that was devastating the country. He had wanted a safe future for his children and believed they would find it in France. It wasn't easy to find work or to legalize his situation in the country. In the beginning, they had survived thanks to support from relatives and friends who had already settled in France, and through perseverance and strength, he had established himself and succeeded in owning a modest apartment near Chapelle Avenue. He felt comfortable in that neighborhood because most of his neighbors were Muslim immigrants like him. Sometimes it felt like the neighborhood wasn't even part of Paris.

His wife felt nostalgic for Algiers, and they had talked about returning a few times, but now that he had his own workshop and work to feed his family, they never found the right moment to leave Paris.

Jamal knew Ali because they'd crossed paths at the mosque and sometimes talked about the difficulties of living outside their countries and having to adjust to a society that was so different.

On the afternoon Noura was to meet Brahim, Aunt Fatima couldn't hide her worry. Noura had sworn to them she wouldn't get married, that the only thing she yearned to do was finish high school and then go to a good singing academy where they could train her voice. She was unwilling to let anyone close off the path she had chosen.

Fatima opened the door at exactly 7 p.m. Jamal came in, followed by Farid, then Ali and Brahim. Abir and Ismail were there too. The men would talk about the details of the arrangement and then they would introduce the young people to each other. It would be a brief encounter, but long enough for them to meet each other.

Jamal had told his wife to cover Noura's hair with the hijab. She needed to appear to be a modest young woman. If it hadn't been for the imam's recommendation, Ali would never have accepted Noura as a daughter-in-law because of the gossip about her.

Abir was nervous. He knew his cousin, and although he disapproved of her behavior, he wanted the best for her. He knew she wouldn't accept an arranged marriage and was afraid of what might happen.

In the small living room, Fatima served cups of tea and sweets she had made herself. Then she left the men alone to talk. They would call her to bring in her daughter to make the introductions.

One hour later, Jamal asked his wife to come in with Noura.

Mother and daughter entered the room. Noura was wearing the hijab, but that didn't ease Abir's mind. He knew she hadn't given up her rebellion against her father.

"This is my daughter, Noura," Jamal said.

What he and the other men didn't expect is that in a flash Noura would snatch off the hijab, leaving her coppery hair visible to everyone, and unbutton the trench coat that covered her body to reveal her slim figure squeezed into jeans and a t-shirt that left her midriff bare.

Her mother screamed and her father pushed her away, ashamed.

"Get her out of here!" he ordered his wife.

"I don't understand…" Ali managed to say.

His son Brahim looked down, trying to avoid looking at Noura. As for Farid, he went to hit his sister, but Abir got between them, urging the girl to leave the room. Instead of returning to her room, Noura pulled away from her mother's grasp and rushed to the front door, opened it, and ran down the stairs. Everything happened so quickly that neither Fatima nor the men knew how to react.

Jamal showered Ali with excuses, and he accepted them with a serious face, though he made it clear that he couldn't consider an engagement between his son and Noura. He thanked him for their hospitality and left politely, followed by Brahim.

Fatima was frightened and cried while Farid, livid with anger, urged his father to take a hard stance on Noura.

"Either you send her to Lebanon, and she can get married there, or you do what you have to do with a woman who dishonors her family. I am prepared to avenge our shame with her blood."

Abir intervened, terrified. He knew what it meant to restore family honor with blood, and he felt guilty for having allowed Noura to behave so shamelessly without telling his aunt and uncle. Jamal and Fatima did not deserve that disloyalty. They had taken him in as a refugee along with Ismail and given them a home, and he hadn't stopped his cousin from doing the same things as the other girls in school, flaunting their bodies and messing around with boys.

"She ... she's not a bad girl. She's just confused. She hasn't done anything different than the rest of her classmates ... nothing serious. They just have different values, they don't have our morals," he said, trying to defend her.

The rage in Farid's eyes made him look away.

"You knew, you were aware of my sister's behavior, and you hid it from us. Is that how you repay my father's generosity? You and Ismail owe him a debt of gratitude that you'll never be able to repay."

Abir felt like his face was on fire, a burning feeling of shame and fury. Farid's words had hit him to the core. He didn't know what else he could say, so he waited. It was his brother Ismail who broke the sudden silence that had settled over the men.

"Where did Noura go?" he asked, to no one in particular.

Fatima cried even harder. She knew then that the real problem was only just beginning. Where was Noura? Where could she have gone? Jamal and Farid looked at Abir, awaiting a response.

"I ... I don't know where she could have gone." the boy dared to say.

"We have to find her," Farid prompted. "She must have gone to one of her classmates' houses. If we don't find her, we'll have to report her disappearance. And if we find her and she doesn't want to return, we'll have to report that too. She's still underage, and even in France they won't let an underage girl wander around wherever she wants," he declared.

Abir wasn't sure if he should speak. If Noura had taken refuge at a friend's house, it could only be Marion's.

His aunt's anguish and his uncle's rage forced him to say it.

"She could be at Marion's house. She's her best friend."

"And where does this Marion live?" Farid asked in a falsely sweet tone.

"Near the Strasbourg-Saint-Denis station," Abir answered quietly.

"Well then, let's go. Ismail, you stay here with your aunt and we will go to this girl's house. You're coming too, Abir."

Abir regretted revealing Marion's address. He knew she looked down on them and would laugh in their faces, and if Noura had taken refuge in her house, she would protect her at all costs.

But there was no turning back now. He had to accompany his uncle Jamal and his cousin Farid.

What would Marion's sister Lisette say? Abir had only seen her once and she seemed obnoxious. She'd come to pick Marion up from school and they'd gotten into a shouting match.

Lissette was prettier than Marion, but lacked her provocative expression and always looked bored.

They took the metro. Abir led the way, fearing the scene that Marion would make, and also wondering what Noura's reaction would be if she were there.

It was Lissette who opened the door, looking them up and down suspiciously.

"What do you want?" she asked curtly.

"My daughter Noura is here," Jamal declared, "I've come to get her."

"Nora?"

"Noura," Farid corrected her.

"Nora, yes, she was here, but she left with Marion."

"Where did they go? Will they be back?" Jamal asked anxiously.

"They went to a lawyer's office. Nora wants to present her case. Apparently, you're trying to force her into marriage, and that's illegal in France. You can lose custody of her for that." Lissette's voice was icy.

Jamal was bewildered by what he was hearing, but Farid lunged forward and pushed the door open, forcing Lissette to step back.

50

"My sister is here. Tell her to come out. No one, not you, or your sister, or the French state can stick their nose into family matters."

"I'm not sticking my nose in. I'm simply informing you that Nora is at the office of a lawyer who specializes in women's rights."

"She's here," Farid insisted, raising his voice.

"Look, she's not here, but you should know that your sister has my sympathy, and it seems monstrous to me that you would all try to marry her to some guy she's never seen in her life. I'm not a lawyer, but I'm familiar with the laws that protect women."

"What about Marion?" Abir asked anxiously.

"Like I said, Marion went with her to the women's center. Now get out of here, I don't have to talk to you. I have my own problems to worry about."

"My daughter is underage." Jamal tried to speak with total certainty.

"I'm aware of that, but it doesn't take away her rights. Quite the opposite. Forcing a minor to get married is an outrage, and punishable by law. Don't forget, sir, we are in France."

Lissette's impertinent tone was just like Marion's.

"You're the one who's harboring a minor who has run away, and you'll have to answer to the law," Farid retorted.

"You have no idea about the law. Your sister isn't here, I already told you, and you guys are the ones who'll have to answer to a judge for abusing a minor. If you don't leave, I'll add another report to the one Nora's making right now."

"Don't call her Nora!" Farid yelled.

"If she wants to call herself Nora, there's not much you can do about it."

"Noura! Noura! Nora is not one of our names." Farid snarled.

"Get out of here or I'll report you for threatening me in my house."

"We haven't threatened you!" Jamal cried.

"That's exactly what you're doing. You're trying to intimidate me, and I won't allow it. If you don't leave right now, I'll call the police."

She shoved Farid out and slammed the door in their faces.

The three men went down the stairs wordlessly, each thinking about what to do. When they got to the doorway, the caretaker let them out.

"You'd better leave, or I'll have to call the police. Miss Lissette just called and said you've been threatening her."

Farid gave a rude response to the woman as they left the building.

Abir didn't dare say a word. Lissette had demonstrated that she had as strong a personality, or more, than Marion. These sisters weren't easy to handle. He saw his uncle's broken expression and felt sorry for him. His authority had been questioned, and it had stirred in him up both fury and pain

On the way to the metro station, it was Farid who broke the silence.

"That woman can say what she wants, Noura has to obey us. Let's file a report that she's run away from home. They'll force her to come back."

"Be quiet, son, you have to know when you've lost. The laws in France are the opposite of ours. They allow a daughter to disobey her father's will. If Noura has told them that we tried to marry her and she refused, they will take her side. They'll say she's a child. I don't know how we'll get her back," Jamal said mournfully.

"What do you think, Abir?" Farid asked, fixing his cousin with a hard look.

Abir preferred not to say what he was thinking. Noura wasn't going to come back, and she definitely wouldn't be getting married. They had lost her forever. But if he said so, he would enrage his cousin and increase his uncle's pain, so he chose to shrug, responding listlessly, "Maybe she'll come back."

All three of them knew this wasn't true.

Jamal and Farid went to see the imam to tell him what had happened, and they sent Abir home to be with Fatima and Ismail.

When they returned, Jamal told his nephew to go to school the next day and try to talk to Marion. He must tell her to convince Noura that she should return to them, that her parents would postpone the marriage. This had been the imam's advice.

The last thing they were expecting was a call from a child welfare office informing them that Noura was fine, but that she was going to be evaluated by a psychologist. There was no need for the family to worry. A social worker gave them an appointment for the following day to make to 'plan for Nora's future.' Jamal protested, saying his daughter wasn't called Nora but Noura, but the woman on the other end of the phone ignored him, referring to her as Nora.

The next morning, Abir found Marion at school, though she tried to step around him.

"Hey, I didn't do anything," he said, putting a hand on her arm to stop her.

Marion jumped as if she had been stung by a wasp. She hesitated, but she decided to listen, though she smacked his hand away.

"I just want to know how my cousin is."

"No. You're never going to find her. The lawyer has taken charge of her case. There are places that take in girls with problems like hers. Luckily, this is France."

"And she's not going to come back to school?"

"She'll finish the year at another school, social services have already told your aunt and uncle. Now leave me alone, or I'll tell the principal that you're harassing me."

"But I'm just asking you about my cousin!" Abir protested.

"You're all … you're all so barbaric! You tried to marry her off and she's only 16 years old! You have no respect for women, you think they're your property. It's so disgusting!" And she turned her back on him.

Fatima burst into tears when Abir told them about his encounter with Marion. She was anxious. She had to accompany Jamal to the youth home where Noura was staying, and she was afraid of what they would ask her, but even more afraid she would never see her daughter again. For the first time, Abir heard his aunt reproach her husband out loud. She regretted ever listening to the imam's advice.

"Noura hadn't done anything wrong!" Fatima screamed.

"Dressing so immodestly, leaving the house without a hijab, showing everyone her hair! How can you just overlook the fact that she was wearing a skirt so short you could see her thighs? And her face. Does it not matter to you that she was wearing red lipstick? She was behaving like a whore!"

"You don't understand, she was just copying her classmates. There are only two other girls in the school who wear a hijab. We live in France, Jamal. If you don't like how the French behave, then let's go back to Lebanon, to Algiers, or wherever you want! But if we live here, our children are going to act like other young people." Fatima's ferocious defense of her daughter left Abir and Ismail in stunned silence. They never would have imagined she was capable of standing up to her husband.

"That's not true! Isn't Farid setting an example? He's never done anything to shame us! He works, he studies, he's becoming an Islamic scholar. He will be a respected imam."

But Fatima paid no attention. She could only feel the pain of losing her daughter. She had no delusions; like Abir, she knew they would never get Noura back.

Abir and Ismail, who shared a small bedroom, would have preferred not to hear their aunt and uncle's fight. After the murder of their parents, they'd built a new life with Jamal and Fatima, and they'd been provided with safety and affection, and above all the semblance of belonging to a family. If it fell apart, their lives would once again become unstable.

"Noura is bad!" Ismail dared to say out loud to his brother.

"No, she isn't. How can you say that about your cousin?" Abir responded angrily.

"Look what's happening, we're all suffering."

"What's happening is that we don't understand her."

"What do you mean, we don't understand Noura?"

"She's different, she wants to be like the other girls here, dress the way she wants, but that doesn't mean she's bad," Abir explained.

"But what she's doing is bad. Good girls don't wear miniskirts or makeup," the boy insisted.

Abir couldn't find any more arguments to defend Noura. Ismail was only reciting what they'd been taught since they were children, what they'd heard from the imam, but still, he refused to accept that his cousin was a bad person. She wasn't. She'd always been kind to them. When Jamal brought them to their home from Lebanon, both Fatima and Noura had welcomed them with open arms, while Farid, though respectful, had never shown any affection.

"Noura is a good person, Ismail, don't ever forget it. Now do your homework, because I know you're not doing very well in French and math."

"I want to be an electrician like Uncle Jamal."

"Isn't it better to go to university? You could be an engineer."

"But I don't want to be an engineer, I just like to fix things."

"OK, but then let me study. I have a chemistry exam tomorrow and with everything going on, I haven't even cracked a book."

It was just after 7 p.m. when Fatima and Jamal returned from the center.

Fatima was sobbing inconsolably, and Jamal looked years older.

"They let us see her, but she refused to speak to us alone. She was with a psychologist. Our daughter says she prefers to stay in that place under the care of the state, knowing they won't let her out until she turns 18. And the psychologist! That woman looked at us like we were monsters, saying that we live in France and that there are laws here to prevent a minor from being forced into marriage. She also said that you can't punish a girl for how she dresses or for wearing red lipstick. She dared to say to me that if they forced every teenager who wore a miniskirt to be married, there would be no girls left unmarried in France!"

Jamal spoke in pain and anger while Farid listened in silence, rage flickering in every muscle of his face.

"There is a lack of respect for our religion and our traditions. We have to defend ourselves as Muslims. We can't allow them to impose customs on us that we find perverse. And then they talk about freedom! Yes, freedom to be like them, but not to allow us to be who we are. Does the state have the right to decide how parents raise their children? That's not freedom!" Farid insisted.

"Why doesn't Noura want to come home?" Ismail asked.

"Because she doesn't want to obey. She doesn't recognize her father's authority to decide her future," his cousin answered.

"They've kidnapped our daughter," Jamal said.

"No, that's not true. We're responsible for all of this," Fatima blurted through her sobs.

Jamal and Farid looked at her in shock.

"Woman, how dare you blame us! Haven't we done what anyone would do when their family's honor is at risk?"

"I only know that my daughter left because she didn't want to get married, and she hadn't done anything serious enough to justify our forcing her into it," Fatima answered, tears streaming down her face.

"Mother, we understand your pain, but that's no reason for you to question Father's wishes. If Noura doesn't marry, our family's honor will remain tarnished," Farid reproached her.

"The family's honor? Because Noura dared to wear a miniskirt? Do you mean to tell me that no family in France has honor? That all the young girls—"

Suddenly, Jamal raised his hand, then pointed an accusatory finger at his wife.

"How dare you question my authority in this house!" he exclaimed. "How dare you defend the girl who has shamed us! My own wife, defending her daughter for dressing like a whore! We don't need to copy the French customs. This country is putrefying little by little like the rest of Europe because they're atheists who don't have any morals. I will throw you out you if you ever say anything like that again! The pain of losing your daughter is no excuse. Now go and make dinner, and don't you dare say another word!"

Abir and Ismail were silent. Fatima's outburst was a shock, they knew that her behavior would have consequences. Jamal would never allow her to question his authority again; she had embarrassed him in front of the whole family.

That night during dinner, Jamal told them what he expected of the family from now on. Nobody could ever mention Noura's name again. They were all forbidden from seeing her or talking to her on the phone. Anyone who ignored these rules would be disowned from the family forever.

"Noura is dead to us," he said, leaving no room for debate.

Fatima served the meal with her head down, her eyes red and her hands shaking. Jamal and Farid would not look at her, but Ismail and Abir couldn't help glancing in her direction. They were both distressed by their aunt's suffering.

Noura's absence left a terrible void in the family. Everyone obeyed Jamal's orders, though Abir tried to get news about his cousin through Marion.

He would approach her in class, begging her to tell him how she was. But Marion always treated him with disdain and contempt, and he allowed her to insult him.

"Leave me alone. I'm not going to tell you anything. And don't stand so close, your breath smells disgusting."

He could stand the insults, but not what happened a few months later, when he watched Marion get out of a tiny convertible driven by a man a few years older than her. He dropped her off at the door of the school and kissed her in front of everyone, oblivious of anyone who might care.

Abir felt a powerful impulse to kill the man, and without thinking he ran up to Marion and grabbed her arm, forcing her to stop and look at him.

"Who is that?"

"How dare you! Let go of me or I'll scream and say you threatened to rape me."

But Abir didn't let go, clenching her arm even harder.

"I don't want to see you kissing anybody. Anybody!"

"You're crazy! I'll do whatever I want, with whomever I want, wherever I want! You're nobody, nobody! Don't you realize how grossed out I am by you? Let me go!"

"And that day in your house, did I gross you out then? Why did you want to do what we did?"

"I've told you a hundred times. I never would have chosen you, I just got unlucky. I didn't push you away because of Nora, she would have been sad if you'd gotten rejected. And I love Nora. She's my best friend, she's like a sister to me. I love her so much that I put up with you drooling all over my face. You're a nobody, Abir, and you always will be. Will you be an electrician like your uncle? Maybe a waiter? I don't know, I could see you working as a streetcleaner. There are so many men like you, losers who are good for nothing but cleaning up everybody else's shit."

Marion shoved him, and still, he didn't let go of her arm. He lunged towards her until there wasn't an inch of space between their faces.

"You will marry me. You won't do what we did with anyone else. I can forgive you for kissing that guy, but you won't do that with any other man!"

"You're an idiot, Abir. You'll never be in my league. You'll always be nothing, nothing at all."

"And what will you be, Marion?"

"I'll be whatever I want to be."

"You know what? One day you'll regret all of this. You'll admire me despite yourself. I'll be someone big Marion, and you'll regret it."

\*

Just before Abir's graduation, Jamal announced to his family that they would be leaving Paris. He couldn't bear the looks from his friends, or the sorrow that had settled on their home. Fatima obeyed him and didn't allow herself to question his authority or defend their daughter out loud. They all followed his orders to never mention Noura.

"Where will we go?" Ismail dared to ask.

"To Brussels. I've been offered a better job than the one I have here. I'm going to become partners with our imam's brother, who lives there. The man is doing well as an electrician and has a business with a few employees. And I have plans for you boys as well. Now is the time to complete your education. Tomorrow, someone important is coming over for dinner, someone you know well: Sheikh Mohsin."

Abir and Ismail each felt a tremor through their bodies. Sheikh Mohsin, the man their parents had given their lives for. His name was respected by upstanding Muslims. They knew his name was connected to the Circle and that he usually took refuge in Afghanistan, in the blessed mountains that always defeated invaders.

Why would the sheikh risk coming to Paris? He could be arrested. The two brothers saw the smirk on Farid's face.

"But isn't it dangerous for him to come to France? The Jews want to kill him. When ... when they came to our house, they were looking for him!" Ismail burst out fearfully.

"He's a brave man, a messenger from Allah to make Muslims greater," Jamal responded. "Yes, he's risking his life coming to Paris. But it's not the first time he's been to Europe. He commands an army of fighters all over the world. Brave servants of the Circle. Every blow that the infidels suffer has been planned by him. It is a great honor that he's coming to our house, and an even greater honor that he is prepared to bring you with him. Farid will accompany you to Afghanistan, and there you will be trained to become great soldiers of Allah."

Ismail was about to protest, to tell his uncle that he didn't want to go to Afghanistan, that he didn't even want to go to Brussels. He felt like his life was turning upside down. But he didn't dare complain, let alone say he didn't want to become a soldier for Allah and would prefer to be an electrician, nothing more.

Abir didn't say anything either. He thought about Marion. If he went to Afghanistan, he wouldn't see her for a long time. The idea made him extremely sad because he feared she would then marry someone else, but at the same time he savored the thought that maybe one day he would have his revenge on all those boys who had treated him with scorn.

Sheikh Mohsin's visit changed their lives forever.

Fatima took great pains in preparing several dishes for the dinner, even though Jamal had warned her that Mohsin was very austere. But she said that for a man of the sheikh's stature, he must be honored appropriately, and even if he didn't eat a single bite, at least he would see how much they appreciated his visit.

Jamal had to admit that his wife was right, and he allowed her to do it.

Six p.m. precisely. Spring had brought with it a rainy afternoon. Abir was studying in his room when he heard the doorbell. He stood up and went with Ismail to the living room.

Jamal came in, followed by Farid and a man that they didn't recognize. Tall, clean-shaven, his graying hair carefully combed back, a well-tailored wool suit in blue —though not extravagant enough to call attention—and a blue polka-dot tie.

Jamal made the introductions and the sheikh embraced the two brothers, addressing them affectionately.

"You are the sons of martyrs. We believers owe a debt to you. That day, you behaved like heroes. I remember it well. That's why I wanted to see you. We need men capable of making the most difficult sacrifices. It's an honor to be here."

The two brothers felt flattered. But was this really the same sheikh? Ismail didn't remember him well, but Abir still had memories of a man with a thick beard, bushy eyebrows, calloused hands and dark hair dressed in worn-out brown pants and a faded green shirt. That man seemed nothing like the person in front of them, who looked more like a businessman than the commander of the *jihad*. Even his way of speaking seemed different to them. The Mohsin they had met in their home in Ain al-Hilweh back in Lebanon spoke quickly with an Afghan accent, whereas this man's speech was very cultivated.

Fatima hid behind the kitchen door, trying to hear what the men were saying in the living room. Jamal had reminded her that Mohsin was profoundly religious, and therefore she would not be introduced to him. Even so, he insisted that she cover her hair well with her hijab in case Mohsin caught a glimpse of her. Farid then muttered that French customs had corrupted Muslims ways when it came to women's roles.

"Fortunately for me," he said, "I don't have to face the shame of my mother leaving the house to work, and if she goes to the grocery store, she always wears a hijab."

During the meal, Mohsin was friendly to the two brothers, but he pressed them on their knowledge of the Koran and didn't seem satisfied with the answers they gave.

"They don't have the adequate knowledge, but we'll soon fix that. We'll make these two into good men and they will have the honor of becoming soldiers of the Circle."

Abir and Ismail listened in silence, not daring to speak against Mohsin. They agreed to whatever he said, though neither of them was able to show enough enthusiasm when he explained what their new lives would be like. Mohsin warned them that they'd have to make do with very little and devote every minute of the day to training. Abir wanted to serve in the Circle, he yearned for it, but he worried about being hardened in the Afghan mountains, where his bed would be a crevice in the rocks, and with no other prospects than praying to Allah and learning to shoot, prepare explosives, and, above all, obey, obey, obey, because his life would be in the hands of the sheikh.

Farid said he was worried about the sheikh's safety in Paris.

"If the infidel dogs found you, it would be catastrophic for our cause," he said.

"They're looking for Mohsin, they're not looking for Nael Safady," he answered with a smile. "My passport is authentic and so is the business I represent. I buy medical supplies and distribute them throughout the Middle East from Lebanon. My credentials couldn't be better."

"Even so, you're risking a lot," Farid insisted.

"Son, Allah protects our leader and won't let him fall into the hands of our enemies," Jamal declared with total conviction.

"Very soon, this country will be trembling, just like all the other infidel countries. We need brothers ready to give their lives to win the final battle. This holy war needs brave, devout men, capable and intelligent men, men who are as disgusted as we are by the sin and depravation of the West. They will lose because they are corrupt, because they are infidels and because they are afraid of us. We will defeat them."

"We will!" Jamal declared, satisfied with Mohsin's words.

The rest of the meeting was spent finalizing the details of the journey that Abir and Ismail would make. The sheikh would become their guardian.

"Their parents died to save my life. I wouldn't be a man of honor if I didn't take care of these two boys. I will return them to you as true soldiers of Allah. They will honor your family, and you will be proud to have them carry your blood."

Jamal's face filled with gratitude. Farid implored the commander of the Circle to let him join them, but he refused.

"We need you here, in the heart of this rotten, corrupt place, to help us defeat the infidels. You're important, Farid. Men with your wisdom and devoutness are an example to the young. There are those who should take up arms, and others whose weapon is their intelligence. This is why you should stay. I'm putting my trust in you."

"I had thought Farid would accompany Abir and Ismail on the trip," Jamal said.

"That won't be necessary," Mohsin said firmly.

The sheikh stood up to leave at about 9 p.m. He hugged Abir and Ismail, reminding them that he would be back to see them in a few days.

When the family was left alone, Fatima came into the living room and took Ismail in her arms.

"Husband," she said, "you didn't tell me that the boys were going to leave. I may be just a lowly woman, but I know they're not old enough for war—"

"Shut up! How dare you?" Jamal cut her off.

"The sheikh is right…we've allowed ourselves to be contaminated by the customs of the West. Mother, when have you ever seen a good wife question her husband?" Farid intervened.

Jamal wasn't the only one who was outraged; the disdain he felt for his mother was written on his face.

"But I'm just saying they're still very young," Fatima insisted.

The fury in Jamal's eyes was enough to make the woman lower her head and return to the kitchen.

Abir and Ismail barely slept that night. The brothers spoke for hours about the future that had been designed for them. While Abir felt attracted to the abyss that opened before him, Ismail admitted to his older brother that he was afraid. He didn't want to be a soldier and he didn't want to fight, he confessed. Abir reproached him. The Sheikh Mohsin himself had taken an interest in them and become their guardian. He was doing them a great honor. He reminded him that their parents had been murdered by filthy dogs and their obligation was to get revenge. They would learn to be soldiers and they would join the Circle. They would avenge their family and, moreover, they would contribute to the expansion and triumph of Islam.

Ismail listened to Abir, ashamed of his fear. For the first time, he realized that he had no control over his own life, and this sunk him deeply into despair, though he didn't dare express his feelings to his brother.

Abir excitedly counted down the days until he graduated from school, while Ismail counted them apprehensively. Abir had finished high school, but Ismail still had a few years to complete. He didn't have that many friends, but he already missed them. He almost always played with other Muslim boys. The French boys, though not much better off financially, avoided him except when they were beating him up. And even though he didn't like studying, Ismail would have preferred to continue his daily life. It hadn't been easy for him to adapt to Paris. When they first arrived, he suffered from the same nightmare every night, watching his father fall to the floor, his mother crouching down, screaming, someone ordering them out of their house, Abir pulling him by the hand. Night after night he would wake up drenched in sweat and unable to contain his tears.

It had taken time for him to understand that his uncle, though distant and not very affectionate, was a good man. He had always feared Farid because he sensed he was unhappy that his father had brought the boys to live with them.


But the women of the house, his aunt Fatima and his cousin Noura, had showered them with affection. Noura had always found time to teach him games, and she confronted the boys who teased him in school. If it hadn't been for her and Fatima, his life in Paris would have been unbearable.


Now Noura wasn't there anymore. She would have argued against them being sent to Afghanistan, although it wouldn't have had any effect; Noura and Fatima's opinions didn't matter. They were women, and in their house the men took the decisions. Ismail would have preferred it the other way around.

*

Some weeks later, Marion arrived on the last day of class wearing incredibly tight jeans and a tank top, a sweater in her hand to complete the outfit. She was dressed like every other girl there.

It was a day of goodbyes. Their teenage years were ending, and they were about to enter adulthood. Many of the kids would never see each other again. Others might keep up their friendships, but the future ahead of them all was still unwritten.

Abir was graduating at the top of the class, just like Marion. The director of the school congratulated them both in front of the rest of the students, emphasizing that with these grades both Abir and Marion would be welcome at any university. When he asked what they planned to do, they both dodged the question. Abir couldn't confess that he was going to become a mujahid in Afghanistan, and Marion closely guarded the secret decision she had made about her future.

"Have you seen Noura?" Abir asked her.

"Yes."

"And is she OK?"

"Yes."

"Listen, I love my cousin, I don't know why you refuse to tell me how she is."

"Because I'm not your go-between."

"My uncle won't let us see her."

"Better for her."

"I don't believe that Noura would shut us out of her life," Abir protested.

"Look, I'm not going to get involved in your stuff. I did enough for her."

"I thought you were best friends!"

"We are…well, we were. It's hard to have a best friend when you never see her."

"When is she getting out of that center where they're keeping her?"

"I guess this week. Nora's about to turn 18, so she'll have to fend for herself."

He was shocked by Marion's indifference towards what would happen to her friend.

"Has she told you what she's planning to do?"

"I wouldn't tell you if I knew. Look, we're all older now and everyone has to figure out their own life. High school friendships stop being so important. Nora's cool, but now she has to figure things out for herself, and I do too."

"But she won't have anywhere to go when she leaves that place," Abir protested.

"Well, I'm sure they'll help her find something. I don't work for social services. Now get lost Abir, I really don't feel like talking to you."

"You know what, Marion? One day you're going to regret treating people so badly. You think you're better than the rest, but you're not."

"I don't care what you think of me. You're a nobody, Abir, a nobody."

"I'm the first guy you slept with. I know you lost your virginity to me."

"Come on, you're such an idiot! I never would have chosen you for something like that."

"One day you'll regret treating me like this. I'll be an important man, Marion, very important."

She started to laugh, her expression dripping with scorn. She turned away without saying goodbye, without even looking at him. To her, Abir didn't exist.


A few days after graduation, Uncle Jamal told the two brothers to start packing their bags. They would travel with a good friend of Farid's to India, and from there they would go to Pakistan and cross the border into Afghanistan. The trip would be long and difficult, but safe. He told them to use only a backpack; where they were going, they wouldn't need very many clothes, just some items for cold weather and a good pair of boots.

Fatima was also packing. As Jamal had announced, they were soon going to live in Brussels. For their uncle, it meant the opportunity of becoming a partner in a small business. For Fatima, it meant sorrow; she would be moving far away from Noura. She hadn't seen her daughter since she ran away, but she was waiting impatiently for her to turn 18 and get out of the youth home. Though Fatima had always obeyed her husband, she was prepared to defy him when it came to her daughter. Jamal had forbidden her from seeing Noura again. "She's dead to us," he told her. Fatima didn't contradict him, but she was determined to see her daughter. She would see her in secret, but she would see her. Jamal's decision to move the family to Brussels, however, would distance her. She feared not being able to say goodbye, and that Noura wouldn't know where to find them. She couldn't confide in her son Farid, with him being so pious and obedient. He thought Noura should be severely punished. Without anybody's support, she was resolved to see her daughter before they left, to tell her about moving to Brussels, and beg her to find a way for them to see each other sometimes.

Fatima took a risk and shared her anguished thoughts with Abir. He confessed that he also didn't want to go to Afghanistan without saying goodbye to his cousin first.

Finally, the day arrived.

Noura asked for a *café au lait*, passing on the croissant. She wasn't hungry. All she wanted was to start her life.

It was her 18th birthday. Her lawyer had told her they could help her find a place at a women's shelter, but she had turned down the offer. Eighteen years old. She was now of legal age, and her father had no power over her anymore. She had come out on top. She was grateful to have been born in France, to be French, and grateful for the country that had protected her from her father's plan to marry her off.

She was looking forward to seeing Marion again. They would make a plan and see it through. She was sure that Marion and Lissette would let her stay at their house, at least until she could find a job that would let her pay for school and a room. She wanted to ask the sisters to let her rent a room at their place. The apartment was big and had four bedrooms. She wouldn't get in their way, and best of all, they would be together.

When the lawyer arrived, she signed all the paperwork that would give her control over her own life.

"Well, Nora, I hope you will take good care. Nobody can make you get married if you don't want to, and I don't know whether you should try to talk to your parents— perhaps they want to reconcile with you."

"I doubt it. My dad is not the kind of guy who changes his mind. He's not a bad person, but he thinks he has the right to decide who I should marry, and to force me to do it if I refuse. My mother is different. She's always obeyed him, never opposed him, but I know she loves me. And deep down, I know that she agrees with me."

When the lawyer walked her to the door and she stepped onto the street, she saw her mother. Yes, there she was with Abir. Fatima was wearing a hijab and a long navy blue coat that covered every inch of her body. They held each other, bursting into tears.

"My little girl! I tried to call you, but they wouldn't put you on the phone. Your own mother! I was so worried. I've been here since 8 in the morning. As soon as your father went to work, we came to wait for you. Oh Noura, what are we going to do?"

They walked until they found a small café. Fatima hesitated. She was afraid to go inside, thinking someone might see them.

"Mother, we're not going to do anything wrong! Let's just sit and talk and have a cup of coffee. I don't think anyone will recognize us, we're nowhere near the neighborhood and anyway, Abir is with us."

Fatima relented, but insisted on sitting inside in a discreet corner, out of sight from those walking by.

"Will you ask your father for forgiveness and come home? He won't talk about you, but he misses you as much as I do."

"You know that's impossible. Father is not going to change, and neither will I. I'm sorry Mother, but I have to try to do what I really want to do. It's never been a secret that I want to become a singer."

"But that's not a decent job! If you do that, you'll never find a husband. And there's something you should know. Your father has decided to move us to Brussels."

"Brussels? Why?"

"Because, well, you know how he is. He thinks your behavior has brought shame on our family and he wants to go somewhere where nobody knows us. The imam's brother has a small business in Brussels. He's older and wants to retire soon. Your father is going to partner with him, and then, later on, he'll buy the business."

"It's good that he wants to do well. He works hard and earns very little, and we were always a lot of mouths to feed. I'm happy for him. But do you want to go to Brussels?"

"I want to be where my family is. Your brother Farid will stay in Paris, but Abir and Ismail are leaving. Sheikh Mohsin wants to turn them into soldiers of Allah."

Noura grabbed Abir's hand.

"Where are you going?" Noura asked, alarmed.

"To Afghanistan," he responded with pride.

"Incredible. I've always known that Mohsin was a leader in the Circle. And he has no problem sacrificing two children. This is horrifying! And my father is allowing it!"

"Noura, it's a great honor, what Sheikh Mohsin is giving us!" Abir interjected.

"An honor? Do you know what they're going to teach you there? I'll tell you. They're going to make you into terrorists."

"Don't say that! Allah won't allow it!" Fatima exclaimed.

"Mother, try to convince Father to bring Abir and Ismail to Brussels with you. As for Farid, my brother is grown up, and he's become a fanatic."

"Don't say that about Farid!" Fatima begged her, frightened by what she was hearing.

"I love him because he is my brother, but I'm sorry, that's how it is. You know the things the imam says better than I do. Farid defends the holy war. He believes that anyone who isn't Muslim is repulsive. I'm sorry that my brother is as much of a fanatic as the imam, and I'm even more sorry about what Sheikh Mohsin will do to Abir and Ismail."

They talked for a long time. Noura asked her mother and her cousin to write and call her at Marion's house. She was going to stay in Paris, but she promised that as soon as she could, she would visit her mother Brussels. The bonds between them would never be broken. Fatima insisted on giving her some money.

"It's all I could save," she said. "I hope it helps you, though it's not much," she said, pressing the bills into Noura's hand.

The cousins hugged, promising they wouldn't forget each other.

Fatima, Abir and Noura took the subway towards Strasbourg–Saint-Denis, but once they got there, they headed in opposite directions. Marion and Lissette lived in a neighborhood that had a certain charm, near the Canal Saint-Martin.

Lissette opened the door and was surprised to see Noura, and even more surprised by the warm hug she received.

"What are you doing here? I didn't know you were getting out today."

"It's my birthday. My 18th! I need to get my life together now. Where's Marion? I can't wait to see her!"

"Marion? She'll be here later. She's leaving."

"Leaving?"

"Yeah, she says she's sick of Paris, and I get it. She's grown up now and has to figure out her life. I'm going to live with my boyfriend, and we've decided to sell the apartment. But she'll tell you about all that. Come in and sit down."

Marion explained everything to her as soon as she arrived. She didn't spare a single detail. She had met a young British man and she was going to live with him in London. She would work, study, and start a new life. Paul—that was her new boyfriend's name—was sharing an apartment with a friend on the outskirts of London, and she was moving in with them.

"But you can't go! What are you going to do there?" she asked in anguish.

"First, I'm going to find a job. Paul says it's not hard to get a job as a waitress. He works as a concierge at the Savoy, and he can probably get me in there."

"But you've always wanted to study…"

"And I will, Nora, I will. I know that if I don't study, I won't amount to anything, that's why my goal is to get into one of the London universities. You know my English is pretty good, thanks to Lissette."

"No, not thanks to me," her sister interrupted, "after all, Papa was the English teacher, and he forced us to speak English at home."

"And with Mamá, Spanish," Marion remembered.

"What a family!" Lissette exclaimed.

"It wasn't Father, it was Mamá who always insisted that English was necessary if we wanted to be something in life."

Noura listened anxiously to the sisters, feeling left out.

"You always did get good grades in English," she offered.

"The only problem is my accent. Paul says I have a bit of an accent. But I'll fix it. I'm sure I can."

"So, when are you leaving?" she asked, afraid of the answer.

"As soon as we sell the apartment. The real estate agent has already shown it to a few people. It's too bad Saint-Denis has gotten so unappealing, even though we live in the best part. No offense Nora, but you Muslims, with all your customs, have changed this neighborhood."

Noura was confused. Marion was suddenly treating her like a stranger. She was talking to her as if they weren't close friends, as if their friendship didn't count anymore.

"And what are you planning to do, Nora?" Lissette asked.

"I … well … I wanted to rent a room. My mother has given me a little money. I thought that—but I guess that can't happen anymore—but I thought that you could maybe rent me a room. I didn't know—you never told me you were planning to leave Paris."

"Come on, Nora, don't be like that! We're done with high school, it's over, we each have to find our own way in life, however we can. Did you think we were going to spend the rest of our lives together? That's silly. School friendships don't last forever. We had a good time, but it's over. Now everyone needs to fend for themselves. Look, if it's OK with Lissette, you can crash here for a few days until you find a place. I'm leaving in four days. Paul has to get back to work, and I'm going with him."

"But … when did you meet him?"

"A month ago. He was in Le Sully having a beer and I was walking past. What happened was I tripped, and he helped me, and … well, now he's my boyfriend."

Noura didn't say anything. She knew this was Marion's tactic when she wanted to flirt with a boy. Tripping on purpose and, if necessary, even twisting her ankle. They always helped her, then she would start a conversation and get what she wanted. She decided to turn down Marion's unenthusiastic offer to stay for a few days. She didn't have anywhere else to go, but she was hurt and humiliated. She had just discovered that their friendship was a thing of the past, and it was going to cost her quite a few tears to get over it.

"I'm glad you have a boyfriend. I'm sure you'll do great in London and that you'll get everything you want."

"So will you stay here for a few days?" Lissette asked.

"No, thank you. You'll be busy packing up. I don't want to bother you. I'll figure something out."

"Yes, one day you'll be a famous singer," Marion said mockingly.

"Maybe, who knows?" she said, and she left without another word.

In that moment, she felt she had lost everything.

Fatima was busy working in the kitchen when Abir came in with Ismail. Their uncle had given them money to buy good boots; he said they were the thing they would need most in Afghanistan. They showed their purchases to their aunt, who barely paid attention, and then Ismail asked permission to watch TV before Jamal got home.

The phone rang and Fatima asked Abir to answer it. Strangely, there was silence on the line, then he heard Noura's voice, asking if her father was home, and then, if they could talk. They met up in a café and she told him about the end of her friendship with Marion.

"I always thought she cared about me, that our friendship was real, and now ..."

Abir felt doubly humiliated. Marion was going off to London with some guy, and even worse, she had hurt Noura.

"I promise you, one day she'll pay for what she's done to us."

"Don't wish anything bad for her, Abir. That's just her nature. I thought our friendship was real. My mistake. I should have understood that Marion only cares about herself at any given moment. You know what, Cousin? I'm glad she never liked you back because she would have just ended up breaking your heart."

They talked for an hour. Then she gave him the phone number of the boarding house where she was going to live.

"I don't know what I'm going to do. Maybe I'll go to Brussels too, to be near my mother. There's nothing left for me here Abir."

The next morning, Abir went to Marion's house. Wearing only the t-shirt she slept in, she opened the door.

"What the hell are you doing here? Look, if you're going to stalk me, I'll report you!" she threatened.

"You acted like a perfect bitch to Noura. You knew perfectly well she had nowhere else to go."

"She could've stayed here for a few days, but she was too proud. I guess your cousin thought we were going to be together the rest of our lives. I don't know where she is, and I don't care. We're done with high school now and everyone has to figure out their own lives."

"You know perfectly well she can never come home! She thought you were her best friend."

"I don't care what she does with her life. Your whole family is so annoying! Anyway, I wasn't her only friend, Nora was friends with other girls in our class."

"Yes, but you were her best friend. Noura loved you and admired you. She followed you everywhere. You decided who she should or shouldn't talk to, and you loved showing off to everyone that you were in charge."

"Wow, what an earful. I didn't know you were capable of stringing that many words together!" she said mockingly.

"Why are you like this, Marion?"

"What am I like what, Abir? I think you and your cousin are a pair of idiots. High school friendships don't matter."

"I was more than a friend to you! You had sex with me!" he screamed with rage.

"Hey, don't yell at me! And forget what happened that day. For me, it's like the whole thing never happened. I already told you Abir, you're a nobody, you'll always be a nobody. Maybe you'll get lucky, and your uncle will teach you how to be an electrician, or maybe you'll get a stall selling second-hand clothes in Le Passage. But whatever you do, just forget about me! You'll never be good enough for me, Abir, never. Get out of here! I've told you more than once you stink and it grosses me out. You reek of spices and sweat. Get out of here, or I'll report you for harassing me!"

"You'll regret this, Marion. I promise you."

"Don't threaten me again or I'll report you!" she screamed.

Marion slammed the door. Abir couldn't hold back his tears of rage.

Many years had passed since that day. Years he spent under the wing of Sheikh Mohsin in Afghanistan. Abir had learned how to fight, how to handle explosives, and how to disappear into the landscape to avoid falling into enemy hands.

It had been difficult and demanding, a training course where the only thing that mattered was staying alive to carry out the next mission. He learned the difference between strategy and tactics. He learned to live with only what was necessary. He learned never to complain. He could now circumvent borders and smuggle weapons from one country to another. He could handle fraudulent commercial transactions and forge documents. He was able to live in hiding. He learned to carry messages to cells scattered around the world. He learned to deceive. He learned to kill. He learned to survive and strike back. Sheikh Mohsin said he was proud of him. He had earned his trust. Abir accompanied him on his clandestine journeys to Europe and the United States. For the sheikh, war had to be waged against the West, and against the infidels.

Abir got out of bed and made himself a whiskey on the rocks. He thought the alcohol might help him fall asleep.

*Tel Aviv.*
*Jacob*

He had come back. He told himself it would be the last time, though maybe it would be worth it to investigate the depths of his psyche. Dr. Tudela greeted him from behind her desk while she typed something into her computer.

"Have a seat."

He obeyed silently. The doctor took a moment to turn off her computer.

"Sorry."

Jacob shrugged. It hadn't bothered him that she took a few seconds of his time.

"I'm glad you've come back," the psychiatrist said with a smile.

"Did you think I wasn't going to?"

"I thought you might be reluctant to come."

"The truth is, I didn't hesitate. At least not today, but I'm not sure what I'll decide in the future."

"You're deciding whether it can be useful or not."

"I'd like to ask you a question: are there others like me? I mean, people who don't really know what it means to be Jewish?"

"You're not alone. This country isn't easy. There are Jewish people here who have come from all over the world. Before they decided to move to Israel, they were French, Russian, German, even Iraqi. They had a different language, different customs, and they had roots in the societies they were living in. Coming here means learning Hebrew, adopting new customs and a different vision of life. Above all, it means fighting for the survival of the country. All of this creates conflict. It's normal. Tell me, do you have any close friends?"

Jacob considered this. Did he have close friends? He sometimes thought that the relationships he'd built lacked depth. Except for Efraim. He and Efraim had met when they were both completing their military service. They had participated in operations in the Occupied Territories and had felt the same unease when facing the Palestinians, young men like them. He and Efraim often thought there wasn't much that made them different from those boys, that they all wanted the same thing, a place of their own. But they were incapable of talking about their feelings and this sense of unease. He explained this to the doctor.

"So, you didn't adapt to the army?"

"I couldn't stop wondering if everything I was doing was meaningless. I don't mean learning to fight to defend Israel—I don't have any doubt about that. This country deserves to be defended, and it deserves to endure, but I think sometimes we're not doing things as we should. Something happened that I can't forget. It's my darkest nightmare, a memory that won't let me sleep, or even live."

"Do you want to tell me about it?"

And so, Jacob began.

"One afternoon, the commander of my unit called us soldiers together. He seemed in doubt, but maybe that was just my impression. His orders had been explicit. We were going to participate in a mission to enter southern Lebanon and capture an Islamist leader. We were told he was one of the biggest arms traffickers in the Middle East, someone who provided weapons to all the radical groups in the region."

Jacob had spoken up boldly and said that the plan was impossible. There was a United Nations force in Lebanon.

He said he couldn't participate, not only because he had no experience with special operations, but he was also incapable of putting anyone's life in danger. The others looked at him as if he had lost his mind. In reality, there was no choice. He would join the task force that was being put together, five men in total. They would secretly enter Lebanon, reach the camp in Ain al-Hilweh, capture their objective, and get out immediately.

"Four of you will enter the house and you, Jacob, will stay outside to ensure no one escapes. The cameras embedded in their helmets will send a visual of what's happening inside to your computer. That's it," the commander said. Then he added, "Jacob, that man, apart from being an arms dealer, has valuable information. We think he's the leader of the Circle, a terrorist organization that—I don't need to remind you—has carried out terrible attacks. So keep your precious scruples to yourself."

Jacob didn't dare ask why he had been chosen for this mission. Later, over time, he'd come to the conclusion that they'd been testing him. On a few occasions prior to this, he'd talked to some of the other soldiers about the discomfort he felt during certain operations, especially those that took place in Palestinian territories. At one point he had even told this to his commander, who had asked in response if his reluctance was a matter of conscience or fear.

The commander had been going easier on him for a few months, he said, but it was another thing to let him weasel out of what he believed to be the responsibility of every Jewish person in Israel.

Jacob shut his mouth. He didn't agree, but he knew couldn't push his luck any further.

Two days later, just after dawn, the five soldiers crossed the southern border of Lebanon. It didn't take long for them to get to Ain al-Hilweh, a refugee camp near Sidon.

That camp was a squalid, miserable place where displaced Lebanese citizens also lived. The five men in the unit felt sure of what they were doing. They took their positions, surrounding a house located a few hundred meters from the camp. Jacob remained back, alert. Soon, the video transmissions appeared on his computer. The men looked around carefully and then quietly entered the house before shattering the sleep of those inside. And then Jacob looked up and saw him. A boy of about 14 or 15, jumping out of the window. He held the hand of a sobbing child no more than 10. A man followed behind them, shouting at them to run. But the boy stopped, pulling on the hand of a woman who had had difficulty jumping from the window because she was wounded and carrying a baby girl in her arms.

The man started to shoot as he broke into a run, leaving behind the woman and the children. The boy remained with the woman who had fallen as she jumped from the window. She was badly hurt. He tried to help her get up. The baby had slipped from her arms and was sprawled on the ground, her face covered in blood. Jacob was frozen, unable to move. Everything was happening in slow motion. Another man appeared in the middle of the confusion, shooting in Jacob's direction.

His commander ordered him to aim at them, though he didn't order him to shoot. Did he shoot? He couldn't remember. The boy then looked at him, lifted up a rock, and threw it in his direction, though it didn't hit him. He then threw another. They looked at each other, the boy with hatred, Jacob transfixed. Suddenly, one of the rocks struck his neck and a trickle of blood started to run down his skin. Two soldiers emerged from the house and ran toward him. Jacob was holding a position near their truck. There was the sound of gunshots. Screams. The voices of women. Then a deafening noise, and that pitiful house exploded into flames. The camp had woken up, people running towards them.

82

That boy and Jacob looked at each other again, and through the noise of the fire and the screams he heard him shout, "I'm going to kill you all!" His face was the image of rage, rage mixed with an intense, deep hatred. Next to him, the woman lay still, the tiny girl she'd been carrying in her arms nearby with her bloodstained face. When the woman had fallen, the baby had hit her head. Or had he killed her? The boy was trying to pull his mother to her feet. Jacob could hear him screaming, "Um! Um!"* and begging her to get up. But the woman couldn't respond, her life having seeped out of her, her open eyes staring into eternity. The boy bent down over her, trying to lift her and failing. Shielding her body with his own, he turned back to look at Jacob, raised a shaking fist and screamed, "I'll find you! I'll kill you all and you'll pay for what you've done, filthy dogs!"

Jacob couldn't move. He felt a hand shove him and a voice order him to get in the truck. He looked back and his eyes met again with those of the boy, now dragging his mother's lifeless body. The mission was over. The mission had failed. The man they were looking for had managed to escape. The inhabitants of the refugee camp were now running towards them, and they would have to start shooting to hold them back if they waited any longer.

"Why did we do that? Did we really need to blow up that house? How many more have we killed?" Jacob shouted at the commander.

"It's us or them, Jacob. They would have killed us if they'd had the chance."

"And the women and children? Are they our enemies too? That boy … that boy will hate us for the rest of his life. I would too."

* *Um* means "mother" in Arabic.

The commander didn't respond. He took out a pack of cigarettes and offered them to the others. Jacob had never been a smoker, but he became one that day. The other soldiers looked at him anxiously. No one spoke. Each soldier was submerged in his own thoughts. What could they say? What could they tell themselves?

When they returned to the base, once again in Israeli territory, he asked the commander who else had been living in the house besides the man they'd tried to capture. He managed to get some information. The people that Sheikh Mohsin had taken refuge with were an impoverished Lebanese family. The father was from a village near Sidon and the mother had been from the north. She was the daughter of a Lebanese woman and the grandchild of a Palestinian refugee. Her sister was married to an Afghan, and this was the person Sheikh Mohsin had come to visit. The sheikh crossed borders like they didn't exist, the commander told him, and he was one of the biggest providers of weapons to the terrorist groups that operated in Europe and the Middle East.

"Get over it!" the commander scolded him.

Much later, Jacob learned that the dead woman, Ghada, was the boy's mother, and that she had protected the sheikh by putting herself between him and the soldiers. The father, Jafar, had died inside the house, having attacked the soldiers to allow the sheikh to escape. The family's last name was Nasr, and there were two sons: a young boy called Ismail, and his older brother, Abir.

"They asked us to do a composite drawing of the boy, but the other soldiers were unable to provide many details; they hadn't been paying attention to him, and he had escaped pretty much as soon as they entered the house. He wasn't the target anyway. But I had seen his face and, worst still, locked eyes with him. I don't know why, but I didn't give many details to the artist. The commander knew that I was lying when I said that I didn't remember, but he didn't push me."

"Ever since, his face appears in my nightmares and I hear his voice saying, 'I will find you, you will pay for what you have done.' I'm sure that he will."

"Are you afraid of him?" Dr. Tudela asked.

Jacob considered this, aware of the doctor's eyes searching his face.

"I wouldn't call it fear, it's more the certainty that it will come true. I think about how I would have felt if I had lived through such a terrible thing at his age. I wonder what kind of person it would have made me. Wouldn't you wonder the same?"

The doctor didn't respond, but lowered her head as she wrote something in her notebook and then looked at Jacob again.

"And after that event, what happened?"

"I started having nightmares. It became harder and harder for me to fall in line with the army's demands. I felt like a stranger. It wasn't my place. I started to have problems with the other soldiers in my unit, except for Efraim, who was my only friend, and still is, although we couldn't be more different.

"Then one day my unit was ordered to cross the Green Line and enter Bethlehem. I told my commander that I would not participate in the mission. I would be unable to deal with the children who threw rocks at us, the horror in the women's faces as they ran from the sirens, and the hateful looks from the men who felt impotent against the superiority of the Israeli army. I had decided that the Palestinians were not my enemies, or at least I didn't want them to be. So I refused, and I was sent to prison.

"My friend Efraim didn't find it as difficult as I did to follow orders, and he tried to talk me out of it when I told him I sympathized with the *refuseniks* and had decided to join the

Courage to Refuse movement. You had to have courage to refuse to participate in the military operations in the Occupied Territories—taking that step made you the worst kind of outcast.

"Efraim tried to change my mind. No, he didn't like what we were doing in Gaza or the West Bank, but it had to be done because we were at war.

"'They'll lock you away,' Efraim warned me. But I didn't care. 'I didn't come to Israel to oppress anybody. Haven't we been oppressed and persecuted ourselves, just for being what we are? We should resolve this problem with the Palestinians some other way. They have to accept that Israel exists, that it's a reality, and we won't be thrown out, but we also have to share this land.'

"It surprised me when Efraim asked if fear was what was behind my decision. I told him the truth. Of course I felt afraid when I faced other men, of course I was afraid for my life, but I was also afraid for the Palestinians. Most of all, I was afraid of not recognizing myself. I was prepared to defend Israel, no question, but only behind the Green Line—in other words, only if we were attacked."

His friend didn't understand, and that put distance between them. Efraim was upset when Jacob joined the other conscientious objectors who'd refused to operate in the Occupied Territories, and disappointed when he appeared together with a group of soldiers protesting against public opinion. Because Jacob wasn't alone. Many Israelis felt the same way. In 2002, they had started *Ometz LeSarev*, the Courage to Refuse movement, just as 20 years before. In 1982, another group of soldiers dissented during the invasion of Lebanon by forming a group called the *Yesh Gvul* (There is a Limit!), and later the New Profile movement, as well as a number of NGOs who tried to help the Palestinians.

No, he wasn't alone, but even so, when they sent him to a prison cell for his actions, Efraim tried to visit him and did whatever he could to talk to whomever would listen, insisting that his friend Jacob was not a coward.

At that time, neither of them imagined they would end up working for Dor, Efraim permanently and Jacob occasionally.

It was his mother who got him out of prison earlier than expected. She knew Dor. At first, she wouldn't explain how she knew him, but it was her fault that the man appeared in his life.

One day, the door of his cell had opened and a tall, strongly built man with a magnetic stare walked in. He seemed able to read a person's innermost thoughts. Thinking he looked like a bear, Jacob wasn't surprised when he introduced himself so plainly.

"My name is Dor."

He then told him that he would be released in a few days and would spend the rest of his military service working for him. The man was intimidating, and Jacob didn't dare ask what the work would involve.

Dor didn't bother to give further any explanation either. For the next hour, he asked him questions about literature, history, international politics and, above all, about his talent with computers while Jacob wondered to himself what he really wanted.

Two days later, a man in civilian clothes appeared in his cell and ordered him to follow him. "Dor is waiting for you," he said without adding anything else.

They went by car to a two-story house hidden among fruit trees and palms. Palm Tree House, where Dor was waiting for him. This would be the second time they'd meet.

"You speak French perfectly and Arabic with a Lebanese accent, which is very good for us," Dor observed.

"I'm Lebanese, and my father was French," Jacob managed to say.

"I know quite a lot about you, Jacob Baudin. Your father André was French, though he lived most of his life in Beirut as a businessman. You were born in Beirut, and you spent the first years of your life there until your father fell ill and decided to return to France at the time when Lebanon stopped being the Switzerland of the East. So you are French and Lebanese, but above all you are Jewish through your mother, just like your mother's parents and your ancestors before them."

There was something strange about Dor, and Jacob couldn't imagine what he wanted until he finally laid it all out. He could spend the rest of his sentence in jail—the commander of his regiment was very angry with him for the bad example he set for the rest of his unit—or he could make himself useful to Israel working for him in the virtual intelligence department. Dor had heard that he was a genius with computers, even his professors had said so.

"War is not just waged on the front. We need people who can think, people who are able to find out what's being said in Gaza, Baghdad and Cairo. Your mission will be to listen."

He then explained that he would have to participate in simple operations, possibly in Lebanon. And no, he wouldn't have to kill anybody, except if his life were in danger, in which case he would have two options: let himself be killed or defend himself. He would leave that up to him.

He didn't know whether to refuse or not. What exactly would these 'simple operations' consist of? He soon found out, and it became clear that the man wasn't trying to do him a favor, but rather use him for the same cause he'd rebelled against.

At that time, he still lived with his mother. She hadn't told him she knew Dor, and he hadn't told her about the man who'd turned up in his prison cell, but eventually they ended up talking about what had happened. She criticized his attitude, telling him, "You owe it to Israel."

He responded that there were many other ways to defend Israel. And anyway, he didn't care about her opinion—it would be better if she didn't waste her breath.

They argued intensely and it became unpleasant. She didn't understand his conscientious objections and berated him in the worst way possible.

Jacob looked at Dr. Tudela, who seemed engrossed in his story. He couldn't help feeling momentarily uncomfortable and wondered if it made any sense to be talking to a stranger, even if she was a psychiatrist.

"Well, that's pretty much it. I probably said a few things that don't matter," Jacob said apologetically.

"You have a good memory for detail. I understand your relationship with your mother is complicated. And from your tone of voice, it doesn't seem like you get along very well with Dor either."

"Do you know him?"

Dr. Tudela hesitated before deciding on an appropriate answer, her lips glued in a smile.

"Yes, we know each other."

"I should have known. They wouldn't have sent me to you if Dor didn't approve of you. Do you sympathize with him?" Jacob wanted to know.

"It doesn't matter what I think of Dor, but rather what you think of him," she stated, still smiling.

Jacob wasn't sure whether to answer that honestly.

For a few seconds, he and the doctor were silent. She waited to see if Jacob would decide to continue. He was wondering how she knew Dor. For him, since he had finished his military service in the Palm Tree House, it was inevitable that they knew each other. Later, when Natan Lewin hired him to work at IAI, he warned him that Palm Tree House was one of their regular clients, along with several leading AI companies.

In fact, Lewin himself had been one of Dor's agents in the past.

"I don't know if I can trust you," Jacob finally replied.

"I'm a doctor. I would be breaking my confidentiality agreement if I shared what you tell me. If you want to know whether I ever collaborated with Palm Tree House, the answer is yes. I work for my country whenever they require it. Occasionally, they ask me to make psychological profiles of certain individuals classified as enemies. But they have never asked me—nor would I agree—to tell them about what I hear in this office. It's about professional ethics, Jacob, ethics for how to live life. And now ... well, I think we should stop for today. You have to think about whether you can trust me, and right now you're not sure if you can. But it's your decision. When you decide, call me."

*Brussels.*
*Abir*

A bir walked casually through the European Quarter. He didn't want to call attention to himself. He was dressed like the young men who worked in the many international organizations in the city. Gray pants, blue striped shirt, jacket and tie, his shoes polished to a shine. He carried a nondescript leather briefcase in his hand. No one seemed to notice him, and that made him smile. He had been in Brussels for two days, but he still hadn't met up with any of the brothers who would help him in his mission. He hadn't even gone to see his aunt and uncle, though he was planning to do so this afternoon. Their apartment was his only home. He crossed over Schuman Roundabout and then passed in front of the Berlaymont building, the seat of the European Commission. He went past the European Council and walked towards Leopold Park, then turned in the direction of the European Parliament.

He liked the city, as much as he would have preferred to hate it, though he wouldn't admit that to the others. Where he saw harmony, others would only see their reasons for fighting. It was the capital of Europe, the capital of the infidels who had once attacked them; there could be no mercy. Their blood would run and purify the place.

Paris was beautiful, but Brussels had something special. He would fulfill his ambition for destruction and in doing so, he would punish them, not just for their cosmopolitan

91

environment and for being the capital of Europe, but for being the headquarters of NATO. Apart from New York, where the United Nations headquarters were, no other city in the world had a higher number of foreign civil servants. And that was very useful for his plans.

After the Twin Towers were destroyed, the authorities had made New York highly secure. Abir knew no objective was impossible, but he preferred not to pursue the highest risk of failure. In his opinion, Belgium was a failing country that was only staying on its feet because its capital housed a good number of European institutions. This was why he had chosen Brussels. Sheikh Mohsin had congratulated him on his choice, though he also urged him to be careful.

"I hope that your success doesn't make you arrogant, and that arrogance doesn't make you blind," he had said when Abir described his plans.

No, it wasn't pride that drove him to complete his mission. It was vengeance. An intimate and irrepressible desire to settle a score with those who had snatched away his parents, his childhood and any future he might have had other than the one he was heading toward.

He would never forget how as a child, his father had told him that if he studied, he could get out of Ain al-Hilweh, that he wouldn't have to live in a place which was only known for its poverty.

"I'll be a doctor, an engineer, or, even better, an astronaut!" he responded, sure of his unwritten future.

His mother smiled proudly. She preferred for him to be an engineer and was sure he would have a good future in one of the Gulf states where, she assured him, they needed talented people.

He wanted to study, but he didn't want to leave Ain al-Hilweh. His parents were there, as were his siblings, friends and relatives. He would become an engineer and he would make Ain al-Hilweh into a beautiful village.

But he wasn't an engineer, a doctor or an astronaut. He was a soldier of the Circle.

He knew he would die young. One day, he would have to give up his life even though he didn't want to die. He longed to keep living. He wondered what it would be like to have a life like the men he passed on the street. A job, a wife, children. Routine.

He knew he couldn't allow it. If he got attached to a woman and she gave him children, would he have the courage to die? Fearing the answer, he preferred to devote every minute of his life to the cause, to being a soldier of the Circle, with no other ambition than striking his enemies as hard as possible.

He thought about Noura. His cousin had become part of the fabric of the city. She had followed her parents to Brussels and only had contact with her mother, the good, sweet Fatima. Jamal refused to see her. He had banished her from his life, just like Farid had. Abir knew that if his uncle and cousin wanted to have the community's respect, they had no other choice. He didn't dare say her name in Jamal's house. Noura had been led astray. She didn't behave like a decent woman. She rejected the hijab and dressed like any other western girl, and there wasn't a trace of decency left in the way she carried herself. She smoked and drank, and never set foot in a mosque. She wasn't one of them anymore. Knowing this pained him, and he continued to miss her.

Walking down the street, for a few seconds he felt free. He was like any normal guy strolling around the city. The beeping of his phone dragged him back to reality. It was a missed call from a phone that would then be destroyed. An alert. Sheikh Kamal had arrived in Brussels. Abir didn't know how they had achieved it, and he wasn't going to ask. Like Sheikh Mohsin and himself, Kamal traveled far and wide throughout the world and his safety depended on no one, not even his own people, knowing anything.

He respected Kamal, but he knew that Sheikh Mohsin left nothing up to chance and had sent him to Brussels to make sure that the operation would be planned exactly as he himself had authorized.

Only once had Abir disobeyed the sheikh.

He had sent him to a meeting about an arms deal in Beirut. It was a city he loved going to, mostly because he stayed at his cousin Gibram's house. When his parents were killed, his mother's cousin Ayman took him in along with Ismail. Ayman was a fighter in the Circle too, and a follower of Sheikh Mohsin, and his sons Gibram and Sami had inherited their father's bravery and commitment, becoming the sheikh's eyes in Beirut.

Gibram was a widower. His wife had been Palestinian and had died during childbirth when their first son was born. He never married again. The wound of his loss had never healed, and he devoted all his energy to fighting in the ranks of the Circle. Abir admired Gibram and enjoyed the time they spent together. In the mornings, they would go out for breakfast and sit and read the newspapers in a café on Gemmayzeh street.

There are some days when destiny strikes. One morning, draining his second cup of coffee while reading a newspaper, he found an article about conscientious objectors in Israel. A few of these objectors, some of them already veterans, had been interviewed about their decisions and their experiences. They were part of an organization based in Tel Aviv. And that's when Abir saw him in the photo.

Yes, it was him. He was sure. His face had been etched into his memory. He had a few gray hairs, but this was the soldier who had stood staring at him as he had fled with Ismail. Yes, this was the soldier he had threatened, who he swore he would kill for the murder of his parents. That filthy dog, explaining how when he'd fulfilled his military training, he had made the difficult decision to refuse to participate in the West Bank or Gaza. 'Participate,' was the word that dog used, masking what actually happened when they 'participated.' 'Participating' meant tanks entering the Territories, the demolition of houses suspected of belonging to Hamas. 'Participating' was the attack on his house in Ain al-Hilweh. 'Participating' was the murder of his parents and aunt and uncle. That was how Israeli soldiers acted. And there, on the pages of a newspaper, that man presented himself as if he had a conscience. Abir spit angrily on the floor as if it were the soldier's face.

He started to think about how he would kill him. It wouldn't be difficult to find him as a part of this veterans' association for objectors. For several days and nights his thoughts were centered on what at first was just a fantasy. Until he made a decision. He wouldn't tell Sheikh Mohsin, only his cousin Gibram. Killing the Jew would be difficult, but not impossible. No border was uncrossable, that he knew well. The Israelis thought they had sealed their border with Lebanon, but he would go right through it. He would find that soldier. And he would kill him.

Gibram urged him to talk to the sheikh. He shouldn't carry out operations without his approval.

"You can't disappear, not even for a few days, without the sheikh knowing. You know he'll find out!" he warned him.

But Abir couldn't see reason. He hoped the sheikh would understand. The Jew had appeared in his life again through the pages of a newspaper, someone who had participated in the attack on his home, responsible for his being orphaned, for losing most of his family. Ignoring Gibram's protests, he took a French passport out of the false bottom of his suitcase. It was a fake, but perfect. He had traveled to many countries with this passport belonging to Rémi Dufort. Businessman. Single. Catholic.

He would go to Jordan, and from there he would slip through the Israeli border.

The following morning, he flew to Amman. He liked that city. He knew many people who could have helped him, but he decided to act alone and not involve any men from the Circle.

He headed to a luxurious hotel, the Intercontinental, and asked for a room. After checking in, he went for a walk. As always, he preferred to wander aimlessly, his feet carrying him to the citadel, Jabal al-Qala'a. It was a long and tiring route, but worth it. From there he could take in the whole city. He knew this place so well, his favorite part being the Temple of Hercules. He sat in thought for a while, the tourists with their cameras around him, trying to capture the essence of this place that had been inhabited since the Bronze age, where Romans and Umayyads had also left their mark.

Without trying, he overheard two girls talking about the trip they were taking to Petra the next day. One said that the citadel ruins were fine, but the highlight of the trip was definitely Petra, followed by Jerusalem.

It determined his plan to get into Israel. He would blend into a group of tourists and cross the border through the Allenby bridge. It would mean being extremely calm and patient, something he had learned in the Spīn Ghar mountains of Afghanistan. Waiting. Waiting with his finger on the trigger. Waiting for hours and days. Waiting.

Sheikh Mohsin said that impatience was the road to disaster. He was right, though it had cost him many tears to learn self-control.

He made his way down from the citadel and decided to treat himself to a large portion of *kunafa*, fried cheese with honey and pistachios, one of his favorite foods. The best place to eat it was the Habibah sweet shop: cheap, discreet, and usually not overwhelmed by tourists.

Once he had eaten his fill, he headed to the coffee shop in Wild Jordan Center. He would spend the rest of the afternoon there until the hour of prayer. He liked to go to the King Abdullah I Mosque, where Westerners were forbidden from entering.

When he got back to the hotel, it was already evening. He asked the concierge to recommend a guided tour to Jerusalem, telling him that he would prefer to go with a group and an expert guide who could explain everything there was to see. His tip was generous, and the concierge was extra attentive. As soon as he got to his room and was removing his shoes, the phone rang. The concierge had found a trip that might suit him.

"The most uncomfortable part is crossing the border on the Allenby bridge. The Israelis make it very difficult, but as pilgrims you might have an easier time of it."

"Pilgrims?"

"Yes, it was the best tour I could find. I have a friend who's a guide and works with groups of French and Italian pilgrims. They will visit the Christian holy sites, and Petra as well. They're usually in Jordan for three or four days, and then another few days in Israel. And you're in luck because this group is all French. It costs seven hundred dollars and includes the hotel in Petra, two nights in Jerusalem and another in Galilee. Are you interested?"

Abir accepted immediately. He would be sure to give the concierge another tip.

"When does the tour start?"

"It's already started—today was their first day. They visited Jerash, the citadel, the modern city, and tomorrow they'll go to Mount Nebo and the castles in the desert, Madaba, and end in Petra."

"What time do I have to meet up with the group?"

"At seven on the dot. They're all staying in this hotel, so you won't have to go far. My friend, the guide, will arrive at 6:30 a.m. It's probably best if you come down to the lobby then, and you can go over all the details with him."

At 6 a.m., Abir was already pacing impatiently in the lobby. He was irritated because the restaurant hadn't opened for breakfast yet. He had slept terribly, and felt shooting pains in his chest and the pit of his stomach.

He started to feel a little better after a cup of tea and a little plate of hummus. He wasn't hungry, but he knew the day would be exhausting and it was better to avoid a rumbling stomach.

At 6:30 he went out into the main hall again and asked for the guide. The man told him to call him Saleh. He was short and stocky with an intelligent face. He made no objection to him joining the group, and Abir responded gratefully with a good tip.

The group wasn't very big, about 30 people, mostly women. Saleh reminded them that one more traveler would be joining their group, Rémi Dufort, a respectable businessman from Paris. Some showed no interest in the new addition, and others seemed suspicious. Abir knew he had to win them over to avoid raising any questions and, above all, appear as an integral part of the group when they got to the bridge. They left at exactly 7 a.m. for Mount Nebo, and although he didn't care about the guide's explanations about the place, a holy site for Jews and Christians, he listened patiently to him saying that this was where Moses had contemplated from afar the Promised Land that he himself would never reach.

They continued on to Madaba, where the guide enthusiastically explained the importance of some mosaic from the 6th century, a detailed map of the Middle East from Lebanon in the north to Egypt in the south. Then he announced that they were in luck—they would attend mass in the church of Saint George.

Abir was startled. He had never been inside a church, except for Notre-Dame during his school days because his history teacher had insisted that they wouldn't be able to understand France without seeing it.

He observed the service without moving a muscle, watching the movements of the rest of the tour group. When they left

98

the church, one of the women came over to him and asked with a smile, "When was the last time you went to mass?"

He wanted to hit her, but he smiled back.

"I have to admit it's been too long. Life takes you away from your childhood beliefs, you know how it is."

"And what made you decide to take this trip?" the woman pressed.

"I want to know if there is still anything left of what my parents taught me."

"I'm Loana Rémilly," she said, holding out her hand.

"Rémi Dufort."

"It's a pleasure, Mr. Dufort. And what do you do?"

He was tempted to tell her to stop being so nosy, but he couldn't. The woman was about 40, tall, thin, wavy hair, sure of herself. He decided to play along.

"I'm looking for business opportunities in this part of the world," he answered. "It's not easy, but one has to try. And then sometimes it's important to stop and look inside one's self. That's why I decided it would be good for me to do a tour of the Holy Land. Who knows, maybe I can get some of my faith back. I would like nothing more."

"Your accent … you speak a very guttural French."

"I spend a lot of time in this part of the world, Ms. Rémilly," he answered, holding in the rage that began to course through his body.

"And where do you live in Paris?"

"I don't live in Paris. I travel constantly. I spend most of my time in Lebanon, our former colony."

"Do you have family? What do they do?"

"And you Ms. Rémilly, what do you do? Where do you live? Are you married? Do you have children? What made you come on this pilgrimage?"

His tone of voice had changed. He would have to cut off this woman's curiosity at the root, or he would end up insulting her.

"Oh, I'm sorry! You must think I'm very rude. It just seemed so strange to me that you suddenly joined our group. Saleh, our guide, didn't tell us anything about it. And ... well ... you don't really seem French."

"If you say so. But you haven't answered my questions."

"Yes, you're right. I'm a doctor, Mr. Dufort. I work at the hospital in Pitié-Salpêtriére, in the 13th arrondissement. Do you know it?"

"Of course. What's your field?"

"I work in the emergency room. It's very stressful."

"I imagine. And where do you live?"

"Well, Mr. Dufort. I don't think that matters."

"Of course not, but you asked me the same thing. Maybe you can tell me what brought you on this pilgrimage?"

Loana looked at him, disconcerted. She knew that her intrusiveness annoyed people and had caused her more than a few problems. Obviously, she had offended him. She had interrogated him, and now he was doing the same to her.

"I'm sorry I was so nosy. That wasn't very nice, was it? Can you forgive me?"

"Of course, and now let's go join everyone else—they're getting on the bus."

They sat together. She didn't leave him any other choice. She could have sat next to the woman she had chattered endlessly to since the start of the tour. He thought about changing his seat, but his rudeness would have caught the attention of the other passengers. He pulled out a pamphlet about Petra began to read. Loana sat quietly next to him, not daring to say another word. The young man intrigued her, though she couldn't say why. Then she remembered—he reminded her of a boy at university. Mohamed, a clever boy from Morocco, the best in the class. A poor Muslim immigrant, and one of eight siblings, he had succeeded against the odds and defied his destiny. Now he was a reputable surgeon, his hands uniquely gifted in opening thoraxes and operating on hearts, while she had become an unremarkable practitioner among many.

Mohamed had never shown interest in her, and she didn't allow herself to feel anything for him, but the memory of him was enough to make her feel drawn to the young man beside her.

The bus came to a stop. "We're going to visit the archeological park of Umm ar-Rasas. Its mosaics are truly spectacular. It . was declared a World Heritage Site in 2004. You'll like it as much as or more than Madaba," the guide assured them, enthusiastically explaining the importance of the archeological remains. "Look closely. This was Saint Steven's complex, with mosaics from the 6th to 8th centuries." He had them stop in front of the remains of a Roman fortress and contemplate the 13-foot-tall stylite tower where the holy men of the desert paid penance and prayed.

Abir managed to keep his distance from Dr. Rémilly, positioning himself next to the guide or mingling with the other travelers. He listened attentively, not just to Saleh's explanations, but also to the comments of the others, who seemed genuinely enthusiastic about what they were seeing. He thought about the many times he had been to Jordan, and yet he'd had no knowledge of what they were visiting. He had never spent time on anything other than clandestine meetings with Islamist leaders or arms dealers. Sheikh Mohsin wasn't someone who would allow himself or his men to waste time on anything but destroying the enemy. He couldn't imagine his reaction to one of the men asking him to spend a few hours seeing the sights. Abir felt ashamed for enjoying the tour—Saleh was good at his job and passionate about the ruins that made up Jordan's history—but he told himself it was necessary for him to be there.

They left Umm ar-Rasas and headed to Kerak Castle, a popular tourist destination. Saleh explained to them proudly how the castle had been in the power of the crusaders until the Great Saladin had conquered it.

Once they had left Kerak, some of the group began to get tired, but Saleh insisted on taking them to visit Shobak Castle. "Not just because it's part of the package," he said, "but because it's unique in the world. It was built by Baldwin I from Jerusalem to control caravans traveling between Syria and Egypt. But the crusaders couldn't fend off Saladin's attacks, and were defeated by him."

Evening had fallen when they arrived in Wadi Musa, the town that had formed around the entrance to Petra. They were staying in the Movenpick hotel, very close to the old quarter. Saleh advised them to rest; they had to be up at dawn the next day. He would be waiting for them in the lobby at 5:30 a.m. and promised them a unique experience: witnessing Petra at dawn. He also reminded them that dinner was included in the tour and that the buffet was about to close, so they should hurry.

Abir headed to his room and after taking a shower, decided to go out. He felt wide awake, and would rather have dinner alone somewhere in town.

He went out into the street and was immediately engulfed by crowds of tourists. There were stalls to buy something to eat, cafés and restaurants, as well as shops with the kind of souvenirs tourists liked. He wandered, feeling unburdened. It had been a long time since he'd felt so free. Ever since Mohsin had taken over his life, he hadn't had a moment to himself. Surviving had become his only goal. The sheikh wouldn't allow him to spend time on anything other than fighting. As he wandered the crowded streets of Wadi Musa, he had an odd sensation, that for the first time since he left his childhood behind in Paris, his time belonged only to him.

A hand suddenly grabbed his shoulder, and he froze.

"What are you doing here?"

Recognizing the man's voice with dread, he turned around and faced him.

"What about you, Mousa? Who are you here to kill?"

The man pulled his hand back from Abir's shoulder and let out a dry laugh. He was taller and stronger than Abir, and also older. Mousa could scare anyone; every inch of his presence oozed cruelty.

"We're committed to the same thing, Abir, fighting the infidels. I'm surprised to find you in Wadi Musa. Should it surprise me?" His tone of voice was as cold as ice.

"I don't owe you any explanations, Mousa." Abir tried to stay calm.

"Fine, don't give me any. But at least have dinner with us. My people are staying in one of the canyons in Siq al-Barid. We have delicious lamb there, much better than any you'd find here. Wadi Musa has been corrupted, it's a city of infidels."

"I am honored by the invitation Mousa, but I can't."

"This is my territory, Abir. You can't walk around here without me knowing what you came to do. Sheikh Mohsin didn't warn us you were coming."

"Do we have to ask permission to travel to Jordan? No, I don't need your permission, but even so I'll answer your question: I came to see Petra, is that so strange to you?"

Mousa didn't answer, but he repeated his invitation, smiling and slinging an arm around his shoulders.

"Abir, you must honor us with your presence. My father will never forgive me if we don't honor you like you deserve. My car is right around the corner. You'll have dinner with us and if you want, you can stay in our encampment tonight and I'll bring you back to Wadi Musa myself. Tell me, did you travel with your real name, or should I call you something else?"

If Abir had learned anything from Sheikh Mohsin, it was that there are moments when it's best not to contradict your enemies. He accepted the invitation.

"All right, Mousa. I am honored by your invitation, even more so in knowing that your father, Sheikh Afaf, is in Siq al-Barid. As far as my name, as long as we're alone or with your people, I'm still Abir."

It took less than half an hour to reach Siq al-Barid. Sheikh Afaf had settled his encampment in a place where he could see and not be seen. He knew the landscape. From the Horn of Africa to the Mediterranean Sea, there wasn't a single meter of land that held secrets from him. He belonged to a long line of men born in the desert, whose ancestors had guided caravans carrying goods and people from one place to another. Afaf had modernized the business, and his main trade was in weapons. Those who had made the jihad their life's mission knew they could trust Afaf, although he refused to let his own men participate in the holy war. He didn't like the infidels, but he didn't hate them either.

He had only one rule when he sold weapons: the buyers could not use them within Jordan. He insisted so intensely that some jihad chiefs thought he was part of the Jordanian monarchy. A loyal Bedouin, he would cut the throat of anyone who dared raise a hand against King Abdullah.

Nearly 50 tents, jeeps and mules formed the encampment. With the sun already set, the valley was illuminated by flickering campfires where lamb was being roasted. Sheikh Afaf seem unsurprised by Abir's presence. He received him like any important guest in the desert, offering him water and food and honoring him by seating him at his side. During the meal, they spoke about generalities, though Mousa did try to get Abir to explain his presence in Petra.

"It's been a long time since Sheikh Mohsin has done business with us," said Mousa.

His father shot him a severe look. Mousa was disregarding the hospitality owed to a guest.

For a few seconds, Abir hesitated over whether to respond, but as he felt Afaf's gaze on him, he knew he was also waiting for an answer.

"Apart from business, Mousa, I assume you're not questioning the respect and esteem Sheikh Mohsin has for your father. The bonds of friendship have nothing to do with business."

Afaf suppressed a smile. Abir had elegantly sidestepped his son without having to give a precise answer. He also wondered what Abir was doing in Jordan. He knew the young man was a soldier. He had fought in Afghanistan, Iraq and Syria, demonstrating his bravery each time. He was intelligent and fast, and Sheikh Mohsin protected him. Abir might be in Jordan for a secret meeting with someone. Yes, that must be the reason he was here and naturally, he wasn't going to reveal it.

When dinner was over, Mousa again invited Abir to stay overnight at the encampment, but he couldn't convince him and had to honor his promise to drive him back to Wadi Musa.

When they got to the hotel, Mousa hugged him like a brother.

"This is our territory, Abir. Remember that."

"I am aware of this, Mousa, and have the utmost respect for your father, and you and your family. I will send your father's greetings on to Sheikh Mohsin."

As the elevator arrived, he could sense the woman's presence from a waft of her perfume. Without even turning around, he knew it was Loana Rémilly.

"Good evening, Mr. Dufort. Did you have a nice walk?" she asked as he stepped in.

"Good evening, Dr. Rémilly."

"It's late. We have to be up at dawn tomorrow."

"Yes. Have a good night."

When he got to his floor, Abir got out without looking at her. That woman irritated him.

The next morning, the tour group gulped down their cups of coffee in the restaurant, which was packed with tourists like them. It was 5:30 a.m., and the sky had not yet left the night behind. The guide rushed them along.

"Let's go, let's go! Don't dilly dally, but make sure you eat breakfast, because it's going to be a long day and you'll need a lot of energy. As I mentioned yesterday, there's an optional activity to visit the ruins by horse. If anyone wants to play Indiana Jones, let me know. For those who don't like to walk, I recommend a rickshaw."

Some smiled, but others hadn't yet shaken off the fog of sleep.

Abir felt tired and his stomach was churning. Maybe he had eaten too much at Sheikh Afaf's encampment. His chest was pounding and he felt short of breath, but he chalked it up to nerves. The meeting with Mousa had been a setback. He'd been unable to sleep thinking of Sheikh Mohsin's reaction when he learned Abir had been in Jordan without his permission. He felt a sharp pain in his side, but showed no outward expression.

"Saleh, should we bring water?" one of the tourists asked.

"Of course, madame. Although you can buy it on the way, it's always best to carry a small bottle with you."

Petra wasn't far from the hotel. They walked together, listening attentively to Saleh's enthusiastic explanations.

"The city of the Nabateans! A market town, but as you will see, the inhabitants were great artists as well as merchants. You may wonder why they built a city in the desert. The reason is that there was water here. In past centuries, it was known as the lost city, but really, it was never lost. The Bedouins and the people from this area knew perfectly well where it was, but the West thought they discovered it in the 19th century when a Swiss explorer—who, by the way, was an admirer of Islamic culture and became a good Muslim—convinced the Bedouins to bring him to the Rose-Red City. OK, everybody all set?"

They walked another kilometer, struck by the extraordinary beauty of the Siq, the gorge that led to Petra. The walls were over 200 meters high and seemed impossible to scale. Saleh waited knowingly for the group's reaction when they came upon the jewel. That communal gasp always produced the same satisfaction. He explained to them that they were looking at a tomb and gave them precise details about its proportions.

"The façade measures 23 meters long by 30 meters wide and…"

Abir couldn't help admiring everything around him and regretted having never visited before, considering how many times he had been in Jordan in his life. His visits never allowed time for anything other than meetings with a jihad leader or checking that a shipment of weapons would arrive at its destination. In his life under Sheikh Mohsin's guidance, there was no room for anything but fighting the infidels. Thinking about the sheikh made him shiver. He knew he would have to answer to him for coming to Lebanon in secret and, even worse, seeking personal revenge without his permission. The sheikh would never have allowed him to be distracted by any activity that wasn't related to their holy war.

Sheikh Mohsin was right about this, and a wise and fair man, but even so, he couldn't help enjoying the tour.

"You don't look well. Are you OK?"

The sound of Dr. Rémilly's voice interrupted his thoughts and spoiled the silence of the dawn.

"Yes, I'm fine," he responded curtly, moving away from her.

They continued to walk, listening attentively to Saleh's explanations.

"Here is the great theater of the Nabateans, which could hold 3000 people. The Romans expanded it. Here are the royal tombs. We will visit the Urn tomb, the Corinthian tomb and the Palace. Ah! And for the brave few willing to follow me, we will climb to a lookout where you can see all of Petra. It will take an hour, but it's worth it to see the top of the Jabal al-Khubtha!"

As they climbed, Abir was struggling to breathe. He grimaced and kept walking. It was just fatigue, he repeated to himself. That was it. Tiredness. When they got to the top, he immediately sat down on the ground.

"Here, drink a little water." Loana offered him a bottle.

"Thank you," he said, unable to refuse.

"I know you think I'm a busybody, but as a doctor, you look unwell to me."

"Nothing is wrong with me, Dr. Rémilly. I'm just tired. I ate dinner too late last night and didn't sleep well," he explained with a trace of irritation that he couldn't hide.

"Maybe you should go back to the hotel and rest."

"And miss all this? Of course not. I'm fine. Don't worry."

"If you insist." Loana moved away, concerned.

Saleh seemed unaware of the situation, and although he would sometimes ask the group if they wanted to stop, he didn't really give them the option to do so. He dragged them from one place to another and had them go up to the cliffs so they could see the details of the tombs. He wanted them to enjoy the view of Qasr al-Bint, Petra's main temple.

"Its walls are 23 meters high and it is dedicated to the god Dushara. It's not carved from the rock face, however, and this is one of its peculiarities."

When Saleh announced that they would stop to buy something to eat before climbing to the monastery, the group applauded. They had been walking since 6 in the morning and had exerted themselves climbing the cliffs. They were all feeling exhausted and enthusiastic at the same time.

Abir wasn't hungry. His stomach hurt but his mouth was dry, and he quickly drank two bottles of water. He felt Dr. Rémilly's eyes on him and heard her whispering with the other travelers as they stared at him.

After an hour, Saleh invited them to continue the journey. "There are only 800 stairs to get to the monastery, and it won't take more than 40 or 45 minutes at the most. If anyone would rather go up on a donkey, it's no problem, though it might be a problem for the donkey," he said, laughing at his own joke.

Eight hundred stairs. Abir counted them one by one as he struggled to climb. He could barely breathe. Suddenly his foot twisted, and as he stumbled everything went dark.

He didn't know it until much later, when he gained consciousness, but he had come very close to falling into the abyss.

"How are you feeling?"

A man in a white coat was speaking to him in English. Where was he? Behind the man, he could make out the shapes of Saleh and Loana Rémilly.

"I...I..."

"Don't try to speak. I'm Dr. Odwan. You gave us a pretty good scare, but the danger has passed. It looks like you're going to make it. You were lucky that Dr. Rémilly was there and had that miraculous pill with her."

Abir didn't understand.

"You've had a heart attack. We thought we'd lost you. Your heart is in very poor condition, and we need to let your family know."

The man was speaking clearly, but it was difficult for Abir to hear him. He couldn't make out what he was saying, though he spoke perfect English.

Loana quickly noticed Abir's confusion and started translating Dr. Odwan's words into French.

"Mr. Dufort, you are in the Queen Rania hospital in Wadi Musa. Dr. Odwan has saved your life. You were showing signs of a heart attack and, well, I always carry nitroglycerin pills in my bag. Part of the profession. I put it under your tongue and that helped to stop the initial danger. You're being well taken care of here, but they will need to operate on your heart and replace the valves. They can do this here, or in Amman."

"No...no..."

"I understand you want to go home, Mr. Dufort, but we don't think that would be advisable. You can't travel. In Dr. Odwan's opinion, they will need to fit you with a pacemaker, and to be frank, I agree. You should know that there are very good doctors in Jordan and the specialists are very competent. I assure you, you will be in good hands. Could tell us how to reach your family?"

Heart attack. Hospital. Operation. Jordan. Family. The words slowly took on meaning for Abir as they hammered into his skull, forcing a terrible headache. He had to think. He had to make a decision. He had to get out of here.

"Mr. Dufort, tell us what city in France you live in. We can call any relative you like. I'm sure you'll feel better once you have your family with you," Dr. Odwan insisted.

But Abir squeezed his eyes shut. He couldn't think or decide, not then.

"Let's let him rest. He's confused," Dr. Odwan said.

"Yes, but we're leaving tomorrow, and I don't think he can accompany us," Saleh said worriedly.

"I'd advise him to stay here for at least a few days. We have to do some tests. In any case, he has to have an operation, though I understand he would probably prefer to do that in his country, near his family," the doctor responded.

"In my opinion, he should have the operation as soon as possible," Loana said.

"I respect your view, Doctor, especially knowing that you work in emergency response, but you have to put yourself in the patient's shoes. It's important that we locate a family member to explain Mr. Dufort's situation. I can't guarantee anything, but I will do everything in my power to stabilize him so that he can return to France and have the operation there, if at all possible."

"I see, Doctor."

"I agree that the most sensible thing would be to treat him here, but you have to understand Mr. Dufort's situation: ill, far from his home, from his family. If it were strictly necessary to act here and now, I assure you I wouldn't allow him to decide. He would already be on the operating table. And now I'm afraid I must leave you, I have other patients to attend to."

After the doctor had left the room, Saleh asked Loana what they should do.

"If I were Mr. Dufort, I would remain here. Dr. Odwan seemed very competent to me and, as I said, I believe there are very good specialists in Jordan. But we can't make the decision for him."

"But is he really fit to travel?"

Loana shrugged. She didn't want to be the one to insist that he should remain in the hospital.

"You're a doctor, and the fact is, you saved Mr. Dufort's life. Make him understand that he should stay here," the guide insisted.

Abir opened his eyes slightly and squinted at them. It had taken him a while to remember that the Dufort they were talking about was him. Rémi Dufort was the name on the passport he was using.

"Please ..." he struggled, "I don't want to stay here. I'm sorry for the trouble I caused, but I want to continue the journey. If I feel bad in Jerusalem, I promise I'll go straight to the hospital. If the doctor says the operation can wait, please allow me to continue."

"Are you sure, Mr. Dufort? You gave us a terrible scare. Having a heart attack on the steps of the monastery wasn't exactly the ideal place," Saleh pointed out.

"Without a doubt, it wasn't the best place, but Mr. Dufort didn't choose it on purpose," Loana interjected.

"Right, but what if it happens again? I can't have that responsibility."

"To my understanding, Mr. Saleh, we will be saying goodbye to you on the Allenby bridge. Once we cross over, an Israeli guide will take over the final three days of our trip," Loana said. "But I must insist, Mr. Dufort, that this is a foolhardy idea."

Abir was silent. He didn't have the strength to argue with the guide or the doctor.

"You decide. I've given my opinion. Tomorrow at midday, I'll see you off on the Allenby bridge. We can wait until tomorrow to see how Mr. Dufort feels. We'll come tomorrow at 9 a.m., and if you think you're fit to continue ..." Saleh voice trailed off.

"I'll pack your things up in a suitcase for you—is that OK?" Loana asked the patient.

"No, that's not necessary. I appreciate your worry. But could you bring me to the hotel?"

"Absolutely not, you will spend the night here," Dr. Rémilly informed him, fully in professional mode.

Abir quickly tried to recall if there was anything in his bag that could give him away. Then he remembered that he had only essential items, and had been planning to buy the weapon to kill the Jew once in Tel Aviv. A carving knife was all he would need.

That night he didn't sleep well. His heart became irregular, and the nurse reported this to Dr. Odwan.

After examining him and ordering some tests, the doctor told Abir he must stay in the hospital.

"I'm sorry, but you can't continue your trip. You should inform your family of your condition," the doctor said.

Abir phoned Gibram, waking him up. His cousin was alarmed to hear he was in hospital, and promised to catch the next flight to Amman. If there were no delays, he would be in Wadi Musa soon.

At 8:30 in the morning, Loana appeared in his hospital room.

"I've come to say goodbye. Dr. Odwan informed us he's not going to discharge you. Can I do anything for you?"

Abir was tempted to tell her the one thing she could do for him was disappear, but he contained himself, promising her that he was fine and was waiting for a relative who was on his way.

"I'm glad you're finally being reasonable. You're very headstrong, but you can't take chances with your heart. I understand you'd rather be treated in Paris, but I promise you, you're in very good hands here. Jordanian doctors are some of the very best. Anyway, here's my card." She said goodbye and left, to Abir's immense relief.

For a second, he thought about ripping the card up, but then revolved to keep it; he might find a way to make use of this woman someday.

Next he called a hotel to reserve a room for at least a few days. He spent the rest of the morning undergoing several tests ordered by Dr. Odwan.

Gibram didn't arrive until that afternoon. He rushed into the room and held his cousin tightly.

"What happened?"

As Abir told him what had happened, and about Dr. Odwan's prognosis, Gibram listened with concern.

"If they have to operate, it would be best to do it soon," he said plainly.

"No, not here. I want to have the operation in Beirut. That's why I need your help."

"You'll have to do what the doctors say," Gibram responded, "and of course Sheikh Mohsin already knows about your little adventure and isn't happy that you didn't consult him. It makes him look bad in front of his men. We soldiers must obey, nothing more."

They argued for a long time. Gibram wouldn't agree to bring Abir to Beirut without Dr. Odwan's assurance that he would be able to undertake the journey, though he insisted that the operation should be done as soon as possible.

Four days later, Sami and Rosham, Gibram's siblings, were waiting impatiently for them at the Beirut airport. Rosham was a pediatrician at Sacre-Coeur Hospital, where, she said, she had arranged an appointment for Abir with a cardiologist.

"But that's a Catholic hospital!" Abir protested.

"It's a hospital where you will get excellent treatment. I work there and have never had any problems being Muslim. The staff are of many faiths, Catholic, Orthodox, Muslim, and the nuns don't show any prejudice against us. You'll be fine. The cardiology team is very good, you'll see."

Gibram didn't seem convinced either, but Rosham was the oldest sibling and always took charge ever since their mother had died.

"I don't like you working in that hospital," Gibram muttered.

"If you two had your way, I'd stay home and never go outside. Fortunately, my husband isn't like you."

"You don't behave like a good Muslim!" Gibram responded.

"You don't get to tell me what a good Muslim is!" Rosham said defensively.

"There's no need to argue. Abir can choose a different hospital. I don't like Christian hospitals either," Sami intervened.

"You decide, Abir. Are we going to Sacre-Coeur or another hospital?" Rosham asked angrily.

"I'd prefer another hospital," Abir admitted reluctantly.

"We could take him to Makassed," Sami suggested.

"Yes, that's a good hospital and it's one of ours," Gibram agreed.

"Ours? What do you mean, one of ours?" Rosham's voice trembled with rage.

"It belongs to the Philanthropic Islamic Association, you know that," her brother answered defensively.

"The Philanthropic Islamic Association has an excellent relationship with the Christian Organizations, I believe. But I'm not going to fight with all of you. It's your heart, Abir, and it's up to you. I tried to help, but none of you seem to need it."

"Come on, Rosham, don't be angry," Sami admonished her.

"I'm not angry, my dear little brother. Just let me out here, we're near my hospital and I have a lot of work to do. I'll call Nabil and ask him to help you."

Sami stopped the car, and Rosham jumped out and marched away without looking back, leaving the cousins feeling bad. Not only did they love her, they also respected her, despite her being so westernized that she almost didn't seem Muslim.

"She has a bad temper," Gibram complained.

Rosham increased her pace. As angry as she was, she wasn't going to stop helping Abir. As her cousin, she knew how much he and Ismail had been through. His uncle Jamal was too rigid and his aunt Fatima too weak, so Abir and Ismail's life in Paris hadn't been easy. Even worse, Jamal had had handed them over to Sheikh Mohsin, who'd turned Abir into a fanatic like her brothers Gibram and Sami. She didn't want to know about their activities, but she assumed that if they were under the sheikh's wing, they belonged to the Circle.

Rosham thanked Allah for putting her husband Nabil Abbadi in her path. They had met as teenagers. Nabil was the son of a businessman her father had bought goods from to sell in their store.

Thinking about her father irritated her. He had never re-married after losing his wife, and so it fell to her to mother her two brothers, and she'd spoiled them. She had failed to instill the right values, to have tolerance and respect for those who think or pray differently.

Rosham had only been able to study because Nabil proposed to her, opening the door to freedom, she thought with a smile. She had found freedom in the unlikeliest way; marriage usually meant giving up any career aspirations.

She had married Nabil when he was already studying neurology, and it was he who encouraged her to go to university. She worked extremely hard to become a pediatrician, and there was no way she would take a single step backwards.

When she finally arrived at the hospital, she went directly to her office and called her husband.

"Nabil, my cousin didn't want to be treated at Sacre-Coeur and has gone to Makassed. They'll be arriving any minute."

"I told you they wouldn't want to come to Sacre-Coeur," he admonished her.

"Yes, you told me, but I still hope that one day they'll stop being so single-minded."

*

Nabil Abbadi greeted his wife's brothers and cousin warmly. He didn't like them very much, but as family they would be given all the help they needed. He was disturbed by Gibram and Sami's fanaticism. He didn't want to know too much about their activities, but just listening to them was enough for him to know that they were part of some jihad group. The two brothers had taken over their father's business in Souk al-Ahad, a furtive, depressing place that had none of the charm of the other souks. They sold everything, t-shirts, perfume, shoes, hijabs—anything could be found in their store.

Sometimes he wondered how the same mother and father could have had such disparate offspring. Rosham was so different from Gibram and Sami. As for Abir, he felt compassion for him and his brother Ismail. Their parents' murder had condemned them to a fate decided by others. When Rosham told him that Sheikh Mohsin had taken them to Afghanistan, he knew they were lost forever.

In the cardiology department, they examined Abir and admitted him immediately. Dr. Haidar, his cardiologist, carefully read the report from his Jordanian counterpart.

"OK, tomorrow we'll do two more tests and when we have the results, you'll go directly to the operating room. As Dr. Odwan's report states, you urgently need a pacemaker. What surprises me is that this never bothered you until now."

Abir looked down. He had noticed some time ago that his heart was not beating normally.

"The surgery is quite straightforward," the doctor added, "and if everything goes well, you'll be out in a few days. I want the device to also have a defibrillating function, but until we do these tests, I can't confirm it."

"So you're going to put two devices inside me?" Abir asked, worried.

"It's actually just one, but it has two functions. The technology has really advanced in this respect."

"Is this all really necessary?" Abir asked him.

"Let me explain. When a person's heart beats too slowly, we call it bradycardia, and it is caused by sinus node dysfunction and a blockage in your heart. The heart beats more slowly than normal, and you are at risk of a much worse scare than the one you just had."

"You should trust the doctor, Abir," Nabil advised him. "This hospital has a very good cardiology team."

"Yes, of course … it's just that I thought maybe some pill could fix the weak heartbeats."

"I'm sorry, but that's not possible," Dr. Haidar replied. "You urgently need this procedure."

Nabil took his leave, with Abir still wondering aloud if the operation was really necessary. He wasn't prepared to argue with them, and Dr. Haidar had made it clear that there was no other option.

"Maybe I should go to Brussels," Abir said.

"Maybe, but from what the doctor said, you can't wait too long to get the pacemaker put in," Gibram responded.

"But he's lasted this long, what's the rush?" Sami cut in.

"I have my doubts too, but we should trust Dr. Haidar. Nabil says he is very competent," Gibram insisted.

Suddenly Abir felt all his strength pour out of him. His heart went into distress again, and he went unconscious.

When he awoke, the first thing he saw was Dr. Haidar's giving instructions to two nurses. He had to concede and let them operate.

Until then, he rarely felt fear, but in that moment he was truly afraid. He was aware that life could stop at any moment, and he remembered the many occasions he had ignored how ill he'd been. Sheikh Mohsin had ingrained in him and Ismail that the jihad only wanted the bravest men capable of sacrificing themselves, of ignoring pain, of not thinking about themselves, not being weak. Ismail had barely coped, but Abir felt proud of having gone on to become part of the sheikh's most trusted group.

He thought about his little brother. Ismail didn't have the soul of a fighter, or the ambition or sense of sacrifice. The time he had spent in Afghanistan had been the waiting room to martyrdom. Abir knew that if it wasn't for him, Sheikh Mohsin's men would have gotten rid of Ismail. But Abir reminded them that as children of martyrs they were deserving of their respect. They couldn't kill the son of a martyr.

This is also what saved Abir from punishment for his adventure in Jordan. The sheikh did however point out his stupidity and warn him that if he ever disobeyed again, he would kill him himself. Abir knew he meant it.

*

Abir shook off the memories of the hospital in Beirut. All that had happened a long time ago, and he was in Europe again. His heart was beating in a smooth rhythm thanks to the pacemaker and defibrillator, which hadn't stopped him from participating in the many missions Sheikh Mohsin had entrusted him with after the operation. And it wouldn't impede him from carrying out his biggest feat to come.

His feet carried him back to the Grand Place and he decided to make a stop at the Cocorico café. He would sit there and think about the conversation he would have with Sheikh Kamal.

Then, he would spend a few days in the apartment that would serve as their headquarters. He would meet Kamal there, along with his brother. Ismail had spent more than a year working in Brussels and was living at his aunt and uncle's house. It was part of his plan.

Abir felt a wave of fatigue pulling him under. Sometimes, his heart still sent him messages.

*Tel Aviv.*
*Jacob*

Day was breaking. The first sounds of the morning announced that the city was waking. It was the best time to run on the beach.

He watched Luna trying to dodge the waves, but he held back from running to her side. He glanced at her now and then to make sure she was nearby. They loved each other. It had been like this since the first night they met. He could remember the day and the time, every detail of what happened.

They ran a little further until the sun dissolved the last shadows of daybreak. He looked at his watch. He was going to be late again. Dr. Tudela had told him to come at 8 a.m. He wouldn't have time to drop Luna off at home, so he decided to bring her with him. He hoped the doctor liked dogs—if she didn't, he would never come back.

He arrived 15 minutes late and had to argue with one of the guards at the hospital entrance about going inside with Luna.

But the doctor's office was on the ground floor and her window looked out onto a garden, so he decided to enter that way.

He tapped on the glass and the doctor spun around, surprised.

"What are you doing there?"

"Do you mind if I come in through the window?"

"Why do you want to come in through the window?"

"Because I'm with someone, and they won't let her in."

Dr. Tudela looked down at Luna and smiled. She opened the window and watched with bemusement as Jacob picked up the dog and pushed her inside.

"You've brought a friend I see."

"She won't be any trouble. Do you like dogs?"

"I don't dislike them."

"That's not an answer."

"I think it is. What's her name?"

"Luna."

"And why did you choose that name?"

"Do you want me to tell you?"

"Why shouldn't you tell me?"

Jacob wondered whether to respond directly to this.

Thinking back, he remembered the whimpering animal, her thick fur entangled in the barbed wire. He was trying to cross the border, and couldn't help turning to look at where the sound came from. Then he saw her. Blood poured down her back, the suffering in her eyes stopping him in his tracks. He approached her slowly and silently. He knew they were following him. He could almost smell the sweat of the man lurking some distance behind him. But Luna's eyes drew him over to her, and taking out his serrated knife, he removed the cruel barbed wire. Then he picked her up and continued, outrunning the danger that loomed behind him.

The border in that area wasn't physically difficult to cross, but an Israeli could be killed in an instant by the Lebanese policeman or soldier, or even one of his own.

The little dog weighed almost nothing, but her whimpering could give him away.

He told himself he was an idiot, that what he had just done made no sense. He was returning from a mission he shouldn't have accepted. In fact, he had refused at first, but his boss Natan hadn't given him any choice.

"You know that we work for official organizations, and if they ask us to do something, we do it. There's very little risk. You can get in and out of Lebanon, no problem. You know Beirut well, and all you need to do is to fix the flaw in one of our devices. You go, you do the repair, and you come back."

And so, he went. The device was being used by a local agent to watch the activity in a general's house from a place next door. It hadn't been easy to fix the problem. He had spent a few days holed up in the apartment, and when he finally went out onto the street he'd had the feeling someone was following him. He cursed his bad luck. He was an engineer, not an agent, even if he had been trained to deal with difficult situations like this. But he didn't have what it took to navigate the world of shadows.

Worried, he walked around the city for a long time, wondering if someone had uncovered the agent. But he couldn't call him, and he definitely couldn't go back to the apartment. He had no other option but to head for the border. They would be waiting for him there. The agreed-upon hour was 11 p.m. As he walked, he thought he could make out four men who were taking turns tailing him. He then hailed a taxi and went to the beach, and from there he took a bus that let him off in a small village in the south, where a man was waiting for him. When he told him he was being followed, the man got scared and refused to take him to the border, leaving him a few kilometers away. The darkness of night protected him. He knew the four men were close behind him, though he was only concerned about one of them, the one he could sense was closest, the one who had left his group behind, sniffing out his target in the dark. It was ridiculous, he thought, that he'd wasted precious minutes rescuing a puppy trapped in barbed wire.

He was risking his life for this stranger, who whimpered in his arms and hampered his movements.

But he was lucky, and he made it across the border, eluding his pursuers and not drawing any attention to himself.

He walked quickly for a few more kilometers, and when he saw the lights of Misgav Am twinkling in the darkness ahead, he began to breathe normally again.

He kept heading towards the kibbutz, but as he got less than 10 meters away, he felt the barrel of a gun press into his lower back.

"You're late. I've been waiting for you for two hours," he heard the man say.

"I decided to take my time, Dan. I knew you didn't have anything better to do tonight."

The man grunted good-naturedly and then noticed the whimpering lump.

"And what's this?" he asked suspiciously.

"A puppy. I think it's female, I'm not sure. She's hurt, that damn barbed wire. She was probably trying to get under it and got stuck."

"For fuck's sake! Your job is not to save puppies."

"Well, as you can see, I expanded the mission to dog rescue. And you need to inform your office that there were men following me in Beirut from the second I left your man's apartment."

Jacob would not leave the dog now. He put her in the car with them and told Dan all the details of what had happened as they drove.

He was tired, and he still felt the fear coursing through his body from being followed. Dan made a call to say he was "delivering the package" to his house and that he had nearly been lost along the way.

He dozed until Dan announced that they had arrived in Tel Aviv.

He went into his building, carrying the dog up to the apartment that had become his home.

He examined her carefully. She wasn't any specific breed; though she had some characteristics of a German shepherd, her color was lighter. He liked that she was mixed, and nothing in particular.

He then tended to her wounds. He put an antibiotic pill in her mouth, thinking she might have an infection. If that antibiotic was good for him, it would be good for her too, he told himself. He decided to take her to a vet the next day.

He put her on the bed, leaving the window open so they could hear the sound of the waves crashing on the beach.

When he woke up, it was still dark. He was surprised to find that she had jumped onto the bed and was sleeping by his side. He touched her and she opened her eyes, frightened.

He checked her wounds and felt satisfied. They didn't look infected.

He took a quick shower and made coffee, then searched the fridge for something to give the little dog, though he knew he wouldn't find anything. She would have to make do with crackers and water. He found a bowl, filled it with cold water and fed her. She wolfed the food down, and he wondered when the poor animal had last eaten anything.

He stepped onto his terrace and breathed in the sea air. He looked at his watch and calculated that he had an hour to run on the beach before going to the IAI offices. He had to report on his 'outing' to Beirut and raise the issue, once again, of them sending him to do a job more appropriate for an agent than a computer engineer. As he prepared to leave, the little dog sprinted to his side and started to whimper. He hesitated, then decided to bring her with him.

Once they were on the beach, he slowed his pace to match the injured puppy's. It didn't leave him much time to run, and it was getting late. Nothing irritated the boss more than his people not being on time.

The little dog tried to keep up, but one of her cuts started bleeding, and he took her back to the apartment. He called his mother and asked her to come and look after the dog.

"A dog? What are you talking about? It's not even seven in the morning and you expect me to come to your apartment and take care of some dog you found?"

"You only have to take the elevator up one floor. It's a female dog. I want you to take her to the vet. I would do it myself, but I have to go to work."

"OK. Does she bite?"

"She hasn't bitten me..., but guess it depends if she likes you," he responded in irritation.

"I don't like dogs."

"I know. You never let me have one."

Joanna let the comment pass, and promised to be at his apartment in half an hour and find a vet clinic.

Not much later, Jacob was parking his car in front of IAI, an avant-garde building of steel and glass. He walked in with a determined stride.

"Natan Lewin is in your office with Dor. They're waiting for you," the receptionist told him.

*

Jacob looked at Dr. Tudela. She appeared to be weighing up what she had heard up until then. He couldn't help feeling uncomfortable and wondered what interest she could possibly have in hearing how he'd found Luna.

For a few seconds, they sat in silence. She waited for Jacob to continue. He was aware that the doctor knew Dor, and that she wouldn't be surprised by what he told her. That if Natan Lewin told him to do something because Dor said so, he would have two options, either accept or resign from his job.

"Anything else?" The doctor pulled him back to the present.

"Well, not much. I'll tell you what other memories I have of that day."

Natan Lewin greeted Jacob with a handshake.

"So everything went well?"

"Well, I'm afraid your man in Beirut has been exposed."

"Yes, Dan told us." Natan nodded.

*

"Dor seemed like he was in a bad mood, but that was nothing new. He always was, though I couldn't care less. Even today, I still wonder why I accepted that mission to Lebanon."

"I think you know the answer," the psychiatrist replied.

Jacob didn't respond, but Dr. Tudela was right. He had accepted it because he needed to prove to himself that he was capable of it.

"Anyway, when I got home that night, I still hadn't decided what I was going to do with Luna. I got home pretty late and found my mother sitting on the terrace with a glass of white wine in one hand and a cigarette in the other."

*

"It's about time!" she said by way of greeting.

Jacob shrugged, looking around for the puppy.

"She's fine. The stitching you did wasn't bad, the vet said. They treated her wounds and gave her I don't know how many vaccines, dewormed her and everything. They think she's a little over four months old. And now, what are you planning to do with her? You can't keep her."

Hearing those words from his mother removed any doubt he had about keeping the dog.

"Well, yes, she's staying with me. She's good company."

"But you don't have time!"

"I have nothing but time," he told her.

"One day you'll have to decide what to do with your life," she responded grumpily.

"That's a decision I might never make."

"You really like annoying me, don't you?"

"No, just reminding you how things are. Thank you for taking care of the dog. We'll figure it out on our own, though you're always welcome to come lend a hand."

His mother stubbed out her cigarette, got to her feet and planted herself in front of Jacob.

"Do whatever you want, but don't count on me. I've done enough today, considering I don't like dogs. Oh, and I left a note on the table for you with all the vet's instructions, and the pills you have to give her. They recommended some type of canned food."

Once his mother had left, and still savoring that he'd gotten the better of her, Jacob went to the kitchen, read the note and took a bottle of white wine from the fridge. He poured himself a glass and with the puppy following on his heels, went to find get some fresh air on the terrace.

"What am I going to do with you?" he said to the dog. "The first thing I have to do is find you a name. A pretty name."

He looked out into the night. The water churned from the wind.

"I know. I'll call you Luna. Do you like it? I think so. I found you at night. You're a survivor. Yes, Luna suits you well."

Twelve years had passed since then. Luna had gotten old, but she was a healthy dog, and protective. Despite her protests, his mother took care of her when he traveled. Luna's presence in his life had anchored him in Tel Aviv.

He was less bothered by his work or the missions he was occasionally forced to participate in. The thing that irritated Jacob most was the feeling that not only did he owe his job to Dor, but that some of the missions entrusted to him by his boss were actually under Dor's command. He didn't really have any complaints about Natan Lewin. He was a man who could be trusted, a computer mastermind who had looked for others like him at the university, and Jacob had earned top grades in computer engineering and quantum engineering. Still, he was sure that Dor's opinion held sway over Natan Lewin.

Jacob excelled in the new discipline of artificial intelligence. He had his own lab in the IAI and a few friends who shared his interests, though not many. In truth, algorithms were his best friends.

*

Silence.

"So you don't like that IAI completes missions from Palm Tree House."

"Not really."

"Or that your mother knew Dor."

"Her way of helping me was to put me in Dor's dangerous hands. She shouldn't have turned to him to get me out of military prison. In our last session, I told you why I decided to be an objector; I knew what was involved. As far as my mother's relationship with Dor is concerned ..."

"It upsets you."

"It was hard for my mother to explain how they really knew each other."

"Can you tell me about that?"

"One day, when I mentioned Dor to her, she couldn't help but smile."

*

"Didn't I tell you we had a cousin in Israel?"

"Yes, but after all these years, we've never met this cousin. You're not going to tell me it's Dor, are you?"

"Well, we're not cousins. But nearly his entire family died in Auschwitz."

Jacob understood then that this united them more than if they were actually related. But what his mother said next surprised him even more.

"I met Dor at a concert in Paris organized by the Jewish Community of France. You father and I clicked with him right away. Dor took an interest in us, wanting to know what our life was like in Beirut, curious about our views on Lebanese politics. On one of our visits, he told me that I could help, that we Jews had to stop anyone from ever killing us again. He didn't need to tell me about the horror of the camps because your father and I had already visited Auschwitz. I told him that I agreed, but I didn't know how I could help.

"He asked me if I would keep my eyes and ears open in Beirut. He knew that your father had important business there and that we mixed with prominent people. It was just a matter of listening and, every now and then, giving him that information."

"And you agreed?" Jacob asked, shocked.

"I told him I would talk it over with your father. Dor said he understood and assured me that your father and I would never be in any danger. It was just listening, nothing else."

"And what did Father say?"

"That, of course, I couldn't do it, that whatever that man said, it would put me in danger and our goal was to build a family, to have children, and to be loyal, yes, loyal to France as our homeland, but also to our Lebanese friends. He was right, and it took a weight off my shoulders. I explained this to Dor, and he said that he understood. But on our trips to Paris, we would run into him at some of the Jewish events. Your father was always reluctant to tell him what was going on in Lebanon."

"And you?"

"I was uncomfortable too, though not as much as your father. If we were chatting with other people and the conversation turned to Lebanon, Dor didn't say anything, or ask anything, but …"

"But you said more than they would have liked you to say."

"Nothing I spoke about was a secret. We didn't have access to privileged information. We would just express opinions about what we read in the newspaper."

"But given you had important friends, your opinions would obviously be tinged by the special knowledge given to those in that circle."

"Your father became an important man in Beirut. His businesses were going well, and he had dealings with ministers, bankers, and businessmen. So yes, we were well positioned. But Dor never asked me for anything, and when he found out that I had decided to come live in Israel, he offered to help me. And he has."

*

The doctor interrupted his recollections, pulling him back to the present.

"I think that's enough for today."

"Of course, though I don't know, all this seems a little ridiculous to me. Why would you have any interest in the story of how I named my dog Luna?"

"It's important to you and it helps me to get to know you and help you. Today I've learned many things about you. Do you want us to see each other again, or would you prefer to close the door and not return?"

He didn't know why, but he now felt comfortable talking to this woman. He had been able to ramble on about Luna and how much she meant to him.

"When can I come back?"

It wasn't until he left the hospital that he realized he had been there for more than an hour and a half. He would be late for work and, even worse, he would have to bring Luna. He imagined his colleagues' surprise when they saw him arrive with her. But he didn't have time to bring her home, and he wasn't going to leave her locked up in the car. He knew that she wouldn't be a bother and would just curl up at his feet.

The IAI security guard checked whether he could allow Jacob into the facilities with a dog. It must not have been easy for the bosses to make a decision; they made him wait at the door for 10 minutes.

When he entered the open-plan office he shared with a dozen other engineers, he tried not to see the smirks passing between them. He told Luna to lay down next to him, and she did so silently, and that was how they spent the rest of the morning. He didn't go out for lunch; he'd been late and he was making up the time, he took advantage of the silence to call his mother.

"How are you?"

"I have a fever, a headache, I'm dizzy and I can't move. This damn pneumonia is going to finish me off."

"You don't have it anymore."

"But I haven't recovered yet."

"Do you need me to bring you something?"

"I have enough food. The only thing is I'm tired and have a headache."

"It's a matter of time. Unless you're getting worse or feeling like you can't breathe, the best thing to do is stay at home and follow the doctor's orders."

"I'm not sure. It's been a month and look at me, I'm so weak."

"I'll be home soon. If you need anything, call me."

Jacob sat on his terrace and Luna came over to curl up next to him. They stayed in that position for a long time, Luna dozing and Jacob thinking about his conversation with Dr. Tudela. He realized that she barely spoke, she only listened, and he wondered what was behind that friendly face and restrained expression. There had to be a story behind her intelligent gaze, but what could it be?

He wanted to try and find out something about her. He picked up his phone and, without hesitating, called Natan Lewin.

After some obligatory small talk, Jacob cut to the chase.

"Why did you recommend Dr. Tudela to me? What's so special about her?"

He heard his boss's dry laugh alongside the snap of a match. Natan Lewin couldn't do anything without a lit cigarette between his fingers.

"For a year, I went to see her every week. She helped me find out many things about myself."

"Right, but who is she really?"

"An excellent psychiatrist. What's going on with you, Jacob? Are you falling in love with her?" he teased.

"Come on, don't joke around. She just interests me. She's the first psychiatrist I've met in my life. I don't know if they all act the same way. I don't know why, but sometimes I start to talk, but I'm not saying anything interesting."

"That's how it is, that's how you unload. You'll see. Dor recommended her to me, and the sessions with her helped me a lot."

"Dor! Damn him! He's always in the middle of everything."

"Come on, Jacob, you know he's a good guy. He comes from a generation that's had many hardships. And maybe you haven't noticed, but he appreciates you."

"I don't like the idea of doing therapy with someone who is a friend of Dor."

"Well then don't go, you know what's best for you. I recommended her because she was very useful to me, but I'm me, and you're you, and you have to decide what works for you," Natan responded, his voice hardening.

"How do Dr. Tudela and Dor know each other?"

"That's none of your business or mine, but I will tell you this: they both lost most of their families in Nazi concentration camps. Dr. Tudela is a Sephardic Jew, and her family lived in Salonika. Her grandparents were taken to Auschwitz. Her mother is still alive but very old, over 90. She was lucky. She'd been only 15 when the Russians liberated the camp." Natan stayed silent for a few minutes on the other end of the line. "Dor's story is similar and, as far as I know, his mother's as well. Those death camps united millions of Jewish destinies forever," he concluded.

*Tel Aviv. 8 a.m. the following day.*
*Jacob*

He was regretting coming here. He slowed his pace and debated whether to leave, and then he ran into her.

"Jacob, good morning. What are you doing here? We don't have an appointment. We saw each other yesterday."

"I'm sorry. I'll go, it wasn't a good idea just to show up like this."

"It's not a good idea or a bad one. If you're here, it's for a reason. Come to my office."

"You're probably busy…"

"I'm participating in a seminar in an hour. I have to give a talk to a group of university students. But don't worry, we have time."

He followed her down the hall to her office and she invited him to sit, watching him curiously.

"So, tell me."

"In one of our conversations, you said that I know the reason why I accept those special operations like the one in Beirut I told you about yesterday."

"Yes, that's right."

"And you believe that?"

"All that matters is what you believe, but I will tell you what I suspect. Somehow, you feel guilty for not being the soldier you should have been, and you have started to wonder if underneath your conscientious objection, you were really just afraid. Am I mistaken?"

Jacob was quiet, observing Dr. Tudela's inscrutable face. "It's possible."

"Both things are compatible—one doesn't preclude the other. You can have scruples and not want to participate in something, and at the same time, feel afraid of it."

"Last night I couldn't stop thinking about why I then accepted another mission from Dor."

"Do you want to tell me about it?"

"Natan sent me back to Beirut on Dor's orders. The mission consisted of accompanying a woman called Rina, but she could have given me any name. Like me, she spoke French and Arabic perfectly. It would be very simple, according to Natan: go to Beirut, to the house of a man who would give us information. While the man spoke to Rina, I had to plant a few microphones around the house.

"I resisted. I reminded him that I was an engineer, not an agent. But Natan used his go-to argument: Dor was one of our best clients, and he wasn't going to say no to him."

"So you didn't get your way," Dr. Tudela commented.

Jacob shrugged, searching for an answer.

"No, I didn't. I didn't want to do it, but at the same time, I wondered if it was from cowardice."

"And then?"

"Rina was experienced and had warned me that it would be risky. The man, she explained to me, had been selling us information until now, but being a good businessman, he could sell us out if someone paid him a better price.

"So the mission wasn't quite as simple as Natan had told us. They gave us a thick wad of money to pay the man we were going to meet."

"From what you're telling me, it was effectively agent work, but you still accepted it."

"We crossed the border just before dawn and a young man was waiting for us on the other side in a truck. He drove us to

Beirut without saying a word. Rina told me to let her deal with the informant.

"The man received us very formally, offering us coffee and sweets set out by a beardless teenaged servant. We wasted a lot of time on small talk before he finally described the type of information he had and the price he was asking for it. Rina agreed and said we would pay him. The man gave us the addresses of where some jihadist leaders were hiding. He also described the clashes going on between some of the leaders.

"I got up in the middle of the conversation on the pretense that I needed the bathroom. I had to plant the microphones somewhere. It wasn't easy because the boy followed me to the door and waited for me to come out. I tried to distract him, asking him about himself and if he was in school, then I dropped my phone on the floor, letting him retrieve it, but I still wasn't able to plant the microphones anywhere except the bathroom.

"Later, while Rina continued talking to the man, I asked to go out to the garden. Rina glared at me. The man smiled.

'Your bodyguard is not very professional,' he said. 'He's bored! Fine, go out in the garden. Yusuf will accompany you.'

"It was impossible to get rid of Yusuf and I couldn't find anywhere to plant the microphone in the garden. Eventually we went back to the living room.

"I didn't say another word after that, and only brought out the payment when Rina gave the signal."

"We then spent a few hours walking around Beirut. The young man taking us to the border would collect us after lunch. We sat in a café and read the Lebanese newspapers. Later, Rina asked me to go to a barber while she went into a beauty salon that was famous for French manicures."

"'Listen,' she advised, 'in barbershops men relax and talk about everything. The same thing happens in beauty salons.

Don't give your opinions on anything, just listen. And if they ask you something you can give them an answer, now that we've just read the papers and are caught up on things.'

"We had lunch in a restaurant near the beach. I would have liked to go to one of the places my father use to love, but Rina was against it, arguing that it was better to go unnoticed.

"My part of that mission had been a failure. Still, I was re-assured that I hadn't put anyone but myself in danger.

"I was sure that Rina had seen my obvious incompetence at carrying out jobs like hers. I wasn't made to live among shadows, and I had no talent for being an agent."

Jacob stayed silent. He had nothing more to say.

"Well, we don't all have the same talents or aptitudes. You needed to prove that you were capable of putting your life at risk. The rest was secondary."

"Yes, I guess you could say that."

"But you're still not convinced."

"What do you think?"

"Jacob, the forging of this country wasn't easy and like everyone else, you have heard many stories about the heroic behavior of those who made modern Israel a reality. But this country also needs people who know how to lay bricks, sow seeds and invent things.

"We can feel proud of those men and women, but we don't have to compete with them. Each of us has a responsibility. I wouldn't be a good agent either, and that doesn't bother me in the slightest. I don't think it makes me any less brave. You can do a lot for our country, for the world, as an engineer. You have your own talents. Dor has his, as does Natan, as do we all. We're all necessary. Without Dor, we wouldn't be able to sleep peacefully. But without what you do with algorithms, we wouldn't progress."

"But is it worth the effort, everything we do to stay here?" Jacob asked her.

The doctor looked straight at him, placing her hands on the table.

"My grandparents and yours, those who died in the concentration camps, would be able to answer that question better than me. This is our homeland, Jacob, it has been for thousands of years. We never stopped belonging to this place. If Israel had existed at the time of the war, there never would have been a Holocaust. You already know this. The question isn't whether Israel should exist or not. The question is whether you want to be part of all this, and fight for us to keep this piece of land. So you tell me."

"Yes. Yes, it's worth it. But you know what? I still dream about that boy in Ain al-Hilweh. His face, his voice, they stay with me. How will he ever forgive us?"

"I'm not a cynic, Jacob, so I won't say that collateral victims are just an unavoidable part of war, even if it does happen."

The door opened and a smiling man poked his head in.

"Dr. Tudela, they're waiting for you. They sent me to find you."

"Yes, I'm coming right now."

Jacob and the doctor said goodbye with a handshake.

# Book II

Book II

*Brussels. 6 p.m.*

"Brother, what is more difficult, dying or killing?"

Ismail waited anxiously for the answer. The visible tension in his brother's jaw worried him. If they'd been alone, he definitely would have gotten a smack on the head, but the men were looking at Abir, and a forced smile flickered across his face before he answered.

"The hardest thing is serving Allah, wherever he needs us. With generosity, without questions. He decides how you are most useful."

"And has Allah already decided what he needs from me?" the young boy continued, even though he knew his insistence would irritate his brother.

"You'll know when your time comes. Now pay attention to Ghalil's instructions. If you don't learn how to handle explosives, you'll end up killing yourself."

Abir looked away from his little brother and beckoned to one of the men to follow him. A bookshelf covered one wall of the room where the meeting was being held. He felt around the shelves for the lever. Like in Ali Baba's cave, the shelves slid open to reveal a small but well-equipped room. It had been soundproofed and simply furnished: a pair of sofas, a plasma TV on a low table, six stacked chairs, and a round table. The only noticeable thing about the room was that it had no windows. Once inside, Abir pulled another lever and the solid wooden panel closed.

"Your brother is too young," the man said to him.

"Don't worry, Kamal. He will follow instructions and he will die when we order him to."

"But you still haven't told him he'll die."

No, he hadn't told him. And he wasn't even going to think about it until absolutely necessary. Telling his brother would only scare him.

Abir ran a hand over his face. He was tired, and in that windowless room he felt short of air.

"Sheikh Mohsin is worried about him," Kamal insisted.

But Abir raised a hand to stop him.

"I trust my brother. If I didn't, I wouldn't involve him in what we're preparing."

"And are you really willing to sacrifice him?"

"Didn't you lose two sons fighting against the infidels? We must all pay a blood tribute to be worthy of the battle that will lead us to establishing the Caliphate for all time."

"May Allah hear you," Kamal responded.

"And may He always protect us. Now let's review the entire operation. I have prepared it painstakingly, but I think your expert eyes will find any mistakes I may have made."

"That's why they sent for me, Abir. There can't be any errors, and you like taking risks a little too much. You think you can outsmart all those who are out looking for you. You trust too much in your good luck, but one day it may abandon you. And then there's your health. With your bad heart, you're looking unwell."

"My heart is holding out. It took me one month, Kamal, one month to recover, fighting to survive. You shouldn't worry about my health or the plan. So far, I've outsmarted every security service in the world. They can't catch me. They don't know what I look like because they don't know who I am. They're searching for a ghost who strikes them in the most unexpected places. They're always trailing behind. When they think I'll strike one city, I strike another. When there's a massacre in a crowded public place, I choose some unlucky bastard who's well known enough to them to make sure his death will show up on every news report on TV. I'm ahead of the game, Kamal."

"Arrogance is a sin against Allah. I'm afraid it will be your downfall," Kamal reproached him.

Abir's mouth twitched, but he didn't respond. Kamal was one of Sheikh Mohsin's lieutenants, and to offend him was to offend their leader. He needed him. He wasn't a lone wolf and didn't want to be; there were already a lot of those, including some he'd created himself.

He wanted to become highly respected man, someone the other soldiers wouldn't just admire for his bravery, but revere him and follow his every command.

"I'll be very careful, Kamal. I know how much is at stake."

"Are you sure your brother will be willing to kill himself?" the sheikh insisted.

"Ismail has been trained to obey. He will do whatever is asked."

"He's a scared little boy," Kamal sneered.

Abir had to contain himself, but he knew it was true. His brother Ismail was scared, even before knowing that this mission would cost him his life. But he couldn't admit this to Kamal.

"Ismail is brave. He has been since he was little. And he will give up his life without any trouble. I guarantee it," he stated more forcefully than necessary.

"Fine, now tell me all the details of the operation."

"The next NATO summit will be held in two weeks and will last three days. Defense ministers from every country in the alliance will be there, and they're also expected to hold a meeting with the Russian defense minister to talk about the tension on the eastern borders."

"I already know all that, Abir," Kamal responded impatiently.

"Yes, of course. In any case, it doesn't matter to us if the Americans and Russians are friends or enemies, we're fighting them both, and both are our enemies. We should make an example of them. I will turn Brussels into a place of hell. But it is only the beginning. The infidels won't sleep peacefully anywhere in the world. They won't know where or when we're going to act. I might also try to kill all the ministers who come to the NATO summit. I'm working out the details," Abir told him.

"You're crazy!"

"It won't be that hard. I've thought it all out. We'll need to sacrifice one of our own, but we'll succeed."

"When many fighters are needed, things go wrong. Leaks happen more easily."

"No one will know the entire plan. Each soldier will have concrete orders, and we will play with the enemy. They feel safe in Brussels."

"No, I don't think we should try this. There are too many risks."

"I'm prepared to die. In fact, that is what will happen," Abir replied fiercely, though he had no intention of putting his life in danger unless circumstances forced him to.

"How are you planning to do it?" Kamal asked skeptically.

They talked for almost two hours, but Abir didn't tell him the most important details. What he wanted was for him to provide more explosives. It wasn't that he distrusted Kamal, but he knew that the success of any operation was based on silence, on no one else knowing a single extraneous detail about the plan.

"Who will be the martyrs?" Kamal wanted to know.

"You'll see. Our men are willing to die if that means shortening the infidels' time in power. Trust me."

146

"Fine, but you must have a backup plan. The NATO head-quarters are housed in one of the most secure buildings in the world. Face every possibility with bravery, but don't be foolish enough to attempt the impossible."

"There are many other organizations in Brussels. The European Commission, for example. I won't rule that out as a second objective."

Kamal nodded, but he looked at him with concern. Abir did not look good and had lost too much weight. His face was haggard from exhaustion. Ignoring Kamal's look, Abir firmly pressed the hidden lever. The bookshelf slid open until they could enter the adjacent room. There they found Ismail and Ghalil, now with an elegantly dressed man in his forties and a woman carrying out a tray.

The woman covered her hair in a hijab and her body with a tunic, not allowing even an inch of her body to be seen.

The man stood up and smiled with a nod of greeting to-wards Kamal.

"May Allah protect you, Zaim," Kamal said, stepping for-ward to embrace him.

"And may He protect you always, my friend. I hope you will honor us by dining in our home. Nashira is a good cook."

Kamal nodded. Although he was naturally suspicious, he knew Zaim Jabib to be a man with a strong sense of loyalty, not only because Sheikh Mohsin trusted him; he had demonstrated intelligence and good judgement during his many years of ser-vice to the cause.

"I see you have meticulously prepared the hiding place for all the explosives and weapons."

"It's taken two years, Kamal, but we have made this the safest place in Brussels. I hope you don't find any flaws. I built it all with my own hands. The living room connects to a win-dowless safe room, as you've seen. It's not very big, but it's enough to hide Abir, if necessary. Nobody will find him here, and he will be able to oversee the rain of hellfire," he assured them, smiling.

The five men stood together talking while Nashira set the table. No one looked at her, and she didn't look at them. She appeared not to be listening.

Nashira was very young, about 20, and had a delicate face. Zaim felt proud of his wife. His parents had chosen her carefully, and she possessed the crucial qualities of a good wife: obedient, modest, pious, and discreet. They had only been married for a few months. Zaim had rejected his previous wife for not giving him any children. It wasn't an easy decision, and he'd suffered, but now he felt content. He and Nashira knew they would become parents soon.

*Brussels. 7 a.m.*

The gray light of dawn poured slowly over Brussels. Ismail walked quickly, sweat plastering his hair to his head. He hadn't slept well the night before. He had barely been able to force down any food at dinner, listening silently to Kamal, Ghalil and his brother talking. Zaim had been polite, but distant.

Ismail's body coursed with fear. What he feared most was his older brother's hate. Abir hated cowards. He arrived at an imposing building of glass and steel and hurried in, distracted. This is what Abir had advised him to do. He took the elevator to the basement and headed down the hall to the building's maintenance area, which also housed the mail room. There were always people coming and going, a beehive of activity.

"You're late, Ismail," a middle-aged woman told him with a disapproving face.

"Sorry, the bus was late."

"Leave your house earlier then," she answered coldly.

Without looking at him, she pointed to a cart stacked with packages. She didn't need to tell him what to do. He would deliver them on each floor, then help the maintenance team make any requested repairs. He went to his locker and jammed his backpack inside. In it was a container of food for later. At the back of the locker, he'd hidden a bag. He took a can of a soda out of the backpack and put it in the bag. He checked that both the bag and the backpack were well positioned, and then he locked it up with a key. The same thing he'd done every day

149

since he'd started the job a year ago. He then went to the elevator and, floor by floor, completed his work. He liked his job, and was even happy with the paycheck he received. His aunt and uncle were proud of him. Though, he hadn't actually gotten the job on his own merit. Abir had insisted that he work in that specific building, and he'd only gotten the job thanks to a recommendation from an acquaintance of his uncle's.

Arriving on the 10th floor, he discreetly pulled an envelope out of his pocket and slid it among the packages. The receptionist talking on the phone ignored him as he placed the delivery on her desk. He then continued to the next floor.

*Brussels. 9 a.m.*

Helen pushed aside an envelope her secretary had left on her desk, the sun glinting on the glass surface. She was distracted and lit a cigarette. Smoking wasn't allowed anywhere in the building, but she didn't care; she needed the hit to her bloodstream.

The short night of sleep she'd had was clearly visible on her face and in her mood. She missed her newsroom in Washington. In Brussels she felt like an intruder, even if the offices belonged to the network. She turned on her computer and skimmed her interminable inbox. She answered a few emails and left others for later. Lucy came in without knocking, setting down a cup of coffee, and Helen thanked her with a strained smile.

"Are you ready for your 9 o'clock? Maybe tell the makeup artist to give you a little more color today. And put out that cigarette."

"Lucy, give me a break! I went to bed late. Andrew wanted to go to the opera, and then we had a drink with Markus and Emma. My stomach is a mess. I can't handle gin and tonic, as you know, but Andrew and Markus insisted we order them."

"Yes, it must be horrible to have to go to the opera and have drinks with two of the company's most important shareholders, one of whom is your husband and also the vice president, poor thing!"

Helen smiled. Lucy was right; she shouldn't complain. Her husband was one of the most important men in the TV industry, and even though she was already a successful journalist, marrying Andrew had been a real boost for her career. They had both been married when they met. She was on her third husband, a fellow colleague who specialized in sports, while Andrew was in a marriage of convenience, his wife pouring all her energy into philanthropy. Neither had been happy, so their divorces were fairly painless for them. Helen knew that many at the network thought she'd married Andrew Morris for her own personal gain. She pushed the thought aside and began to focus on the day ahead of her.

"Is Benjamin here yet?"

"Yes. Ever since he got divorced, he's become punctual again, and since we're in Brussels, and not New York, he doesn't have as many distractions. He did tell me that he had dinner last night with some civil servants from the U.S. State of Defense who've come to the NATO summit. He's waiting for you in the meeting room, and Lauren and the rest of the team are with him. You'll be the last to arrive."

"Lauren's going to be pissed off," Helen observed without the slightest hint of concern.

"Yeah, well, she's your producer and always wants everything to be perfect. Take your coffee and get out of here already."

"What about this envelope?"

"It was addressed to you and Benjamin. The delivery boy brought it."

Swallowing her coffee, Helen tore open the envelope. Inside was a thumb drive, but no note.

"What is this?" she asked out loud.

"Exactly what it appears to be," Lucy answered, looking down at her watch.

"Let's see what's inside," Helen answered, plugging the device into her computer.

"You'll be late," Lucy warned.

A few seconds later, they saw the image of a man in a ski mask, his eyes hidden behind black sunglasses, surrounded by other masked men. His monotonous voice startled them. "Infidels, we demand the freedom of our brothers incarcerated in Guantanamo prison. For every day that passes without their release, your blood will flow. For every brother you have imprisoned, one of you will die. There won't be a single place in the world where you can sleep peacefully. We demand that you share this recording so that the corrupt nations of the world will know that our fury will also reach them. We expect to see this message aired on *The World at 7* tonight. Vengeance will be ours!" the masked man shouted, shaking his fist menacingly.

The man's face disappeared from the screen, and they then saw the recording of a young man being decapitated with an axe. Five more followed. The video then showed the symbol known to represent the Circle.

The two women froze in silence. Helen's fingers clenched her coffee cup, and Lucy's eyes stayed locked on the computer screen.

"Oh my god! They're insane!" she blurted.

Helen took a few seconds to react.

"Jesus Christ. Lucy, tell Lauren and Benjamin to get over here now. They have to see this. Then call Foster's office in Washington and get ahold of his secretary. We have to talk to the boss right away." Helen spoke calmly even as waves of shock rolled through her.

"It's three in the morning in Washington. Everyone will be in bed!"

"Well, wake them, Foster's the head of the network—now!"

Helen stood up and walked quickly to the bathroom to vomit. She glared at her reflection in the mirror, preparing herself. She didn't like how she looked. Her chestnut hair was dry and a map of wrinkles had appeared around her eyes. She held her mouth in a twist of fear.

Nausea rose in her stomach and she threw up again. She promised herself never to drink gin again.

When she came out of the bathroom, Lucy handed her a glass of water.

Suddenly the door swung open and Lauren Scott stepped in, glaring at the two women. Immediately, she saw there was something going on that had nothing to do with the diva-like behavior of one of the network's stars.

Benjamin came in behind Lauren.

"What the hell is going on?" he shouted.

It was Lucy who responded.

"Sit down, Benjamin, and you too, Lauren. We've received a file."

Then she clicked on the video and waited as Lauren and Benjamin watched.

"My god. What should we do with this?" Benjamin asked. "If we air it, we'll get a record audience, but we'd be turning ourselves into a loudspeaker for these nutjobs."

"Yes, this goes beyond covering the news. It's … well, it's doing what the terrorists want," Helen responded, holding in another wave of nausea.

"Well, we have to do it, we just have to fully explain the context and warn the viewers that they're going to see some very difficult images. Don't you agree?" Lauren said, looking expectantly at Helen and Benjamin.

"Yes, of course, it's clear we can't keep this news to ourselves." Helen's words were barely audible.

Just then her phone began to ring. Joseph Foster was not at all happy. He asked what could possibly be so important that Lucy had to wake him up at three in the morning.

Helen explained, promising to send over the contents of the pen drive right away.

"Don't any of you do anything! First, I'll watch it and then let you know exactly what we'll do. And we'll have to inform the White House."

"Yes. But Lauren, Benjamin and I are all in agreement that it must be aired. We can't keep this to ourselves." Helen's voice was firm.

"Don't even think about moving a muscle without my permission!"

Foster hung up and Helen stared at the phone in her hand.

"What did he say?" Lauren wanted to know.

"To do nothing without his OK."

"He'll have to let us air it. It would be a scandal for the network to cover up news like this," Benjamin argued.

"He'll greenlight it. But he said that would talk to the White House press office," Helen explained as she encrypted the file to email it to Foster.

"Have you talked to Andrew?" Lauren asked.

The question annoyed Helen. Her professionalism was being questioned. Being married to Andrew Morris didn't make her a less serious journalist. Everyone seemed to have forgotten that she had made a name for herself in television before she had even met her husband.

"I haven't spoken to him yet, but he'll surely find out from Foster first," she responded irritably.

"We'll have to talk to W.W. He's the chief correspondent in Europe after all, and we're on his turf. It's one thing for us to set up here to air the program, doing things our way, but it's another thing for us not to inform him about what's going on. Walter White is not exactly an easygoing guy," Lauren stated.

Barely a minute had passed before Walter burst into the office.

"Were you even planning on telling me? Foster had to call me from Washington to inform me that you, my illustrious and unwanted guests, have a bombshell story, a message from who knows what jihadist faction threatening to kill who knows who. It's completely unacceptable that I had to find out from the head of the network!" he reprimanded them.

"OK, calm down W.W. I don't know why it bothers you so much that we've come here to do the program for the NATO summit. There's a lot at stake—our country might abandon the alliance and leave the Europeans to fend for themselves," Benjamin shot back.

"We don't need you in Brussels!" Walter shouted.

"Of course not, and as far as I know, no one is going to interfere in the running of your bureau. We'll do our thing, producing the program from here. Is it really so hard to lend us a couple of workspaces? You're going overboard, W.W." Benjamin told him calmly.

"I want to see this shit they sent you," he demanded from no one in particular.

Helen clicked on the video and they were all silent, scrutinizing the threatening image of the man promising that rivers of blood would flow.

Walter watched Helen light a cigarette and decided to join her, no longer caring about building regulations. Benjamin took out his own pack from his jacket pocket, and Lucy couldn't resist borrowing one.

"Fine, we'll put it in the midday report. Brussels will be paralyzed."

"Has Foster given the go-ahead?" Helen asked.

"We're journalists. We can't cover this up. Foster can't force us to do that. I'll tell my people to get to work. I'm taking the thumb drive," Walter answered.

"I think you should watch the message again. It was sent to Helen and to me. To our program. He says it very clearly. They want their demands aired on *The World at 7*. And that's what we're going to do." Benjamin leveled his gaze with Walter's.

"Since when are you in charge of the Brussels office? As far as I know, Foster hasn't fired me. I'm the director here, and I will decide how and when we air it." Walter's voice had turned to ice.

"But they sent it to us!" Helen protested, her stomach churning.

"This is a television network, there is no 'us' and 'them' among us. There is only news, and we as directors decide when it is delivered. You are in Brussels, not in Washington, and I'm in charge here. You can help my team or do nothing, I don't care. But what I say goes.

"Of course," White looked directly at Helen, "you'll probably pull some strings to get your way. We know how you operate."

"You're a bastard!" Benjamin leapt up to stare Walter down.

"Both of you, calm down!" Lauren intervened, stepping between the two men. "You know what, Walter? Benjamin might be right, but that's not important right now. We need to know what we're going to do with this video. I'm scheduling a conference call with Joseph Foster. Everyone can give their opinion, and we'll see where we end up."

Helen was still and silent, counting to 20. It had cost her a small fortune in therapy sessions to be able to contain the rage that would fill her when someone attacked her marriage. Finally, she responded, "You're a piece of shit, Walter, and even worse, you think we're all like you."

At that moment her phone rang and she could see it was her husband. She considered letting it ring, but after a few seconds she answered.

Andrew was angry. He'd heard about the thumb drive from Foster, and wanted to know why she hadn't called him.

Helen responded in monosyllables, embarrassed in front of her colleagues.

In the meantime, Lucy had Foster on the phone, saying he was already arriving at the network's main offices. He would connect in a few minutes to the videoconference. In Washington, the heads of the other news channels had been alerted and were ready to get to work as soon as they were given the signal.

W.W. left the office without a word. No one asked where he was going or if he planned on coming back, but they assumed he would return with the most trusted members of his team.

An hour later, Foster told them his decision. There was no doubt that they had to air the video on *The World at 7*. Helen Morris and Benjamin Holz had won that battle. But they would work under W.W.'s orders as he was fully in charge of the correspondents in Europe.

"Wow. Am I not the producer of *The World at 7*?" Lauren Scott asked drily, glaring at Foster's video image.

"You are, Lauren. But tonight's program will be unlike any other. We'll work as a team and put our egos aside. I've spoken with the White House press office, inviting them to make a comment. They didn't waste a minute sending over the NSA and have alerted the CIA too. Right now, there's a long line of people waiting outside my office. Do you all understand what I'm saying? I will not allow your personal disputes to come first when we have a real problem on our hands. Some son of a bitch has decided we should be the official channel for his insanity!" Foster was clear that he would be the one to decide how the game would be played.

"That's all fine, Joseph. I have a visitor as well. NATO's secret service has come for the thumb drive," W.W. explained. "They don't want us to air it, but I've already told them that's not negotiable. In the past hour, I've received a number of calls asking us not to collaborate with terrorists. The Belgian government have also requested a copy of the thumb drive, and the European Union's counterterrorist service have added themselves to the list."

"Fine, we'll collaborate with the authorities, but we're going to air that goddamn tape," Joseph Foster shot back. "Our duty is to inform the people. The intelligence services have the duty to catch the terrorists. To each their own."

"My people are comparing other files to try and figure out who the man in the video recording is," W.W. reported.

"They're doing the same thing in the newsroom in Washington," Foster replied. "We'll check in every two hours, unless one of us has something important to share. I want you to send me the copy that Helen and Benjamin will read ASAP. Be careful with the tone, we don't want it to be too alarming," he asked everyone.

"It's going to be difficult not to alarm people when they hear that if the U.S. government doesn't start releasing prisoners, people will die," Benjamin replied darkly.

"We will report that every intelligence service is working to prevent an attack, and that there is no greater danger today than there was yesterday," Foster answered. "Interview someone high up in the Belgian police force, and a security expert from NATO. I expect that the White House will also release a statement."

Jacob was making a salad when the buzz of his cellphone startled him.

"Get over here right now. It's urgent. I've already called Natan. If he hasn't called you yet, he will soon. He's already on his way."

After so many years, Jacob was still unused to Dor's brusque ways.

"What happened?"

"There's no time for stupid questions! Do you think I'm going to tell you anything over the phone?" Then he hung up.

Jacob put food in Luna's bowl and checked that she had fresh water, looking at his watch.

"I have to go. Be good and wait for me."

Luna stared at him. Jacob was sure she understood him. He cursed Dor. For months, Natan hadn't given him any of those assignments, and he had slept peacefully. He knew that other colleagues were being called on by Dor; as an artificial intelligence company, IAI was at his beck and call. He felt his stomach turn over. Artificial intelligence and algorithms were his world, though there were things that could be done with them that he wanted no knowledge of. But this was Israel, and there was no avoiding it.

He thought about Gabriella, who he had met on a night out with some friends. He had planned to have dinner at her place that night. The only problem with Gabriella had been that that she also worked in artificial intelligence. He suspected that she worked for Dor, and knew he wouldn't be able to handle it if she turned out to be someone other than what she seemed. He had learned that anything was possible in the world of shadows.

Within half an hour, he'd arrived at Palm Tree House. Dor was with a group of men he knew, including Natan. Four of them worked together in artificial intelligence programs for businesses connected to the army. The other two, Maoz and his friend Efraim, worked directly for Dor. The room smelled of coffee and smoldering cigarette butts.

Dor barely glanced, up, gesturing for him to sit next to the others around a table. He turned the lights off to show them a video on a computer screen and began to watch the image of a man who had covered up every inch of his face.

Then Jacob heard his voice and went cold.

Dor's phone suddenly rang, and he paused the video. The image of the man remained frozen on the screen as Dor spoke in English with someone who must have been important.

Jacob felt Efraim's eyes on him, and later he could feel Maoz looking at him too. He knew them well, or at least he thought he did. Maoz was already over 70 years old, though he looked like a much younger man. Dor considered him one of his best agents. He was a specialist in operations that went behind enemy lines. A tough guy, but also an expert in ancient history who could speak half a dozen languages perfectly and play the double bass. Maoz could have been a great musician if he had been born under different circumstances. He had grown up on a kibbutz, and it was his mother, a Czech violinist, who had fostered his love of music. And Efraim, despite their differences, was still Jacob's best friend.

As they waited for Dor to finish the call, he closed his eyes, and, for a few seconds returned to a place he never wanted to return to: Ain al-Hilweh. Again, he saw the boy running, throwing stones and screaming, "I'll find you! I'll kill you all and you'll pay for what you've done, you filthy dogs!"

Memories were assaulting him randomly. He knew he was in Dor's office, but he felt it all happening again, the past mingling with the present. His head hurt and his hands trembled.

*How long have I suppressed the memories of that day? Why are they suddenly coming back? Can the others tell what's happening to me? Probably—those looks from Efraim and Maoz. They're experienced agents, but the rest are engineers like me and probably not skilled in psychology, not like the people who play mind games every day behind enemy lines,* he thought as he tried to calm himself down.

Dor finished the call and then gestured for them to keep quiet as he clicked on the video to continue.

He listened. Dor played the video again until they had watched it seven or eight more times.

"The Americans have asked us to examine this file. Apparently, the voiceprint hasn't been found in their database, or in NATO's or in those of any of the allied countries. We haven't found it yet either. All of you here today were born or have lived in Arab countries, and you are very familiar with many of the regional expressions and accents. But you're also experts in artificial intelligence and utilizing devices that give you the powers of a crystal ball. I want your opinions. Where is the man from originally? We will try to create a profile, and take it from there. I want you to go through our voiceprint library, compare files, and tell me who this individual is. The Americans have asked us to help them."

Dor's eyes gleamed and Jacob felt them penetrating his soul. He realized he hadn't moved a single muscle. He had always tried to appear indifferent in front of him, but the sound of that voice had shaken him, making him appear visibly anxious.

One of the men said the man's accent seemed neutral to him. Another thought that he dragged his Rs as if he had studied French. Someone else was positive that the Arabic the man spoke was influenced by Afghan vernacular, but that accent ...

Jacob felt Dor's watching him.

"What do you think, Jacob?"

For a second, he considered not revealing who it was. He felt it would be a betrayal to the boy he'd never stopped thinking about. Could he live with that betrayal?

"Do you have any ideas?" Dor persisted.

If he didn't say what he knew, would he be betraying the country his mother had worked so hard to make her own? He had to choose who to serve, either that boy or the men waiting expectantly for him to speak. He had to choose, and though it hurt him, he answered, "I think I know who he is."

Silence fell. Dor looked at Jacob incredulously. He hadn't called him in because he thought he would know that voice; he simply expected him to analyze the voice recording with one of his devices.

Jacob could feel the rest of the men waiting for him to continue.

"We're waiting, Jacob," he heard Dor's voice filter in through his cloudy thoughts.

"It's Abir Nasr."

"Abir Nasr? And who is Abir Nasr?" one of the men asked.

"He's Lebanese. Years ago, we killed his parents in Ain al-Hilweh, a refugee camp in south Lebanon. I was there. It was supposed to be an easy operation, but ..." he managed to say.

"And how do you know it's him?" Dor's voice sounded more hoarse than normal.

Jacob didn't know how to respond. Was he really sure, or was his brain playing tricks on him?

"Search every file—now!" Dor ordered.

"You told me about that family yourself. His mother's name was Ghada and his father's, Jafar. They weren't the tar-

164

gets, it was Sheikh Mohsin. They were all living in a rundown house together," Jacob blurted out flatly.

"Yes, that was 14 or 15 years ago. We were trying to catch Sheikh Mohsin, someone who was and continues to be the biggest arms dealer in the Middle East, and who acts as an intermediary between the Caliphate and certain individuals in Gaza. He escaped us," Dor confirmed, looking at Jacob as if it were his fault.

"Why do you think it's Abir Nasr? Did you talk to him? Have you seen him in the last few years?" Maoz asked.

"He was a child at the times, maybe 14, 15 years old. He watched his parents die, and fled with another little boy, holding his hand," Jacob continued without looking at anyone.

"But have you talked to him? How can you recognize his voice?" Maoz asked.

"No, I haven't spoken to him. But at the time I heard him curse and swear that one day he would kill us all. I've never forgotten it. He was a just a poor kid.

"The operation was a failure. What happened was that one of the women in the house woke up and started to scream, and then it was just chaos. The women defended Mohsin with their lives, so did the father," Jacob explained.

"And it wasn't possible to do it better?" one of the men asked.

"My job was to make sure nobody escaped the house. I was outside monitoring it all on a computer screen, but the images weren't very clear. Those women ... yes, it was Abir's mother who had woken up and seen the shadows of our soldiers and then started to scream. The kids were sleeping next to their parents. I saw how the father ordered his children to run, but Abir hesitated. He pulled on his mother's hand, he wanted to bring her with him, but she tripped. She held a baby girl in her arms and used her body to shield Mohsin and stop him from being killed. She saved his life. I then saw him jump out of a window and run off."

"Kill him? Dor said the objective had been to capture him."
Maoz seemed determined to get every detail out of Jacob.

"Yes, but he and the other men started firing their weapons, and we had to defend ourselves. I … we … had no other options." Jacob tried to keep his voice neutral.

"So Mohsin escaped, and it would appear that the boy has now become a man who has decided to make us notice him. Is that what you think, Jacob?" Dor concluded.

Efraim was unconvinced that Jacob could recognize the voice of that little kid from so many years before.

"Are you sure? How can you remember his voice?"

"I really believe it could be him."

"Come on Jacob, you can't know that. I'm sorry to say this here, and maybe I shouldn't, but that experience changed you. I remember when you told me about it. It was deeply traumatic for you, a trauma that's left its mark. You can't possibly know whether that voice belongs to the boy." Doubt flooded Efraim's face.

"I'm not ashamed to admit that what happened affected me. I will never get used to the image of children having their homes destroyed or their parents killed. Never."

"Yes, we know," Dor responded, "but now we have a problem, and if we don't resolve it, people will die. Start going through the files, and you, Jacob, you'll be joining the team. Maximum priority. Natan, I suppose you don't have any objection to Jacob collaborating with us. After all, it was you who suggested I call him. It's lucky your business is our business. You'll have to get by without us until we find these people. Did you all sign confidentiality agreements on your way in? Then get to work. You have been mobilized, Jacob. Stay here a minute."

Dor lit a cigarette as the other men filed out. Smoking was banned in every public building in the country, but this place was more like his home. He spent more than 16 hours a day here, and no one would make him follow the rules.

"You're so sentimental, Jacob. I'm really not sure you could match that voice to a boy you heard speak for a few seconds so many years ago. Efraim says that mission really affected you, but the truth is every mission affected you. You can't handle reality."

"Reality? What reality? For me, the only reality is that there are people who have no future. There are children who see how we destroy their homes, how we take away their parents, how their people die! They hate us and I get it. That's reality for me."

"Right. So in order for you to be happy, so you can sleep at night, with your morals and your ethics so superior to ours, we should let them kill us. You know, we aren't the ones who started this."

"It doesn't matter who started it, the question is what happens here and now. What are we doing to try to stop this nightmare? Do you really think we can live like this forever?"

"No, I don't think so. The politicians are doing their job, but in the meantime, I'll do mine. My obligation is to stop them from killing us. But this case isn't about the Palestinians and us, it's about something else. The problem is that there are some people out there who say they represent the Caliphate and they want to destroy the West. Men who behead anyone who doesn't agree with them. Human lives are worth nothing to these guys. We are fighting against an organization that is made up of millions of people who live among us and who can therefore attack us whenever they feel like it. The next step of an army can be predicted, but not that of a single soldier. That's the war we're fighting."

"Yes, of course, but our American friends are the ones who decided to kick that part of the world while they were down by invading Iraq. That's where the Caliphate, or ISIS, or the Circle—whatever you want to call it—was born."

"Look, I'm not here to argue with you about geopolitics. You're a goddamn pacifist who doesn't want to see reality. I don't care who kicked the wasp's nest. All I know is that there are guys out there ready to blow us all to pieces and my job is to stop them from doing that."

"Is it that simple?"

"It's that complicated, Jacob. That's what you don't understand."

They sat in silence for a few seconds. Dor lit another cigarette.

"I don't understand this country, you're right about that."

"Well, you have two options: you either leave or you stay. If you stay, you'll have to do the same as everyone else: fight so they don't throw us into the sea, so we don't disappear. If you don't like that reality, get into politics, go to the parliament and tell them how you think they should do things. Write articles, or keep marching for peace like you do sometimes. I suppose that alleviates your conscience. Go for it. But in the meantime, answer me this question: should we let them kill us? Should we let the Caliphate put bombs anywhere in the world, setting off massacres? Why don't you ask minorities like the Yazidis how their ISIS brothers treat them? Why don't you ask the women kept as slaves to satisfy the glorious soldiers? Tell me, what should we say to stop them?"

Jacob didn't know how to answer. He knew there was no answer, or at least, he didn't have it.

"You're an expert on artificial intelligence. A genius. You're one of the best. If you hadn't said you recognized that individual's voice, I would have told you to get out of here with your scruples and go cry somewhere else, but you claim to know the voice of the man in the recording, so now you have to collaborate with us whether you like it or not. You'll go to Brussels to support our people there, and you'll have to work with the information services from NATO, the European Union, the CIA and whoever else they say is necessary."

"To Brussels? When?"

"Now. Right now, so get going."

As soon as Jacob was out of the room, Dor lit one more cigarette. He'd always thought he'd be killed during a mission, but now he was sure he would die of cancer. He had already smoked four packs that day, and had been feeling some pain in his chest for a while. But he didn't even think about going to the doctor or quitting smoking. He wasn't ready to give up the fight, even if he had to do it from Palm Tree House.

A minute later, Maoz came into his office.

"We have to find Mohsin. Through him, we might be able to get to the man Jacob named, Abir Nasr. Mohsin is as slippery as an eel and has escaped us several times."

"Yes, it's rather hard to find someone in the Afghan mountains," Dor responded bitterly.

"He's not just in Afghanistan. We know he moves around Europe, but we haven't been able to catch him."

"There haven't been that many opportunities. He controls everything from Afghanistan, and when he travels he does it in countries that are difficult for us to operate in. But our priority now is this Abir Nasr. If Jacob's right, that man is our target."

"Jacob is too sensitive for this work. He believes that it's easier, morally speaking, to direct a drone or a plane with no pilot to bomb a target. But direct action is another thing. When he thought he recognized Abir Nasr, he became highly anxious, as if he were betraying him. He's too squeamish for the job."

"You know something, Maoz? When I started in this business, I went to a conference with a retired colonel who had been part of Mossad. Of everything he explained to us that day, one thing's stuck in my mind. He said that for the dirtiest jobs, you need the men with the cleanest hands. He was right. Otherwise we'll end up becoming thugs or murderers. I don't like men who enjoy pressing the trigger, or who sleep well after a mission. I don't trust them. Jacob's scruples annoy me, but they are a guarantee that this country hasn't lost its soul."

Maoz shrugged, but he didn't argue with Dor. They had a mission ahead of them: stopping the man who was threatening the world.

"I should go to Brussels with Jacob. I would be more useful there than here. The CIA's put Austin Turner in charge. He's not an easy guy, but we're friends."

"We have people in Brussels. Ariel Weiss is experienced and he'll know how to manage Turner."

"Some of our friends in the CIA have an issue with us not telling them everything, and Turner is one of them. He's a very distrusting guy. I know how to handle him, and we'll waste less time if we can all collaborate with each other. Ariel Weiss won't be bothered by me going—he served in my unit when we were in the army."

"Yes, but now he's our man in Brussels. He's in command."

"I have no intention of interfering with that. I know that I can help."

"I would rather you to go to Lebanon. We need to know what happened to Abir Nasr after his parents died. We need to try to find some answers in Ain al-Hilweh. It won't be easy."

"You're assuming that Jacob is right, that the voice belongs to that guy from so many years ago, Dor. It's almost impossible to remember a voice that precisely."

"I know. But it's all we've got for now."

"Are you going to tell the Americans?"

"Not yet."

Maoz nodded. Maybe Dor was right, and they had to start in that camp in south Lebanon. If Abir Nasr had turned into a terrorist, it would have all started the day his parents died in Ain al-Hilweh.

"I agree with you Dor, but I still think I'd be more useful in Brussels. We have people in Lebanon."

Dor hesitated. He didn't want to ignore Maoz's request. A specialist in jihad, he was the best agent that he had ever had in the Arab region, capable of melting into the background. His Iraqi-Jewish parents could barely speak Hebrew when they were forced to leave Baghdad after the war in 1948. His parents were still alive and spoke Arabic at home, and though he was born in Israel, it was Maoz's mother tongue.

"I don't know if we should neglect other operations," Dor responded.

"All operations are now the same operation now: finding out where they're going to strike next," Maoz replied.

"All right. Within the hour there will be a plane leaving for Brussels. Call me when you get there."

Maoz nodded. "In my opinion, Efraim could take charge of the operation in Ain al-Hilweh," he said on his way out.

"Yes, he could ... how ironic that a refugee camp could be known as the sweet water spring."

*Brussels.*
*Studios of the International Channel.*

They mentally rehearsed the timings they would use to tell the world the news. They knew the White House, the Kremlin, the European Commission headquarters, and Downing Street, among others, would be hanging on their words. There wouldn't be a single center of power that wasn't on high alert. As producer of the program, Lauren was in charge together with W.W. as the network's director in Brussels.

It had been a difficult day. There'd been endless arguments and shouting among the team of *The World at 7*, W.W. and the network heads.

Lauren had struggled to get Washington to accept her proposal to send an email to the main news agencies informing them that the program would be breaking the news. W.W. opposed it, arguing that it would give the rest of the media a head start, but Lauren said that it was about creating expectation. Joseph Foster, the director of the network, finally broke the deadlock by taking Lauren's side, but with one condition: they would send the message only half an hour before *The World at 7* would air. That way, no one would have time to investigate the video, but it would create enough excitement that editors-in-chief around the world would be on alert.

The red tally light switched on with the camera focused on Helen and Benjamin sitting behind the news desk with grave expressions. Helen was the first to address the viewers.

"Good evening. Tonight, we are reporting on terrifying threats that have been sent to our studios on a thumb drive."

She looked over to Benjamin so that he would continue.

"It consists," he began, "of a statement from an Islamist terrorist group claiming to represent the Circle. In the recorded message, they state that if the United States do not release the prisoners of Guantanamo Bay, they will carry out a series of executions. For every imprisoned terrorist, they have threatened to take the life of an innocent person."

The camera turned to Helen again.

"While we are distressed and disturbed by the video, The International Channel and *The World at 7* have decided to air it for two reasons. Benjamin?"

"First, our program and our network are committed to informing the public on everything that is relevant to you."

"The second reason," Helen continued, "is to respond to the terrorists with the message that society condemns their actions. The authorities are working to protect us all and they will surely succeed."

"In tonight's program," Benjamin added, "we will look at the identities of the terrorist suspects currently being held in the U.S. and in Europe, their crimes and their sentences. We will also report on the Circle, the group responsible for today's death threats. Then we will hear from experts on Islamist terrorism. But first, we will watch the recording."

The studio held the silence of a tomb. Helen imagined the same terrible hush in every embassy and intelligence center, in the White House, the Kremlin, though in all those places they had already known about the video for hours. She felt another wave of nausea. She glanced at the control room, everyone packed in like sardines. There were people she didn't recognize. She knew they would be agents from Belgian intelligence forces, from the CIA and from NATO. W.W. had already warned them about it. She and Benjamin had even had to be interviewed by the Americans about the thumb drive. Her eyes unwillingly connected with those of one of the strangers. He looked at her curiously, making her uncomfortable. The minutes passed by slowly.

When the video finished playing, they began the report on detained terrorist suspect, and then Benjamin took the lead by presenting two experts in Islamist terrorism, a professor from the University of Brussels and the president of the Association of Transatlantic Friendship, a think tank on global politics. They finished the program by interviewing the Belgian head of security.

When the red light clicked off, Helen realized her whole body was drenched in sweat.

Lauren Scott walked over, her hand making the sign for victory.

"Great show," she said.

"Thanks Lauren, we couldn't have done any of it without you," Helen answered.

"Well, that's what producers are for, conducting the orchestra. By the way, along with the CIA guys, the Belgian antiterrorism unit, the NATO security services, and the representative from the European Union Intelligence Center, we have some new friends just arrived from Israel. Except for Russia, the gang's all here."

Helen had already noticed one of the Israelis. She took in his missing tie, badly fitted jacket, sweater, and ripped jeans, then admonished herself for being so superficial at a time like this.

Lauren was remarking on the tension of the last few hours, and the feeling of having produced the most important program of her life. She was sure that *The World at 7* would never get a higher rating than it did tonight.

"Ah, and W.W. had asked us to meet in his office. The new arrivals want to talk to you both."

*Brussels. The home of Jamal Adoum.*

Jamal lit a cigarette and inhaled. Ismail stared with fright at the screen as his brother smiled and changed channels. European, American, Asian, African—all the world's news presenters were giving alarming accounts of the video shown by *The World at 7*. Each channel reported on Islamist terrorists detained in their particular country; the number was always high.

Abir knew they would never comply with their demands to liberate their brothers that very night. *The World at 7* certainly hadn't given any indication of it, quite the opposite in fact. The director of Belgian security had said that no civilized country would accept terrorist blackmail, and that they would work together to prevent the threats from being carried out.

No country could ever entertain the idea of giving in to blackmail, especially not publicly. It was now time to play chess and win. He was sure that western intelligence services were now trying to identify the voiceprint that they had no record of in their files. He also had no doubt that, despite their intense mutual distrust, a protocol for joint action among those countries would have been established. Even the Russians would cooperate. He looked at his watch. Before dawn, they would take the first life. The uncle and nephew looked at each other with satisfaction, then Jamal formally embraced Abir.

"I feel very proud of you. You're very brave, Abir," his uncle said, "and you, Ismail, you always honor your brother by obeying him."

A few timid taps on the door announced Fatima's presence. She looked afraid.

"Jamal, Abir, my dear, have you seen the news?"

"Yes, but you shouldn't worry," Abir responded.

"But if people die, the others will hate us even more. They'll blame all of us as Muslims. You could all lose your jobs."

"Woman, you shouldn't give your opinion. It's not proper!" Jamal cut her off.

"I'm scared. I don't like violence." Fatima looked at them, her face twisted with worry.

"You're a woman—it's normal that you're scared," Abir said. "But you have to understand that without violence, we'll never be free, and they'll never stop humiliating us. We have brothers who are fighting and sacrificing their lives for our future. Aunt Fatima, we must not dishonor their sacrifice."

"But Abir, you shouldn't think like that!" she cried.

"Just leave it be, Aunt Fatima. You don't understand these things."

"Woman, don't come to us with your fears. You know nothing, and you understand nothing. And you, Ismail, go outside, go into a café, and listen. Listen to what people are saying," Jamal instructed him.

Abir smiled at his aunt. He knew she wouldn't a problem, and his uncle wouldn't be either.

Fatima left the room to answer the phone. It was obvious from her tone of voice that she was arguing, and Abir was sure it was with Noura. Though his aunt tried not to speak softly so her husband and Abir wouldn't hear her, her agitated tone floated out to them. Once again, mother and daughter were fighting.

Abir's cousin had never forgiven her parents' behavior. She was exactly the opposite of his cousin Farid, who was a good

Muslim and who worked as an electrician like his father and aspired to be an imam. He had married a woman named Ayra who his father had chosen for him. She was a respectable wife, covering herself with the hijab and a trench coat that stopped at her feet. She had given Farid four children, honoring the meaning of his name, 'the unique'. While Ayra was a gentle woman who knew her place in the world, Uncle Jamal complained about the misfortune of having a daughter like Noura and blamed it on his wife Fatima.

When they were younger, Abir admired Noura. But now, while he still cared for her, he deplored his cousin's behavior. Any good man would be miserable with her. If she had married Brahim, he would have had to lock her up or maybe even kill her for her brazenness. Abir had to admit that Noura had a beautiful voice, but Allah didn't give her that gift to please so many men—it should have been only for her husband.

It had been years since Noura had run away from home, but that didn't mean she had stopped worrying about her mother. She would phone her when she knew her father wouldn't be home. They argued. They always argued. Fatima tried to convince her to get married and stop working in sinful places. Noura responded that she liked singing in the club and wasn't going to stop. That was how the conversation between mother and daughter always went.

Abir turned the volume higher on the TV and flicked through the channels, enjoying his triumph. An hour later, he heard the voices of his uncle Jamal and his brother Ismail as they burst into the room.

"Abir, Brother, we did it! The infidels are scared. I did what you asked and listened to people's conversations. They're afraid there will be an attack."

Ismail hugged Abir, who was glad to feel his little brother's admiration. Then he headed to where his uncle was sitting, taking off his shoes. When Jamal saw his nephew, he stood up and folded him in his arms. There was no need for words; their looks were enough. They wouldn't want to say anything in front of Fatima either.

They spent dinner talking about Jamal's work while Fatima attentively served them. When they were finished, Fatima went back to the kitchen and cleaned it. Then, following her husband's orders, she went to her room. It was the men's time to be together.

Jamal took a cigar out of his pocket and handed it to Abir, then lit one for himself.

"Today is a good day, we must celebrate," Jamal declared.

"May Allah protect us," Ismail said.

"Everything we do is in His name," Abir answered.

They turned up the volume on the TV and watched the screen closely.

Ismail admired his brother and uncle equally. He loved his cousin Farid too, but Farid never paid very much attention to him. He was always so busy studying the sacred texts. He didn't want to admit it, but when Farid got married and left his aunt and uncle's house, Ismail was relieved. As a teenager, Farid would yell at him if he didn't think he was praying with enough devotion, or if he was late for Friday prayer. His uncle Jamal was strict, but not as strict as his son, and his aunt Fatima was always kind to him, keeping his mistakes a secret so he wouldn't be punished.

His uncle and his brother were talking in low voices muffled by the sound of the TV. The image of the masked man threatening the entire world played over and over on all the channels, and Ismail felt proud to know that it was his brother, his brave brother.

He remembered his parents murdered by the Israeli soldiers. He remembered his brother Abir shouting at the filthy dogs that he would kill them. He would keep his promise. He was keeping it.

In the frigid nights of the Afghan mountains, he and Abir had often remembered the details of that early morning. Neither of them would ever forget it. The tragedy wasn't just part of their nightmares; that day in Ain al-Hilweh had also written both their futures.

The doorbell made them jump. Jamal looked at his nephews. There was no fear in his eyes, but there was caution.

"Who could it be?" Ismail asked.

They heard women's voices and a moment later the living room door was pushed open by Noura. Her mother gripped her arm, trying to stop her. The three men looked up at her in surprise.

"It was you!" Noura shouted at Abir.

Jamal got to his feet and grabbed her hair, yanking her head to the floor.

"How dare you show up here! You're dead to me! You're not my daughter anymore! Get out of here, you dog!"

Noura held in her tears as her father hit her and her mother screamed, trying to get in between them.

It was Abir who intervened, separating father and daughter.

Noura sat on the floor as blood ran from her eyebrow and into her eyes. Fatima tried to help her up, but her husband pushed her away and tried to order her out of the room.

"You gave birth to an animal!" he shouted.

Ismail was frozen, unable to handle the violence.

"What did you come for, Noura?" Abir asked.

"To stop you! You're all insane! You're murderers!" she screamed.

Jamal gave his daughter another kick, and she recoiled in pain.

"How dare you come to our house and insult us!"

"It was him. I know his voice. It was him on every TV channel, threatening the world. Did you think I wouldn't recognize you? As much as you tried to disguise your voice, I know it was you!" she swore, looking at Abir and curling up to avoid another kick from her father.

Fatima cried as she snatched at her daughter's hand, wanting to get her out of the room.

"No, it wasn't me. You hate me so much, you're willing to accuse me of anything," Abir responded, unfazed.

"No, I don't hate you, I could never hate you, but I know it was you!" she said.

"Well, if you believe that, go and turn me in. It's no problem for me because I'm innocent. But when my innocence is proven, what will you do then? Will you crawl back to beg for forgiveness?" Abir's voice was as convincing as it was icy.

Ismail looked in shock at his brother. Abir was capable of lying so convincingly that even he would have believed him if he hadn't known what he knew.

"Go turn me in, Noura," Abir repeated, looking calmly at his cousin, who was still crouched on the floor. "Do it if you think I'm a murderer. It's your duty."

"It's not him, my darling, it's not him! You're wrong!" Fatima said with more fear than conviction.

"I know his voice, Mother," Noura managed to say.

"I do too, and I swear that that voice is not your cousin's. Think about the harm you could cause, not just for him, but for us too. Until they discover the truth, they will mark us all as terrorists … even you," Fatima put her arms around her daughter.

Abir fixed his cousin with a hard look.

"You know what, Noura? If I were a terrorist, I'd have to kill you right here and now. But I'm not. I don't even know why you think it's my voice. Maybe it sounds similar, but it's no excuse to accuse me. I forgive you, Noura, I forgive you because you're a woman and you don't know what you're talking about. I forgive you because I owe everything to your parents. I forgive you because I've never stopped caring about you."

No one spoke. Fatima looked at her nephew with fear and knowing in her eyes, but her next words contradicted her heart.

"Listen to him, my darling. If he were guilty, he wouldn't talk like this."

"Get her out of here! If she ever comes back, I'll kill her. I have every right. That's what I should have done when she dishonored us the first time," Jamal said, his voice shaking with rage.

Fatima struggled to help Noura to her feet.

"Let me clean her face. She can't leave here like this," she pleaded with her husband.

Jamal said nothing. When the two women left the room, Abir put a hand on his uncle's shoulder to soothe him. Then he asked him to go rest. The next few hours would be very eventful. Ismail wanted to stay with his brother for a while, but he said no. Then they heard the sound of the door closing. Noura was gone.

Abir went to his room and lay down. Once again, his cousin had caused an earthquake in the family. He thought that if she persisted, there would be no choice but to kill her. He knew her well; she hadn't believed him at all. He wondered if she would turn him in now. Noura had turned herself over to the infidels. She lived like them, she thought like them and she sinned like them. She had stopped being Muslim a long time ago. He didn't understand how it could have happened.

Ismail came into his room. Fear filled his face.

"I'm … I'm worried."

"About Noura? Don't worry. She's not dangerous. She won't say or do anything," Abir answered, trying to fill his voice with a certainty he didn't feel.

"Do you trust her?"

"Trust her? Come on, Ismail, don't ask stupid questions. Noura can't turn me in because she doesn't know anything."

"But she recognized your voice."

"No, she didn't, she suspects it, but she's not sure. Go on, get out of here. You have things to do. We'll see each other soon. Tomorrow's an important day."

"But Noura could turn you in!"

"She won't," Abir swore, waving him out of the room.

Ismail left his brother's room. He heard Uncle Jamal's severe tone and his aunt Fatima's sobbing.

Meanwhile, Abir smiled with satisfaction, his gaze fixed on the TV. The dogs were scared.

He thought about Noura. He hoped he'd planted a seed of doubt in her mind. There was no going back now. He felt like his life didn't belong to him, like an actor who had been cast in a role by a demanding director, a role he didn't want but would inevitably have to play.

Fatima came into her nephew's room with a glass of water, and her presence calmed him.

"Did you take your medicine?" his aunt asked.

He avoided her gaze. His eyes were glued to the screen as he moved from one channel to the next. He took the glass of water, then rummaged around on his bedside table for a box and took a pill out.

"Thank you, Auntie."

"Abir ..."

"Don't say a word, Aunt Fatima."

"But I'm scared."

"You shouldn't be scared. You're a believer and your life, like that of all believers, is in Allah's hands."

*Brussels.*
*Studios of the International Channel.*

W.W.'s office was sizable but austere. Helen, Benjamin, Lauren and Lucy sat around a large circular table with the various authorities. There were three representatives of the Belgian security force, Louise Moos, Gilles Peeters and Arthur Dubois, along with the Israelis, Ariel Weiss, Maoz Levin, and Jacob Baudin, and two Americans, Anthony Jones from NATO's intelligence services, and Austin Turner of the CIA. They were joined by Alba Fernández, a Spaniard from the European Union Intelligence and Analysis Center. It was obvious that the Americans, Turner and Jones, had the most clout.

"There are only a few hours left before the terrorists' deadline. European security forces are on high alert, as are those in the U.S., Canada, and Japan. But we don't know where they're going to strike us," said Louise Moos, the director of the Belgian security services.

"They'll strike here," Alba Fernández cut in.

"Here or on the other side of the world, that's what we don't know," Austin Turner retorted.

"The most logical thing is for them to attack Belgium, given that they made the threat here," she insisted.

"That's just an assumption," Louise Moos insisted, her unpleasant tone making it clear she disliked the Spanish woman.

But Alba Fernández wasn't scared off. She forced a smile as she fixed her dark eyes on the Belgian woman. "Ms. Moos, at the moment everything we say is based on conjecture. We'll see in time which one of our theories is accurate," Alba answered, unfazed by her Belgian colleague's disagreeable manner.

"And you, Mr. Weiss, what do you think?" Turner asked him directly.

"I agree with Ms. Fernández. It will happen here," the Israeli agent responded.

Austin Turner was bothered by the unwavering assertions from the representative of the European Union Intelligence Center, but he didn't want to contradict her either, especially since her hypothesis had just been supported by the Mossad agent in Brussels. He preferred not to make any mistakes. But he could see that the Spaniard was not the kind to back down.

"The real question," Benjamin Holz interjected, "is whether you all can stop the attack or not."

The agents glared at the journalist. Benjamin showed little trust in them.

"Absolute safety doesn't exist, Mr. Holz. You should know that. What happened on 9/11 is proof of that. Not even a country as powerful as yours can prevent it," Alba declared dryly.

"It's not about what happened, Ms. Fernández, but about what could happen," Benjamin retorted, irritated by the European's reproach.

"I'm wondering what else we can do," Lauren said to the room.

"We have to wait. There's nothing else to be done," Louise Moos cut in, looking at the Israelis with distrust. "I can assure you, every single member of the police and the security forces of Belgium are looking for clues that could lead us to the terrorists. And as you can see, we have the support of the CIA, the NATO intelligence service, and this strong representation from Israel."

"And from INTCEN, Ms. Moos, the European Union Intelligence Center," Alba added, leveling her gaze with Louise.

"Yes, that too," she reluctantly admitted.

As the dialogue continued, Jacob scrutinized the faces around the table. The tension between Louise and Alba was obvious. They couldn't be more different, and not just because of their age, with Louise well in her fifties, and Alba Fernández a decade younger. While the Belgian director of security was elegantly dressed as a high-ranking civil servant with a suit jacket, silk blouse and pearl necklace, the Spaniard was more informal in black jeans, a gray cashmere jacket and a turtleneck sweater.

The men present in the room could also be distinguished by their clothes. The NATO representative wore the perfect navy blue suit of an official. Turner, from the CIA, wore a shiny tie. The Israelis, meanwhile, looked like they had just come from a field operation.

Jacob was also aware that, unlike him, the other agents seemed uncomfortable speaking in front of the journalists. Journalists had been his allies in finding support within Israeli society to protest the settlement policy. Still, he knew that their actions were often more driven by ratings than ethics.

The agents had to regularly excuse themselves from the room to get news and updates on the phone.

That night, Brussels seemed calm and quiet, like a place where nothing ever happened.

It was 9 p.m. before Austin Turner decided to end the meeting. They agreed to keep open channels of communications with each other. Helen and Benjamin were asked to immediately inform them of any further messages they might receive from the terrorists.

The group was about to say goodnight when W.W. suggested they go and eat something first.

"We have a ton of sandwiches and coffee here," he said, "though I think we've already had enough coffee for one day."

They all accepted W.W.'s invitation. No one had eaten and they were starving. They knew there would be little time to rest going forward, that night would seep into morning, and so forth. The terrorists had the advantage over them.

Not being seated around a table allowed the conversation to flow more easily.

Without knowing why, Jacob went over to Helen Morris.

"You've barely said anything."

"What can I say? I'm not a security expert. Nothing I could add would be important," she told him.

"I disagree. Sometimes inexpert eyes can see what we don't. Too much information makes you lose perspective."

"Will they stop people from getting killed?" Helen wondered.

"No, I don't think so. It will be difficult. The terrorists will have planned it perfectly. They're not going to improvise, and they'll have already chosen their victims and location."

"Don't they have any ideas?"

"It's not about coming up with a good idea. It's about finding the man in the video."

"Doesn't anyone have any idea who he could be?" she asked gloomily.

Jacob didn't want to answer that question. How could he tell her that he thought he knew exactly who the terrorist was and that's why he was here?

"Why do you believe they chose your program to communicate their threats?" he asked.

Helen was taken aback. Jacob could see she was offended.

"You must know that *The World at 7* is the most watched international political program worldwide. For decades, it has become the standard for broadcasting, even for the President of the United States. It is seen by most of the leaders of the free world, and a very prestigious program."

"Right, well, I guess the terrorists were looking to reach those decision-makers, and your program was a guarantee that everyone would find out. And now the world is holding its breath waiting to see what they might do."

"Yes, I guess that's why they chose us."

"How long have you been co-host?"

Helen was again surprised by his question. She assumed that most well-informed people knew she had replaced Samantha Bryan. Helen was the star of the network, a well-respected journalist recognized by the general public.

It hadn't been easy replacing Samantha. She'd had to prove she was just as worthy as her predecessor, and for two years she'd had to live with comparisons. It had also been a challenge to work with Benjamin Holz. Samantha had presented on *The World at 7* alone, but when they made her retire, Joseph Foster had decided they needed two presenters. Benjamin Holz also believed himself to be a star journalist.

It had taken a lot of patience, but now they got along well and made a good team. Helen realized that she hadn't answered the Israeli agent's question.

"Five years. Benjamin and I have been the show's presenters for the past five years."

"Have you ever interviewed a jihadist?"

"What kind of question is that? We've reported on the jihad, of course."

"So you've met some jihadists."

"Once we did a program from Syria where we managed to interview some fanatics, yes. That program was a success. You should watch it," she shot back defensively.

"Of course. For now, I'm afraid there's nothing left to do but wait."

"Wait for what?"

"For them to carry out the first attack."

"You're assuming they can do it."

"Yes, unfortunately they will. Anybody who goes out in the street with a weapon can kill."

Alba Fernández came to where Helen and Jacob were standing.

"Am I interrupting?"

"Mr. Baudin is convinced that the terrorists will manage to kill someone." Helen's voice gave away her anxiety.

"It's not hard to kill, is it, Ms. Morris?" the Spanish woman agreed.

"But you have to stop them!" Helen almost shouted.

"We'll try, we're all trying, and we'll probably end up arresting someone, but it might not be until after the terrorists have killed someone," Alba told her.

"Jacob," Maoz's called, "We must go. We'll keep in touch, Ms. Fernández, Ms. Morris."

Without speaking, Jacob followed Maoz. They said goodbye to Jones and Turner. Relations with the Americans were friendly, but not completely open.

Ariel drove them to a building where he kept a small office that to the public eye appeared to be a consultancy firm. Their conversation was light and inconsequential until they reached their destination. Jacob was aware that both Weiss and Maoz were seasoned intelligence agents, and that his own role would be limited to guiding them toward the voice he thought he recognized.

"Dor called me 20 minutes ago. Our people still haven't found a single trace of Abir Nasr."

"He's here in Brussels." Jacob was sure.

Both men looked at him, weighing the words they'd just heard. They didn't contradict him, but they weren't going to agree either.

"He could be, or he could be on the other side of the world," Ariel said.

*Ain al-Hilweh, Lebanon. Evening.*

Mohamed wiped the sweat off his face with the sleeve of his shirt and heard his wife's footsteps.

"It's getting late and the girls are hungry."

The man slid out from under the car. It was so dented and coated in dust it didn't seem worth the effort of repair.

"If they're hungry, give them dinner. I have to finish this."

"Can't you leave it until tomorrow?"

"No, Salma, I can't. Now leave me alone, or I'll never finish."

The woman pressed her mouth together, but she didn't respond. It wouldn't make any difference. She went into their house, if you could call it a house: thin walls topped by a sheet of corrugated metal. Her daughters, three and five years old, were the light of her life, though she prayed to Allah to give her a boy. And though Mohamed loved his little girls, he never stopped complaining; a man, he told her, wasn't complete without a son.

She put a handful of rice on to boil, singing softly. Suddenly a hand clamped over her mouth and she could barely breathe. A hold on her neck made her lose consciousness. Her last, rushed thought was for her daughters.

The little girls didn't have time to scream. The men had snatched them up from the floor, covering their mouths. Silent tears fell down their cheeks. One of the men whispered a few words, the other two dragged the woman and the girls to the only bedroom in the house.

Mohamed was still under the car trying to pinpoint the problem. He wouldn't rest until he did. He was unscrewing a part when he felt something cover his face. A smell he didn't recognize clouded his senses. He couldn't speak or move, and became lifeless.

He didn't know how much time passed. Someone had dragged him to the back of the shed. He struggled to shake off the fog in his eyes, squinting to make out the shape of a man aiming a gun at him.

"Don't move. If you do what we say, nothing will happen to you, your wife, or your daughters."

Cold fear trickled down his spine. His wife. His daughters.

"It all depends on you. You just have to answer my questions. Abir Nasr. I want to know everything. Where he is and what he's planning."

Mohamed opened his mouth, trying to form the words.

"I don't know who that is," he managed to say.

"Mohamed, I don't put up with lies. Right now, you have to make a choice. Either you're loyal to Abir Nasr and your friends in the Circle, or you're loyal to your family. If you tell us everything, nobody will ever know. We'll go and leave you in peace. If you don't want to talk, well then, you'll come with us."

"My wife and my daughters," he moaned.

"They'll come too, except, well actually, they aren't really useful to us. We'll have to see what we do with them."

Mohamed insisted he did not know who Abir Nasr was.

"It's a pity you've decided not to save your family."

The man took a small phone out of his pocket as it beeped. The image he showed Mohamed was alarming. A man, his face covered, pointing a gun at his wife and daughters, who appeared to be unconscious.

"We're taking your wife and your daughters. As for yourself ..." The man took out a knife and pressed it to his throat.

Mohamed started to cry. His mind raced, trying to figure out who the man was. He thought he could be Israeli, but decided against it. His Arabic sounded local. He was Lebanese, Mohamed was sure. But what Lebanese man would threaten to take his wife and children, and take them where? He shook harder as he felt the knife move against his neck.

"A hundred meters from your house, your neighbor Jafar once lived with his wife Ghada and their two sons, Abir and Ismail. They shared a house with Ghada's sister and her husband. Is it coming back to you now, Mohamed?"

Mohamed remembered and told them. He knew that for a while the two orphans had stayed with some relatives in Ain al-Hilweh, but eventually they went to live with a cousin of their mother in Beirut. The kids had come back to visit a few times. They'd seemed sad, but who wouldn't be after seeing their parents murdered right in front of them?

Later, an uncle of their father's took them in. Jamal Adoum seemed to be doing well in Paris. There had been a family dispute, and they had all wanted to have custody of the orphans. In the end, they reached an agreement. Abir and Ismail would spend time with each of the families. Nobody ever asked them what they wanted.

A trickle of blood started to run down Mohamed's throat, a sign that what he had told them wasn't enough. They needed more.

He stumbled over his words as he told the man that Abir and Ismail were now fighters under Sheikh Mohsin, that they had trained in Afghanistan and that they came to Lebanon frequently. They had become good men. No, he didn't know their uncle's address in Paris, only that he was an electrician and a good friend of a very well-known imam, Adel Allawi, a wise and fair man who helped Muslims survive the difficulties of settling in France.

Then Mohamed said more. He explained that Jamal Adoum didn't live in Paris anymore and was in Brussels, and that he ran a small electrician business there. Yes, he had two children: Farid, who had become an imam and still lived in Paris, and Noura, who the family never spoke of because she had stopped being a good Muslim to live like a European. The girl had greatly dishonored the Adoum family.

A dark, starless night had fallen. The man eased the pressure of the knife on Mohamed's throat.

"Nobody has seen us. Nobody knows that you've spoken with us. Only your actions will determine whether your own will consider you a traitor. If you say nothing, nobody will ever know. Whatever has to happen, will happen."

"And my wife and daughters?"

"Your daughters are asleep. They saw nothing. Your wife barely had time to realize what was happening. It was a bad dream. A nightmare. You are the man of the house. If you order them to keep their mouths shut, they will obey you."

As he said this, he pressed a point on Mohamed's neck and he lost consciousness. He would be out for a while, long enough for the men to disappear.

Ariel Weiss opened a device and decrypted the file containing the report they had sent him. "Abir Nasr. His parents and younger sister were killed during an operation in Ain al-Hilweh in southern Lebanon. For a time, he and his brother Ismail lived with relatives in Ain al-Hilweh. Later, his mother's cousin Ayman brought them to Beirut. Ayman was widowed and had three children, Gibram, Sami and Rosham. Abir became a difficult, taciturn boy without many friends. His younger brother Ismail was ill for a time. He went mute from the trauma of his parents' death. An uncle then decided to take them in at his home in Paris. We still don't have much information about the years Abir spent there. His uncle, Jamal Adoum, is married to a woman named Fatima, of Maghrebi origin, and they have two children, Noura and Farid. We are waiting for more detailed information from Paris. An imam, Adel Allawi, holds a lot of influence over the Adoum family, so much so that Farid became an imam himself. Now the whole family, except for Farid, live in Brussels. Sheikh Mohsin shows up in this history as well. He eventually took Abir and his brother to Afghanistan. Abir now travels frequently to Lebanon and visits Ain al-Hilweh whenever he can. But he has changed his last name to his uncle Jamal's."

"What about his brother Ismail?" Maoz wanted to know.

"We are still piecing the puzzle together," Weiss responded.

"So you're going to give this information to the Belgians

and the Americans?" Jacob said more as a statement than a question.

"Of course not. We have to confirm your hunch. You claim the terrorist's voice belongs to that of a man you saw years ago for a few minutes during an operation. I don't know, Jacob. We'll investigate Abir because we have to start somewhere. I have my people on the streets. I hope that within a few hours, we'll be able to find out more about Jamal Adoum." Ariel Weiss's tone was harsh.

"Is that all?" Maoz asked.

"For now, yes."

"Paris is very close to Brussels," Jacob observed.

*Brussels.*
*Abir*

Abir rose out of bed. He had to leave. He really shouldn't be here at all. But he knew he had an advantage over those who were looking for him. He looked around the room. He would never return here. Last night was an endpoint on the life he had been living until now. He went to the door. His uncle hugged him while his aunt cried.

"May Allah protect you," his uncle said.

"Let it be so. We're never going to see each other again."

"I know. Don't look back. You must go and face your destiny. The sheikh will be very proud of you, just as your cousin Farid and I are. You will help our cause greatly, Abir. You will be the pride of all believers, and your name will be remembered for centuries."

Fatima tried to wrap him in a hug, but Abir moved away. He couldn't show any emotion.

"Ismail left a little while ago. He'll be waiting for you. Be careful," Jamal said.

Abir left the apartment and merged into the shadows of the night.

Nora's eyes were fixed on the TV screen. She had called the club to say she felt sick and wouldn't be coming in to work.

She knew that the hooded man who had threatened the entire world with retaliations of death was her cousin Abir. But she couldn't report it. She wouldn't be able to live the rest of her life carrying that burden. She would feel infinite shame for having endangered her family member. But if she stayed silent, she would have to live with the weight of the deaths her cousin would cause.

She hadn't seen Abir in years. She barely knew anything about him, only the bits of news she got from her mother every so often. She had never seen her father again either, not since that night when she ran from their home and ended up in a youth shelter. When she got out, she didn't return to her family. She couldn't have lived again under their oppressive rules. She had paid a high price for the rupture. Her father had disowned her, and her brother Farid had threatened to kill her to avenge the family's honor. She had only her mother, who didn't understand her but was still wanting to see her, just as Nora was unwilling to distance herself from her mother.

They saw each other in secret. Jamal had decided that Nora was dead to the family. Nobody was allowed to talk to her. But Nora knew Fatima's routines well and managed to run into her where there were no eyes around ready to betray them. Some meetings only lasted a few minutes, but sometimes they found a stolen hour together, knowing it could be their last.

Finding work in Paris had not been easy. Nora didn't want to become a backup singer—her dream was to be the main attraction. She worked in a store during the day and in the evenings she took singing and guitar lessons.

Madame Poulin had been an opera singer. She had even performed at the Paris Opera, and while she never became a bel canto diva, but she hadn't failed either. By the time she had reached her 50s, and was thinking about what the future held, she decided to look for another way to earn a living. She opened an academy near the Opera Garnier. Although she hadn't been very well known, she was very good at training voices and discovering talent. She accepted Nora as a student, though she warned her she'd have to work hard with her mezzosoprano voice. She also didn't mislead her into thinking she would be a star.

"You have a nice voice, but it's quite ordinary. You'll never reach the top, but if singing is what you like, you can do it," the woman told her. Nora was uninterested in being in the opera; what she wanted was to be a melodic singer. She understood that she needed more than willpower to do that, if that she didn't train her voice, she would never be anything more than an amateur.

Her mother tried to convince her to ask her father for forgiveness and come home. She never conceded, but when Fatima told her they would move to Brussels, she made the decision to follow them so she could be close to her mother. Before she experienced the loneliness of being her own master, she hadn't realized how much she needed her mother. Once in Brussels, Fatima felt sure Jamal would eventually find out about their secret meetings.

She arrived in the city ready and determined not give up on her dream to become a singer. Madame Poulin had recommended her friend Ivette, an old colleague from the Paris Opera who had found the perfect husband in Monsieur Leblanc, a banker who loved music and had enthusiastically helped her open an academy. Through her former teacher, Nora began to study with Madame Leblanc, and this turned out to be serendipitous in her new life.

She helped her find work as a cashier in a supermarket and recommended her to a widowed friend who rented her a room in Matonge, an old neighborhood with a large African community. Nothing in the world could have made her live in Molenbeek, the neighborhood where her parents lived. It had become a Muslim microcosm.

Madame Leblanc was as honest with her as Madame Poulin had been. "You have a pretty voice," she told her, "But it's not very powerful." Madame Leblanc's words didn't bother Nora because the only thing she yearned for was to make a living singing the songs she composed on the guitar she had worked so hard to purchase in Paris. After a few months, it was also Madame Leblanc who recommended she go see an acquaintance of her husband, who had opened a place in Les Marolles, an old working-class neighborhood that had become more bohemian in recent years.

"It's not a dive, but it's nothing to write home about either. My husband says you can trust Mathis Discart. They're not close friends, but they've known each other for years through the bank. Monsieur Discart no longer wanted to spend the whole day stuck behind a desk and decided to become an entrepreneur. He's done well for himself. First he opened a hamburger restaurant, then a pizzeria, then a cabaret, and now he's the owner of a live music coffeehouse, I'm not sure what exactly that is. Anyway, you have nothing to lose going to see him."

Mathis Discart was over 50, tall, with salt-and-pepper hair, a strong complexion, and a shrewd look. He seemed polite, though in reality he could be very brusque.

He gave her an audition. Nora sang a few songs she had composed on her guitar. He listened to her in silence and then without a moment's hesitation told her she was hired. The pay wasn't much, but it would be enough to live on without the supermarket job, and she would be able to rent a studio in Matonge itself. Despite Madame Leblanc's misgivings, Le Rêve de Marolles, as the place was called, was a charming café that offered live musical performances. Mathis offered his space to young musicians who were starting out in singing, and he also had a pianist, a violinist, and a bassist who livened up the evenings. Nora became a full-time singer and started creating a name for herself in the artistic circles of Les Marolles.

The young woman had adapted her look to Le Rêve de Marolles. She wore her copper hair short and dressed like a Gauche Divine singer in tight black suits or black pants and sweaters, with carefully done makeup and red fingernails.

Mathis let her sing the songs she'd written herself, but he also insisted she include Juliette Greco's songs in her repertoire, because she resembled her so much.

What Nora hadn't known was that Mathis Discart was attracted to her. She also never would have imagined becoming her boss's mistress, but this is what happened. Discart was married with two daughters, and had no intention of leaving his wife. His mother, a widow, also lived with his family and got along well with his wife.

"My wife and I are a good team," he explained to Nora, "she's just happy to be financially comfortable and take care of the kids and my mother, and she turns a blind eye to anything I do on the side."

Madame Discart, it would seem, was untroubled by Nora becoming something more than an entertainment for her husband.

Nora didn't just help run Le Rêve de Marolles. Occasionally, they would also share a long weekend in Paris, Amsterdam,

Strasbourg, or Berlin. In the summer, Mathis even found a way for them to spend a few days together at the beach in Spain.

She got used to that life. She told herself that one day someone important from the music industry would come into the bar, listen to her sing and offer her a good contract. She would record an album that would become a worldwide success. But time passed, and no music magnate ever wandered into the café.

But her cousin Abir had.

She still shuddered when she thought about the night three years earlier. Abir had come into Le Rêve de Marolles with two other men and sat at a table in the corner, waiting for her to begin her performance.

That night she had worn a long, low-cut black dress. As she sang she felt an intense gaze on her skin, and then she saw him. Abir, with his serious, disapproving face. She suddenly felt almost naked, and she regretted choosing the dress that Mathis liked so much.

Nora sang badly and left the stage earlier than she was supposed to.

"What the hell are you doing?" Discart shouted at her. She explained in a daze that her cousin was in the audience and that she had to talk to him. She didn't give him time to protest and made her way through the tables to them. She didn't know whether to touch him in greeting in any way. She could see in his eyes that he was no longer the teenager who'd kept her secrets. The eyes of the man in front of her showed no affection at all. He could have been a stranger.

"Abir, it's—"

He gestured for her to be silent and sit down next to him. She obeyed. The two men got up but stayed nearby, never letting them out of their sight.

"What are you doing, Noura?"

"As you can see, I'm a singer."

"You're putting yourself on display to these people like a loose woman."

They looked at each other. It was hard for Nora to recognize the cousin from her adolescence in those words.

"I'm not doing anything wrong, Abir. I always wanted to be a singer—you know that. This is a decent business. Normal people come here. Men don't come here on the hunt for women."

"Men don't need to go to a special place. Women like you are on offer for free. And don't make excuses—do you really think the men don't notice your cleavage? Why wear that dress, Noura, if not?"

"I think you've become a fanatic. Is this what Sheikh Mohsin has done to you?" she responded bitterly.

"Don't you dare say his name. Your mouth will pollute it."

"What about Ismail? Where is my cousin?"

"With Allah's help, he is learning to be a good believer."

"What have they done to you, Abir? Why are you talking like this?"

He didn't answer at first, looking at her for a while before he spoke.

"Your mother, my dear aunt Fatima, poor innocent woman, told me where you work. You've really deluded her. She thinks you have a decent job. If she only saw you here! And your father—he should kill you for the shame you've brought upon them."

"I am already dead to my father."

"He's a respectable man. If they knew he had a daughter like you …"

"Don't worry Abir, we haven't seen each other since Paris, and I've never set foot in Molenbeek."

"But your mother meets with you."

"She always comes to my apartment. No one can see us there."

"Don't you feel ashamed to dress like that?"

"No, Abir, I'm not ashamed of my body. Why should I be? It's you men who try to make us feel impure so that you can control us."

"So you've become a corrupted woman like all the Westerners."

"Oh, come on! Women who don't hide their bodies are not evil. Don't waste your time on me, Abir. I've paid a high price for my freedom. Do you think it doesn't hurt to have to see my mother in secret and know that my father hates me? And now I see you. How have men like the sheikh convinced young men like you to hate women? What scares you so much about us? Maybe you only feel like men when you're controlling us? Do you have so little self-esteem?"

"Shut up, Noura! You sound just like the degenerates."

"I'm sorry, Cousin, but you're the one who's confused. I always thought you would get away from the tradition of ignorance they want to drown us in. But I can see they've brainwashed you."

"One day you'll pay for your impiety, Noura."

"I'm still Muslim, Abir, but I don't believe the same things you do. Even so, know that I love you, Cousin. I'll always think of you with affection and be glad we had those years together with you and Ismail. I love you more than Farid, my own brother."

"Farid is a fair and respected imam."

"Farid is a fanatic! Don't you remember you once said so yourself?"

"I didn't know then what I know now. I was confused."

"I think you're confused now, Abir. What did you come here for?"

Despite the words that had come out of his mouth, Abir wanted to tell her that he still cared very much for her, that he'd admired her determination when she left home to find a way to be herself. But he refused to say anything that she might interpret as an endorsement of her behavior. He stood up and touched her hand in a second of weakness. They looked at each other and Nora knew that somewhere deep down the cousin she had loved like a brother was still there.

Abir strode out, flanked by the two men, and they hadn't seen each other again until she confronted him that night.

Nora couldn't deny what was happening. When she saw the man on the TV reading the statement in the name of the Circle, she recognized the voice. His voice, Abir's. She knew she had to go to her parents' house, but still wondered how she had had the courage. There was no doubt in her mind that the man was Abir, and that her parents would know where to find him. But she'd never imagined he would be right there with them.

Her poor mother was a frightened creature, and her father was someone she despised and loved at the same time. He was her father, but fanaticism oozed from every pore of his skin, and it had only taken him a few seconds to respond when he saw her coming into his home, and how his wife received their daughter tearfully, as if there hadn't been years of distance. Rage had flooded him when he saw her head for the living room, as if she had known Abir would be there.

For three hours, she'd been contemplating her life, the image of the terrorist threatening to leave a trail of blood and death intruding her thoughts. She was sure that Abir would carry out his threat, and it tortured her not knowing what to do.

No, she couldn't report him. She wouldn't just be putting his life in danger, but it would also destroy her parents. They would arrest them, possibly even torture them to find out what they knew about Abir, and they would never be able to prove they were innocent because of their family ties. And what about her? What would happen to her? She would also pay a price. The life she had worked so hard to build would evaporate like cigarette smoke. She would no longer be a singer-songwriter performing in a café in a bohemian neighborhood waiting for someone to notice her talent. She knew the world would see her as the Muslim relative of a terrorist, or even a terrorist herself.

But if she did nothing, if she said nothing, her silence would make her complicit in the murders her cousin was planning.

It was nearly midnight when her phone rang, making her jump. Mathis.

"Are you feeling better?" he wanted to know.

"No, not really."

"Are you watching the news?"

"Yes, I have it on," Nora said.

"There was hardly anyone in the club tonight. Four tables and they all left early. People are scared. Who knows what those crazy Islamists are going to do?"

"Where are you?" she asked worriedly.

"At home. My mother and my wife went to bed a while ago, same with my kids. We were all glued to the television. But I can't sleep."

"Me neither."

They had nothing more to say, so they hung up. In that moment, she felt the same anxiety of millions of people all over the world, waiting in fear for the attack promised by the hooded man. But Nora was alone in knowing his name.

Jacob's phone vibrated. His mother. He hesitated, then answered.

"Is something wrong?"

"You left in such a hurry—are you OK?"

"Yes."

"Is there any way you can tell me where you are?"

He didn't know if he should tell her, and decided not to respond.

"Take care of Luna."

"Yes, I have her here with me. She misses you."

"I miss her too. I'll call you soon." And he hung up.

Maoz looked at him curiously but didn't ask any questions, though it wouldn't have been hard for him to figure out it was Joanna. He knew Jacob's mother, and was aware that Dor was close to her. This was what had made him protect Jacob.

They were reviewing the information Dor had sent from Tel Aviv. Jacob and Maoz knew that Efraim was behind the report from Lebanon. Dor had entrusted him with the operation and based on what they were seeing, it had been a success. It was much more than they could have hoped for. Dor had instructed them to share some of the information with the Belgians and the CIA, but not all of it. Ariel had argued with Dor. "If we don't tell the Belgians everything we know, we'll never be able to find Abir Nasr. We should share it with the European Union Intelligence Center too. Their head, Alba Fernández, is very competent. We have to show our cards, Dor." But Dor insisted; they were to tell only what was absolutely necessary, not a word more.

Ariel was relieved when they could finally share some information with Louise Moos. He then mobilized his agents in Brussels and spoke with his colleague in Paris, a woman named Orit Singer that everyone deeply respected. She was a legend within Mossad. Few field agents could compare with her and what she'd accomplished, though it was all highly classified. Paris had been a golden reward, with Dor making her the head of the section. Orit was battling cancer, but she would never give up the game.

She assured Ariel that they would get precise information about Imam Adel Allawi and Farid, Abir's cousin. She had mobilized her people.

Just then, Maoz beckoned Ariel and Jacob over to read what had come in on his computer. "Look. It turns out two of Abir Nasr's cousins are persons of interest: Gibram and Sami," he murmured, "members of the Circle, experts in arms dealing. There's more information about them—our people in Beirut have been following them for a while. They often receive visits from men we have trouble tracking down, who appear and disappear without leaving us time to act."

"Interesting. If someone makes the effort to cover their tracks, it's for a reason," Ariel observed.

"The only one who seems clean is the sister. Rosham, a pediatrician. She works in the Sacre-Coeur Hospital in Beirut. Apparently, she stays out of her brothers' activities and is married to a doctor named Nabil Abbadi, a neurologist. He has a practice at the Makassed Hospital," Maoz read aloud.

"That's a good hospital. It's run by the Islamic Philanthropic Association," Jacob interjected.

"Is it a religious hospital?"

"No, it's just an institution. They maintain good relationships with other religions," Jacob clarified.

"But not the Israelis," Maoz added.

"It's a good hospital. When my father got sick, he was treated there. They have some excellent specialists," Jacob insisted.

"There's more here," Maoz continued, looking at the screen. "Apparently, a few years ago, Abir Nasr's underwent a heart operation at the Makassed. We don't have all the information, just that they operated on him. In the next few hours, they may find out something else."

"Good work from our people in Beirut," Ariel declared.

"They risk their lives every day," Maoz responded.

"Let's hope Jacob is right, and we're not on some wild goose chase," Ariel said.

"I'm sure that voice is Abir Nasr's." Jacob was tired of his colleagues' skepticism.

"It'd better be because we're focusing everything on following his trail, and if it's not him, we'll have wasted vital time trying to find the wrong man," Ariel shot back, looking at him sideways.

"It's Abir Nasr, and he's in Brussels," Jacob insisted.

"You might be right that it's Abir Nasr, but why do you insist that he's in Brussels?" Ariel asked, annoyed tone.

"He's here. I don't know how I know, but I know. He chose to send that thumb drive to an American news program that had come here to report on the NATO summit. He wants to strike here. He's capable of outwitting every intelligence service and acting right under our noses. He knows NATO will not cancel the summit because it can't show weakness. And he knows that if he strikes here, it will be a humiliation for NATO. How can they defend the world when they can't even defend the city where their ministers are gathering? But there's another reason, something we're missing ..."

"Jacob, in the intelligence service, you can't just go by your gut instinct," Ariel admonished him.

"I disagree. Some intelligence operations move forward based on a hunch," Maoz interrupted.

Ariel was unconvinced, but he respected Maoz and knew that he was one of the best agents behind enemy lines. "In any case, Dor believes Abir Nasr might be our man. We'll see if Jacob is right and the target is here," he concluded.

The door opened, and a woman came into the office, her head covered with a hijab. Ariel Weiss got to his feet and went to her while the other two men waited expectantly.

The woman took off the scarf and shook her head, letting her long brown hair loose.

"I spent an hour walking around, just in case," she said by way of greeting.

"Did you find anything?"

"Maybe. Abir Nasr's aunt and uncle do in fact live in Molenbeek. The husband, Jamal, owns an electrical shop and Fatima, a housewife, is discreet but friendly, and well liked by her neighbors. Their son Farid still lives in Paris but visits often. They live a simple life, nothing remarkable except that Jamal never misses a single day of prayer at the mosque."

"Nothing else?" Ariel pressed.

"Jamal often visits or receives friends, some of whom are foreigners. But until now, he's never done anything to attract attention."

"And his nephew Abir?"

The woman shrugged.

"Nobody I spoke to knows him. He could be any of the men who visit Jamal. The only nephew they've ever introduced to people is Ismail, Abir's brother."

"OK, Miriam, you can ease off," Ariel told her.

"No," she said, "if this Abir Nasr is in Brussels, the best thing to do is get back out on the street to look for him. The only place he could be hiding is Molenbeek. The problem is time. And it's hard to go around there asking questions without attracting attention."

Jacob observed the woman, curious. Nothing stood out about Miriam. She wasn't tall or short, thin or fat, pretty or ugly. She looked unremarkable. Dor would say it was the perfect quality of an agent.

Miriam looked back at Jacob and smiled.

"Are you sure that Abir Nasr is in Brussels?" she asked him.

"Yes. I believe his first attack will be here, and he will want to be close by," he affirmed.

"I think you're right. We have to keep looking for him."

Ariel considered Miriam's words. She was his best agent and knew Molenbeek like the back of her hand. In fact, she lived there. She passed for a widow who worked for well-to-do people, and used that excuse to come and go without attracting any attention. She even went out at night, claiming to be babysitting. Brussels was a city of civil servants of many nationalities, and it was normal for these people to be out at dinner parties.

"So you're going back to your house, at this hour?" Ariel asked, concerned.

"Yes, I can't keep walking around or someone will notice. Oh, I forgot! I went into Les Marolles, the café-concert or club or whatever it is where Noura Adoum works. She's Abir's cousin. The girl wasn't there. They were actually closing because they didn't have any customers. The city is terrified of what could happen. People are at home waiting."

"I hope you changed your appearance," he said.

"Didn't you know I'm a music lover?" she responded with a smile.

"Did they tell you anything about the girl?" he asked.

"Just that she was sick and hadn't come in."

"Do you have her address?"

"I got her phone number from a waiter, telling him I was the assistant of a music manager and I was interested in getting in touch with her."

"And he just gave it to you like that?"

"Sometimes simplicity is the easiest way. Yes, he believed me. Here it is. You'll have to trace it to find out where she lives."

"Please be careful. Don't draw attention to yourself," he told her.

"Tonight at the mosque the women were very upset. They came with their husbands, who were just as nervous," Miriam commented.

"They open the mosque at night?" Jacob asked, surprised.

"No, but the imam had no other option but to receive the faithful. So many people wanted to ask him what could happen, with the general alarm caused by the video. Many are afraid that there will be xenophobic attacks on them. Others seem happy that the hooded man has the West by the throat. In any case, people are being cautious, and nobody is saying a word except to their closest friends."

Jacob had always felt a certain fascination for field agents, especially those who passed as Muslim. He couldn't imagine the pressure of living life as an imposter, pretending to be someone else.

"How do you do it?" he asked Miriam, giving voice to his thoughts.

"Do what?" she looked at him expectantly.

"Go to mosque, pray like them, be their friend. Betray their trust."

Ariel looked at him with surprise. He wondered what kind of professional could ask that question.

"When I pray, I do it with my heart. When I'm with them, I feel I'm among friends. I empathize with their problems, just like anyone's. You can't do this work if you're not capable of

216

thinking like them and putting yourself in their shoes, feeling what they feel. If you don't do this, they will discover you, and you will fail. Maoz can explain it better than me —he's the master."

Silence followed. Maoz, the master, didn't say anything. He wasn't there to answer Jacob's soul-searching questions.

"Take care," Ariel Weiss finally said, breaking the tension.

"I'm going home. I'll call a friend. Let's see if the echo of some rumor will reach me."

Miriam left and Ariel went to make coffee. There was no time to rest. They had no other option but to wait.

An hour later, Orit called from Paris. Ariel put her call on speaker so everyone could participate in the conversation.

"I have a friend in the French police force. They don't know much about what's happening, but all the security forces are on alert. Louise Moos hasn't told them about Abir Nasr, or Abir Adoum, which he goes by now, but she will in a matter of hours. I think she's afraid of a leak. I laid a bit of a trap there— if we're not able to collaborate on this matter, it's going to be very difficult to catch Nasr. You'll have seen on the news that the Elysée has decided to deploy the army, to calm people down more than anything. I have asked my friend to report on what's happening at Imam Adel Allawi's mosque. We will need to hack his phone."

"Your people couldn't do that?" Weiss asked.

"Not with so little time. I know you don't like it, but we can't do this alone," Orit responded sharply.

"You're right."

"Of course I am. The Sécurité already had a tap on the phones of Imam Adel Allawi and Farid Adoum, actually. They've been watching them for a while."

"And have you, Orit?" Maoz asked.

He heard a dry laugh.

"My dear Maoz, one of my people always goes to Friday prayer in Imam Allawi's mosque."

"What about Farid Adoum?"

"He's slippery. They're both dangerous. They're usually careful in their sermons, spreading ideas without saying them explicitly. They often gather privately with the faithful. We have someone in one of those groups, and even though they express sympathy for the Circle, the imam has never even implied he is actively involved with them."

"Do you think they know something?"

"If Jacob Baudin, who is there with you all, is right about that voice, it wouldn't be strange for his fanatical cousin and that devious imam to know more than they appear to. We'll find out, Maoz. I'll call you as soon as we have anything."

"We have six hours before the first deadline they gave in the video statement," Weiss reminded her.

"Let's not fool ourselves, Ariel. We all know that without some incredible stroke of luck, we will not find this man in six hours. There will be deaths."

"I hope you're wrong, Orit."

"We're experienced professionals, Ariel. I don't believe in miracles."

Orit hung up, and the three men were quiet for a few seconds. They knew she was right. They only wished they believed in miracles.

Helen tore open another pack of cigarettes, her third since that morning. Her husband looked at her with concern.

"You smoke too much, and you really should rest a little," he said, knowing she wouldn't listen.

"Can you rest, Andrew? No, none of us can," she snapped.

"Tomorrow you'll have to be on camera. You have to keep reporting on whatever happens. Who knows how long all this will last. You're a professional, Helen. You know you need to save your strength so you can keep going."

"Exactly, a professional. So that's why I can't sleep knowing there's a guy out there who has threatened to destroy the world. And he will, Andrew, I'm convinced he will."

"I think so too, but who knows, maybe he's bluffing."

"No, this guy is all in."

Andrew looked at his wife anxiously. The grim expression on her face made her appear older, or maybe it was just fatigue.

"Every police force in the world is looking for him, every secret service. They'll find him, Helen. Sooner or later, they'll find him."

"And how many will he kill before they do?"

"You can't assume that they're really going to be able to carry out their threat. It's possible, yes, but right now every single country is on alert. It won't be so easy."

"What did Foster tell you?" she asked.

219

"Joseph? You already know, you heard the conversation. He's in constant contact with the White House. And you've spent practically the whole day with those security teams, the CIA, Mossad, the NATO agent, and that Spanish woman from the European Union Intelligence Center. They all seem very competent."

"Joseph said that the White House has concerns about whether we should air any other messages, if they send them to us. He's the director, and it worries me that he thinks the same thing," Helen said.

"Well, the truth is as vice president of the network, I pretty much agree with him. We can't turn ourselves into the loud-speaker of a group of terrorists. They want us to dance to their tune, and we have to decide whether or not to do that. It's a very serious matter, Helen. What's happening here goes beyond the news. I know that for you, journalism is everything, but there are some issues that go beyond our profession. I'm sure that Joseph will make the right decision. We can't disregard the White House on this matter."

"Politicians have no right to tell us what we should say and what we shouldn't! Our obligation is to report, whatever it may be. Good news isn't news, Andrew, you know that better than me."

"But this isn't just bad news. It's blackmail that some Islamist terrorists want to spread around the entire world using our network. Come on, you need to rest. And stop smoking, at least for a little while."

"I don't want to stop smoking, Andrew."

He shook his head. He had always admired Helen's passion for journalism, but he also knew that she was incredibly stubborn and would push past Joseph and any obstacles that might stop her from airing new videos. For her, reporting the news was more important than anything. He understood this. The terrorist group behind the hooded man had chosen *The World at 7* to spread their message, and for Helen it was a powerful news story. But he knew that if terrorists sent another message and the White House asked them not to air it, it would create conflict within the editorial team. Helen and Benjamin would, of course, fight hard to air. Joseph Foster was respected by the editorial team and he knew how to talk to his journalists, but this time Andrew wondered if he would be able to handle them. Helen could be very combative, and it put him in a difficult position as vice president of the network and one of its biggest shareholders, though his fortune hadn't only been made in television. He had too many interests and commitments not to consider the consequences of going against the White House and the rest of the shareholders. He wouldn't sleep that night either; he would be waiting to hear the phone ring with news of an attack.

Helen sat on the bed in a robe, her eyes glued to the TV screen. The room reeked of smoke.

"I'm going to order something from room service. You haven't eaten all day."

"I'm not hungry," she said.

"It doesn't matter. I'll order soup and some sandwiches. It will do us some good."

Half an hour later, a waiter carried a tray into the room. Helen wanted to resist, but she had to admit her stomach was empty. She wolfed down the food and leaned back on her pillow. She was exhausted, and gave into sleep. Andrew didn't dare move and wake her, and eventually he fell asleep as well.

Ismail stretched. It was time. He hadn't been able to sleep, though Abir had insisted he rest. How could he?

The bedroom door opened and he saw his brother in the shadows.

"Get up," he ordered.

"I'm already awake."

"Good. Get dressed or you'll be late."

"I still have time."

"I've made coffee. It will do you good."

"Yes, I'm just going to wash."

Abir left the room. Ghalil was waiting to give Ismail his final instructions. He had spent weeks explaining to him how it should go. They exchanged a look. Abir's face was full of determination, Ghalil's completely void of any emotion.

None of them had slept that night. They hadn't even tried.

At that moment, everything depended on Ismail.

"I'm ready," they heard Ismail say, coming out of the room.

His facial expression contradicted his words. Ghalil could tell that the boy wasn't ready to die but that he wouldn't dare defy his brother, and that he hated death the way only youth can.

"May Allah be with you, brother. I admire your bravery. From now on Ismail, you will be revered as a martyr."

"Abir, I—"

Abir stopped him with an embrace as Ghalil looked on, frowning.

"If you're going to chicken out, it's better for you to tell us now, Ismail. If they arrest you, we'll all go down." he said.

"Are you doubting my brother's bravery?" Abir snapped, clearly offended.

Ghalil looked at him. He did doubt Ismail's bravery, and Abir's sanity. He didn't understand why Mohsin had allowed them to devise this plan. Not because the infidels didn't deserve it. But up until recently, Abir had conscientiously followed the sheikh's instructions. Now he wanted to pull the strings himself.

Ismail felt his brother pull away from the hug, but he held on tighter. He'd felt protected by Abir ever since the night the soldiers burst into their house in Ain al-Hilweh.

"Go or you'll be late. I won't cry for you, Ismail, because today you will enter Paradise. You will be much happier there than we ever have been here. We'll see each other soon, Brother."

Ismail walked slowly to the door. He turned back, his eyes pleading to his brother to save him, to not send him to become a martyr. But Abir only smiled, putting a hand on his chest.

Ismail walked to the subway. Police were everywhere in the city. He tried not to look at them. Ghalil had instructed him well. He had to look calm. His route to the glass building that housed so many offices, including the International Channel, took him near the new NATO headquarters.

When he got there, the police presence was even more intense. He walked briskly. He just had to do the same thing he did every day, Ghalil had told him. He reached the building and headed to the staff door, but the security guard sent him to the main entrance, where a security line was set up. He had to empty his backpack, which contained only a cheese sandwich and an apple. It took him more than 20 minutes to get to the maintenance office. He apologized to his boss. "I wasn't late, but security is moving really slowly," he explained. She nodded, a worried look on her face. "Better for them to go the extra mile with searches than for us to have any nasty surprises. You must have seen how those bastards from the Circle threatened us yesterday," the woman declared.

Ismail would have loved to tell her that those who wage the jihad weren't bastards, but martyrs for Allah.

He went to his locker and opened it slowly. There was no one else in the room, so he took out the shopping bag he'd been keeping there and put in the backpack he'd brought that day. He headed to the bathroom and locked himself in a stall. There was the belt. He just had to assemble the explosives he'd been smuggling into the building each day. Ghalil had showed him what to do. It wouldn't take long. He began to sweat as he heard two of his colleagues come in. They were talking about the *fucking terrorists* and how if they managed to catch them, there would be no mercy. Ismail's hands trembled. He had to assemble the belt as quickly as possible. He heard toilets flush and water running in the sink. They were leaving. Ghalil had spent months instructing him, making him assemble and disassemble the belt until he was sure he could do it. During this period, he'd smuggled in the pieces one by one in soda cans that Ghalil had adapted. He breathed heavily with fear as he put on the belt. No one could tell what he was hiding underneath. The gray sweater he wore would disguise it. It was ragged because he wore it all the time, and loosely fitting.

He came out of the bathroom and went to get the mail cart.

His boss shot him an angry look. "You took your time," she scolded him.

He pressed his mouth together and made up an excuse.

"I have an upset stomach."

He pushed the cart over to the elevator. First floor. The receptionist at the cosmetics company greeted him with a smile.

"Hi Ismail, crazy day, huh? Everyone is hysterical, like it's going to happen in Brussels. But those terrorists on TV didn't say anything about attacking here. I think they'll do it wherever's easiest, and Brussels, especially on the eve of the NATO summit, is armed to the teeth. I don't know about you, but I'm pretty calm about the whole thing."

What could he do but nod and agree with her?

Second floor. Third floor. Fourth floor. Ismail made his way up the building, dropping off envelopes and packages with office receptionists until he got to the 16th floor.

It was 8 a.m. and there were more people than usual in the office of the International Channel. A pair of security guards stood next to the reception desk.

W.W. came out of the bathroom attached to his office, having just showered and shaved. He'd been at the network for 24 hours, and he always kept a change of clothes there.

He was exhausted and needed more coffee, though he'd already lost track of how much he'd had since the day before.

He decided to go to the editorial department. A few of the writers who had gone home to rest were returning. Behind them was the mail boy he never bothered to acknowledge. A second later, he heard someone scream, "Allah is great!" and then he plunged into nothingness.

*

Noise. Blood. Smoke. Screams. Helen was on her way into the building when she heard the explosion. She ran toward the elevator, but the security guards stopped her. "Everyone must evacuate the building," they told her. Ignoring them, she skirted around the area. Everyone in the lobby was running, trying to get away. Helen found the door to the stairs, determined to climb all 16 floors as she called the newsroom. No one was picking up. She felt like she was drowning. She dialed W.W.'s number, but there was no answer. She stopped to catch her breath. Air refused to go into her lungs. She still had 12 floors to go.

She called Benjamin and listened to his stammering voice.

"Benjamin, it's Helen, where are you?"

"Here. It's horrible, I—"

"Are you OK?" she asked anxiously.

"No, no, I'm not OK! I don't know—"

"Where are you?"

"The machine, the coffee—"

"Stay right there, I'm on my way."

Without knowing how, she sprinted up the stairs until she reached the right floor. She heard a distant sound of sirens. Opening the door to the hallway that led to the International Channel offices, she saw the glass doors had been destroyed. She heard desperate screams. Her eyes then focused enough for her to understand what she was looking at, and a ragged cry flew from her mouth. The floor was covered with human remains, blood coating every square inch of the place. She froze, not knowing what to do. Then slowly and fearfully, she went forward, the bloodstained glass crunching under her shoes. She tried to avoid the bodies and looked through the rubble that had been the newsroom. Where were Benjamin, W.W., Lauren and Lucy? She heard people talking, men giving orders. She turned and saw security guards through the haze. Someone was ordering her to stop, but she didn't, she couldn't, she didn't want to.

A hand gripped her shoulder.

"We're going to get you out of here," a guards said to her.

"No, no, I'm staying! My colleague Benjamin is here, I just spoke to him—"

"Don't worry, madame, we're getting everyone out. For now you must come with me, you can't be here. It's dangerous."

"It was him!"

"What do you mean? Who are you talking about?" The guard looked at her closely.

"Him! He said that if we didn't comply, he would start killing people."

"Calm yourself, madame, and please come with me."

But Helen shook off his grip and ran towards the editorial department.

"Stop! Don't! That woman is out of her mind! We have to get her out of here right now."

Helen leapt over the bodies. She didn't want to look. She just needed to get to the break room, a cramped space with a vending machine that sold coffee, snacks and sandwiches. Maybe she could find Benjamin there.

A man was running behind her, but Helen was fast and knew the offices well.

Benjamin sat on the floor, his body slumped against the wall. Next to him were the bodies of two men, and nearby lay three injured women, immobilized by shock. Helen reached her hand towards him and he struggled to his feet. She hugged him, bringing him back to himself.

"You were here when it happened," Helen murmured.

"I couldn't sleep. I came to the office at five. I talked to W.W. for a while, then Lauren came in, charged up with the day. Lucy got here at six. We were arguing about how we should prepare the program for today. Then Lucy and Lauren went to the editorial room, and I stayed here to have another cup of coffee. Then—"

Benjamin hugged Helen again. She stroked his head to soothe him. Firefighters and police officers suddenly filled the room.

"We've got to evacuate you. Are you OK? Is anyone injured?" they heard a firefighter say.

Helen held onto Benjamin's arm and they made their way through the wreckage and the gore. The smell of blood and bombs was overpowering and clawed at their lungs so that they struggled to breathe.

They led them down to the lobby. There were several officers in masks and disposable gloves handling the victims' blood-soaked remains. Where was Lauren? Where was Lucy?

"You have to let us do our jobs. You can't stay here. There are some survivors, but most of them are badly injured. You were lucky, monsieur, like those two ladies who were with you. For everyone else, it was a massacre."

Words, words, and more words. They were led to the main entrance of the building, which had been almost entirely evacuated by now. Helen saw her husband at the door. Andrew was talking to a woman she recognized, yes, it was Louise Moos, the head of the Belgian security services, who they'd interviewed the day before.

When Andrew saw Helen, he ran to her. She went into his arms and let the tears stream down her face.

"It's all right now," Andrew soothed her.

Louise went over to them, her face impassive.

"Ms. Morris, I would like to speak with you."

"Yes, of course," Helen responded.

"Does it have to be right now?" Andrew asked. "As you can see, my wife is in shock."

"I know and I'm very sorry, it will only take a few minutes. We need to know if the terrorists have contacted you in any way. Perhaps another thumb drive or a phone call." Her voice was dry and professional, as if the blood and the chaos had no effect on her.

"No. Yesterday when I left our meeting, I went to the hotel but could barely sleep. I came to the office first thing this morning. As you can imagine, we have all been anxious wondering if they might decide to send us another statement."

"What time did you arrive?" Louise asked.

"I'm not sure, it was not long ago. I was here in the entrance of the building when we heard the blast. The security guards asked all of us to get out immediately."

"But they found you on the 16th floor."

"I didn't listen and took advantage of the chaos to climb the stairs. You have to understand my distress, I was afraid that the explosion—"

Helen made an effort to contain her tears. Andrew put his arm around her shoulders and turned to face the head of Belgian security.

"Is it really necessary for you to interrogate my wife?"

"Mr. Morris, I have to do my job. I understand your wife is in shock, but anything we find out could be useful."

"I'm fine, Andrew," Helen said, recovering her composure. "As I climbed the stairs I called the office, but nobody answered. Not even W.W.'s phone. Then I tried my co-anchor on the program, Benjamin, and he did answer. It was terrifying, he could barely speak. I ran up all those stairs, I don't know how I managed it, and I went into the office. It was horrible! What I saw—"

"You weren't authorized, Ms. Morris," Louise Moos rebuked her dryly.

"No, I wasn't, that's true. But I'm a journalist, and I'm not going to start asking permission to find out what's going on. And my colleagues were in there, Benjamin was in there, and I had to get him out," Helen responded with a hard look at the director.

"That's what the firefighters were there for, and they had already arrived. A wall could have collapsed on you, or the roof."

"I didn't think of that, Ms. Moos. I had to see what had happened. I had to help my people. Wouldn't you have done the same?"

Louise didn't answer.

"Now, Ms. Morris, I kindly request that you leave here. We'll speak again later. We have a job to do."

"I know that. I'm a journalist and I have to report it. I need to find out which of my colleagues have been affected by the explosion, and what's left of the network office. I also have a job to do, Ms. Moos, and I hope you're not going to stop me from doing it."

The two women glared at each other with mutual determination and dislike.

"Helen, maybe you should let someone else take over," her husband said.

"No. I'm staying here, Andrew. It's my obligation. I have to speak to Joseph, though I imagine he'll have already heard what happened."

"Of course, I spoke to him a few minutes ago. I'll take care of everything," Morris replied.

"Well, the first thing we have to do is find out who and what has survived and then start broadcasting."

Benjamin Holz came over to them, a bottle of water in his hand.

"How are you holding up?" Andrew asked him.

"Alive and ready to report on what happened. Helen, we have to rent some equipment and start sending video to Washington. There are already many journalists out there, but I was the one inside when it happened. Let's get to work."

Helen and Benjamin held each other for a moment, an invincible team.

"OK," Andrew said, "you'll soon have your cameras, and a place to do the program."

"Was anything saved from upstairs?" Helen asked.

"You can't go up there, Ms. Morris," Louise interrupted again angrily. "That's not important right now. There are several dead and injured."

"Ms. Moos, we'll make sure not to disturb anything. You have to understand, it was our television network the terrorists attacked."

"I will not authorize any of you to go up," Louise said firmly.

"Jack!" Helen ran over to a man with a camera on his shoulder and arguing with the police blocking his way into the building.

"Oh my god, it's Jack!" Benjamin exclaimed, following.

"You're going to have to let them in, Ms. Moos," Andrew declared.

"Mr. Morris, I understand that you have a job to do, but only under the condition that it doesn't interfere with mine. We're dealing with a blast site—making a television show is the least of my concerns."

A police officer took Louise to speak a few steps away. But Andrew could still hear what he said.

"It seems the cause of the explosion was a suicide bomb."

"They've really gone too far!" she exclaimed.

"The count right now is 14 dead and 25 injured, seven of them in critical condition. In terms of the damage, I would say it's pretty substantial—hardly anything was left intact. The firefighters are examining the structure."

Andrew went over to Louise and the police officer.

"Ms. Moos, please have the firefighters take out any equipment that is still working."

"No, I'm not going to ask them to do that. You may be the vice president of this network, but I'm the head of security in this country, and my duty is to avoid putting anyone in danger. I will not send any firefighters to rescue television equipment. I'm sorry."

Louise turned and walked toward a group of men who had just arrived. Austin Turner from the CIA and Anthony Jones from NATO stood talking to Ariel Weiss, Maoz Levin and Jacob Baudin. Agents from three of the most powerful intelligence services in the world who were then joined by Alba Fernández.

232

"I took a look at the upstairs floors. It could have been worse," she said evenly.

"You shouldn't have gone up! You're not authorized," Louise reproached her. "That was foolish. The firefighters and emergency teams are doing their jobs. Couldn't you wait for the official report? I can give it to you personally within a few hours."

"I would, of course, appreciate an official report, Ms. Moos, and I will also give you mine. This case goes beyond your mandate. My duty at the European Union Intelligence Center is to investigate, and I hope I can count on your cooperation," Alba declared, fixing Louise with a hard stare.

Jacob stifled a smile. He instinctively sympathized with the Spanish agent, while the Belgian head of security seemed impossible to work with. They couldn't be more different.

"This is Belgium, and I'm directing the investigation," Louise reminded Alba.

"Yes, Ms. Moos, there are representatives from every European organization here as well as NATO. This attack is not an internal matter for Belgians. If we cooperate, it will be easier for us to fight the terrorists."

"Ms. Fernández is right," Jacob declared, ignoring the glares from Weiss and Maoz.

Alba gave Jacob a look of thanks.

He could see that the two women would continue to clash.

*

Jack Sander was an exceptional cameraman. Hardened from covering many conflicts in the Middle East, he often went with Helen and Benjamin on their trips. He was the best. That night, he'd barely gotten any rest, having spent it running around Brussels getting shots of the city, especially in Molenbeek. It was cutaway footage that he knew they needed for that night's program. Only a few minutes before, the sudden news alert on his phone about the attack had sent him running to the building with his camera.

Helen approached Louise.

"Ms. Moos, you must let us go up to the 16th floor. We need to get some footage, and Benjamin is going to report from there about the moments before and after the explosion."

"No, absolutely not. The bomb has caused structural damage, and we still don't know the extent of it."

"I'm sorry, Ms. Moos, but unless you'd like to arrest us, we're going to go up there," Benjamin jumped in. "You can't stop us from reporting on what happened to us. Any risk we take is our responsibility. We know what we're exposing ourselves to. We're journalists."

"I'm sorry, no," she replied.

"I think you should let them, Louise," Turner intervened.

"So the terrorists can enjoy the spectacle?" she responded irately.

"So the world can see what those bastards are capable of," he responded.

"You're in charge, Ms. Moos, but I think Austin is right," said Anthony Jones.

The Israeli agents stayed silent. Ariel had no intention of intervening in the showdown between Moos and the journalists, who now had the backing of the Americans.

Andrew walked over to the group. In a quietly confident manner, he turned to Louise and said in a serious tone, "I believe that the White House is going to ask your government to allow us to do our work. We have a duty to fulfill."

Wordlessly, Louise signaled to one of the police officers and told him and two firefighters to accompany Helen, Benjamin and Jack to the 16th floor.

"Clearly, you all will take full responsibility for the risks you're taking."

When the journalists were gone, Louise could no longer contain her rage.

"The arrogance! They think they have the right to do whatever they want. I hope a wall doesn't collapse onto them, but if it does—"

"You wouldn't lose any sleep, right, Louise?" Turner said.

The woman limited her response to a terse smile.

Abir felt exhausted and euphoric all at once, but his eyes stayed fixed on the TV. The night had been long, and the dawn, glorious. The infidels had paid for their impiety. He was very proud of his brother. Ismail had behaved courageously, sacrificing his life for the jihad. Although he'd always sworn to the sheikh and Ghalil that he was a brave man, secretly he had always had his doubts. He'd never stopped seeing him as a fragile, frightened boy since the day the Jews killed his parents. In Afghanistan, Ismail would hide away to cry. He wasn't made to fight, to slit a man's throat, to withstand the noise of bomb blasts, to survive without eating or drinking. Though he would look at him imploringly, he never complained. Abir knew how desperate he was, but did nothing to help him. Sheikh Mohsin wouldn't allow weakness, and expected the men under his command to be invincible. Sometimes he questioned whether Ismail was capable of fighting in the holy war.

Now the sheikh would have to recognize Ismail's bravery and martyrdom. From that day on, his name would be venerated by all believers.

Ghalil sat in a chair drinking coffee.

"You should go out and see what's happening," Abir said.

"No. We shouldn't leave this room for now. They're looking for us, Abir. Right now, you're the most wanted man in the world. You devised this plan yourself, and you said that patience was the key. We're safe here."

He knew that Ghalil was right, but he frowned in annoyance. This place was his life insurance, and he had been the one who'd decided they should stay hidden there. Nobody would look for them in this apartment because Zaim and Nashira were model citizens, he an electronics engineer, and she an early childhood teacher. They both passed as integrated, modern Muslims. She never took off her hijab in public, but her husband told her to dress in European clothing at work, wearing jeans that were never too tight, and blouses that covered her arms. He wore expensive suits. They lived in the best part of Molenbeek, the most central and least troubled area. Some Belgians still lived on their street and in their building.

Abir turned back to the TV and smiled when Helen Morris and the Jew Benjamin Holz appeared on the screen. *The World at 7* was reporting from 'ground zero' of the attack. Where the offices of the International Channel had once been, now there were only dead bodies.

Helen looked like she'd aged 10 years, her makeup failing to mask the tension and exhaustion on her face. Holz appeared to be in a daze, but he answered his colleague's questions, trying to explain to the viewers where he had been and what he felt when the explosion happened.

"I was at the back of the office in the coffee room, talking to a sound tech and an assistant, and there were other people nearby. Suddenly, an explosion threw us to the floor. The blast left me deaf for a moment, and I couldn't see clearly. I began to hear screams, and for a few seconds, shock stopped me from thinking. I couldn't understand what was happening. I couldn't get up, couldn't get my legs to respond. I thought I was dead. I don't know how much time passed and then I heard the far-off sound of a phone ringing. I was able to answer it, and it was you, Helen, you were telling me not to worry, that you were coming, and that I shouldn't move."

Helen and Benjamin then took turns recapping the events of the day before, when they'd received a thumb drive from an Islamist terrorist group with a message threatening the entire world. They knew they would attack, but they never imagined that the International Channel would be their first target. Benjamin warned that intelligence services would find these terrorists sooner rather than later. After replaying the video message, they moved to their colleagues in Washington, who were reporting from the White House.

The live program was going to continue nonstop. Intelligence agencies around the world were on alert; the terrorists could attack again anywhere, at any time.

Abir watched the screen intently. Helen was looking directly into the camera.

"What the terrorists need to know is that no country will allow blackmail. None of their friends in prison for acts of terror will be released. And they should also know that soon, they will be sharing a cell with them."

"That woman is such an idiot," Ghalil said.

"They say what they're told to. Anyway, you weren't really expecting them to release any of our brothers, were you? They never will. If they had had any intention of doing so, they would have asked to negotiate in secret. They're afraid their citizens will view them as weak. But I promise you, Ghalil, if they do try to negotiate, we'll make it known."

The hidden sliding door opened slowly, and Zaim entered the room.

"Congratulations, Abir! It was a success. Your brother is a hero, and we will never forget him."

"Ismail has avenged my parents and all the brothers who have suffered at the hands of the infidels."

"I know I shouldn't ask, but what happens now?"

"No, you shouldn't ask Zaim. You should just follow orders."

"Right. My train to Paris leaves in an hour."

"You will go to your work meeting, then you will go into the Café de Flore, order a coffee, and go to the bathroom."

"Yes, I know."

"Do whatever you would normally do in a bathroom, but it's essential that you take out a comb and comb your hair. Don't look at anybody, don't catch anyone's eye if they're looking at you. Just comb your hair."

"That's what I'll do, Abir. I should tell you that my boss almost canceled the meeting with his partners in Paris. The security checks in the stations and airports are exhaustive, and everyone is scared."

"But he didn't cancel it, did he? So do what you have to do."

Once Zaim left the tiny room and the wall panel closed again, Abir turned his eyes back to the TV screen.

Think like them. Feel like them. Miriam's words had taken root inside Jacob. It took all his effort to put himself in their shoes. As a teenager, he'd tried to understand the other boys his age, why they acted a certain way and why they thought he was different. What he'd felt when his mother brought him to live in Israel, and he'd had to learn what it meant to be Jewish, was that he wasn't one of them. His mother had constantly reproached him. "Jacob," she would say, "you should feel at home. We are Jewish—you can't reject who you are." But the fact was that he could. He'd never been able to relate to being Jewish, though he didn't deny his identity.

He wanted to put himself in Abir Nasr's shoes, but he couldn't do it.

He secretly spent hours thinking about it, trying to understand the man's journey to becoming a murderer.

They had had different lives and had opposing moral codes, but they had something in common: they were both from nowhere, having had their roots ripped out. *You stop being who you thought you were*, he realized, *and from that moment on, you're looking for yourself within the confusion*. The report that Dor had sent them said it all, although whoever had written it had probably not considered that behind the objective facts was the story of a boy who had been robbed of everything he knew to be true one fateful night. Would he have become a different person otherwise? Jacob wasn't sure.

He knew that every person was different, and when faced with the same circumstances, feels and reacts in a different way. Nasr could have chosen the opposite path to terror, but it was also true that vengeance was an understandable choice. He wouldn't admit it, but if one morning some men had come into his house and killed his parents, he's not sure he would have done the same thing. It was a question he'd posed to some of his friends, and most of them had avoided answering.

But he couldn't think about his conscience anymore. He needed to figure out what to do about Nora Adoum, now that he had convinced Ariel to let him talk to her.

"You're not a field agent," he had said. "You have very limited experience with terrorism. I know you participated in a few operations when you were in the army, but this is on another level, Jacob. Computers are your thing, that's what you're good at."

Ariel was right. He wasn't an intelligence agent used to risking his life in the field. Dor had eventually accepted that he would never be a good agent and decided to use him where he really shined in artificial intelligence.

Jacob took a taxi to Nora's apartment after getting the address from Louise. The woman's phone had already been tapped for hours.

He was surprised when he saw Matonge, the neighborhood she lived in. Most of the residents had settled there from a wide range of African countries, and there was a feeling of calm on the streets, as if no one was concerned about a terrorist attack. Women dressed in vibrant colors sold food in stalls, and many business signs made references to the diverse regions of that continent. The cafés and shops bustled with a melting pot of cultures.

The gray apartment building where Nora lived was unremarkable. A woman with a child tied to her back passed him as he entered. As he pressed Nora's doorbell, he realized he had no plan. He didn't know what he was going to say to her, and he was surprised when she opened the door a crack without asking who it was, though the chain was still attached.

"Noura Adoum?"

"What do you want?" she asked.

"I'd like to talk to you. Don't be scared."

"Should I be scared?"

"Can I come in?"

"Who are you?"

"It's about your cousin, Abir."

Nora was quiet. They looked at each other.

"I won't bother you for very long."

"Are you a cop?"

"Not exactly. I'm one of the people investigating the attack on the International Channel."

"I can't help you."

"Yes, I think you can. Abir could be the person behind it."

"Says who?"

"It's a possibility."

"Get out of here!"

"I'll go if you want me to, but just know that if you don't talk to me, the police will come instead, and, well, they'll take you down to the station to question you."

"Isn't that what you're trying to do right now?"

"You don't have to talk to me. I don't have a warrant or any legal authority to make you. You can decide."

"You still haven't told me who you are."

"I'm someone who is part of the team looking for the terrorists. I think you can help us."

"Help you? Are you accusing me of having something to do with what happened?"

"Miss Adoum, I was hoping we could talk, and that maybe it would be a better option for you. But I won't bother you any further."

"So as soon as you leave, the cops will come, right?"

"I'm afraid so. They will interrogate you, along with the rest of your family."

"What do I get out of talking to you?"

"Nothing. You won't get anything. I can't promise you anything."

"Then what's the point?"

"I'm sorry to have bothered you."

Jacob turned around feeling ridiculous. What would Efraim or Maoz have done? Would they have broken down the door? Would they have forced her to talk?

"Come in," he suddenly heard behind him.

He turned and saw she'd unlatched the chain and was holding the door open.

"Thank you."

The apartment was small. A living room with a kitchen along one wall and a door that probably led to a bedroom. Nora was attractive, with her copper *garçon* hairstyle, enormous eyes and delicate frame.

"Please sit down. Would you like a coffee?"

Jacob nodded and was silent as Nora brought it to him.

"My cousin is not a terrorist," she began.

"Do you know where he is?"

"I don't."

"But you do know that he's spent the last few years training in Afghanistan, that he participated in arms deals, and that he's part of a radical Islamist terrorist group called the Circle. You must also know that he never got over the death of his parents."

"Why don't you call it what it really was: the murder of his parents. They were killed in cold blood right in front of him and his little brother."

Jacob tried not to let his face betray his feelings.

"What did you think when you saw the video on the threatening to turn the West into a living hell? Did it worry you?"

"How do you think I felt? Do you think I'm not human?"

"Did you recognize the hooded man's voice? It wasn't disguised. It could have been recognized."

"That's what you want, right? For me to say I recognized the voice?"

He realized she had an advantage. He didn't dare push her or accuse her of being her cousin's accomplice and avoiding his questions.

"They will find him, Miss Adoum. You must know that. And everyone who is related to him and hasn't cooperated will have their share of the responsibility."

"So, you're accusing my cousin of being a terrorist and you're accusing me of working with him? Does that about sum it up?"

"You're very intelligent, but you're not answering my question. I'll leave my phone number with you. If you think of anything else and want to talk, give me a call."

"Didn't you say the cops were going to show up any minute?"

"Yes. They will."

"Then what good will your number do me?"

"Maybe nothing, if they get here before you call me."

Nora dug her nails into the sofa. She wasn't going to betray Abir. Never. But that meant betraying herself and allowing more innocent people to die. She was sure that it was Abir who had started to carry out the threats, and before they caught him many people would die. Could she live with knowing she could have prevented it?

"I have nothing to say to you, sir."

"Abir Nasr is in Brussels," he said confidently, though in his mind he wasn't sure at all.

A twitch of fear crossed Nora's face, confirming this.

"If you're so sure of it, why don't you find him and ask him?"

"I won't bother you anymore, Miss Adoum." Jacob stood up.

"Give me that phone number," she said, immediately regretting it.

Jacob took a slip of paper out of his jacket pocket, gave it to her, and left without another word. She didn't see him out.

When he got onto the street, he was tempted to ask a Black man pushing a fruit cart for a cigarette as he already had one hanging out of the side of his mouth, but he resisted and decided to walk back.

An hour later, he arrived at the office and found Maoz transfixed in front of the computer screen.

"Where's Ariel?"

"Louise Moos summoned him. As you know, Dor has officially informed the CIA, NATO and your friend in the European Union Intelligence Center of our well-founded suspicions that Abir Nasr could be the terrorist behind the attack. Moos has put Abir's aunt and uncle under watch, as well as his cousin Nora. Their phones are tapped. Now we wait."

"OK. For the record, Alba Fernández is not my friend, but I like her and she seems like a person we can trust. So have we learned anything yet that could provide some clues?"

"Jamal Adoum's phone conversations are innocuous. His son Farid called him from Paris, but they didn't even mention the attack on Brussels."

"Which is not normal."

"No, it's not. We also have a conversation between Nora Adoum and her mother."

"From just now?"

"No, you were on the way to her house. Nora seemed anxious and made plans to meet her mother in the Molenbeek market. She insisted they see each other. The mother said she would try to go. Her husband has forbidden her to see her daughter.

It seems Nora is the black sheep of the family. What did she tell you?"

"She didn't tell me anything, but she knows the man in the video is her cousin. And she knows he's in Brussels."

"But she didn't tell you that."

"We had a strange conversation, a conversation between two people who know the truth, but neither one will say it out loud. She won't betray him, but I'm not sure how far she's willing to go to protect him. She seemed like an intelligent woman, an interesting person. I'm not sure she would talk if you people decide to interrogate her."

"Are you excluding yourself from something like that?" Maoz asked him harshly.

"No, it's not that."

"But you don't think we should interrogate her, is that it?"

"I think that without speaking, she told me that the man we want is Abir, and he's here in Brussels. I think she might even know where he is."

"Then we have to question her."

"I suppose so. Who will do it, Belgian security or us? I think Moos lacks a certain ... I don't know ... empathy. She's too high strung. If she talks to Nora Adoum, she'll scare her."

"Let's wait for Ariel to get back. In the meantime, read the briefing from Palm Tree House. We already knew that Abir Nasr had a heart operation years ago, but now we also know that they fitted him with a Medtronic device. It's a defibrillator and a pacemaker in one. The device serves—"

Jacob interrupted him and recited the information as if it were a lesson.

"... to measure the activity of the heart. If it detects an altered rhythm, it emits a shock so the heart will go back to beating normally. Interesting."

Maoz raised an eyebrow and waited expectantly for Jacob to continue.

"There are security problems with defibrillators."

"How so, Jacob?"

"A few years ago, the company that made the device realized they could be hacked. It was actually the FDA, the U.S. agency in charge of product regulation, who sounded the alarm."

"Is that really possible?"

"It's not impossible," Jacob replied.

"Explain it to me in detail."

"It's very simple. Software is used to program the device and later monitor the condition of the patient's heart, all from the computers at the hospital where the patient was treated. Have you ever seen the TV series *Homeland?*"

"No."

"It's a show about spies that I really enjoyed, and in one of the episodes in the second season, the bad guys decided to hack the pacemaker of the U.S. vice president and kill him. When I saw that episode, I thought it was worth investigating whether it could actually be done."

"Are you telling me we can control someone's heart with a computer?"

"Well yes, at least in theory. But it wouldn't be easy. You see, what the defibrillator does is it makes sure the heart is beating at the correct speed. If it suddenly beats irregularly, the device will send it a shock. But if everything is working correctly, and you reprogram the device through a computer, you can cause the heart to start beating harder. That could kill the patient. The hacker would have to be not very far from the person with the device. This is just a theory of course—nobody has actually proven it. Some defibrillator companies are remotely monitoring the implanted devices to make sure they're working, and if one needs reprograming, they can do it right away. In my opinion, they're just saying this to reassure their patients. Wi-Fi-enabled technology opens many dangerous doors."

"Jacob, is it then possible to cause a full-on heart attack in someone who's wearing a pacemaker?"

"I don't know for sure, but I think so. If a hacker can access your computer from the other side of the world, then they should be able to access a computer at a medical center, wherever that may be."

"And might that be tested?"

"Well, it's never been done, but yes, I think that if you hack the computer base you can manipulate the defibrillator and … What are you thinking?" he asked, alarmed.

"I'm going to ask you again: can it be done from a distance?"

"God, I don't know. I think so."

"I'm going to talk to Dor. Or better yet, you talk to him and explain it."

"But Maoz, what are you planning on doing?"

"If possible, we will kill Abir Nasr."

"No no, we can't kill him!"

"Jacob, it's either him or countless innocent people."

Nora walked briskly towards the metro. She asked Allah to make sure her mother got there all right. She mentally reviewed the conversation she'd had with the stranger. She worried she'd said something that could be a clue for the police. His visit confirmed to her that they already suspected Abir and that they were going to put the whole family under surveillance to find him. Knowing they could be listening to her phone conversations made her feel naked. A few minutes after he'd gone, before she left her apartment, she had called Mathis. He had repeated how much he needed her and how much he had missed her the last few hours. He said a few intimate things that made her uncomfortable. He then asked her advice on whether to open Le Rêve de Marolles that night. She had told him she didn't feel well and that either way she wouldn't be able to go to the café-concert. "But you're our star," he'd protested, and Nora made an excuse saying that a stuffed-up star with a headache would be a disappointment for the customers.

Her mother was walking with an absent expression. She looked lost. Nora went up to her and touched her shoulder, startling the woman.

"If your father finds out we've seen each other …"

"How is he?"

Fatima struggled to describe her husband's mood.

"He says that what happened is Allah's will, that we should defend ourselves from the infidels."

"Is Ismail OK?"

"I don't know, he's not home. Your father says I shouldn't worry."

"But he works in the same building as that television channel."

"Your father says there's no reason to be concerned."

"And Abir?"

"I don't know where he is. He left."

"You know as well as I do that it was him."

"Don't say that! No, it couldn't be him. Your cousin isn't evil."

"I'm telling you, it was him. Where is he?"

"I don't know, Noura, I don't know. They never tell me anything I don't need to know. He came home, he was there for a few hours, and then he left."

"They're hiding him. Father will know."

"No, no, your father doesn't know anything."

"He has so much hatred, Mother."

"He hates the infidels. He says they humiliate us, they abuse us. He's right, Noura, I see it on TV."

"Mother, Abir has murdered more than a dozen people and has threatened to kill more."

"Don't say that! It wasn't him, Noura! You can't think that about your cousin!"

"I know him, and I know it was him. I know why he did it too."

They stared at each other, not speaking. Fatima took her daughter's hand and gripped it. She was scared.

"Noura, darling, please. Let's not do anything that could bring on a tragedy."

"Do anything? Abir already did it, Mother. And Father knew what Abir had planned. You know I'm not lying. They're watching us. I'm sure they have our phones bugged."

"But, why? Your father is right, we are always under suspicion just for being Muslim."

"If only there weren't crazy people who kill in the name of Allah."

"What can we do?"

"I don't know, Mother, I don't know. I love you so much and I couldn't bear anything happening to you because of Abir. I love my cousin, but between Father, Farid and Sheikh Mohsin they've converted him into a murderer."

"Noura, what you're saying is terrible, you shouldn't even think it. You shouldn't say these things about your father, or your brother or your cousin. They love you, Noura."

"They want me to be deaf and mute, just like they've forced you to be."

"Noura, please—"

"Mother, go home and don't worry about me. But be careful."

Nora dropped her mother's hand, turned away and let herself get lost in the crowd. She didn't know what to do. She had to choose between endangering her family and betraying them or allowing other people to die in the next few hours. Whatever decision she made, she would never forgive herself.

When she got back to Matonge, she distracted herself by buying fruit from a stand in the street. She knew the vendor, a kind woman originally from the Ivory Coast with a husband and five children.

Looking up, she saw a guy who didn't fit into the neighborhood. He was dressed like everyone else in jeans, a sweatshirt and a jacket, but he looked nervous and out of place. She didn't stop to see if there were more guys like him; she was sure he was a police officer.

Once Nora got to her apartment, she turned on the TV. She knew she would spend the rest of the day anxiously watching the screen.

Brussels.
*Helen*

Helen glanced at her watch. Four p.m. It was already 4 p.m. They were going live again. Benjamin straightened his jacket as he waited for the light on the camera to turn on.

They had nothing new to report, but in Washington they were six hours behind and the network wanted to keep people watching, so once more they described the attack, their dead colleagues and updates on the injured. They interviewed terrorism experts who had nothing new to say, only the conviction that the man from the Circle who'd launched the attack would strike again. It was anyone's guess where. Brussels was trembling, its citizens waiting anxiously, fearing they could be the next victims. A few minutes before, Helen had had an argument with Louise Moos. The Belgian head of security had refused to give her any information. Her response to every journalist was always the same. "We are investigating, and we hope to detain those responsible for the killing."

Helen and Benjamin demanded to have more information than the other networks. The terrorists had chosen them to release their message and had attacked their offices, cutting short the lives of many of their coworkers. They could have been amongst the victims themselves.

"You just don't get along with her," Benjamin told her later. Helen had responded that Louise Moos was arrogant and lacked empathy.

She couldn't get her husband to back her in her confrontations with the Belgian director either.

As vice president of the International Channel, Andrew Morris had been taking charge. His first task had been negotiating with a Belgian television channel to rent them a studio and offices where they could continue broadcasting. They had to put together an improvised team after losing so many of the people who worked at the channel in Brussels. Joseph Foster had arranged for a chartered plane to send them half a dozen journalists, camera operators and producers, but it would still be a few hours before they arrived. Joseph had also decided to bring over some of his journalists from Paris and London.

Helen and Benjamin continued to be the faces of the channel. They had broken the news of the threat, and they had to continue to be the first with new information. The fact that the terrorists had targeted the International Channel put them in a unique situation with respect to the rest of the media.

Andrew was in direct communication with Austin Turner and the Washington director of the CIA as well as the White House, the Belgian authorities and the European Union Intelligence Center. Morris agreed with Helen that Alba Fernández was easier to work with than Louise Moos.

Helen had been resistant to Andrew taking control. She insisted that she and Benjamin could handle the situation. But her husband had made it clear that what had happened exceeded her capabilities. The network's shareholders wanted assurances. They wanted someone who wasn't a journalist to be in charge. Andrew was honest with his wife. "I'm a businessman, the authorities will talk to me differently than they will to you. You and Benjamin are journalists. You have other codes of conduct. All you care about is the news."

But for Helen, what had happened was more important than the news. Walter White and Lauren Scott were among the victims and her assistant Lucy had been badly injured. The doctors were not optimistic about her recovery.

She wouldn't allow herself to cry. At least not until the nightmare was over. If Lauren were alive, she would order her to put on a good show. It was the only thing left that she could do for her.

The red tally light turned on, and Helen tried to compose herself. She was sure that the hooded man would be watching. It wasn't long before the second deadline to release their friends from Guantanamo would arrive.

*Paris.*
*Zaim Jabib*

Zaim Jabib was tired. His meeting had lasted much longer than expected, and he hadn't even taken a break to eat. His boss trusted him and would send only him to the complicated ones. They knew it was going to be difficult to sell electronic devices to an African country. Difficult and expensive, because every sale required 'kickbacks' for the intermediaries. It annoyed him to return to Brussels without a signed contract. "I need one more week to think about it," they had said. One more week.

But he didn't consider the trip a total loss. At least he'd accomplished what Abir had asked of him. He arrived in Paris on the 9 a.m. train and headed straight for Café de Flore, which was near the office where the business meeting would take place. He looked for a table off on its own and ordered a tea from the waiter. Then he got up to go to the bathroom. Abir hadn't explained much to him, only that at a specified moment he had to comb his hair, and that if a man did exactly the same as him, he should let his comb fall to the floor. He was to hand over an envelope and later collect another before he returned to Brussels.

A couple of men were washing their hands, and he did the same. He dried them and then took out a comb which he ran through his hair. One of the men left, but the other stayed. They looked at each other and Zaim let the comb drop.

"You seem to have dropped something."

Both crouched down and Zaim took advantage of the moment to quickly hand him the envelope Abir had entrusted him with.

The man stood up and left without looking at him, and Zaim did the same. The waiter had left a tray with a cup of tea and a glass of water. Two minutes later, he went into the building where his meeting would be, satisfied with himself for making the delivery. The envelope he'd just handed over contained instructions for the Imam Adel Allawi, a friend of Abir's uncle.

But that had been in the morning. Now he had to collect an envelope sent by the imam. The instructions were the same. When he went back into the café, he looked around, expecting to see the same man. But he only saw a group of tourists. He repeated what he'd done that morning: he headed to the bathroom, washed his hands, and took out a comb. He wondered when the other guy would show up and give him his envelope. Barely a second later, the door of one of the stalls opened and a man was at his side, taking a comb out of his pocket.

They carried out the same movements, though this time a quick look was enough for Zaim to know that the man was from the Maghreb. He was dressed discreetly in black pants, a gray sweater and a raincoat in a muted color. He didn't have a beard or anything that would make him stand out.

There was nobody in the bathroom, which may have been why the man dared to speak.

"As you can imagine, all communications are tapped, so this envelope needs to get back to our mutual friend. It contains important information."

"OK."

They didn't exchange another word. Zaim thought that what the man had said was unnecessary. Abir, Sheikh Mohsin and the other leaders of the Circle only communicated in person. None of them carried a cell phone. The use of technology would have made them vulnerable.

He looked at his watch and hurried out of the café. He had done what was expected of him as a courier. He planned to return to Brussels on the 16:55 train. In just over an hour, he would be home. His wife Nashira would be back already. He felt proud of her. Her commitment to the Circle was as strong as his.

The hours crept by too slowly for Abir and too quickly for the security agents, who continued to try to determine where and when the terrorists would attack next.

In Israel, Dor waited impatiently for his men in Beirut to obtain more concrete information about the pacemaker Abir Nasr had in his heart. He was hoping they would be capable of cloning the computer in the hospital that contained the device's code. If necessary, he told them, they should steal it. He knew what he was asking his men was nearly impossible, especially since he hadn't even given them enough time to come up with a solid plan. Efraim was coordinating the operation and he trusted him, but they both knew it was likely to fail.

At the same time in Brussels, Jacob decided to go out for a walk. He needed to think.

"So, you have to walk to be able to think," Maoz said.

"Yes, it's when I do my best thinking. I need to understand Abir Nasr's logic."

"Logic? Do you really think there's anything more to it than terrorizing the world?"

"There could be. Anyway, you don't need me here."

"Ariel wants us here in an hour to go to a meeting he arranged with Louise Moos. Austin Turner will be there and probably that guy from NATO too."

"Anthony Jones."

"Yeah, that's the one. I don't know if he asked Alba to come too. I think Andrew Morris will join us later. He seems like a good guy."

"And Helen Morris and Benjamin Holz?"

"No, as you've seen, they've spent the whole day in front of the camera. Holz seems calm despite having almost lost his life, and she has nerves of steel. She's exhausted but refuses to rest," Maoz remarked.

"Well, it's no wonder. First the terrorists send a video to be broadcast on their program, then they bomb their offices, killing their colleagues. But there they are, biting the bullet. I think they're going head-to-head against Louise Moss," Jacob concluded.

"They are journalists, at the end of the day."

"Yes. The good ones are cut from a different cloth. I'm off, Maoz, I need to think. There's something we're missing," he said.

Maoz nodded. If he'd learned anything during his many years as a field agent, it was the importance of listening to your gut, to that thought that jumps up at you when you're immersed in a case. He wouldn't be the one to deny Jacob the chance to organize his thoughts and identify whatever it was that was slipping through their fingers.

"The meeting is in Moos' office. You can show up whenever you want."

"I'll call you. Listen, would it be all right if I tried speaking to Nora Adoum again?" Jacob asked.

"We're in an extreme situation. I wouldn't worry too much about the rules. Do what you think you must, and then we'll see."

"Thank you."

Jacob left their office and began to feel better as soon as he got out onto the street. He knew he needed Nora's help for the missing puzzle piece, but she also needed time to resolve her own inner conflict: betray her cousin or allow him to keep killing.

As the hours passed, exhaustion began to overpower everyone. Helen refused to rest, and Benjamin followed her lead. He eventually asked Andrew to help them.

"We need a shot of something to keep us awake. Can you find a doctor?"

"You're both crazy! You have to sleep, even just for a few hours. This insanity could last for days, and you can't be in front of the camera 24/7 without a break. If necessary, I'll fire both of you," Morris replied, angry.

Helen argued with her husband, but lost. Andrew was in no mood to put up with his wife's stubbornness.

"You and Benjamin are going to the hotel to sleep for a while. In four hours, I'll send a car to pick you up."

"What if they kill someone else? Who will report it? No, we can't leave."

"I'll fire you if you don't, Helen, believe me. We already have our journalists from Paris here, and they're doing a good job. Paulette Fontaine is here. She's good in front of the camera. She can take over the live feed while you rest."

"That girl has no clue!" she responded, outraged.

"Come on, Helen, she's a good journalist. She hasn't stopped since she got here, and she knows Brussels well. And Noël Morin is reliable, they're the best from our bureau in Paris."

"But this is our story! Don't you get it?" she shouted.

"Your story?"

"God, Andrew, you know this story is Benjamin's and mine! I'm not going to let you push me out."

"I'm not pushing you out, Helen. That's exactly why I'm telling you to rest for a while. Four hours, Helen, just four hours."

"And what will the viewers say? Do you think they want to see Paulette? No, you know they want to see Benjamin and me there on the screen. They trust us."

"I'm not arguing that it shouldn't be you and Benjamin, that's why you need rest. Four hours."

"No."

"Then I'll fire you and I'll tell Paulette to take over everything. And if Benjamin refuses to rest, I'll fire him too. You should see yourself. You look like a zombie."

Helen knew when Andrew wasn't bluffing. In that moment, he was capable of firing her, sending her home, even divorcing her. He wasn't acting as her husband, but as the vice president of the company. Four hours then, but not a minute more.

When she got to the hotel, the first thing she did was run a bath. A bath was all she would do to rest. Then she would get back to the newsroom.

Benjamin agreed with her that though they were exhausted, it wouldn't be professional to sleep while the terrorists controlled what happened next. Andrew didn't understand, but he was the vice president and challenging him would only lead to being fired. But they thought Andrew would settle for them disappearing for a couple of hours, and not the full four he'd demanded.

It wasn't until she'd sunk into the water that she noticed every inch of her body ached from tension. She had been awake for more than 24 hours. She wouldn't let herself close her eyes, and got out after only a few minutes. Then she chose the clothes she would wear for who knew how long, a finely cut Armani suit in charcoal. She shoved a pair of shoes and another jacket into her bag, and ate the chocolates that had been left on the pillows. Then she called Benjamin's room. He assured her he was ready too.

When Andrew saw them reappear two hours later, he was angry. But he said nothing: they had followed at least part of his instructions.

"Paulette is doing great," he told them by way of greeting.

"Good for her, but the replacements are here. She'll be more useful to us reporting from the street," Benjamin responded, gulping down his coffee.

The hours crawled by excruciatingly slowly. Networks across the world were still broadcasting live, but there was nothing new to tell. Experts on terrorism and political commentators appeared on the programs over and over again, and they aired reports on the attack nonstop.

It was six in the morning. Abir stretched. Ghalil was dozing on the sofa. They'd been awake for hours.

"Do you have the belt ready?" Abir asked.

"Yes, you know that. Do you think he'll go along with this?"

Abir didn't respond. Ghalil was the best explosives expert they had, but he was very apprehensive. He found it hard to trust anybody, and he had little faith that any of their brothers were capable of carrying out their missions.

"We need coffee. I'm going to take a shower."

Ghalil got up and turned the lever that hid the room from the rest of the house. They could hear a television. Like them, Zaim and Nashira must have spent the night watching the news. He headed to the kitchen and filled the coffee maker with water. His eye caught a tiny movement behind him. He spun around and came face to face with Zaim, who was still in his pajamas.

"You're up early," he said, smiling.

"It wasn't a night for sleeping," Ghalil responded.

"You're right. The infidels are desperate. They don't understand what happened."

"Do you want some coffee?" Ghalil asked.

"Yes, Nashira will make another pot. She's getting dressed. She leaves for work at eight."

Ghalil was about to say something, but instead he nodded as he searched on the shelf for a jar of cookies. Then he placed the coffee, the cookies, a sugar bowl, and two cups on a tray.

"Well, we're going to have breakfast."

"And I'm going to shower. See you later."

When Ghalil came back, Abir had already showered and was dressed in clean clothes.

"You eat breakfast while I get ready."

At 7 a.m., the hidden panel opened and Zaim appeared, smiling. Behind him they could see Nashira pushing a vacuum around the living room.

The three men discussed what they had seen on the news for the last few hours, and when Zaim was about to leave, Abir motioned for him to sit down.

"Zaim, you know how much we appreciate your commitment to the war against the infidels. Only the bravest soldiers have the honor of participating in this war that will lead us to victory. And you're one of the chosen ones. Sheikh Mohsin always praises your intelligence and, above all, your unquestionable faith. War requires sacrifices."

Zaim listened uneasily to Abir's words. He knew that this speech was just a prologue to something else, but what else could Sheikh Mohsin or Abir ask of him, when he had already done so much? He waited anxiously, terror darting up and down his spine.

Ghalil watched them without a word, waiting for Abir's signal. When he turned to him and raised his hands, Ghalil went into the bedroom and came out a few seconds later with a belt. A belt that he had personally prepared with the precise attention to detail needed for manipulating explosives.

Zaim's face blanched with dread. He knew exactly what that belt meant, and he looked at the two men in fear.

"My friend, only a man with your devotion can sacrifice the most precious thing he has. In this time that we've shared your

270

home with you, we've seen how brave your wife Nashira is. You chose well, Zaim. Nashira isn't just an exemplary wife, she is also a believer who knows the importance of the jihad. Her enthusiasm and support have been an asset to our cause."

Abir paused, observing Zaim's horrified look.

"Only the chosen have the honor of handing over our most beloved. I can't stop mourning my brother Ismail, but I ask forgiveness for doing so because I have no right to lament his death. I can't deny him the honor. And now you, Zaim, you will be blessed by the sacrifice that we are asking Nashira to make. A sacrifice that will glorify her and honor her for generations."

In that moment, Zaim understood, to his great sorrow, that Abir had decided to kill his wife. He searched for words to fight his decision. How could they ask him to send Nashira to her death? She was barely 20 years old and dreamed of having children like the ones she took care of at work. No, he couldn't ask his wife to hand over her life.

"Zaim, tell your wife to come here," Abir ordered, hardening his voice.

"No."

"No? Are you defying us, Zaim?"

"I'm not going to let you take her. Why her?"

"And why my brother, Zaim? Why the children, husbands, wives, friends of others? I'm not asking you for anything I haven't already sacrificed myself."

"Why not offer yourself then," Zaim said, rage overtaking him.

Abir leapt to his feet and hit him across the face.

"Coward! You deserve to die for your betrayal!"

Nashira came into the room, alerted by the voices, just as Abir hit her husband. She stood very still, frightened and looking down, waiting for them to speak to her.

"Are you as much of a coward as your husband?" Abir sneered.

She tried to meet Zaim's eyes, but he avoided hers. How could he look at her if he couldn't save her?

Ghalil stood up. It was time to intervene before Abir lost control.

"Nashira, you have been chosen to become a martyr. Your name will be remembered throughout the centuries for contributing to the defeat of the infidels. It's an honor for me to help you."

She looked at them uncomprehendingly. She wanted to defeat the infidels, she had no doubt about that, but did Ghalil just say she must become a martyr? What did that mean?

Abir turned his head toward her and smiled, making the girl blush. She didn't understand what was going on and looked over at her husband again, but he was looking down.

"I've prepared a belt for you. It's very, very easy, Nashira. You won't even notice you're wearing it," Ghalil said.

"A belt?" she asked, trying desperately to make eye contact with Zaim.

"In a few minutes, you'll leave the house to go to work, just as you do every day. Say hi to any neighbors you come across, go to the tram stop and get on it like you always do. It's a very crowded line, isn't it Nashira?" Ghalil asked.

"Yes, at this hour there are many of us on our way to work. And ... and there are also mothers taking their children to school—"

"Good mothers, no doubt, but infidels. Their children are not worth more than our children. How many of ours have died because of bombs and criminal attacks from the infidels? We can't feel compassion for them, because they didn't feel compassion for us."

Nashira started to shake. She was finally absorbing what Ghalil was telling her.

"I ... I ... Zaim—"

"Zaim will feel proud of you. To have married a brave woman who didn't hesitate to give her life to defeat the infidels is an honor that not many men can have."

"My life! Give my life! No, I don't want to die! Zaim!" Nashira's ragged screaming forced Zaim to take his wife and hold her tightly.

"I gave my brother's life! Do you think you're worth more than Ismail?" Abir's voice rang through the room.

"Enough arguing!" Ghalil cut in. "We all have to comply with what is expected of us. Today that means you, Nashira. You're going to be late, so put on your coat and go. I'll explain what you have to do. It's very simple. When the belt explodes, you won't even notice, you won't feel any pain. You're one of the privileged." Ghalil's tone of voice left no room for a reply.

He strapped the belt laden with explosives on her. Then he helped her put on her coat. They had planned for the possibility that she wouldn't cooperate; the belt was programmed to detonate in half an hour and was locked so that she couldn't take it off.

"I would prefer to sacrifice myself," they heard Zaim say as Nashira went out the door of the apartment, but neither Abir nor Ghalil were going to change the plan. Zaim was not allowed to say goodbye to his wife. Goodbyes might have stopped them from accepting what was already written.

Nashira got into the elevator, went out the door, and walked towards the tram stop. She recognized the faces of the people who traveled with her every day at this time. There were no free seats, so she stood. Ghalil had told her to press a button on the belt, but she stuffed her hands in her pockets. She didn't know what she could do, but she knew that she didn't want to die. She thought of Zaim and felt a terrible pain. He had allowed them to take her life, and she wondered what kind of husband didn't protect his own wife. The tram made its first stop. Nashira recognized a mother she saw every day with her two sons. Two boys no older than ten with sleepy, grumpy faces. At the second stop she saw a familiar elderly couple. At the third stop, the same group of teenagers she saw every day clambered on. And at the fourth stop, the attractive young man in a suit and tie like so many of the officials who worked at international organizations in the capital. The man smiled at her and she lowered her eyes, shouting, "Allah is great!" as she felt the click of the detonation. Agony surged through her for a split second before she plunged into nothingness.

*

"A tram has exploded near the European Union Court of Justice!" a producer yelled, running towards the studio where Benjamin and Helen were reporting on events up to that moment. The news was already breaking online and alerts were popping up. There had been an explosion on a tram, the cause still unknown. Authorities feared that there were many casualties. The camera focused on Helen, who had hunched toward her laptop at that precise moment.

"We are getting reports of a terrible event. Just a few moments ago, an explosion on a tram line…"

Helen continued talking in autopilot mode. The hooded man had made his threat a reality once again. There was no doubt in her mind that the explosion was another terrorist attack. Benjamin announced that a team from the International Channel were already on their way to the explosion site and that very soon they would have live images.

While Benjamin addressed the viewers, Helen made a decision. She wouldn't stay in the studio. She wanted to report from there live. She interrupted him to announce she would reconnect from the site of the explosion. Benjamin nodded.

Maoz put a hand on Jacob's shoulder, jolted him awake immediately. He had fallen asleep on the sofa in Ariel's office, having wandered aimlessly around Brussels the night before, wanting to return to Nora's apartment but knowing that she was still undecided about what to do. Pressuring her wouldn't help.

He rubbed his eyes as Maoz urged him to get up.

"We have to go. A tram has exploded. Louise told Ariel that she is sure it was a bomb."

"A tram?"

"Yes, a tram full of people at rush hour. I happened at 8 o'clock, and now it's 8:30. Apparently, one of the cars flew through the air, and the tram was derailed. There are many dead and injured. And guess where it was: right before the stop for the Court of Justice of the E.U."

"Abir!"

"It could be him, or it could be someone else."

"It's him, Maoz, it's him. He's not afraid. He's still here. He's sure we won't find him. I'm going to his cousin's house right now."

"Louise Moos wants to arrest the whole family. She says the time has come to put some pressure on them."

"No, that's idiotic! He'll go deeper into hiding, and then we'll never find him. If you arrest them, we'll lose our only lead."

"You're too sure of yourself, Jacob."

"I'm not wrong. I know I'm not wrong. Talk to Ariel and Dor, to your friend in the CIA, to Louise. Talk to whoever you need to, but don't let them arrest Abir's family or we'll lose him. We have only one way to reach him, and it's only because Nora can't bear to be complicit in her cousin's murders."

"OK. Let's call Ariel. He was having breakfast with Austin Turner when it happened."

"And what do they think?"

"Turner is an intelligent guy. He's not like those oafs from the CIA. Both he and Alba are open to your theory that Abir Nasr is the man we want. Alba stood up to Louise when she proposed arresting the Adoums. She says that we have to give them enough rope to hang themselves, that it would be a mistake to make arrests and show our entire hand. Louise has the support of Anthony Jones. At NATO they don't believe that all this is the work of one man alone."

"Abir has help. He's not alone. He's intelligent and knows how to manage his people. I bet you another so-called martyr blew up the tram."

"You have five minutes, let's go."

"You go ahead, try to convince them. I'm going to try to talk to Nora Adoum."

"Now?"

"Yes, now."

*

Police were blocking the onlookers who were approaching the site of the attack. Emergency workers were searching for injured people inside the tram cars. There were still no numbers on the victims.

Helen reported live on the chaos. Serious and professional, she told the world in a retrained voice what had happened on that street in Brussels. Even though it was the middle of the night in the United States, she knew that the president himself would be in front of the television.

The terrorists were carrying out their threat, there was no doubt. They would only stop the slaughter if the jihadists held in Guantanamo prison were released.

Occasionally, they would cut to Benjamin in the studio to give Helen time to talk to the police and emergency services and try to get information without the camera focused on her.

*

Jacob blended into the crowd. As he arrived at Nora's building, he saw her walking quickly out the door with a frantic expression. He decided to follow her, even though he feared she would discover him. He wasn't a field agent, and he lacked the knowledge necessary to make himself invisible on the street. But she seemed unaware that he was following her, perhaps because she was beside distressed and walking so fast that she didn't notice her surroundings. He even got on the same subway car. Keeping his distance, he got off behind her at the Grand Place and followed her to the site of the attack.

Suddenly, Nora stopped. She seemed to be looking for someone. Jacob wondered whether she thought Abir would be there in the crowd. Then he saw her crashing through the hordes of people, not caring who she pushed out of her way, heading towards the stream of ambulances arriving to take away the wounded and the dead. He stopped and stood, watching. From where he was, it would be difficult for her to notice him.

Then she saw her.

"Marion!"

The woman turned around, stunned. They stared at each other for the first time in many years.

"What are you doing here?" Marion asked.

"A friend called me and told me there had been another attack."

"And you think—"

"I think the same as you, Marion."

"Have you told anyone?"

"No. Have you?"

"What could I say? No, there's nothing to say, Nora. Nothing."

"But we both know that—"

"Shut up!" Marion ordered her, panicked.

Nora obeyed. Things between them were still the same as in high school. Marion was in charge of their relationship, even after so many years.

"Your fucking cousin. I always knew he couldn't be trusted."

"He was in love with you. You were his first love, maybe his only love," Nora dared to say.

"Nobody asked him to fall in love."

"But that day in your house. It was very important to him—you have to understand that."

"Don't be stupid. It was a game. We were teenagers. Nothing we did was important. We were at an age to break rules, experiment—"

"Maybe, but for him what happened between you wasn't an experiment."

"What do you want, Nora?"

"Nothing, nothing! What could I possibly want from you? I want to do something to stop all this, but I can't. What about you?"

"Your cousin has nothing to do with me."

"But you think the same as me, that all this is his work."

"Shut up!"

"The voice of that hooded man. When I heard it on TV, I was absolutely sure. Weren't you?"

"Why won't you just go away, Nora? I have nothing to do with any of you. We happened to meet in high school, that's all. Afterwards, everyone followed their own path. I never thought I'd see you again."

"Well, as you can see, we haven't been able to avoid it."

"Really Nora, just leave me alone. I don't want to talk to you. I don't want to know anything about you. Nothing. Understand?"

"Shouldn't we do something?"

"I don't know who the terrorist is, there's nothing I can do."

"But you're here!"

"Just like you, just like everyone who came to see what happened."

"Marion, are you scared?"

"Don't be ridiculous, of course I'm not scared."

"I'm sure he's not doing all this just to liberate his brothers in the jihad. He's been waiting his whole life for the chance to do something to get your attention, to impress you, so you'll never forget him."

"You're still such an idiot! I don't know who the hooded man is. Even though your cousin is as stupid as you, I don't believe that after all these years since high school he would decide to carry out these attacks just so I would notice him. You were always very simple, Nora. Where is your brain? Now leave me alone. I have no interest in talking to you. You're a nobody, Nora, a nobody. You don't exist to me. Never come near me again, OK? Never."

Marion spun around and barged into the crowd. Nora stood still, watching her leave.

Jacob hadn't gotten close enough to hear the conversation, but he could see the tension between them, as well as something else: fear. He'd managed to take a few photos of them on his phone.

For a moment, he thought about calling Maoz and telling him what he saw so that Louise would order them both to be questioned, but he didn't. He decided to investigate the women on his own, or rather, with the help of his computer. But first, he wanted to talk to Nora. He would at least try to coax her in confessing that she knew the other woman. Maybe it would help them get to Abir Nasr.

He found Nora still standing, frozen, observing the tragedy the terrorists had caused.

"Good morning, though we should probably not say that on this particular day."

Nora panicked and tried to get away from him, but he gripped her wrist with his hand.

"Either talk to me or the police. I'm not going to give you another chance."

"I don't know who you are! Leave me alone!"

"I've already told you. I'm part of the group investigating the attack."

"What group are you talking about?"

"Miss Adoum, right now there are security services from all over the world collaborating to find the man and his friends who are behind this."

"And you belong to one of those services. I'm guessing the French Sécurité, because you're obviously French."

"You're right about that, I am French."

Jacob told himself it wasn't a lie. One of his identities was French, as deeply rooted in him as it was to be Lebanese and Israeli. This was one of the things he and Abir had in common: being uprooted and having to construct a new identity, though this meant they became people from nowhere.

"So you're from the Sécurité."

"No. I'm actually not an agent from any service. I'm just collaborating to resolve this crisis that your cousin has caused."

She looked at him closely, surprised by his sincerity. Who was he exactly and what he was doing?

"We have to stop this. You have to help me find your cousin."

"Stop accusing him! What proof do you have? None. You're just taking a shot in the dark. Why would my cousin be the cause of … of all this?"

"I can't tell you what proof we have, just that we have it."

"You have nothing. Nothing!"

"I know how important blood ties are, and family, but there are moments when we have to make a choice."

"And what choice do I have?" she responded angrily.

"Between loyalty to your family and protecting your cousin, which means living with the terrible guilt of all these innocent deaths, and deciding to prevent more death and destruction. It's in your hands."

Nora glared at him again. He was making her feel disoriented.

"You're wrong. I can't prevent anything because I don't know anything, and I'm not going to allow you to accuse my cousin. I have no reason to believe you have any proof against him."

"OK. Up until now I've done everything I can to stop them from arresting you and your family, but now I don't have any other choice. You know what an arrest will mean for you and your parents, especially if they can prove that you knew something about what was happening. You'll be scarred by it forever."

She knew that, of course she knew that. She didn't need some stranger to tell her that her life would be shattered, and her parents would become infamous. She thought of her mother. Could she withstand an interrogation? Would they torture her to make her talk? She felt a pain deep in her stomach just imagining how they might abuse her.

"So, you're going to order us to be arrested, to be interrogated. Anything else?"

"No, I'm not ordering anything, Miss Adoum. That's a decision someone else will make. It's logical. We have a suspect, and the normal next step is to question the family of the suspect."

"And you're saying you can prevent it?"

"No, not exactly. Maybe it will help so that things aren't so difficult for all of you, if you're innocent. And I think you are."

Nora thought about her father. She knew he hated Westerners, infidels, as he called them. It was a hatred that had grown from the frustration of being an immigrant who had to carve out a place for himself in a society with very different values than the ones he grew up with. A society that watched him with suspicion, never trusting him. A society that he considered morally rotten. A society he disdained, that he was eager to humiliate as much as he felt they had humiliated him. He would never belong, even if some self-righteous people claimed multiculturalism was possible. It wasn't possible for him. Either you accepted their rules, or you would always be seen as different, provoking a deep anger.

Nora knew this, and it was the reason she had chosen to integrate. This society had offered her a door to freedom, to try to be who she wanted and not be conditioned by customs or religion and to control her own life. She preferred being part of it. It wasn't a hard decision in this sense; religion had never occupied a central role in her life. She saw it as a set of rules that oppressed her, prevented her from being, doing, feeling, deciding. She wasn't an atheist, but she had decided to do without religion.

But her father was a believer who had become a fanatic after the experience of emigration and because of more person reason, the murder of his nephew by the Jews. They were the guardians of the West in the East. Her father said this repeatedly, and she believed it. And the Jews had stormed Abir's house, scattering death behind them. They had condemned

Abir and Ismail to be orphans, destroying their future. And now they wanted to hold them accountable for their hatred. The injustice of it, Nora thought.

Jacob waited, respecting her silence. They stood together, surrounded by people and their trembling conversations, watching the injured and the corpses emerge from the bomb site.

"Leave me alone. Arrest me. Do whatever you want," she muttered.

Jacob didn't answer. He just disappeared into the crowd, leaving her disconcerted. Nora thought the man would insist that she give herself up, but he had barely put up a fight.

She searched for Marion and saw her deep in the crowd. She hadn't changed. She was still pretty, arrogant, sure of herself. Marion always seemed to know what she wanted and how to get it. But she was also still brilliantly intelligent, the best student in class. She had never hesitated, never allowed herself to be intimidated. Her looks had made her believe that the world belonged to her and that she could have anything she wanted. Nothing could stop her.

Nora still wondered how she'd been allowed her to be her friend, her, the daughter of immigrants, even though she'd been born in Paris. The truth was that was being Marion's friend that had given her the strength to flout her upbringing, to break the rules, to dare to be free and to say no. Marion always said that the only people who were free where those who could say no. And she had said no to the rules, to the traditions and religion of her parents. She had said no and put herself in a no man's land, though she intimately enjoyed her freedom, a freedom she paid for with loneliness. She didn't belong to her community anymore. She was alone.

It hurt that Marion treated her with so much disdain, as if their friendship had meant nothing. She treasured her memories of high school, the years where Marion taught her many things, though the friendship had been one-sided. People were just circumstances in Marion's life. She wondered if her friend had ever loved anyone, and decided she probably hadn't. Poor Abir had fallen in love as only a teenager can, completely surrendering himself to it with blind confidence. Yes, poor Abir, who she was sure was still wounded by Marion's disdain, who couldn't understand how that goddess had seduced him only to reject him later. That rejection had plunged him into bitterness.

This was the same Abir they'd trained to hate, to become a soldier in a war against the West, and who now savored his triumph in sowing terror and shedding blood. Nora was sure that his show of force was also intended for Marion. He knew that she would recognize his voice and that even if she hadn't loved him, she would at least fear him. Marion would realize what he was capable of. She had belittled him, telling him he would never be anything, and now she, like so many millions of Westerners, trembled under his power.

"Stand back. You're blocking the paramedics from doing their jobs," she heard a police officer say, and she moved away.

She decided to call her mother. She was afraid for her. If that man was telling the truth, they would be arrested soon. Her father could bear it, he might even enjoy being converted into a martyr. But her mother … her mother would be frightened. She wasn't capable of lying, and what she said would be enough to put away the whole family. She had to save her, to prevent her from being interrogated. Yes, her mother was the weakest link. Her father would assume the police would leave his wife alone. She was just a woman. And women might see and hear, but they keep their mouths shut.

*Brussels.*
*Nora and Fatima*

She got away from the bomb site and when she got to a quiet street, she called her mother.

"We have to see each other."

"I can't, your father isn't well."

"I wouldn't ask you if it wasn't important. It's not for me, it's for both your sakes—tell that to Father."

"Tell him what?" Fatima asked, not understanding her daughter.

"That you have to see me, that it's about something that affects the both of you, not just me. Tell him, Mother. Please."

"But you already know he forbids me from seeing you. If he finds out we're talking ... you know what he's like!"

"Yes, I know. But we can't let his foolishness stop us from talking. Tell him, Mother. I'll be waiting for you at my apartment."

She walked to the metro station. She had to get home before her mother arrived.

**"W**here are you, Jacob? Ariel needs you at the meeting."
Maoz's voice sounded serious through the phone.

"I'm at the site of the explosion."

"What are you doing there? We need you here."

"I think I'd be more useful working on my computer."

"What you think isn't relevant right now, you have to do this. It's important, Jacob. They're making decisions you should know about."

Maoz hung up. Jacob knew that he couldn't get out of following orders. But he would have to convince them to give him some leeway. He could do more than attend meetings, if they let him. For the moment, he obeyed.

"We're going to question the Adoum family," Louise announced as soon as he came into the meeting room.

"I still think we should wait a little longer," said Alba.

"I agree, you should wait," Jacob reiterated.

"Wait for what? We've already argued about this, Ms. Fernández. And Mr. Baudin, are you sure that it's Abir Nasr's voice? If you are, we must follow that lead and arrest the people closest to him," Louise retorted.

"Jacob, with the exception of Alba, we all agree that we have to act," Austin intervened.

"Waiting is a kind of acting," Jacob argued.

"You all know as well as I do that in intelligence operations, you have to leave the suspects room for movement. If you arrest the Adoum family, Abir Nasr will disappear," Alba insisted.

"We can't stand idly by waiting for something to happen that apparently only you know about," Louise interjected, glaring at them both.

"I just spoke to Abir's cousin," Jacob said. "I think she's closer to cooperating with us. I can't guarantee it, but that's the impression she gave me. She's scared. She's struggling between loyalty to her family and her conscience," he explained, hoping she would be more patient.

"You should have consulted us first," Louise reproached him. "But we can't just sit here while that woman makes up her mind."

"I'd like to know if she called anyone after talking to me," Jacob said.

"Let's find out right now." Louise left the room and returned 10 minutes later. "We're going to listen to a recording," she announced.

They heard the phone conversation between Nora and her mother.

"We've got her!" Jacob exclaimed.

"Maybe, I'm not sure." Louise said cautiously.

"You don't catch fish on the first cast. That woman is worried. She's scared for her family," Alba said.

"Have you bugged her apartment?" Maoz asked.

"Yes, but Fatima Adoum hasn't arrived yet," Louise replied.

"Then we just have to wait for her to get there and listen to the conversation between mother and daughter," Austin concluded.

Louise had to reluctantly agree.

Fatima was unable to lie to her husband when he asked her why she was going out.

Jamal usually went to his shop early, an hour before they opened, but that morning, like so many other people, he'd stayed home to watch the news. He had woken at six and after dressing he'd sat in his armchair flicking the channels until he got to the International Channel. He kept looking at his watch impatiently, waiting for the news that hadn't come yet.

Fatima served him breakfast. At exactly 8 a.m., the presenters of the news program made an announcement that she didn't understand because it was in English, but she was surprised to see her husband smile. She stayed silent and didn't dare ask why. She hovered in the doorway to the living room watching the screen. Then they showed the images.

"A tram was derailed because of an explosion," Jamal explained to his wife. "There are probably many injuries and deaths."

Fatima fearfully ventured to ask about Ismail. He hadn't come home since the day before. But Jamal told her to shut up while he translated what he heard.

"The police and the emergency services are heading to the area. They don't want to say what caused the explosion yet." Jamal seemed to be talking to himself.

"An accident? Is it an accident?" Fatima asked, frightened.

Her husband looked at her with contempt and ordered her to do the housework. She lowered her head, left the room and went to the kitchen in search of a tiny radio. She turned it on low so her husband wouldn't yell at her. It was Jamal's, and he didn't allow her to use it.

In the middle of the morning, when Noura called her, Fatima decided to ask her husband permission to meet her daughter.

"No! I forbid you from seeing that degenerate! We don't have a daughter!"

"Jamal, she ... she's scared. She says she needs to talk to me, that it's about our family, not her, that she has something to tell me. Let me go, Jamal. If it weren't important, Noura wouldn't have dared to call us."

"Dared? Didn't she dare show up here two days ago? You let her in! You let her see Abir. You put him in danger and it's that degenerate's fault. May Allah protect him so you don't have to regret anything happening to him."

"But Jamal, I ... I don't understand. What could happen to him? Noura would never hurt him. She is loyal to the family and she loves her cousin."

"She doesn't respect anyone or anything!" he shouted.

"Don't say that. She respects you, Jamal, and she respects her brother and her cousins."

"How can you still defend her, woman? Don't you understand the evil things she has done?"

"Jamal, I'm begging you to let me go see her. She has something important to tell us. She ... she was scared the other day, and that's why she came here."

"And disturbed Abir's peace."

"Noura wants to help, that's all. Let me go."

Jamal was quiet, his gaze lost in the images on the TV. Maybe Noura did know something. Maybe she'd be able to warn them. But what? Nobody knew the man in the video was Abir. Nobody. Not even the group of men who appeared at the end of the video. They had all covered their faces, without even an inch of skin left exposed. But somehow his daughter had known and burst into his home to point at Abir.

"I don't know what that crazy woman could tell you. Go, but be wary, Fatima. She's your daughter, but she's not to be trusted. She has chosen to turn her back on who she is. I hope this doesn't cause us any problems."

Fatima rushed out of the apartment before her husband could change his mind. She had been surprised that he hadn't objected more strongly. Maybe Jamal was scared too. Scared of what he knew. Scared of what could happen to Abir. He wasn't fooling her. Even though Jamal never consulted her or shared any of his worries with her, especially not about the things he said were only for men, she knew that his beliefs had become an obsession. He wanted to punish the infidels, to make them suffer, to humiliate them. He wouldn't rest, he often said, until the day they were on their knees begging for compassion that they would never receive.

*

Louise had deployed a discreet operation around Nora Adoum's building. One of her men alerted them when Fatima entered the door. From that moment on, the microphones planted in the apartment would pick up whatever was said between them.

Nora opened the door and hugged her mother. They let it last longer than usual.

"I made some coffee."

"I don't want anything, just tell me what's going on. Your call worried me. I told your father that I was coming to see you."

"And he let you come?"

"Yes."

"He's scared."

"Scared? No, why would he be?" Fatima's voice made it clear that she at least was.

"Because of everything that's happening. Abir, Mother, Abir is responsible. You know it, and Father does too."

"Don't say that, sweetheart, you know it's not true. How can you accuse your cousin of such a terrible thing? Abir is a good Muslim, just like your father and your brother Farid."

"Abir wasn't like that before, Mother. It's Father and Farid's fault for sending him away with Sheikh Mohsin. I know that man turned Abir into a fanatic."

"Noura, how can you say that!"

"Mother, why won't you stop lying to yourself? Why do you insist on not seeing or hearing or thinking?"

Fatima stayed silent. She felt exhausted. Not seeing, not hearing and not thinking wasn't as easy as her daughter thought.

"I recognized Abir's voice, and you did too. Don't try and tell me you didn't."

"Noura, please, don't say anything."

"Where is he hiding? Two days ago he was with you. What about now?"

"He just came to visit us, to talk to your father. I don't know where he is."

"Right. They wouldn't tell you anyway."

"Your father doesn't know either, Noura. Abir, well, Abir never tells us anything when he leaves. Not now, not ever. He appears and disappears, and we never even know when he's going to come."

"But Father has to know something."

"No, he doesn't know anything."

"But he must have some way of getting in touch with him."

"No, Noura, he doesn't."

"They're going to arrest all of us, Mother. Father and you and me, maybe even Farid in Paris. They're looking for Abir, and they think we know where he is."

"But that's not possible! We haven't done anything!"

"Tell Father. Tell him to find Abir, to hand him over, or it will bring tragedy to all of us."

"But your father is innocent!" Fatima's voice broke in fear.

"We're Abir's family, and he carried out these attacks!"

"No! No! I forbid you from accusing your cousin."

"Mother, you know the truth as well as I do. Father has spent his whole life thinking you're a simple woman, but I know you're not, even though you're submissive."

"You're scaring me, my darling."

"I'm scared too. Talk to Father. I don't know how long they'll wait to question us about Abir, but they're going to do it."

"That can't happen, Noura."

"It's going to happen, Mother, believe me."

*

"Congratulations," Austin said, turning to Jacob.

"You were right, it's Abir Nasr," Ariel said.

"Impressive," added the CIA agent.

The praise made Jacob uncomfortable. He hadn't been looking for applause or to be told he was right. He had just been sure. It was the image carved into his memory, the teenager screaming *I will find you! I'll kill you all!*

Weiss patted him on the back and even Maoz let a smile flicker across his face. The veteran agent noticed Jacob's discomfort.

"It's time to do what Nora Adoum warned her mother about and arrest them." Louise announced.

"No, no, that's not a good idea," Jacob protested.

"Why not?" she replied impatiently.

"We need more bait to reel Abir Nasr in. Nora's mother will tell her husband what her daughter said. Jamal Adoum will start getting nervous for sure. Whether he knows where Abir Nasr is or not, he will try to get a message to him. He has to let him know he's under suspicion. Then, we can find out who else is working for Sheikh Mohsin, the head of the Circle," Jacob explained with exaggerated patience, irritated by the director's stubbornness.

"Your reasoning isn't bad for someone with no experience as a field agent," Maoz remarked.

"Jacob is right. What we have to do now is follow the thread that will take us to Abir Nasr," Alba said, looking over at him. "Louise, if you arrest the Adoum family, you will have nothing, just a few accomplices, but he will vanish."

"Listen," Louise said, her voice was as cold as ice, "we have terrorists threatening to attack us every single day until we accept their conditions, but you all think we should allow them to continue with the slaughter so we can get to the leader and his instigator, Sheikh Mohsin. Do I understand correctly?"

"Louise, we each have a job to do." Alba sounded like a patient professor speaking to a student. "You are responsible for the safety of your country, so you have to keep looking for Abir Nasr. I admit that it's a risk not arresting his relatives, but if we do, we could lose Nasr forever."

"So you propose that we just let the blood keep running in the streets," she responded.

"Aren't you being a little melodramatic?" Alba couldn't hide her irritation any longer. "Do you think we're a bunch of amoral people who don't care about the fate of innocent citizens? This is a high stakes game, all or nothing, and there's no room for hesitation."

"I will have to consult with my government and explain what we have and what you all are proposing, though I warn you, I will be recommending that we immediately arrest the Adoum family. We must also ask our French colleagues to arrest Farid, the oldest son," Louise concluded, deeply irritated.

Ariel spoke up in a conciliatory tone.

"I understand, Louise. It's not easy playing the waiting game with a terrorist knowing that it could mean more attacks. It's a dilemma that we've all faced at some point."

"No, I've never faced the dilemma of letting a terrorist keep killing people just to find clues about other terrorists. What you are proposing is morally unacceptable," Louise concluded, standing up to show the meeting was over.

"I have a plan, but I need a little time," Jacob interjected.

"A plan?" Austin looked at him with interest.

"I have to talk to Tel Aviv. I need them to help me get some information, and depending on that information, we might be able to catch Abir Nasr very soon."

"What is the plan?" Louise asked.

"I'm sorry, I can't explain it yet. You will all have to trust me," Jacob told them.

"Trust you? Why should we do that? No, I'm not giving my blind support. I want to know what you want to do, why, and how. If not, don't count on us." Louise was livid.

"How much time do you need, Jacob?" Ariel asked.

"A few hours. Ms. Moos, please, let me tell you what I would do in your shoes. I would keep listening to the Adoum family's conversations. I would follow them everywhere and make a map of their contacts. That would be very useful to us, though not enough."

"Well, if it's not enough, why are you asking me for it?"

"Because it's important, but not our main goal. I'm not going to ask you to trust me. You don't know me, and you have no reason to do so, but at least give me a few hours to draft my plan. A few hours, Ms. Moos, that is all," Jacob implored her.

"No. There are security protocols that are unnegotiable. We now know that Nora Adoum believes she recognized Abir Nasr's voice, which means we have to arrest her and her family. The conversation we just heard between her and her mother suggests that Jamal Adoum might have information on how to find his nephew. So, thanks to you, Jacob, we now have some certainty, and my obligation is to act on all the information gathered."

Turner and Weiss looked at each other. They weren't going to bother contradicting the head of Belgian security, but Jacob could read on their faces that they had their own plans.

Maoz tried to get Louise to reconsider her decision one more time.

"Ms. Moos, if the terrorists stick to their pattern, they won't carry out another attack until tomorrow. I think we can take a few hours to let Jacob activate his plan, it's just a few hours."

"You can't be sure that the terrorists aren't going to act at any moment!" she retorted.

"I think you should give us the chance to try," the veteran Mossad agent insisted.

"Louise, please. They're asking for a few hours, that's all," Alba interjected.

Louise Moos tried to hide her displeasure at the Spanish woman's insistence on calling her by her first name. She turned to Jacob.

"OK. But I want you to inform me of every step you're going to take."

"I can't for now, it's not possible," Jacob said, unwilling to lie to her. "Give me some time and I'll explain everything. I have to figure out this puzzle. I think I have almost all the pieces, but I need to put them together."

Louise didn't answer. She had risen in her political career by strictly complying with the rules. She had always disagreed with people who argued that strict compliance with the rules sometimes prevented the desired results. She would rather let the criminal go free if the price for catching him was breaking the law. She knew that there were those in the security services who didn't appreciate her, because she had held to account people who were unscrupulous with law enforcement. For Louise Moos, there were no shortcuts. And here these other agents were determined to dodge protocol in the hope of arresting Abir Nasr. Collaborating with the CIA had always been an uphill battle for her, and as for Alba Fernández, she felt an uncontrollable dislike towards her. Her relations with the Israeli agents were even worse. She didn't like Jews—it was something she knew she could never admit to anyone. However, Jacob Baudin was different. At least he didn't seem Jewish like Ariel Weiss or Maoz Levin.

"It's now noon. You have until 9 p.m., Mr. Baudin."

She left the room without another word.

"She's a very difficult woman," Austin observed.

"Yes, too rigid for the profession she has chosen," Alba muttered.

"I'm going to the office," Jacob announced.

"Are you really not going to tell us what you're thinking of doing?" Turner demanded.

"Yes, of course, but not right now. I need to call Tel Aviv and work on it alone before I can explain anything."

"Well then, get to work. Let's go to the office," Ariel ordered.

Jacob left the meeting room followed by Ariel and Maoz. It didn't bother him that Maoz was there, maybe because he was careful with his words and didn't waste time on useless arguments. And he had helped him convince Louise for the chance to try his plan.

When they got to the office, Ariel turned to Jacob.

"Now you tell me what you've got and what you're looking for."

"Not yet. It could be nothing."

"OK." He frowned and he left.

Jacob sat in front of a computer that he knew had a secure connection. Maoz asked if he could help.

"You could ask Dor if they have the computer from the cardiology unit at the Makassed Hospital in Beirut yet, or if they've at least been able to clone the program."

Maoz nodded and went to the other end of the office.

Brussels.
*Jacob*

One hour later, Maoz touched Jacob's shoulder, finding him lost in thought in front of the computer screen.

"They've got it."

"They have?"

"Yes, but it wasn't easy. A team managed to steal the cardiologist's computer, and they even swiped a few extras, just in case. Dor is confident you'll have it within a few hours."

"They didn't need to steal the other computers, I just need the one the cardiologists use to control their patients' pacemakers."

"Right, but it would have been suspicious if only one computer disappeared, so they took seven, plus a bunch of medical materials, and broke open the safe in the administrative office. Jacob, you should know that our people took a huge risk."

"How did they do it?"

"With the invaluable help of a group of criminals with expertise in impossible robberies."

"Wow!"

"People have risked their lives so you could have that damn computer. I hope you can make use of it before tonight. In the meantime, they're going to send you all the information they found. They've already hacked it. Call Palm Tree House. Efraim will explain how you can access it all."

"I'm not sure my theory is right."

"Well, it had better be. You think it's easy going to Beirut and stealing from one of its most prestigious hospitals?" Maoz asked, tension edging into his voice.

"No, I don't. But I never said that what I'm theorizing is a sure thing, just that … well, that I had an idea and we should see if it's feasible. I need a little more time, Maoz. I'll need to talk to Dor later as well."

*Brussels. The terrorist's house.*
*Zaim*

Zaim Jabib was still in shock over his wife having voluntarily put on a suicide belt to carry out a massacre. He wondered how Nashira could have obeyed Abir's order. When she left the house, he thought she would head straight to the nearest police officer on the street, show him the belt and explain to him that she didn't want to die.

He couldn't take his eyes off the television screen, the images of the horror she had caused playing over and over again.

Ghalil came over to him.

"We're leaving."

"Yes, that's for the best. You should go. I never want to see any of you again."

Suddenly, he felt Ghalil's hands close around his neck. He tried to defend himself, but Ghalil was stronger than him and little by little he sank into the pitch black of nothingness.

"All set," Ghalil said to Abir, who'd just come into the room.

"You sure he's dead?"

"Yes."

"Then set the timer on the bomb. We have to get out of here."

Ghalil double-checked that Zaim had stopped breathing. Then he propped him up in a chair and fastened an explosives belt around him with a timer programmed to go off in half an hour.

"OK, we've already wiped all our prints, even though I doubt they'd be able to find a single one after he goes off. I put in all the explosives you ordered, so the blast will definitely go beyond these walls. More people will die, at least in the two neighboring apartments. That'll drive the police crazy."

Abir shrugged. He couldn't care less if the neighbors from the apartments next door were killed by the bomb. So far, the plan was going smoothly. The whole point was to plant terror and death all over the city, and they were succeeding. They left the building and went in opposite directions. They would meet again an hour later.

Police officers were everywhere, but they paid no attention to the old man slowly moving two large bags with rolls of cloth poking out. Nor did they pay any attention to the man in a suit with a briefcase who could well have been an employee from any bank.

The old man shuffled along until he reached the street that marked the invisible border between upper and lower Molenbeek.

Entering lower Molenbeek meant going into another reality. It was a world of newly arrived immigrants, of boys with nothing to do but lurk in the streets, of being able to buy any drug imaginable and hear the most radical ideas on Islam. It was a nightmare for the Belgian government.

The old man's destination was a flea market on those streets. The owner of a second-hand clothes stall perked up when he saw him arrive and beckoned to another man who seemed very interested in the shirts folded on the table.

"I brought a few things to sell, Abdel. I hope you can give me a good price," the old man said.

The man nodded and politely asked him to move to one side while he examined the clothes on offer. As he did this, he chatted with the old man and watched for potential customers drifting by the stall. After half an hour, they reached a deal with a handshake, and a few bills along with a bag passed between them.

Meanwhile, the young man in the suit had sat down in a café and was looking vaguely around him. When he saw the old man pass by, he got up, paid for his coffee, and casually walked behind him.

The journey wasn't long. Their route led them to a building that was both ugly and nondescript. Two women in hijabs were arguing angrily in the entryway.

The old man went in without even glancing at them. The young man in the suit stopped outside to tie his shoe, and after a few seconds went through the same door. Two minutes later, they both entered a warehouse full of clothes piled high on rickety shelves and even on the floor. There was only one door into the warehouse, the one they had just come through, and there were no windows to the outside.

"Any news, Ghalil?" Abir asked as he watched his lieutenant shed his disguise.

"Abdel promised me that everything we needed was here. It's a safe place, as you can see."

They both examined every corner of the warehouse, which was really just a medium-sized room. Abdel had arranged a couple of mattresses in one corner, plus a table, two chairs, a mini-fridge, a television and a transistor radio on a crate. A door led to a tiny bathroom with a battered sink.

Ghalil opened a box on the other side of the warehouse. He smiled when he saw what was inside.

"Is everything there?" Abir wanted to know.

"Yes, Abdel never lets us down. If you look closely, you'll see the walls are soundproof," he said, satisfied.

"They better be, Ghalil," he replied as he switched on the radio.

"There has been an explosion in upper Molenbeek. The cause is still unknown. It is feared that there are victims." The voice of the announcer sounded distressed. "The area has been cordoned off. The police are already investigating the cause.

Ambulances are on their way. The city still hasn't recovered from the impact of this morning's attack."

"They have no idea what they're in for. They're going to experience hell on earth," Abir said to himself.

B enjamin Holz had just announced to the viewers that another explosion had taken place. They were waiting to connect to a mobile unit that was arriving on the scene.

Andrew stayed seated in one corner of the set. A few minutes before, he had spoken to Helen, asking her to come back to the studio. But she had insisted her place was on the street. "You know I'm always the one who goes out on location, and Benjamin directs it all from the studio. For a journalist, there's nothing more important than being where the news is happening," she'd argued.

*She's right,* Andrew thought to himself, even though it irritated him. What had captivated him about Helen was her passion for what she did. Her first priority was journalism, and if she had any strength or desire left after that, she would show interest in everything else, including him.

He had to admit that the viewers appreciated her being the one to report on location. They probably didn't even notice the bags under her eyes darkening her face; she looked beautiful regardless, though he knew her appearance didn't matter to her. "I'm committed to telling them what happened, I'm not a contestant in a beauty pageant," she would often say when the channel reminded her that image is a big part of news. "Of course, the image of the news is important, but not mine, I just say what happened." That's how Helen was. Perhaps she got away with it because she was secure in the knowledge that her look was on par with her talent.

Benjamin decided with Helen that she would stay at the site of the tram bombing, and Noël Morin would go to upper Molenbeek where the explosion had happened. Helen accepted on one condition: if it turned out to be another terrorist attack, she would go too.

*Brussels.*
*Mossad Office*

A riel hung up the phone. Maoz watched him expectantly while Jacob kept his eyes on the computer screen next door.

"That was Louise Moos. She's furious. She was practically blaming us for the new explosion."

"How many dead?" Maoz asked.

"So far, a woman and her daughter, a retired couple, and two young men. Six deaths in total, and many injuries. The explosion happened in the apartment of a Muslim couple. They were well liked by the neighbors, a perfect marriage. He worked at an engineering company and she worked in a nursery school. But it would seem that neither of them went to work this morning."

"Maybe it wasn't such a perfect marriage after all," Maoz observed.

"What?" Ariel frowned at his colleague.

"What if the suicide bomber this morning was that likeable woman, and the second explosion was caused by her charming husband."

"We don't know what happened yet, Maoz. We only know that on the tram a woman yelled, 'Allah is great!' and then caused the explosion. As for the apartment explosion, Louise didn't give me much information. I hope Jacob can tell us now once and for all what he's working on, otherwise that woman

309

is going to take us out of the game. I'll talk to Austin Turner. Maybe he can get Louise to give Jacob more time."

Just then, Jacob looked up from the computer and shouted, "I've got it!"

The two agents went over to look.

"What do you have?" Weiss asked.

"The key that will force Abir Nasr out of his hiding place," Jacob answered.

Ariel and Maoz waited for him to explain.

"It wasn't easy. This morning Nora Adoum was talking to a woman. A woman who was bothered, or more likely startled, by Nora's presence. They argued and it was obvious they knew each other. They spoke as if they had some unfinished business."

"And who was the woman?" Ariel wanted to know.

"Marion Cloutier," Jacob responded with a satisfied smile.

"OK, so we have a Marion Cloutier, a friend of Nora Adoum. What else?" Ariel became irritated. It seemed like Jacob was taking pleasure in keeping them in the dark.

"I'm going to Paris right now to talk to her sister, Lissette Cloutier. I managed to track her down. I don't know if she'll want to talk to me, but I have to try."

"So you're going to Paris. Thanks for letting us know," Ariel responded sourly.

"I need her to tell me a few things before I talk to Nora Adoum again."

"What if she doesn't want to talk to you?" Maoz asked.

"Well, she doesn't know I'm coming to see her. If I catch her by surprise, it will be harder for her to refuse. I also found the address and phone numbers of two of Marion's classmates from high school."

"Why is this Marion Cloutier so important?" Weiss insisted.

"I have a feeling she could lead us to Abir Nasr."

"Well that is certainly new. And why?" Maoz was intrigued.

"It's a triangle. Nora, Marion and Abir have a shared past. They went to the same high school."

"Right, but they left their teenage years behind them a long time ago. People don't always keep up their friendships from back then. Nora is Abir Nasr's cousin, but Cloutier? Has she stayed in touch with the two cousins?"

"I don't think so. As I said, when Nora went up to Marion this morning, she was surprised. She didn't want to talk to her. I couldn't hear the argument, but they were both agitated. My guess is that they both recognized Abir's voice in the video. In fact, I'm almost sure of it," Jacob explained, sharing the information in small doses. "That's why I'm going to Paris. Lissette Cloutier could tell us many things."

"She'll probably refuse to talk to you. Why would she want to?" Ariel asked.

"I'm not saying she'll want to, just that I'm going to try."

"So this Marion hasn't stayed in touch with Nasr or Nora?" Maoz asked.

"I already said, I don't think so," Jacob answered, glancing at his watch.

"I'll inform Orit Singer that you're heading to Paris. You're going to need her help," Ariel said in a tone that left no doubt in Jacob's mind that it was an order.

*Paris.*
*Lissette*

When Jacob arrived in Paris, Orit was waiting for him at the station. He wondered how she had recognized him, considering they had never seen each other before. But she headed straight over to him, and when she reached out her hand, he was surprised by her strength. She was at least in her 60s, but she had aged well. She wasn't pretty, Jacob thought, but she had that certain appeal of a woman whose life hadn't been ordinary. She was about 5'6" and slender with shoulder-length brown hair peppered with gray. Under her coat she wore gray pants and a camel-colored cashmere sweater.

"I will accompany you to see Lissette Cloutier," she informed him.

"I think I can handle it alone. I'd feel more comfortable doing things my way."

"And what is your way?"

"Well, I think it would scare her less if I went alone. If we both show up, she might refuse to talk."

"OK, but I'll wait for you nearby. She lives on Rue Sainte-Marthe in the 10th arrondissement, and works at an art gallery right by her apartment," Orit said. "Let's hope your intuition yields results."

"Don't you follow your intuition?"

Orit smiled as she fixed him with a steely look.

"Gut feelings have saved my life a few times. But intuition needs to be rationalized. Have you done that?"

"I think so. Did you have any time to do that? Were you able to find out anything else about her?"

"A few things. They gave us an hour, the time it took for your train to arrive from Brussels. Let's see. The gallery she works in is about to close because they don't have many customers. But we're about to find out a lot more. Now, I'm going to wire you up with a microphone that will transmit the whole conversation to me. We'll be recording it."

"OK. Anything else?"

"That's enough for now."

\*

A glass door allowed a glimpse of a small space accented by bright colors from the different paintings hanging on the walls. A few sculptures on high tables were dotted around the room, and Jacob could see a woman absorbed in a newspaper. The woman, who must have been in her 40s, was dressed casually but elegantly. She was attractive, and very Parisian.

Orit waited for him outside, a few meters from the venue where she could watch.

"Good afternoon." Jacob's voice made the woman look up.

"Good afternoon. Can I help you?"

"Yes. Are you Lissette Cloutier?"

"Yes, and you are …?"

"I know your sister and her friend, Nora Adoum."

Lissette tried to stay expressionless, but a small tic in her right eye revealed her shock and worry.

"And you came here to tell me you know my sister?"

"No, I came so you can tell me about the relationships between your sister, Ms. Adoum, and Abir Nasr."

"But who are you? I don't know what you're talking about."

"Yes, you do know what I'm talking about. You're Marion's older sister, her only sister in fact. You always protected her. Then she set out on her own path far from Paris. Your sister's traveled a lot, London, Brussels, Berlin, Shanghai, New York. But I'm not here about any of that. I only want to discuss the relationship she had with Nora Adoum and Abir Nasr."

"How dare you! Get out of here or I'll call the police."

"Fine, I'm sure the Sécurité will be very interested in interrogating you."

"Me? You're insane!"

"No, Miss Cloutier, I'm not insane, I'm collaborating with the team that is investigating the attacks in Brussels."

"And what does that have to do with me and my sister?" she answered in a tone charged with confusion and fear.

"Your sister met Nora and Abir in high school. She and Nora were friends. I want to know everything about the relationship between the three of them."

"I'm calling the police right now," she threatened without much conviction.

"Listen. If you do that, your sister will have to publicly explain her relationship with Abir Nasr and, as far as I know, she hasn't yet gone to the authorities to inform them she knows him."

"But what are you saying! This is insane! Are you accusing Abir Nasr of being behind the attacks in Brussels? The newspapers are saying that the police are investigating, that they don't know who's behind it all, except that it's an Islamist terrorist group called the Circle," she answered, waving her hand at a page of the newspaper she was reading.

"Indeed, Ms. Cloutier, Abir Nasr is a member of the Circle. And if you're about to lose your job, it'll be difficult to find another one if your name appears in the newspapers connected to the Circle."

"But I'm not connected to the Circle!"

"Well, that all depends on how you look at it. You're Marion's sister and she was a friend of Nora and Abir. Someone could easily assume that you and your sister know more than you claim."

"You're threatening me!"

"Yes, Miss Cloutier, I'm threatening you. You have two choices: either answer my questions or your photo is going to be printed in the newspapers connected to the Circle and the attacks in Brussels."

"Get out of here!"

"Are you sure?"

"I have nothing to do with what happened in Brussels, or with Abir, or with my sister! It's been years, many years, since we've even spoken. She chose her path and I chose another. We're not in touch. Marion has always done her own thing. The rest of us are just rungs on her ladder. She uses people and then she tosses them aside when they aren't useful to her anymore. She left me in the dust too. Every time I've asked her for help, she's just ignored me. I'm not part of her life," she explained bitterly.

Jacob had managed to make Lissette nervous, pushing her to talk and tell him precise information without knowing it.

"OK, I'll assume you're telling the truth. But I need to know what Marion's relationship was like with Nora and with Abir. We're not asking for much, Miss Cloutier."

"Who are you?" she repeated, trying to stay calm.

"I already told you. I'm collaborating with the team that is investigating the attacks in Brussels. I can stop them from bothering you, or I can go the other way and get them to mark you as a person of interest in the investigation. Your life will become difficult, and you'll never find a job again. I think you understand."

"Let me see some ID. Give me some proof that you're a cop."

"I'm not a cop. You'll just have to trust me."

"No, I don't trust you. Why would I? I don't know who you are or what you want, I don't know anything!" Lissette was becoming distressed.

Right then, the door opened and Orit walked in.

"Good afternoon, Ms. Cloutier."

Jacob looked at her, annoyed. They'd agreed she wouldn't intervene.

"What do you want?" Lissette asked with an edge of panic.

"I'd like to remind you that you have many reasons to collaborate. You're not exactly an unimpeachable woman. Ali Amrani, your boyfriend, is a known drug dealer in Paris's bohemian circles. And you stupidly let him use you. Remember when they arrested you for possessing a pound of hash? That's what happens when you get involved with certain people. It's not so strange that your sister Marion didn't want to get mixed up with you and your boyfriend when you turned to her for help."

"It's been years since we've seen each other. She won't even pick up the phone when I call," Lissette admitted.

"Look, if you don't cooperate, your photo will appear in every newspaper reporting that you yourself were arrested for trafficking drugs and that your boyfriend is a known dealer who has been in prison where, by the way, he met some Islamist extremists—quite the story!"

"Ali isn't a fanatic! He has no interest in religion. Everyone knows that."

"Do you believe that? Like my colleague said, everything depends on how you look at it. And now, let's not waste any more time. Are you going to answer our questions, yes or no?"

Orit's hard tone sent Lissette over the edge.

"Get out of here!" she shouted hysterically.

"Fine. Within 10 minutes, you and your boyfriend will be arrested," Orit replied.

"What do you want me to tell you?" Lissette surrendered under the insistent harshness of the woman's implacable stare.

"Tell us about the relationship between Marion, Nora, and Abir. That's all. Do you think you can do that?"

"Marion has always been a leader. She studied, got good grades, and was the best in her class. She was brilliant, ambitious, sure of herself and attractive. She was the prettiest girl in school and all the boys were in love with her. But Marion used them, did whatever she wanted with them, and they did whatever she wanted. My sister was always bold, never intimidated by anything. When she wanted something, she got it. Her shallowness was just a mask for her ambition. She had her path mapped out. She's always pushed aside everyone she couldn't use to get her way. That's what she did to me. She didn't care about seeing me ruined. She's always run from everyone else's problems, especially if they could make her look bad."

"Yes, as you said, she doesn't want anything to do with you," Jacob remarked.

"Nora was her best friend. Well, she was more like her servant, always at Marion's beck and call. They were inseparable for the last two years of high school. Nora did whatever my sister asked. For Nora, being accepted by the most popular girl in high school was like winning a prize. She disobeyed her parents for Marion. She took off her hijab as soon as she left the house, wore lipstick and miniskirts that my sister lent her. She even let Marion change her name from Noura to Nora. All just to please her. As for Abir, that poor guy was in love with my sister. He followed her like a dog, willingly enduring Marion's contempt. Some weekends he would stake out the doorway of our building just to get a glimpse of her when she came out, and Marion wouldn't even look at him."

"But something more must have happened between them," Jacob insisted.

"No, Marion never cared about them, although I think one time something did happen. She jumped on the chance to throw a party at our apartment when I was away one weekend. She told me about it after. Apparently, she invited a bunch of her friends from school and Nora showed up with Abir. Nora's father was very strict and didn't let her out unless she was accompanied by her cousin. At that party, my sister had a really perverted idea. She turned off the lights and had everyone pair up in the dark with the person they were closest to, whoever that happened to be. And everything was allowed, I mean, they could have whatever sexual experience they wanted. Marion happened to pair up with Abir. When she told me about it, she laughed. It was the boy's first time—he lost his virginity to her. He thought that made her his girlfriend, that they would get married, but Marion snubbed him even more. She liked humiliating him, telling him that she had recognized him by his stench, that he had had no idea what to do with a girl. She turned him into the laughingstock of the whole school, but even through all that he was still in love with her, convinced that if they had had a sexual experience, it was because she loved him. Abir was very naïve.

"Right before they graduated, something bad happened. Nora's father saw his daughter in the street right outside the school. Marion told me about it, but I don't remember all the details. I think Nora wasn't wearing her hijab. She was in a miniskirt and was wearing makeup. The man almost died from shock. He tried to lock her in their apartment. Well, he actually decided his daughter was practically a prostitute and that she could only recover her good name if they married her off. They found a husband for her, I think the son of some friend, but Nora escaped. She came to our house. Marion convinced me we'd be getting in deep shit, and that the best thing to do was take her to a lawyer. Since she was a minor, the authorities took her to a youth home and she was able to get out of being forced to marry. She didn't get out of that place until she turned 18, when school ended.

"Nora came back to our house, thinking we would take her in, but Marion refused. She told her their friendship was over, that everyone had to find their own life, that friendships from high school were *passé*, and that she never wanted to see her again. She brushed her off. Nora had to realized that Marion wasn't her friend. She suffered. I don't think Nora went back to her parents, they couldn't force her to anymore. Abir showed up at our apartment to talk to Marion, insisting they had a future, that they should get married. She treated him terribly and that was the last time they saw each other. He told her that one day he would be an important man who would go further than her, that she would end up throwing herself at his feet and regret ever having rejected him. She laughed and threw him out. I assume they never saw each other again.

"Marion decided to leave me too. She met a boy who had a job in England and she went with him and started studying and working in London. They got married, they got divorced, and then she married the assistant of a Belgian MEP. She lived in Brussels for a while, and seemed to have settled down, but then she met a businessman, a rich man, and left her second husband. The businessman gave her an apartment near the Grand Place, but he was married, and in the end she left him for another member of the European Parliament, a German this time, who was also married. Then she met a Canadian writer and moved to Shanghai with him. It didn't last long, and she went back to Brussels for a while. I think she was on vacation in Mallorca when she met another guy, the manager of a restaurant. She never seemed satisfied in her relationships with men. She always wanted more and more. I don't know. We fell out of touch. Everyone has their own life. Later, when I needed her, she refused to talk to me. I belong to the past, in the present there's no place for me, and especially not for my problems."

"So, Abir Nasr prophesied that one day he would be important and that she would regret rejecting him. Seems like he kept his promise," Jacob declared.

Lissette looked drained. She had spoken without looking at Jacob or Orit, as if she were reciting her memories out loud. Suddenly, she burst into tears.

Jacob reached out to take her hand, but Orit waved it away. They sat quietly while she recovered.

"What happens now?" she asked, her voice trembling with fear.

"To you, nothing. Forget we were here. Nobody will ever know," Orit assured her.

"Why should I trust you two? I don't know who you are!"

"We're nobody, Lissette, nobody. Do yourself a favor. Don't even tell your boyfriend about this conversation. It's for your own good."

"But I trust Ali."

"It's your call, but I wouldn't if I were you. Ali has a lot of friends, and it's possible one of them might be interested in knowing that you're running around talking about Abir Nasr's business, and that could cost you your life," Orit told her.

"Ali doesn't have extremist friends, I already told you he has no interest in religion," she insisted angrily.

"My dear, your boyfriend deals to anyone who can pay him or do him a favor. You're an adult, Lissette. Maybe you should start thinking for yourself. But it's up to you," Orit insisted.

Jacob turned to her.

"Lissette, it's better if you don't say anything to Ali. Your life could be put in danger. Listen to us. Forget we were here and what you told us. You're the one who will end up losing if you talk."

"Get out of here, please," she begged.

When they went out onto the street, Jacob let out a sigh of relief. Lissette's tale confirmed how important Marion was to

Abir Nasr. He now needed to set the second part of the plan in motion.

"Now what are you planning on doing?" Orit asked him.

"We will ask Marion Cloutier to be the bait to catch Abir Nasr."

"Given how Lissette described her, I don't think that's going to be easy."

"No, it's not. I'll have to make her understand that she can either collaborate or lose everything she's achieved in her life."

"Who is she, Jacob?"

"You would have found her the same way I did. Though actually, I just happened to come across Marion. If I hadn't seen Nora Adoum heading over to a woman who was watching the aftermath of the tram explosion, if I hadn't been close enough to see them arguing and read the tension on Marion's face, I never would have stumbled upon her. It was a coincidence, Orit, a huge coincidence."

Jacob took out his phone and showed her the photograph he'd taken in Brussels of Nora and Marion arguing.

Orit looked at the phone screen for a few seconds.

"Yes, I know that sometimes success or failure depends on coincidence. But tell me, what else can I do from here?"

"Exactly what you're doing. Ask them to reinforce the fence around Farid, Abir's cousin, and around his teacher, the imam Adel Allawi. I'm convinced Abir is in touch with them somehow."

"The Circle's way of operating is always the same. They don't use computers or cell phones, only letters, and in exceptional circumstances like now, letters aren't delivered in the mosque, but through staged encounters with their contacts so they don't attract any attention," Orit declared.

"Maybe chance will play in our favor again," Jacob said, smiling.

"Don't worry, we'll do our job. I'll take you to the station. We don't have much time."

As they walked along briskly, a middle-aged man approached them. Jacob tensed up, but Orit seemed calm.

"I didn't want to call you. The Belgians already know the names of the suicide bombers from today's attacks: Nashira and Zaim Jabib. They still don't have the complete list of dead and wounded.

"With the attack on the International Channel, they already have the names of all the wounded, but they still have a lot of work ahead to identify the dead. The DNA tests are still pending. The perpetrator is suspected to be a young man of Lebanese origin, a Muslim who worked in the building. They have images of him from the security cameras. He was in charge of delivering the mail and packages to all the floors. There is an image where his back can be seen before the explosion. Either he blew himself up with his own belt or he's a victim. His colleagues say he was very discreet and never talked about politics. For now, the Belgian police don't want to reveal his identity in case he was the suicide bomber, but Ariel Weiss has found a name on the list of people who worked in the building: Ismail Adoum. They're looking for more information.

"As for the latest attacks, as I mentioned, this morning's was carried out by a young woman, Nashira Jabib, and this afternoon's by her husband, Zaim Jabib, a marriage that had been considered a shining example of integration. Young and attractive, he worked as a business executive and she was a nursery teacher. Their neighbors found them to be kind and polite. They always expressed moderate opinions and lamented the bad reputation Muslims had gotten because of radicals. Both used the same kind of explosive, only in his case it seems the suicide was not voluntary. They helped him make the decision," the man reported as he walked alongside them.

"I've always said we shouldn't trust those who appear to be friends," Orit responded with a trace of irony.

"Yeah, I know, but you're not always right," the man reminded her.

"I almost always am. Danger hides where it's not obvious. Who would have suspected such a polite, friendly couple? I'll never tire of saying it—we must first investigate those who are free of any suspicion."

Jacob listened to Orit with respect. The woman was fascinating. He felt a sudden sense of pride that they belonged to the same tribe. She reminded him of his mother. They had the same determination, strength and confidence.

"Did you say Ismail Adoum?" Jacob interrupted, suddenly remembering.

"Yes. They don't know anything about him yet. Ariel wanted Orit to know and he wanted you to know too."

"Ismail Adoum! Abir Nasr sacrificed his brother! Adoum is their uncle Jamal's last name, the one who adopted them," Jacob explained.

"So it's possible that Abir Adoum or Nasr, or whatever he's called, ordered his brother to blow himself up with a suicide belt," Orit suggested.

"I think so. Ismail was Abir's younger brother, the only sibling he had left," Jacob said.

"Maybe that's why he gave up his life. The leaders have to be an example, they can't ask others to be martyrs if they're not willing to sacrifice themselves or someone in their family. Think about it," Orit added.

"I don't follow that logic," the man responded.

"If we don't think like them, we'll never be able to defeat them," his boss told him.

They arrived at the station and Jacob was able to get a train that was leaving for Brussels in 15 minutes. The day had slipped by without him noticing. He couldn't stop wondering what

Abir's next move would be. He had already produced three suicide bombers at least.

During the train ride, he spoke to Ariel and Maoz on the phone. He learned that the computer with the coordinates of Abir's defibrillator was now in Brussels. Thinking Jacob might need help, Dor had sent another agent.

"You already know her. You'll need her to handle the computer," Maoz explained.

This wasn't a surprise to Jacob. He'd told Dor himself that he would need the help of a computer expert with medical knowledge.

The other news since he had been away was that the conflict between the security agencies and Louise Moos had intensified. Alba Fernández was driving Louise Moos up the wall, but the presence of the Israeli agents was irritating her much more.

Austin Turner had convinced his CIA bosses that either the White House had to intervene to persuade the Belgian government to tell their security chief not to rush into arresting Abir's family, or else the operation that was underway would fail.

"Turner has gambled on you, Jacob. I hope you're not wrong, or this will be the end of your career and ours," Ariel warned him.

"I never said I was totally sure," Jacob said defensively.

No, he hadn't said it, but too many people had decided to bet on his line of action. They were playing for all or nothing.

Brussels.
*Studios of the International Channel*

Makeup couldn't hide the exhaustion on Helen's face. For the past hour, she'd been sitting in the studio presenting the program. Andrew had convinced Benjamin to take a rest for a few hours. He estimated that it would still be many days before the intelligence services could find and arrest the terrorists. That is, if they were able to find them at all. The International Channel's audience had skyrocketed. People wanted to see Helen and Benjamin on screen, but they had to stop and rest from time to time.

During a commercial break, Andrew came over to Helen.

"You have to remember to rest a little too. Louise Moos thinks the terrorists won't act again until tomorrow. Paulette Fontaine and Noël Morin can take over the program."

"Right now? You know this is the best slot. In the United States, most people will be in front of the TV right now," she protested.

"But there's nothing new to report, and if you want to continue with this, you'll have to rest. Go to the hotel for a few hours, take a nap and then come back."

"What about you? Are you coming with me?"

"No. I have an important meeting. All this is costing us a lot of money, Helen. Joseph Foster and Mike King have just landed."

"God, you didn't tell me the heads of the network were all meeting in Brussels."

"We thought that given the circumstances, it was better for Joseph to come for a few days so we could talk about what we're going to do, him being the director of the International Channel. Mike, as you know, likes to micro-manage everything, and he has too many shares in the channel to stay behind in Washington. I already found some offices where we can get set up temporarily. We can't keep renting these studios from the Belgian television station. I hope we can move there in a few days."

"I guess I should feel lucky you're even telling me this," Helen told him sarcastically.

"You have your job and I have mine," he replied angrily. "Now go to the hotel. I'm not asking you, I'm telling you. We all have to save up our strength."

Helen knew when she had lost a battle. Andrew wouldn't let her go beyond what he thought she could do. As shareholder and vice president of the network, he was her boss, and that's how he was speaking to her.

"Fine. You're right. I hope you understand where I'm coming from. It's difficult for a journalist to rest in a situation like this."

"But even the best journalists are human. I recognize your calling makes you sacrifice yourself for your work, but I won't allow you or Benjamin to appear on screen looking exhausted. Fatigue will lead to mistakes and poor performance. And now, please, let Paulette and Noël take over."

Helen pressed her lips together tightly. She knew this was a huge opportunity for Paulette. It didn't matter as much to Noël. But for her, during that timeslot, the majority of Americans would be watching, and if Paulette did well, and she was sure that she would, she could become a dangerous rival.

"When will I see Joseph? I assume he'll want to speak with Benjamin and me."

Andrew didn't answer and continued to accompany her out.

Minutes later, a taxi was waiting for her at the door of the Belgian national radio and television station to take her to the hotel.

*Brussels.*
*Mossad Office*

When Jacob entered Ariel's office, his eyes met Gabriella Sabatello's, and he froze. He'd always suspected her of being part of Mossad, or some other part of Israeli intelligence. He'd even asked her once, but she'd denied it, and yet here she was.

"You already know each other," Maoz said.

"Yes, we do," Gabriella admitted.

"You'll be working together as you're both experts in artificial intelligence," Ariel explained.

"Well not exactly, I'm an expert in medical computing," Gabriella cut in.

"That's why you're here. Jacob will need your help," Maoz told her.

"Where's the computer?" Jacob asked, refusing to look at Gabriella.

"It's already set up in the van, just like you asked. It wasn't easy on such short notice," Gabriella answered dryly.

Jacob continued to ignore her.

"These are high stakes, Jacob. Going behind Louise Moos' back will have consequences," Ariel warned him.

"What does Austin Turner know?" Jacob asked.

"Not everything. But this time I can't leave the CIA out of the loop entirely. Turner's watching me like a hawk. He knows we're hiding something. I'll give him small pieces of information, but not the whole picture."

"How much time do I have to carry out the plan?" Jacob asked.

"I'd say time is running out. Moos wants to interrogate the Adoum family tonight," Ariel replied.

"I need a few more hours. Just a few more."

"Yes, clearly you need more time, but a lot of people have died and all we've got so far is that the man in the video might be Abir Nasr. Louise won't sit idly by. The whole world is watching what the Belgians will do, and they've never exactly been known for their effectiveness in the fight against terrorism," Maoz interjected with a tone of irony.

"Oh, and they still won't confirm whether the terrorist who set off the suicide bomb two days ago at the International Channel might be—you'll never guess—Ismail Nasr, Abir Nasr's brother. Officially, his last name is Adoum. Apparently, young Ismail worked in the building as maintenance staff, delivering the mail. No one has seen him since that morning. His colleagues say he had to deliver a few packages, one of them to the International Channel. Do you understand now why Louise can't give you more time?" Ariel couldn't hide his concern; the situation could easily get out of control.

"I'm off," Jacob said.

"Might you tell us where you're going?" Weiss asked.

"To launch the next part of the plan. I need you to give me more time. You have to convince Louise to wait until tomorrow."

"I asked you where you're going." Ariel was demanding an answer.

"I'm going to Nora Adoum's apartment. The van needs to be ready when I call you."

"The Belgian police are watching her. There are microphones in her apartment and her phone is bugged," Maoz reminded him.

"I know, but I have to talk to her."

332

"I'm sorry Jacob, but you need to tell us what you're planning to do. We can't act on the fringes of the law in Belgium or we'll end up having a diplomatic problem. Louise has convinced the foreign minister, and rightly so, to get in touch with Tel Aviv and light a fire under us. Dor has your back, Jacob, as long as we know what you're planning to do. Explain it, or it's over." Ariel wouldn't take no for an answer.

"OK. I have a plan, but I don't know if it's going to work. I want to help catch Abir Nasr just like everyone else, but I need you to guarantee that, during the arrest, no one will even put a finger on their triggers."

"Fine, that's no problem. In Belgium, they don't usually get anywhere near their triggers, but in any case, we can't intervene in the arrest, it's out of our jurisdiction," Ariel explained.

"I don't want them to kill him," Jacob said, disconcerting everyone in the room.

"Enough, Jacob. Tell us what's going on, what cards you're holding or I'm sticking you on the next flight to Tel Aviv," Ariel couldn't hide his anger anymore.

"Abir Nasr is here. His cousin knows it, and so does Marion Cloutier."

"Yes, we know that already," Maoz said.

"Marion was very important to Abir."

"Orit already explained everything to us, since you haven't exactly been forthcoming about the details of your conversation with Lissette Cloutier."

"Then you already know that Abir swore to Marion that one day he would become an important man and that the world would surrender to him. That day has come, and Marion has to give him the opportunity to boast in front of her, face to face. Abir needs to humiliate her."

"Goddamn it, tell us once and for all what you're going to do," Ariel insisted.

"I'm going to convince Marion to send Abir a message

through Nora, proposing a meeting. I'm sure he won't be able to resist. He'll emerge from his hideout. It will be his moment of glory. He'll want to see her defeated."

"Based on the phone recordings, Nora doesn't know where her cousin is," Maoz said.

"Nora doesn't, but I'm sure her father, Jamal Adoum, does. He's a fanatic, just like his son Farid. To hide in Brussels, Abir needed the Circle's silent army."

"And why do you need the computer that stores the codes to his pacemaker?" Ariel wanted to know.

"If Abir accepts the meeting with Marion, we will have to be close by in a place where we can connect to his device and cause a cardiac problem. In that state, he can easily be taken down and arrested. That's why I asked for a medical expert on defibrillators, because they can decide on the best way to alter Nasr's heartbeat."

"You're planning to interfere with his pacemaker?" Gabriella asked coldly.

"Yes, that's the idea, to cause a problem without killing him. It just needs to take him out of the game, that's all. I don't want anything irreversible to happen. You must know how to do it. The manufacturers have admitted that there are holes in their security, and that a hacker could reprogram the device, with all the danger that entails. So we need an expert, which you apparently are," he said, glaring at Gabriella.

"Yes, but I'm not sure it's going to be that easy. The device can connect to the computer that programmed it."

"The one you stole," Jacob added.

"Well, I didn't steal anything, though I did help hack it," Gabriella snapped.

"Could you alter Nasr's heartbeat if we were close enough?" Jacob asked.

"I don't know. Aren't you a little old to believe something you saw on a TV show? What you're proposing was on *Home-*

*land*. That's fiction, Jacob, just fiction. Things don't work like that in the real world," Gabriella admonished him.

"The only way to find out is to try."

"This is absurd, Jacob. If Abir Nasr comes out of hiding, Louise will have him arrested. There's no need for such an elaborate operation," Ariel protested.

"If he realizes there are police surrounding him, he won't go to the meeting. The only option is for us to be close enough for Gabriella to try and cause a minor problem in his heart. After that, they can arrest him."

"You're right," Maoz said. "Before he meets up with Marion, if he agrees to do that, his men will make sure the meeting place is clear. If they suspect anything, Abir won't let himself be seen. But are you sure that Marion will want to help us?"

"Yes," Jacob said without hesitation.

"It's too complicated," Ariel insisted, "we'll have to tell Louise."

"If you tell her, it will destroy the operation," Jacob warned him.

"This isn't our operation, it's the Belgians' operation!" Ariel had lost all patience now.

"Let me try. If it turns out badly, they can arrest Jamal Adoum, his children and all his friends."

"We're going to make an enemy of Louise Moos forever," Ariel predicted with resignation.

"You've never cared before about what other countries think when you're doing things you shouldn't be doing. I need time, Ariel. Just find it," Jacob shot back.

"Well then don't waste it, and get going already," Maoz urged him.

"What about me?" Gabriella asked.

"I'll call you and tell you where we should meet. Be ready. We won't have much time."

Nora sat in front of the TV in worn-out jeans and a baggy sweater. She wasn't wearing any makeup. She'd decided not to go to work. Mathis kept telling her that life goes on and that he couldn't shutter his business just because some fanatics had declared war on the whole world.

"They'll catch them, *chérie*, they'll catch them," he'd told her on the phone. "Any minute they're going to make an announcement that they caught the terrorists. And I can't close the club. Every day that Le Rêve de Marolles stays closed I lose money. And you are the main attraction. I don't have anyone else."

But Nora didn't give in, even when he threatened to fire her. "If you don't come in, I'll replace you. There are a ton of girls desperate to be given an opportunity like this. I can't shut my business down just because you're scared."

Nora hung up. Maybe the time had come to dump Mathis and find another job.

The sound of the doorbell made her jump. When she looked through the fish-eye lens she recognized the nameless guy who wouldn't stop following her.

She opened the door.

"Now what do you want?"

"Let's for a walk. Come with me."

"You're crazy! Why won't you leave me alone?"

"Because I'm trying to stop these fanatics from killing again. Believe me, I want to do this about as much as you do. But we're going to do it anyway. Put a coat on, it's cold."

Nora hesitated, but her instincts told her she didn't have any other choice. This man could destroy her life. She tugged her coat off a hook, grabbed her bag and followed him.

When they got down to the street, he gestured for her to look around.

"I don't know if you noticed, but your building is surrounded by police, just like your parents'. Your time is nearly up, Nora. Either you help me now, or you'll all end up in a high-security prison. Don't doubt for a second that the United States will have you and your family extradited. Attacking an American television network doesn't come for free."

"My family and I have nothing to do with the attacks," she responded shakily.

"I believe that you're innocent, but with your family, you'd have to prove it. Your obligation is to cooperate with the authorities."

"You're not an authority."

"No, I'm not. It's what I told you before—my mission is to collaborate in the capture of your cousin, Abir Nasr."

"I don't know where he is."

"You may not know, but maybe your father does. There has to be some way of getting in touch with him."

"Why won't you leave me alone?"

"Because more people are going to die. You have to make a decision: either you're complicit in these deaths or you can help prevent them. It's a simple equation to solve: either you have an ounce of moral conviction, or you just don't care about innocent people dying."

"I can't do anything to prevent it."

"Yes, yes you can! You and Marion Cloutier can do something."

Nora froze and looked at him, frightened. What did this man know about her relationship with Marion?

"Your cousin swore that one day he would be important, and that Marion would regret how she treated him. That day has arrived. Abir has the whole world on alert because of what he's done and what he could do next. Marion knows it was Abir who organized the attacks. She knows it, just like you and me."

"Marion! She doesn't know anything—"

"Yes, she does, that's what you talked about when you met on the street. When you saw her, you hesitated about whether to approach her or not, but you did, Nora, you went up to Marion and you spoke. It doesn't seem like you kept up your friendship. She wasn't happy to see you."

Jacob noticed his words had made an impression, that he had been correct in his assumption. He bolstered his words by showing her the photo he'd taken of them on his phone.

"We met in school, but that was a long time ago, and everyone took their own path after that. High school friendships don't last."

"But when you saw Marion, you went over to her to remind her that Abir was keeping his promise, that he was going to show her that he could be a powerful man."

"You don't know what we were talking about! I just saw her and went over. What's so special about saying hi to an old school friend?"

"It wasn't a very friendly hello. You were both tense. Only you two can get Abir to come out of wherever he's hiding. I hope you'll help us, otherwise I can't stop the police from arresting you and your family. It's up to you, Nora. Think about it."

They fell silent as they walked. The streets were almost empty. For 48 hours, fear had been coursing through the city.

After a few minutes, Jacob made her stop.

"Have you made a decision?"

"What do you want me to do?"

"We're going to see Marion. Hopefully, she'll agree to my plan. You'll tell your father to tell Abir that Marion wants to see him, that she's ready to meet up with him. Alone."

Nora smiled bitterly and fixed her dark brown eyes on Jacob's.

"Do you really think, after so many years, that Abir will agree to whatever Marion says? You're really overestimating the importance of our teenage years."

"You know that Marion was very important to your cousin, and you also know, just like I do, that she probably still is. This is his big moment to show her that he's not a nobody, that he can take down the whole world."

"Marion always looked down on Abir, she was never nice to him."

"That's exactly why he decided to prove her wrong. We can't waste any more time, Nora. They have to arrest Abir."

"And if they do, what will happen to him?"

"You know the answer to that. I know he's your cousin and you care about him, but he's a terrorist and a murderer. You can love him, but don't let him keep killing."

"You're asking me to betray him."

"Yes, exactly, I'm asking you to choose between your cousin and the rest of the world. Abir is responsible for the attacks. Children have died, children that got onto that tram with their mothers to go to school, and lived in the building where another suicide bomber blew himself up and took his neighbors with him."

"Do you know what Abir has been through? They murdered his parents in front of him and his brother when he was only a boy."

"I know."

"You do? Don't you understand he has his reasons for revenge?"

"Revenge on whom? Has he gotten revenge on the soldiers who shot his parents? Is it revenge for him to kill his own brother and a bunch of innocent children?"

"His brother? Ismail? What are you saying?"

Jacob was immediately sorry to be the one to tell her that Ismail was dead. He himself found it hard to believe that Abir could have convinced his brother to put on that explosive belt and attack the International Channel.

"Ismail is fine, he has to be fine! I'll call him right now!" Panic flooded Nora's expression.

It was then that he realized that this piece of information he had let slip could persuade her.

"They haven't announced it to the public yet, but the man who blew up the International Channel office was Ismail Nasr. So you didn't know your little cousin was going to commit suicide?"

Nora started to sob, letting Jacob hold her. They stayed that way for a few minutes, then Nora pulled away, drying her tears.

"It's not true! Abir would never sacrifice his brother!"

"You know I'm not lying. More people will die, Nora. You're our only chance to stop him."

"No! You can't put all that responsibility on me! You can't blame me for all the deaths!"

"OK, Nora. It's over. I won't bother you anymore. In a few minutes they'll arrest you, and your parents too. I don't know if your father knows where Abir is, but if he does, I can assure you they'll get him to talk. As far as your mother, I feel bad for her, but they're not going to spare her from any interrogations."

"What do you want me and Marion to do?" she asked angrily.

"Like I said, let's go see her. If she agrees, which I'm sure she will, you'll go to your father's home and give him Marion's message for Abir. Your father will know how to get it to him."

"And what will that message be?"

"A request for a meeting, a meeting between Marion and Abir."

"A meeting where they'll catch Abir and arrest him. Isn't that what you want?"

"All I want is to help end the slaughter. That's all, Nora."

"That's very noble of you, but where were you when the Jews attacked my uncle's house in Ain al-Hilweh? When they made Ismail and Abir orphans?"

"Do you really want to know?"

The question surprised her. She just wanted to point out his hypocrisy.

"No, I don't want to know," she answered.

Jacob was about to tell her he was there, that he could have shot Abir but didn't, that the memory of that early morning had become a nightmare. But he didn't say anything.

"OK, OK. I can't take any more of this. But I want you to promise me that if they arrest him, they won't extradite him to the United States. They have the death penalty there."

"I can't, Nora. I'd be lying if I said I could do that."

"So what do I get in return?"

"Nothing. I can't offer you anything except possibly a better treatment of your parents, but I can't even guarantee that. The police are investigating, and if they decide that they know something …"

Jacob let his words trail off, and they both kept walking in silence.

*Brussels.*
*Marion*

Marion was woken by insistent knocking on her door. She had been sleeping lightly and it startled her. She looked at her watch.

Without bothering to put on a robe, she went to the door. She was irritated to see Nora's face through the fish-eye lens.

"How dare you come here to bother me! Get out of here! I don't want anything to do with you!" she shouted.

"Open the door, Marion. I'm not alone."

She could only make out half a man's face though the small hole.

"Go away! I have nothing to say to you."

"Please, open the door, I'm with someone investigating the attacks."

Silence fell on both sides of the door. Marion was confused and angry. Nora had always been an idiot who she'd once manipulated as she pleased. Now she was back from the past. Reluctantly, she opened the door.

"I can't believe you would come here. And you" she said, fixing her eyes on Jacob, "what is it you want?"

"We want your help to capture Abir Nasr."

She let them in. Turning her back, she walked to the living area and sat down on a sofa. She didn't invite them to sit, but Jacob did so anyway, and then so did Nora.

343

"Abir Nasr, your goddamn cousin. He was already a nightmare in high school."

"And you know, just like we do, that he is the terrorist in the video," Jacob said.

"No, I don't know anything. How would I know that?" Marion tried to feign indifference.

"Because anyone who knows or knew Abir Nasr knows that voice, the voice of the hooded man who is threatening the world."

"No, I don't know that! Do you really think I could remember the voice of someone I knew when I was a kid?"

"Abir will kill again."

"You seem convinced that the terrorist is Abir, and Nora does too. Even if that's true, what does any of it have to do with me? Are you going to talk to everyone who went to our high school? It's unbelievable that you'd come here, at this hour! Get out of here, I'm going to call the police as soon as you leave. And you, Nora, stop following me around like a puppy!"

Marion looked at her former friend with disdain.

"You have two choices, Marion. Either cooperate with me, or the whole world will learn that you were friends with this terrorist and even recognized his voice, but didn't tell the police. I'm afraid you would have a lot of explaining to do," Jacob said.

Marion looked at him, clenching her jaw with rage.

"Are you threatening me?"

"No. I'm explaining to you that if you don't cooperate with me, I will go directly to the head of Belgian security services. I'm sure she'll find it very interesting to know that you recognized the voice of the masked man and didn't tell the police. The truth is, you and your friend Nora have committed a crime. They could accuse you of conspiring with the terrorists."

"Don't be ridiculous," Marion said, rising from the sofa.

"I'm not," Jacob replied, irritated.

"Do you think I want to hurt Abir?" Nora asked, looking at her one time friend.

"I don't care what you want. Abir is your cousin, and neither of you have anything to do with me."

"OK. Let's go." Jacob stood up and headed towards the door. Nora followed.

"Wait." Marion's voice was drained of certainty.

Jacob stopped, but didn't look back, though Nora did.

"What do you want me to do?"

Sitting back down, Jacob explained his plan to them.

"Nora is going to talk to her father. She will ask him to get a message to Abir from you proposing a meeting at the location of his choice. You'll tell him you're coming alone."

"That's ridiculous. He won't accept. Why would he? The police are looking for him. He's not going to come out of hiding," Marion told him.

"You're assuming that my father knows how to find him," Nora said anxiously.

"Their phones are tapped, and sometimes overly innocent conversations give clues, Miss Adoum."

"My father is not a terrorist."

"Your family is close to Sheikh Mohsin who, as you both know, is one of the leaders of the Circle. The day Abir's parents died, they had been looking for him. Do you want me to go on, Nora? I've been very patient with you, but there's no time left now. You know that your father is a radical, and so is your brother Farid. If Abir is in Brussels, he will know how to get him a message."

"What if he refuses to see me?" Marion wanted to know.

"Then I will be wrong. But I doubt he'll be able to resist seeing you humiliated in front of him or having the chance to brag about his importance."

"And then they'll arrest him?" Nora asked.

"I can't answer that question."

"Nora is so simple, she always has been," Marion scoffed.

"Here is the plan. Marion, you will write the message, and we'll wait for a response at Nora's house."

"Is that necessary?"

"Yes."

"Why do I have to write anything? If it goes wrong, I could be accused of having a relationship with a terrorist."

"Trust me."

"I don't trust you or anyone else."

"Well, you're going to have to, for once in your life. Write."

The note was short and concise.

Abir, I want to talk to you. I think the conversation could be interesting for both of us.

Marion

It took them a while to find a taxi, which stopped first at Nora's apartment building in Matonge. She gave them her keys and then continued on to Molenbeek in the taxi by herself.

Nora was nervous when she arrived at her parents' apartment. She didn't know how she would tell them what Jacob had asked her to say, or how they would react. She pressed the doorbell with trembling fingers.

Her father opened the door, and she was surprised to see that he was already dressed. He looked her up and down in disgust.

"How dare you come to our home, at this hour!"

"Father, let me in. Please."

Entering, she found her mother was sitting in the living room crying. Nora went over and put her arms around her.

"Mother, why are you crying?"

346

Fatima lifted her head without answering.

"What do you want?" Jamal asked.

"I have a message for Abir and you have to make sure he gets it."

He was quiet for a few seconds, surprise and anger rushing across his face.

"What are you saying?"

"You know where he is, or at least you can make sure he gets this message."

Nora picked up her bag and took out the folded piece of paper with Marion's writing.

"You're crazy," her father muttered.

"No, I'm not the crazy one, you are! All of you have sunk into this madness. Sheikh Mohsin and you made Abir into what he is. And we'll all pay a price for it. They're going to arrest him and they'll arrest all of you. Your lives will be shattered forever. Did you really think you could win?"

"Shut up you degenerate!" he shouted, slapping her across the face.

Fatima leapt up to try to protect her daughter, but Jamal pushed her off.

Nora didn't cry, though her father's handprint burned on her face.

"The note is from Marion Cloutier. She's asking Abir to meet with her wherever and whenever he chooses."

"She's a whore who deserves to die," Jamal responded, spitting on the floor.

"If Abir finds out you didn't give him a message from Marion, well … do whatever you have to do, Father, but make sure it gets to him."

Fatima went back over to her daughter and in barely a whisper, asked her to leave.

"We don't know where Abir is," she said, her voice choked by tears.

Nora held her and helped her into a chair.

"I'll wait for the answer here."

"Get out!" her father ordered.

"No. You think I don't know you sympathize with the Circle, just like my brother Farid, that I'll just ignore the fact that Abir is the terrorist on TV threatening the entire world?"

"You're lying! How dare you accuse your cousin!"

"Enough already, Father. Get the message to Abir, and he can decide."

The conviction in his daughter's voice made Jamal waver. He detested her, and thought he should have killed her. Maybe the time had finally come to do it. He would discuss it with Abir.

"Do what Noura asks," Fatima said in a trembling voice.

Jamal opened the door and went down the stairs. He didn't have to go far, just one floor down. He knocked on the door. The man who finally opened it looked at him suspiciously.

"Take this message to Abir."

"A message? From whom?"

"From Marion Cloutier. You already know who she is."

"You want me to put myself in danger, and put Abir in danger, to give him a note from some woman? You've lost it, Jamal."

"Do what I tell you. He'll have to decide what to do."

"I just got home. I can't do anything until tomorrow, when the market opens. The police have eyes all over Molenbeek."

"Abdel, nothing is stopping you from going out. Make sure he gets that note."

When Jamal got home, Fatima was with Nora in the kitchen, putting water on to boil for coffee.

"Go home," Jamal said to his daughter.

"Will he get the message?"

"He'll get it."

"When will I have the answer?"

"I don't know."

"I'll wait here."

"I don't know if there will be an answer."

"It's better if I wait here, Father."

Abdel entered a room where he kept several large bags stuffed with clothes on top of a bed. He took one and placed it on a wheeled cart, pushing it outside. He knew Molenbeek like the back of his hand. For 30 years, the neighborhood had been his home. He walked along slowly, pushing the cart. It didn't take long for him to reach the warehouse where he kept his merchandise. He met a neighbor coming out the door.

"How was business today, Abdel? Seems like a lot of people stayed home scared."

"Not many people are venturing out, it's normal," Abdel responded, shaking his head sadly.

"Yes, my son could have been one of the victims, but he was home sick with the flu."

"Wow, that's what I call good luck."

The two men said goodbye and Abdel opened the warehouse door with his keys. It was silent and the lights were off. He was about to turn them on when he felt a cold blade against his neck.

"It's me," he struggled to whisper.

Someone blinded him with a flashlight.

"It's me!" he repeated, frightened.

"What are you doing here?" Ghalil asked irritably.

"Jamal sent me here," he said, not daring to move.

"Jamal?" It was Abir who spoke.

"Yes, your uncle. He's sent you a message. He told me it's important."

"I hope he's right," Abir said stormily.

Ghalil took the knife from Abdel's throat. He tried to get his breath back, his heart pounding.

The dim bulb barely lit the room. Abdel took the paper from his pocket and handed it to Abir. He suddenly feared this young soldier who he admired for his courage in fighting against the infidels. Tonight there was something in Abir's voice and eyes that disturbed him.

Abir took a few steps back and read the note. He looked up and let out a laugh, dry, bitter and harsh.

Ghalil and Abdel waited.

Turning away, Abir began to pace from one end of the warehouse to the other, absorbed in thought. Then he stopped dead and turned to Abdel.

"Take this answer to my uncle: the woman who wrote this should go to the market tomorrow at 10 a.m. and wander between the stalls. She must not carry a cell phone. That is all."

"Yes, I will tell him," Abdel managed to say.

"And now, this is what we will do ..."

The two men drew closer to Abir obediently and listened to his plan.

*

Abdel arrived home, shaking. Abir wouldn't forgive any mistakes.

When he to the Adoum's apartment, he was shocked to see Noura there.

"You can talk," Jamal said. "She's taking the message back."

"Abir wants that woman to go to the market tomorrow at 10 a.m. She cannot bring a cell phone. She should walk from one stall to another. Nothing else."

"Nothing else?" Nora asked.

"That's it. It will be what it will be."

Abdel left without another word. When Jamal closed the door, he looked at his daughter with a mix of apprehension and contempt.

"You have your answer. Now get out."

Nora kissed her mother and turned to face her father.

"We're gambling with our future, Father. They'll catch him, and when they do, we'll pay a price for being related to him, for helping him."

"Are you asking me to turn your cousin in? How dare you suggest something like that!" Jamal was about to hit her again.

"I don't know what you should do, Father. All I know is that we'll pay dearly for the deaths Abir has caused. We no longer have a future."

"Future? There is nothing for us except taking down the infidels," Jamal declared, shoving his daughter.

"You're wrong. We could have had a different future. You worked hard to give us an education. We could've had a peaceful, normal life. But Sheikh Mohsin didn't allow it. That man convinced you all that you have to die. But what about him? Would he ever put on a suicide vest? No. He sends others in his place. They have to sacrifice their lives while he just gives the orders."

Jamal struck his daughter again, knocking her off balance. When Fatima ran over, he pushed her away.

Nora rose up and left her parents' home, a rush of tears nearly blinding her vision. She hailed a taxi to take her back home. She didn't have the energy to get on the subway. She was hurt and tired. Opening the door to her apartment, she saw that Jacob and Marion were waiting impatiently.

"We have an answer. Tomorrow at 10 you should go to the Molenbeek market and start walking between the stalls. You cannot bring your phone. Nothing else."

"So, he accepted," Marion said quietly.

"That's his answer," Nora said, unable to hide her exhaustion.

"It's logical," Jacob observed. "He wants to make sure it's not a trap. His men will be everywhere, watching for unfamiliar faces in the market."

"If they notice anything suspicious, the meeting won't go ahead," Nora told them with a confidence she didn't actually feel.

"So what now?" Marion asked.

"Now we wait until tomorrow. We can't do anything else. Nora, are you OK?" Jacob asked.

"No! I'm not OK and I'm never going to be for the rest of my life. How could I? I'm helping you arrest my cousin, I'm destroying my parents' lives and mine!" She broke into tears, no longer caring what the others thought of her.

"Your dear cousin is a terrorist who doesn't care about killing innocent people." Marion's voice was cold as ice. "What about the lives that have been lost? Are those lives worth less than yours? You haven't changed, Nora—you're still so stupid."

"And my relatives' lives? Does no one care about what happened to Abir's parents? Who decided to destroy Iraq? And what about Syria? None of it matters. It's impossible for us to understand one another. There are too many deaths, too much blood spilled by all of you, by all of us. We'll just keep killing until there's no one left."

"Don't be so melodramatic!" Marion replied. "Focus on what's happening here and now. Your cousin has decided to become a mass murderer to get himself noticed, to be a hero to your people. He wants to feel important when he's really worthless, a nobody." Marion's voice was filled with contempt.

There was so much tension in the air that Jacob was worried that Nora or Marion might back out.

"This isn't the time for insults or trying to prove who's right. What we have to do is prevent more deaths. Please," he pleaded.

The women were silent, trying to control their anger. Then Nora's phone rang, making them jump.

"It's my boss."

"Answer it," Jacob told her.

Marion and Jacob could overhear the conversation between Nora and Mathis Discart. He was insisting that she had to come in to work, but she refused. When he threatened again to fire her, and it was all she could do not to cry. As she hung up, she looked at Marion and Jacob with embarrassment.

"You're still so weak," Marion told her.

"I—I don't feel up to going there and singing."

"Well, you should. Weren't we told to keep up appearances? I think it's time for me to go."

"I'll help you get a taxi," Jacob offered.

"Yes, do that. I don't like this neighborhood," she responded.

They left Nora's apartment and walked for some time before Jacob found a taxi.

"Will you go tomorrow?"

"Yes, of course I'll go. But will I have protection? I mean, will your people be there making sure that nutjob doesn't do anything to me?"

"Do you think he's capable of hurting you? He was in love with you."

"That's just it: he *was* in love with me, when he was 16 or 17. But now there may be only hate. If he agreed to see me, it may only be because he thinks he can get revenge. Don't you get that?"

Jacob hadn't considered this. He looked at Marion and felt a sudden respect for her.

"Do you think he could try to hurt you?"

"Yes."

"Then how—"

"They say that you can't make an *omelette* without breaking a few eggs. To stop Abir Nasr, we're all going to take risks, especially me."

"Why are you doing it, Marion?"

"I have no other choice."

"Yes, yes you do."

"I could say no to you, but not to myself. It would be cowardly on my part. I'm used to taking risks—don't go thinking my life has been so easy. I've paid a price for everything I've achieved. No, I won't back out. I can't."

"I don't understand."

"Of course you don't. You know nothing about me. Sometimes I think I don't even know myself. And now I need to mentally prepare myself to face tomorrow."

"I'll see you first thing in the morning."

Marion slipped into the taxi and left the neighborhood behind her.

*

Jacob hurried to the office. They had to organize the operation that would protect Marion and allow them to arrest Nasr. Ariel was waiting impatiently for him to go to a meeting with the rest of the crisis team: Louise Moos, Alba Fernández, Austin Turner and Anthony Jones.

Ariel knew that Louise's patience had run out. She wasn't going to allow Jacob's solo operation to continue. Putting together the task force was going to be complicated. Molenbeek was Nasr's territory.

"Before we go, we need to call Dor," he announced.

They spoke for a few minutes. Ariel told him what they were going to do and then he passed the phone to Jacob. Dor listened to him in silence, then responded that he hoped he wouldn't regret what was going to happen.

"Because people will die, Jacob. It's inevitable. We might get Abir Nasr, but more people will die, and as the person who came up with this plan, you'll have to live with that for the rest of your life."

"Yes, I know you can't achieve a greater good without paying a price," Jacob replied, remembering Marion's expression about eggs.

Louise was displeased as she listened to Jacob and looked

carefully at the photo of Nora Adoum and Marion Cloutier on the phone. If the CIA and the European Union Intelligence Center hadn't pressured her government, she would never have approved the Israeli computer engineer's operation. They had also been pestered with demands by several other European countries' agencies. As if that weren't enough, the media had started to question the effectiveness of Belgium's security services, including the International Channel, which was watched by the U.S. president and every other world leader.

At that moment, Benjamin Holz was doing a live interview with a so-called expert on international terrorism who kept repeating, as if it were a mantra, that the jihadists had a big advantage over the police. He also expressed doubt about the effectiveness of the Belgian security services in preventing future attacks.

Her closest colleagues had tried to convince Louise that it was normal for them to receive criticism for what was happening, and for the International Channel to give even more prominence to such criticisms. After all, they had been targeted in the attack.

Her colleagues may have been right, but she still felt a deep aversion toward journalists, and Helen Morris and Benjamin Holz had only worsened this feeling.

To top it all off, the Secretary General of NATO had decided to call a meeting between the defense ministers "because we cannot hide under the bed and let those damn terrorists believe we're afraid of them." So she was facing two challenges: capturing the man who had undermined European security and, at the same time, ensuring the safety of the ministers, including a Russian delegate who had been invited to that special session. "The same old propaganda and idle posturing that politicians love so much," the Belgian security official muttered.

"The human element is the determining factor," Alba Fernández had told her. Louise hadn't replied, but she wished she could have told the Spanish agent she so thoroughly detested that this was not a psychoanalysis session.

What Jacob proposed was for a discreet security cordon to be established around Marion Cloutier from the moment the woman arrived in Molenbeek.

"We'll do it, but there can't be more than three or four agents. Everyone in the neighborhood knows each other, and if they start seeing strange faces they'll let Nasr know, and he won't come out of his hiding spot," Louise told him wearily.

"But don't you have agents who have infiltrated the community?" Austin asked.

Louise shot a hateful look at the CIA agent. She wouldn't tolerate another lesson on how things should be done in the intelligence world. The CIA had quite a few failures behind them, and they were in no position to preach, she thought. She dug her nails into her left knee, which was protected by her skirt.

"Yes, we do, and the Belgian police have agents there too," she said flatly.

"Abir Nasr has proven to be fairly intelligent, and he won't take any big risks," Jacob insisted.

"We know, Mr. Baudin, we know. We'll do everything we can. In any case, it's important for Marion Cloutier to understand the danger she's exposed to. We can't deceive her and tell her this is safe," Louise insisted.

"She knows she'll be putting her life at risk, she's quite intelligent herself," Jacob replied.

"Who will be inside the van?" Maoz asked.

"Together with Gabriella and myself, it would be good to have an agent and another medical computing expert," Jacob proposed.

"We were already planning for that. As I'm sure you can understand, an Israeli agent can't go around on European territory like it's his own backyard." Louise wasn't hiding her dislike of Jacob either.

He did not respond to the woman's comments. He knew Louise Moos had a rigid mind. She would never break the rules, and the operation was putting her abilities to the test and her position as the Belgian security director at risk.

"In any case, Mr. Baudin, I want you to know that some of the best computer experts are even unsure you can pull this off. They have explained to me that although the defibrillators are connected to the computer of the doctor or the center that fitted it inside the patient, to adjust it—or in this case, to manipulate it—the patient has to be in the hospital or very close to where the computer is located. Maybe you watch too much TV." The Belgian security director's tone was decidedly sarcastic.

"I never said my plan was airtight. It's true that what I'm proposing happened on a famous TV show. That might have been fiction, Ms. Moos, but I can assure you that experts have confirmed it's feasible. In 2017 the Abbott company and in 2019 the Medtronic company both admitted that it was possible, though extremely difficult, to hack their devices."

Louise clenched her teeth. She wasn't going to start an argument.

"Well, we hope your theories prove to be true, Mr. Baudin. Two of my men will accompany you," she said with an air of reluctance.

Alba looked at Jacob, then chose to speak. She had made a decision too.

"If you don't mind, Jacob, I'd like to accompany you in the van. I won't bother you and I might even be able to help. I was planning on going to Molenbeek to provide security to Marion Cloutier, but Louise is right, the presence of too many strangers in the neighborhood will tip off Abir Nasr."

"I'd be happy to have you with us. I'm sure you'll be very helpful," Jacob responded.

*

It took two more hours to finish outlining all the details of the operation. After they were finished, Louise summoned them for a few more hours in her office.

"We have to meet with Marion and prepare her for what she's going to face. Then we'll continue the operation from here."

They were all tired, but they would have to work through the night.

Ariel suggested they go back to the office and rest for a few hours, it was the only chance they would have. Maoz agreed, but Jacob was reluctant.

"I'm going to go to the club where Nora Adoum sings."

"At this hour?" Ariel asked, surprised.

"It'll be open. I'm worried Nora might change her mind and back out. She's not as strong as Marion."

"But will she want to talk to you?" Maoz asked.

"I don't know. Maybe not. But I think if we leave her on her own, her fear will only grow."

Ariel offered to drive him to Les Marolles, and Maoz went with them. At that hour, a few bars were still open and snatches of music drifted out as they drove by.

He pulled over just before the door to Le Rêve de Marolles.

"This is not a very smart idea, and we shouldn't be letting you do it. Abir could have ordered his cousin to be watched. I would if I were him," Ariel said.

"You're right," Jacob admitted.

"Of course I am. We can't risk the whole operation."

"But we can't risk Nora changing her mind either," Jacob responded.

It was Maoz who finally decided it.

"Here, take my hat and scarf. Walk naturally, like you're on your way home. If you see someone, don't stop—keep going. We're going back to the office. We'll sleep there for a bit."

Jacob climbed out of the car and walked at a moderate pace. The cold weather allowed him to cover his face with the things Maoz had lent him. His outfit didn't draw attention either; he was wearing black jeans and sneakers.

He crossed paths with a couple of Asian men as they ducked into a rundown bar right before he reached Le Rêve de Marolles. When Jacob went in, no one even looked up. There weren't many people. Three or four tables were taken by couples, and there were a few others sitting alone at the bar. Nora was singing on the tiny circular dance floor that functioned as a stage. Jacob was surprised by her voice. He hadn't expected her to sing so well. It was a melancholy song, the story of being downtrodden. The applause at the end was lukewarm. She saw him and approached the bar.

"What are you doing here?" she asked, irritated.

"I wanted to make sure you were OK."

Mathis came over swirling whiskey in his glass.

"You haven't been very cheerful tonight," he scolded Nora, ignoring Jacob's presence.

"I told you I wasn't in the mood, but you insisted."

"You think the whole world should stop just because a few madmen decided they're going to kill everyone if we don't give in to their demands?" he responded dismissively.

"I don't have an opinion, Mathis."

Suddenly, the club owner noticed Jacob.

"And you are?" he asked.

"A friend of Nora's, and you must be her boss."

"Yes, you could say that. I'm her boss as well as other things, right, *chérie*?" he said smugly, putting an arm around Nora's shoulders.

Nora blushed and slid out from under his embrace.

"Woah, where's this coming from?" Discart grabbed her arm and refused to let go of her.

"I don't think it's a good night for anyone," Jacob observed.

"Maybe not for you, but why wouldn't it be for us? I'm going to have to ask you to leave. You're not welcome here."

"I have no intention of staying, but maybe Nora would like me to walk her home."

"Are you looking for trouble, or are you too dumb to see she's my girl?" He had let go of Nora and was ready for a fight.

Jacob continued to lean on the bar, giving no indication that he was bothered by the man's bravado.

"Look, if Nora wants to stay, I'll go. But if she'd rather I walk her home, I'll wait for her."

"Get out of here or I'll throw you out!"

The two men glared at each other while Nora stood paralyzed for a moment before finally reacting.

"I'm going. I want to go home."

"You're not going anywhere!" Discart yanked her arm, making her lose her balance.

"Let me go! I want to leave!" she cried.

"What's gotten into you? Is this guy your pimp or something?"

Jacob's punch left him dizzy for a second, but he had enough time to react by grabbing a bottle.

Moments later, Mathis Discart was on the floor with a broken arm and a sprained ankle. Jacob had surprised himself by what he'd done. Until then, *krav maga* had never been anything other than a way for him to stay in shape.

"Get your coat, Nora. We're leaving."

The waiters looked fearfully at the man who had just knocked their boss down with a couple of swift movements. They weren't sure whether to try to stop him or let him go. They opted for the latter as the nervous customers asked for the bill, hoping to get out of there as quickly as possible.

Nora walked briskly, forcing Jacob to do the same. She wanted to get far away from Le Rêve de Marolles. Mathis wasn't a thug, but she knew he would never forgive what had happened. They'd have to take him to a hospital, and maybe he would report her or Jacob.

"Don't worry. I'll make a few calls and that guy won't cause us any trouble," he assured her.

He immediately called Maoz and explained what had happened. The veteran agent didn't admonish him, but he did advise him not to walk Nora home.

"Get in a taxi and come here. You have to rest, and she does too. And don't even think about going to her apartment. I'm sure that Nasr has it under watch."

Jacob reluctantly agreed. He knew that Maoz was right, but it was difficult for him to say goodnight to Nora.

*Brussels. Molenbeek neighborhood.*
*Marion*

The taxi driver was caught by surprise when the elegant Parisian woman, her hair covered by a wool hat, asked him to take her to Molenbeek. He tried to make conversation, but she couldn't be bothered to respond. Marion was trying to recall the instructions she had been given by those strangers, who didn't really seem like police. They had gone over repeatedly what she should do until she became irritated. The person who bothered her most nervous was the director of Belgian security, who since the morning began had asked her at least five times if she was sure she wanted to risk herself for this operation. All five times, she'd answered that her mind was made up. This was true, though she was afraid but loathe to acknowledge it in front of these people.

She hadn't slept all night wondering how Abir Nasr could still be obsessed with her. She hadn't spent a single second thinking about him until three days ago.

She had no other option than to force him to bring their lives full circle, and to do that she had to risk her own.

She wondered if he would make a mistake that could give her an advantage. When they were teenagers, Abir had never stood out to her in any way, and she wondered if that boy, now a man, was moved only by rage and resentment, or if he had a talent for anything other than killing.

One of the agents had placed a micro-transmitter in her shoe so they could track her at all times. If that failed, they had inserted another in the handle of her purse. She also wore a pin-sized microphone sewn into her coat lapel.

Abir's instructions had been precise. She wouldn't carry a phone.

Marion had asked several times how many agents would be there to protect her, but they hadn't answered her question. She tried to reassure herself. Jacob had promised that even if she couldn't see him, he would be nearby with Alba and another woman he had introduced her to, Gabriella Sabatello, who would be trying to hack Abir's defibrillator. That was the plan. To put it in practice, they needed her to get Abir to come out of hiding so that they could manipulate his pacemaker from a distance, causing a strong tachycardia. She would be with Abir when he started to feel unwell, and then he would be arrested.

The taxi driver slammed on the brakes, offended by Marion's unfriendliness. She paid without looking at him, and when she got out of the car, she headed toward the Molenbeek market. Sellers had begun to put out their wares on street stalls.

She could feel the looks of surprise from the people she passed in the improvised passages formed by the stands. She wore a white cashmere sweater and black pants, and her black coat, like her shoes and bag, was simple and understated. But they still looked at her, looks that told her she wasn't part of their world, even if they couldn't glimpse a single strand of her hair. They were right—she wasn't one of them.

Among so many women in hijabs and those tedious trench coats that hid their bodies, she didn't know that one of those women was an Israeli Mossad agent. Jacob had asked Ariel not to leave Marion's safety exclusively in the hands of Louise Moos. Maoz then suggested that Miriam trail her. After all, she was just another neighbor in Molenbeek, and, in that market, she was known as a good Muslim believer.

Marion had entered the market at exactly 10 a.m. She walked slowly, stopping at the stalls, asking about prices, smiling and moving on. She had been meandering for almost an hour when at one of her stops in front of a second-hand clothing stand, a man she hadn't even noticed next to her whispered to keep walking and go into a café she would find on the next street.

"Pretend you're thirsty or tired. Order a coffee from the man at the bar and ask him where the bathroom is."

She tensed, but followed the instructions. Walking slowly, she put a hand to her face. She looked over at the little café as if she had just discovered it. She went in, ordered a coffee and asked the owner for the restroom. The man pointed to a staircase going down at the back.

The hallway was short but very dark. She took a few steps and just as she was starting to get used to the gloom, a hand closed over her mouth and another grabbed her arm and wrenched her backwards. How long did this last? Seconds? Minutes? She didn't know because the whole time she felt only terror. They shoved her into a room. And when she got her balance back, she saw him.

"You've changed, Marion. You used to be more beautiful."

"You haven't changed. You're still exactly the same," she responded scornfully as she tried to recover from the shock of the situation.

He laughed bitterly for a second, and then slapped her before ripping off the hat that covered her hair.

"You and I have unfinished business, Marion."

"You're so pathetic, Abir. You think you're important because you hit me, or because you're capable of killing innocent people? You think that's going to make me believe you're worth something? No, you were worth nothing before, and you're worth nothing now."

Abir hit her harder, knocking her to the ground. Marion felt a sharp pain in her head. Her vision blurred, but she didn't cry.

"We don't have time, Marion."

A man appeared out of the darkness and forced her to her feet. Another grabbed her arms and together they took off her clothes. Abir stared at her naked body while the men searched her clothes until they found what they were looking for: the tiny transmitters.

"So basic. A transmitter in a shoe and another in your bag. I was hoping for a bit more imagination." Abir seemed to be enjoying the moment.

Ghalil and the other man wouldn't take their eyes off Marion's body. She managed to stand perfectly still despite her revulsion.

When they had finished, they ordered her to get dressed. Relief flooded her body when she realized they hadn't found the microphone.

"Now, I'm going to give you a very special present. You won't like it, of course. It's not like the Louis Vuitton belt you're wearing, but I promise you, it's much better. Ghalil made it specially for you. And I promise you, Ghalil is the best."

Abir's laugh made her flinch more than his malice. She felt his hands on her body as he fitted the suicide belt around her.

"See? It fits you perfectly. It makes you look a little fat, but it's not too bad," he said, still laughing.

"You're insane, Abir!" Her voice gave away the terror she felt as she became aware of what was happening. They had turned her into a walking bomb!

"And now let's go, Marion. Just you and me. Tell me, how many of those infidel dogs are out there trying to arrest me?"

"No one's out there, Abir, no one. I followed the instructions you gave Nora."

"Don't be stupid, Marion. You want me to believe you got those devices all by yourself, and no one is tracking you? We've seen at least three men and two women who aren't from around here. Molenbeek doesn't belong to Belgium anymore—they should know that."

He hit her again. Her lip split and blood filled her mouth.

"As for my cousin, she'll have to die too. Her father should have killed her himself. I'll settle things with her. But that doesn't matter to you. Noura was just your lapdog."

"What will killing me achieve?" she dared to ask him.

He laughed again, grabbing her arm.

"Let's go, Marion."

*

Miriam had followed Marion to the café. She hadn't gone in because it would've been too obvious. But when she heard them leave, she spoke into her hidden microphone to inform the others. "She's with Abir. He's dragging her by the arm. They must have hit her. She has blood on her face." Miriam's words put Jacob on edge from his position a few meters away in the van with Alba, Gabriella and four other agents. He'd been disturbed by the parts of conversation between Marion and Abir that they had been able to hear. He wished they could back out, and cursed himself for coming up with this operation.

One of the agents said the last thing Jacob wanted to hear.

"They've put a suicide belt on her."

"No, it can't be, they didn't mention bombs."

The agent rewound the tape and Jacob let his head fall. The belt Abir was talking about couldn't be anything else.

"We have to arrest them," Jacob asked.

"We'll ask for instructions," the agent answered.

The man spoke to his superior while Jacob tried to convince Ariel by phone that they had to do the impossible to save Marion.

"It's too late, Jacob," Ariel responded. Louise Moos was at his side talking to the agent in charge of the operation who was with Gabriella and Jacob.

"The operation will continue as planned," he reported.

"No, we have to change the plan! They're going to kill her!" Jacob shouted.

"If we try to arrest him, he may detonate the belt. We have to wait," Alba said, putting a hand on Jacob's arm.

"We must get closer," Jacob said.

"We can't go out on these streets. We'll wait to see where they go," Alba proposed.

"Ms. Fernández is right," one of the agents said.

"We could lose them!" Jacob could barely stay calm.

"If we don't get closer, I won't be able to control the defibrillator," Gabriella warned.

"Miriam, don't lose sight of them," Jacob asked.

"I'll try. There's a man who's been following me for a while."

"One of Abir's men?"

"Could be. I'm not exactly beautiful enough to be followed by anybody else," the agent responded sarcastically.

"OK, just be careful."

*

Abir forced Marion to walk quickly with Ghalil behind them until they reached a street where a black car was stopped. They opened the door and pushed her inside. The driver smiled.

"Where are we going?" Marion asked, trying to hide the overpowering fear in her tone.

"Brussels is an interesting city, as you know. What's your favorite building? Eurocontrol, the European Commission, or the NATO headquarters? You pick, Marion, I'm feeling generous today, and I want to grant you one last wish."

*One last wish.*

Abir's words terrified her to the core, but she stayed silent, trying to feign indifference. With the explosives around her waist, she knew she was going to die.

"Surely the men who told you they'd protect you are thinking that the NATO headquarters is my target. I actually considered it, but I wouldn't even dream of it now. Too obvious. The defense ministers are already meeting and tonight the Secretary General will invite them to dinner. Every inch of that building will be surrounded by police. They're definitely expecting us to blow it up. But I've thought of something better. You'll definitely like it. What do you think of the Parlamentarium? Or maybe the European Committee of the Regions? Or the European External Action Service, or the Economic and Social Committee? I know! The European Commission! I don't like bureaucrats, they're all completely useless and live off everyone else's hard work. We have the president of the Commission there, the vice president and a dozen commissioners. The world would keep turning without them, don't you think?"

His laugh continued to chill her spine.

*

Inside the van, tension was apparent on everyone's faces.

"We have to evacuate all those buildings," Alba shouted.

"There's no time, and it will cause absolute chaos," one of the agents said.

"Tell Louise! Now!" The Spanish agent insisted.

Gabriella typed frenetically on her keyboard, paying no attention to the commentary from Jacob or any of the agents with them.

"Hurry, the microphone isn't working very well, we're going to lose them," Jacob insisted.

"There's nothing more I can do—I'm not sure it's going to work," Gabriella said through clenched teeth.

"It has to work!" Jacob shouted.

"I can't make it work! You do it if you're so sure!"

"Gabriella, all you have to do is increase his heart rate so he feels like he's choking and he can't breathe."

The Belgian agents accompanying them looked at them, silent. They had no plans to intervene in this argument, and stared at Gabriella's fingers.

The driver of the van swerved so they wouldn't lose sight of the black car.

"We're being followed," Ghalil said.

"I'm not surprised. I figured that would happen. Is it the black van?" Abir asked.

"Yes," Ghalil answered.

"How far are we from the European Commission?"

"Two minutes," answered the driver.

"Allah will receive you in Paradise," Abir said to the driver.

Marion watched them from the corner of her eye, still not fully understanding the situation and why Abir was saying goodbye to the man. She was the one wearing the explosives.

Suddenly, Abir put his hand on his heart. He looked like he was being strangled. Pain in his chest preventing him from breathing.

"What's happening to you?" Ghalil asked, alarmed.

"I ... don't ... know. My heart!"

"Stop!" Ghalil told the driver.

"We're only one minute away, I can already see our brother Ahmed's car out front. I'll stop to give you time to get out."

"I think I've got it," Gabriella said.

"Be careful, you could kill him. We want them to stop the car, for him to feel like his heart is leaping out of his mouth, not for it to explode," Jacob told her.

"I know what I have to do," she snapped.

370

"Stop, Gabriella! You're going to kill him!"

"Be quiet," she said evenly.

Abir could barely breathe. His heart was beating so fast that he knew he was dying. He managed to turn his head toward Marion. He could see the triumph in the woman's eyes. She was smiling like she had won the final battle.

"You whore! You're coming with me to hell!"

Abir used his last ounce of strength to pull the ring on Marion's belt right just as Gabriella made Abir's heart burst inside his chest.

Jacob's scream was lost in the noise of the blast. Gabriella felt someone shove her away from the computer. She staggered and fell to the floor of the van. The agents jumped out of the vehicle and ran towards the explosion. Alba and Jacob followed closely behind. Sirens wailed in the distance. The officers asked them not to get too close to the flaming car.

"They're all dead," one of them said.

"Marion?"

"She is too. She was wearing the suicide belt."

Gabriella went over to Jacob to try to calm him, but he rebuffed her.

"You wanted to kill him! He knew he was going to die, that's why he killed Marion," he berated her.

"Jacob, I had my orders."

"Orders? Did they order you to kill Abir Nasr?"

The woman turned on her heel and walked away without answering.

There was no future for them.

Jacob was silent. He felt Alba's hand on his arm. Chaos swirled around them. Screaming, sirens, running, fire, smoke.

For a few seconds, he felt like he had entered a nightmare, that nothing he was seeing or hearing was real. It couldn't be.

It didn't have to be this way, this wasn't what he had planned.

They tried to get closer to the bombsite, but Jacob suddenly stopped dead. He was scared to see for himself what he already knew. Abir Nasr was dead, and he'd taken Marion with him. He felt nauseous and started to cry.

Alba held him.

"Jacob, don't blame yourself. Nobody could have predicted what was going to happen. In field operations, you have to make decisions. We don't always make the best ones."

"But she, Gabriella—"

"Look over there, Jacob. That's the European Commission. If they had gotten a few meters closer, we'd have a lot more dead right now."

"Yes, but this isn't what I wanted."

"None of us wanted it, but we're not responsible for what happened."

"Then who is?" Bitterness had taken over his voice.

"Abir Nasr, and no one else," Alba said.

"Maybe he didn't have a choice either."

"You're wrong, Jacob, we all have a choice. You've told me of his circumstances, everything he had to face to survive, to feel like someone, but that doesn't make him any less guilty. There are so many people out there, Abir, millions of people, who feel like they don't have a present and that the future has been snatched from them, but as desperate as they are, they don't become murderers."

Jacob was quiet as he listened to her. She was looking at him kindly, clearly not allowing herself to be dragged down into his negative view.

"But he—"

"He had a choice, don't ever forget that. He wasn't a child. He was a man who had been kicked around in life, but that doesn't justify his revenge. Come on, let's go, there's nothing more for us to do here."

"Marion trusted me and I failed her."

"Marion knew the risk she was taking, and she made a difficult decision, but she was an intelligent, brave woman. Life forces us to make decisions, and she, like you—like all of us—made hers."

"And now she's dead, Alba. Marion is dead, and I drove her to her death."

*Brussels. One day later.*
*The office of Louise Moos*

Ariel listened coolly to Louise Moos' stream of complaints. He, Jacob and Turner, along with some other security officials, had been in her office for an hour.

"You do know what's going to happen, don't you? I don't know what your Mossad superiors will say, but here in Europe this will come at a cost. There will be inquiries. The White House will wash its hands of all of this, saying it was a European operation. The press will ask for our heads and they will have to hand them over. And you, Jacob. You are responsible for Helen's death. All this madness was your idea."

It was Turner who finally stopped her.

"Ms. Moos, the operation was a success. Abir Nasr is dead and we've saved many lives. Marion Cloutier was collateral damage, and that was very unfortunate, but it's part of reality. Need I remind you that you approved this operation?"

"You think this is over?" Louise addressed the CIA agent furiously. "We haven't solved anything. There will be other Nasrs. They'll kill again, maybe here or somewhere else, but they'll keep doing it."

"You're right, Ms. Moos, this is war. They'll kill again, and we'll defend ourselves again, until one of the two sides wins," Turner responded.

"No! No one will win, that's exactly the problem! We'll keep killing each other, but no one will win. There will be no final battle." Jacob's broken voice was followed by a painful silence.

"Well, there are a lot of people waiting out there. We owe them an explanation," Louise Moos concluded.

*

An assistant opened the door to the Belgian security chief's office and gestured for Andrew to go in. Joseph followed. Everyone stood up, but no one could find the words to give their condolences.

Louise took a deep breath and held out her hand out to Andrew.

"They told me there was no danger ... they promised me ... they deceived her ... they deceived me ..."

She could barely speak.

Jacob then turned to him.

"I'm sorry. It was my plan. We thought Abir Nasir would come out of hiding, and he did. We thought we could arrest him, but he ... he ..."

"But he took Helen," Andrew finished sadly.

They were all silent. Uncomfortable. Repentant.

"Someone owes me an explanation. Why would Abir Nasr want to see Helen? Because she's the best journalist on the best international news program? No, you owe me an explanation. My wife promised me that once everything was OK, she would explain why Abir Nasr wanted to see her. She couldn't keep her promise, but you can do it for her."

They looked at each other, not daring to break the silence. Louise cleared her throat, preparing to speak. But Jacob saw Alba looking at him, tilting her head towards Andrew.

"Mr. Morris, your wife Helen had at one time been known as Marion Cloutier. Actually, her birth name was Marie-Hélène Cloutier, but as a teenager she went by Marion, a version of

Marie. By the time you met her she'd long since dropped the name Marie and went by Helen. She was using her third husband's last name, Hill. Before that, as you know, she was briefly married to a British man and carried his name.

"Your wife is—was—an exceptional woman. Brave, determined, never handed anything in life. She told me herself that she'd paid a high price for everything she'd achieved."

"I don't understand, Mr. Baudin," Andrew interrupted him.

"Your wife is originally French, as you must know. She spent her childhood and teenage years in Paris. In her last years of high school, she had a close friend, a girl of Lebanese-Maghrebi origin, Noura Adoum. Abir Nasr's cousin. Abir fell hard for Marion, but she never gave him the time of day. Her painful rejection of him was something he always carried with him."

"Are you trying to tell me that this terrorist killed my wife because he had been in love with her as a teenager? You're insane, Mr. Baudin."

"It's the truth."

"But she ... I don't understand why she would have agreed to meet with him."

"When Abir Nasr sent that thumb drive to her show, she heard his voice and recognized him. He then sent his own brother with a suicide bomb to her office, killing many of her colleagues. She knew all along that he was trying to get to her, impress her and terrify her, and that there was only one way to stop him. She agreed to meet him to prevent more deaths. Because of that, because of all of those things, Mr. Morris, she did what she did."

"Are you telling me that I didn't know my own wife?"

"You knew Helen Morris, but not the girl she had left behind. Marion Cloutier, for her, no longer existed. Helen didn't want to be anyone else."

Andrew buried his face in his hands for a few seconds, long enough to push back his tears. Joseph patted him on the back and looked around at the room as he tried to put his thoughts in order.

"Helen is now a journalistic legend. We can never, ever reveal the story of Marion Cloutier and Abir Nasr. This is what happened: Abir Nasr wanted publicity, and targeted the most important show on international politics. That's why he sent Helen and Benjamin the video with his threats. Helen proved to be smarter than the police and secret services put together, and through her various contacts she arranged for an interview with Abir Nasr. When he saw he was being followed and felt cornered, he turned the interview into a suicide mission, killing her as well. That's what happened. Marion Cloutier didn't exist, only Helen Morris. Do you all agree? If you don't, well, you will all have to assume responsibility for this tragedy and, for Helen's murder."

Joseph's sober retelling of the events made an impression on everyone gathered there. They all agreed. It was the best version that they could give of what happened. Helen would be considered a heroine, and the reputations of the intelligence services would stay intact.

It was a good deal.

After Andrew and Joseph had left, Louise asked if there really wouldn't be any leaks. There was no doubt: they all committed to sticking to the version supplied by the head of International Channel.

"It's for the best. But Mr. Baudin, tell us one thing. Who really gave her life to catch Abir Nasr, was it Helen Morris or Marion Cloutier?" she asked.

"Ms. Moos, for someone like you who only has one life, it's impossible to understand a woman like her. It's too much for you."

There was no harshness in Jacob's response; he was simply stating reality. He got up and left the room and Alba followed him.

"You'll recover," she whispered, taking his arm.

"And Nora?"

"They've arrested the entire Adoum family. But since she cooperated with us, she won't be charged. I promise, I'll do everything I can to help her. Maybe one day you'll be able to look each other in the eyes."

"You know that won't happen, Alba, you know it won't. She feels deceived by me. I never told her I was Jewish. She thinks I doubly betrayed Abir."

"Perhaps someday, Jacob, that will change."

# Epilogue

*Tel Aviv.*
*Jacob*

A month had passed since Jacob had returned to Tel Aviv. Dor and Natan had advised him to take some time off work and visit Dr. Tudela, but he felt incapable of talking to anyone except Alba, who had called him a few times. She didn't try to console him—she was just there for him in his pain, and he appreciated that she didn't pity him.

He spent the days running on the beach with Luna, with Abir's last words echoing over and over in his mind.

*You're coming with me to hell.*

He hadn't just taken Marion with him. He'd taken Jacob too.

Abir Nasr had won the game.

# Acknowledgements

To David Trías, Núria Tey, Virginia Fernández, Leticia Rodero and the entire team of Penguin Random House who have been by my side, book after book.

My thanks as well to Núria Cabutí for her support.

To Isidre Vilacosta and Asun Cascante, thank you for always responding so patiently to my questions.

And to Fermín and Álex, thank you for always being nearby.

I learned much about the *refusenik* movement by reading *Breaking Ranks: Refusing to Serve in the West Bank and Gaza Strip* by Ronit Chacham.

And I could never forget Argos—thank you for accompanying me in the writing of this novel.